THE TELLTALE TWITCH

Charlotte stepped to the side to better see Dare's groin. She was familiar enough with male anatomy to know what she was looking at. She waited, watching for the sign.

"That I married you proves I have honor. That I refuse to touch you until such time as I desire it proves I am in control of my life regardless of your plans otherwise. I will not have a woman, any woman, dictating to me what I shall and shall not do. I realize you want children someday, that you . . . er . . . embrace the physical side of marriage, but you must understand that I will be the master in my own home." Dare paused for a moment, his breath hissing through clenched teeth. Charlotte leaned closer, her eyes on the tautly stretched fabric concealing his manly instrument. Her fingers itched to touch him.

"WHY THE HELL ARE YOU STARING AT MY CROTCH LIKE THAT?"

Charlotte jumped at the bellow, her gaze snapping up to meet infuriated blue eyes. "I was waiting to see if you twitched," she explained. The man certainly had a lot to learn about marriage if he didn't know all the specifics about bedding his wife. Everyone knew there had to be twitching before the bedding could begin.

Dare ran a hand through his hair, his eyes blazing, his broad, manly chest rising and falling with quick breaths.

"Twiched? Did you say twitched? Do I understand you correctly? You are watching my crotch to see if my . . . er . . . *twitches?*"

Other books by Katie MacAlister:

IMPROPER ENGLISH
NOBLE INTENTIONS

NOBLE
DESTINY

KATIE MACALISTER

LEISURE BOOKS NEW YORK CITY

A LEISURE BOOK®

October 2009

Dorchester Publishing Co., Inc.
200 Madison Avenue
New York, NY 10016

ISBN 10: 0-505-52848-7
ISBN 13: 978-0-505-52848-3

Visit us online at www.dorchesterpub.com.

NOBLE
DESTINY

Chapter One

"You can't leave me now! Not when I need you! How selfish is it to leave just when I need you most? I forbid you to leave! I absolutely forbid you to leave me in my time of Great Distress!"

"I have no choice. I must leave now."

"Widdle, Mama."

"Stop just where you are, Gillian. Don't you dare take another step toward this door!"

"Charlotte, give me the key."

"Shan't!"

"Mama, want to widdle!"

"Char, Dante needs to use the necessary before we leave. Now please, if you have any love for me, hand over the key. Noble's going to be in a terrible fury if he finds out you're holding us prisoner in his library, and I can assure you from experience that Dante does not announce his intention to widdle

1

unless that event is nigh on imminent."

The petite blonde blocking the two oak doors cast a hesitant glance toward the figure of a three-year-old child doing an urgent dance before her. Two thin furrows appeared between her dark blond brows.

"It's a trick. You've taught him to say that. You're using your own child's plumbing as a weapon against me, cousin, and I find that a completely nebulous act."

"The word is *nefarious,* Charlotte." Gillian, Lady Wessex, picked up her son and pointed him toward her cousin. "If you do not unlock the door and release us, I shall allow him to widdle upon you."

The child giggled in delight. Lady Charlotte di Abalongia *nee* Collins, sucked in a horrified breath and leveled a defiant glare at her cousin. "You wouldn't!"

"Gillian? Wife, where are you hiding? This is no time for play, woman. We should have left an hour ago!" The doorknob rattled ineffectually.

"Papa, have to widdle!" Dante squirmed in his mother's arms.

"Now you've done it," Gillian nodded, stepping backwards. "Now you've annoyed Noble. I would advise you to move away from the doorway since he is sure to—"

Three sudden bangs against the door at her back caused Charlotte to jump a good foot off the ground.

"—want in. We're in here, my love," Gillian called. "Charlotte seems to have misplaced the key. We won't be a moment finding it."

"WANT TO WIDDLE!"

"What's that? Charlotte? What the devil is she doing here? I thought she ran off to be some Italian's mistress years ago?"

"I didn't run off, we eloped!" Charlotte bellowed at the door. "We were married in Paris. It was *romantic!*"

"It doesn't matter. Open the door! Gillian, we have to leave. *Now!*"

"WIDDLE!"

"Charlotte," Gillian said, her voice low and urgent. Charlotte eyed the door with alarm as the Black Earl pounded on it, demanding immediate entrance, but she paid heed to the steely note in her closest friend and relative's voice. "I understand you're terribly upset, and I know you've had a horrible time returning to England from what sounds like a perfectly ghastly old ruins in Italy, but my dear, I have a son full of widdle, two impatient children in the carriage with Nurse, and a husband who—" she paused as a particularly loud barrage of swearing accented the increased pounding on the door, "—is fast losing a temper that has been extremely tried today. Please, please, Char, give me the key before Noble is forced to take drastic measures."

Charlotte glanced from the squirming child to the look of concern in Gillian's emerald eyes. Tears had always worked well for her in the past. Perhaps if she could work up a few, her cousin would see how serious she was. She waited for the peculiar prickling sensation to indicate that her cornflower blue eyes would soon be becomingly framed in a pool of tears, and allowed a note of raw desperation to creep into her voice. "Gilly, I need you. I truly do. You're all I have left. There's no one else left who will receive me. Papa saw to that. I have nowhere to go and no money. I sold what remained of

Mama's jewels just to buy a few traveling gowns and passage to England on a merchant ship. You're the only one in the family who will acknowledge me, and now you are sailing to the West Indies. . . ." Her voice cracked as she brushed at the wetness on her cheeks, surprised to find her crocodile tears had suddenly become real. "Oh, Gilly, please stay. Please help me. I've never been alone. I don't know what to do."

Gillian shifted the child in her arms and squeezed Charlotte's hand. "You know I will do everything I can to help you—"

Charlotte shrieked in joy and hugged her cousin, widdly child and all. "I knew you wouldn't leave me!"

A tremendous splintering noise reverberated through the room as Noble Britton, known by the (in Charlotte's mind, understated) sobriquet of the Black Earl, burst through the doors, followed by a tall, bewigged man with a hook where his left hand should have been, and two smaller footmen in livery.

"Are you all right?" the earl asked his countess, rushing to her side.

She smiled reassuringly. "Of course we are. Charlotte just needs a moment or two of my time, and then I will be ready to be off." She forestalled protests on both her husband's and cousin's lips by thrusting the squirming child into his father's arms just before she grasped Charlotte firmly and tugged her toward a nearby emerald and gold damask couch. "While you're taking Dante for his widdle, I'll speak with Char. Crouch, please take Lady Charlotte's things up to the Blue Suite. She'll be staying here for a time. Dickon, Charles, tell the other carriages to start, we'll be along directly."

Noble shot his wife a questioning look before settling a glare on Charlotte, who was profoundly thankful it was a short glare as she never could stand up to one of the earl's scowls. Both father and child hastened away when the latter announced his intention to widdle right there in the library.

"You have five minutes until I must leave," Gillian told her cousin sternly. "You are welcome to stay here for as long as you like. Now, what else can I do to help you?"

Charlotte's heart underwent a peculiar motion that felt suspiciously like it dropped into her jean half-boots. "You're leaving? You're still leaving me?"

"I have no choice," was the calm reply. A burst of pain flared to life within Charlotte's breast at her cousin's defection, but a moment's consideration led her to admit that Gillian really could not remain behind while her husband and children sailed to their coffee plantation. She shoved down the pain of abandonment and focused her energies on explaining what a shambles her life had become.

"Very well. You received my letter that mentioned Antonio died of sweating sickness in November?"

Gillian nodded. "And you wanted to leave Villa Abalongia because you had a difficult time with his family, but you mentioned going to Paris, not home to England."

Charlotte's eyes threatened to fill once more with scalding tears that she suspected would leave her with unattractive swollen, red eyes and a nose that would require much attention with a handkerchief. "And I don't even have a handkerchief anymore," she wailed, unable to stop the tears. Charlotte seldom had recourse to real tears, but they were just as uncomfortable as she recalled. "Everything's gone, everything! The contessa took it all for her two horrid, fat daughters. She said I wouldn't need my fine gowns when I was in mourning for Antonio. She said I'd have to go live on a tiny little farm in the mountains and tend a bunch of smelly goats, that I wasn't welcomed to stay in Florence as I wasn't truly a member of the family, all because I hadn't given Antonio an heir!"

"That was very cruel of her."

"Yes," Charlotte sniffed. "It was. Especially since it wasn't my fault. I wouldn't have minded a child—you seem to enjoy yours so much—but Antonio refused to do his husbandly duty by me."

Gillian's eyes widened. "He . . . he refused?"

Charlotte nodded, her eyes filling again at the memory of such a grave injustice. "It was all he could do to consummate the marriage. After that . . . oh, Gilly, he wouldn't even try. And the contessa was forever making nasty remarks that I was not doing *my* duty properly! I tried, I honestly tried! I wore naughty nightwear, I allowed him to catch me *en dishabille* on many occasions, and I even sought advice from the local strumpet as to how to arouse the passion of Antonio's manly instrument, but to no avail. His instrument resisted all my efforts. I think it hated me," she added darkly.

"Oh, I'm sure that wasn't—"

"It wouldn't even twitch for me!"

"Well, really, Charlotte." Gillian looked a bit embarrassed. "It's not as if it were an animal trained to jump on your command."

"I know that, but the strumpet said it should at the very least twitch once in a while, and not lie limp and flaccid like a week-old bit of blancmange. It wouldn't make even the slightest effort on my behalf. If that's not cruel and petty minded of a

6

manly instrument, well, I just don't know what is!"

Gillian blinked once or twice before patting her cousin's arm and handing her a lace-edged handkerchief. Charlotte viewed it with sorrow. "I used to have handkerchiefs like this," she cried, mopping at her eyes and blowing her nose in a less-than-dainty manner. "But that evil woman took them away from me, just as she took everything else, even my husband!"

"Oh, surely she couldn't have taken Antonio's affection from you—"

"Not his affection," Charlotte sniffled loudly. "He was fond enough of me, although he never dared act so before the contessa. No, she took him away and sent him to a nasty little town on the Mediterranean for his weak lungs. And he died there!"

"Char, I'm sorry about Antonio. I know you must have loved him greatly. . . ."

Charlotte stopped dabbing at her eyes, a look of utter astonishment on her face. "Love him greatly? Where did you get that idea?"

Gillian stopped patting her cousin's hand. "Well . . . that is . . . you eloped with him! You dismissed all your suitors and eloped with the son of a minor Italian nobleman. Why else would you sacrifice everything you held dear if you didn't love him greatly?"

"Oh, that," Charlotte responded dismissively, gently prodding the region below her eyes to ascertain whether they were swollen from her recent tears. "It was my third season, and I didn't care for that year's suitors. Antonio was just like the hero in *Castle Moldavia, Or, The Dancing Master's Ghost*. He was so very romantic, but Papa was being stiff-rumped about my marrying him, threatening to cut me off without a shilling if I didn't marry someone suitable

7

instead. Papa became ever so tiresome, and the Season was really quite boring, so I did the only sensical thing."

"Sensible not sensical," Gillian corrected automatically, staring at her cousin in disbelief. "Are you telling me you ran off to marry knowing that your father disapproved of your husband, knowing he would disinherit you, knowing that such an elopement would cause a scandal that would even now keep all of the doors of Society closed to you, and yet you did it not for love, but because you were *bored?*"

Charlotte frowned. "Most of the doors of Society, not all, and I don't see what that has to do with anything. You said you would help me. I really don't think spending my five minutes discussing the past four years is helping me. I don't see how chastising me for actions viewed by some as romantic and daring—"

"Not to mention heedless, hen-witted, and hasty."

"—is going to benefit me now," Charlotte finished, ignoring the interruption. "As I said, I simply cannot see my way out of this dreadful moil."

"Coil." Gillian chewed on lower lip for a moment. Charlotte watched hopefully; whenever her cousin got that peculiar light to her eyes, it meant she was about to come up with a truly magnificent plan. "What of Lord Collins?"

"Matthew?" Charlotte snorted the name. "He's cut from the same cloth Papa was. When Papa died almost four years ago, Matthew took up the banner of ostriching me."

"Ostracizing, Char. You really should make an effort to use the correct word."

"Pheasant feathers! Language should be fluid, it should work for me, not the other way around. And don't distract me, I have only a few minutes remaining. I wrote Matthew when Antonio succumbed, but all I received back was a terse note to the effect that I was reaping what I had sown. There will be no help from my brother or the rest of the family."

"Hmmm. Well, you do have certain assets we can work with. . . ."

Charlotte's dark lashes fluttered as she smiled depreciatingly and gazed down at her hands in what she knew to be an extremely fetching approximation of modesty. "Yes, of course, that's very kind of you to say, especially considering the fashion is for dainty, blonde nymphs not red-headed, green-eyed amazons like yourself."

Gillian gave her a puzzled look. Charlotte allowed her dimples to peek out in a manner she had been told by several gentlemen was utterly charming. "My appearance."

Gillian's look of puzzlement deepened as her cousin explained. "You mentioned my assets, Cousin! It would not be meet for me to point out my many and various charms, but I am not so foolishly modest that I don't recognize them. If you recall, Lord Darnley *did* write a sonnet to my eyes."

Gillian rolled her eyes. "Oh, that."

"He called them limpid pools of ceruzean, whatever that is. And Lord Beckstand composed several lines about the gilt tones of my hair."

"It's *cerulean*, but I wasn't speaking about something so trivial as your appearance, Char. I was speaking of your assets, your *true* assets."

"Trivial!" Charlotte recoiled from such blasphemy. "Trivial! Cousin, marriage has addled your brains! There is nothing trivial about one's appearance. Why, without a comely countenance, one would have no suitors! No *inamoratos!* Society would shun one! No invitations to balls and routs and breakfasts would be forthcoming! One simply could not attend the opera nor the theatre, nor expect to be received by anyone of discerning taste. . . ."

Gillian was nodding even before the words dried up on Charlotte's lips. "Exactly. You are the picture of loveliness, and yet you find yourself in a position exactly as you describe, hence my comment on the trivial nature of something so shallow as beauty. What you need is to focus on your assets, namely, your status as a widow, your good breeding, your congenial manner, and—" she took a deep breath. "—your willingness to marry again."

"Marry?" Charlotte blinked in surprise at her cousin's words. "Who said anything about my marrying? You just said my widowhood was an asset, why would I want to give it up?"

Gillian cast a quick glance at the door. Voices could be heard in the hallway beyond. "Charlotte, you have limited choices. You can either resolve the argument with your family . . ."

"I've tried. Matthew is just as bull-headed as Father was."

". . . or come with us to the West Indies . . ."

Charlotte made a moue of disapproval. "It's hot there. I would perspire all the time, and I cannot think of anything worse than being in a continual state of perspiration."

". . . or find a position as a companion to an elderly lady . . ."

An unladylike snort answered that suggestion.

". . . or you can marry again."

A frown wrinkled Charlotte's brow as she smoothed out the drab olive green traveling gown her limited funds forced her to buy en route to England. "Marry. I hadn't thought to marry. All I wanted to do was to come home. Marriage means . . . well, there would have to be a husband, wouldn't there? I'm not sure I want another husband."

"Well, what *do* you want?"

Charlotte tried on a little pout. "I want what I had before Antonio swept me off my feet and dragged me to that godforsaken castle in Italy. I want to be the Season's reigning Incomparable, I want my court of suitors, I want lovely gowns and dancing and stolen kisses in the garden!"

"But you're not eighteen anymore, Charlotte," her cousin protested. "You're a grown woman. Surely you want something more meaningful than the mere glitter of life in the *ton?*"

"There's nothing wrong with glitter," Charlotte objected, her pout dissolving into another frown. "It's bright and pretty and it entertains."

"It's also shallow, unsubstantial, and unimportant. Oh, Char, I want you to be happy, but I don't see how that's possible if all you want—"

"WIFE!"

Gillian rose as the voice in the hall took on a strident note. "Blast! I really have to go now. I'm sorry I can't help you. Crouch and the other staff will take care of you here at Britton House for as long as you like, and I'll have the household funds put at your disposal. If you get in a terrible bind and need advice, write to me."

"It will take forever to hear from you, not to mention the fact that you'll only lecture me and say improving sorts of things that are of no practical use whatsoever." Charlotte plucked at the ugly trim on her equally ugly gown and tried not to covet her cousin's smart green-and-white-striped gown with matching green pelisse.

"It wouldn't hurt you in the least to listen to a bit of improving advice, Charlotte. Do think about what I said—I wouldn't wish for you to be in another unhappy marriage, but it's the only solution I can see."

Charlotte nodded sadly and accompanied her cousin to the hall, kissed Gillian's and Dante's cheek, tried not to flinch under the earl's stern, disapproving look, and rallied a smile and a wave as the last of her familial connections drove off in a sleek black and scarlet coach.

"She's left me here alone with no one but the servants. Damnation!" Charlotte swore as the carriage disappeared from view.

"Ye can say that again," a voice muttered behind her, but when she spun around to pin the ears back on the speaker, she was faced with a line of servants wearing faces so innocent they could have doubled for cherubim.

"Hrmph," she snorted, eying the collected servants. "Much as I would like to dissolve into tears over my desperate and completely tragic situation, I shall give in to a well-earned megrim at a later time. Right now I have a more important dish to fry. Crouch, fetch me writing paper, and have the footmen standing at the ready."

"Eh . . . fish to fry, d'ye mean, m'lady?"

Charlotte raised her brows in the manner that had never failed to intimidate Graveltoes, her father's butler, but it appeared that the giant pirate the Wessexes employed was made of sterner stuff. No doubt it was the hook that made him feel superior. "I simply do not understand this unreasonable fixation you and Gillian and others have with something so unimportant as language, Crouch. It's unwholesome. I urge you to get over it. And don't think you can put on airs as you do with Gillian, I shan't tolerate it as she does. I'll have enough of that as I contrive to make my stunning reappearance in the drawing rooms and ballrooms of the *ton*."

She shooed Crouch on his way and marched upstairs to take possession of Gillian's personal sitting room. It wasn't going to be easy re-establishing herself after the scandal, but that was four years ago, and certainly people must have forgotten the details by now. With a little finesse and sweet-talking to the right matrons, the doors would surely open to her again. It wouldn't be pleasant to be forced to listen to lectures by the very same women who called her foolish and headstrong all those years ago, but she could endure a few "I warned you!" comments if necessary. Besides, there were the gentlemen to think of—she had charm and vivacity, and despite her cousin's doubts of the effectiveness of a pretty face and a neat ankle, Charlotte had always found she could have her way if she fluttered her eyelashes and dimpled just so.

"It will be as easy as taking honey from a flea," she predicted, sitting down to write her letters.

"I can't believe it! I just can't believe it! How dare she refuse me a voucher! How dare she tell me I am not welcome to her blasted masquerade ball next week! How dare she tell me that no polite person will recognize me!" Charlotte ripped a cream-colored sheet of paper to shreds and threw it into the unlit grate. "Who would have thought that Lady Jersey had a memory like . . . like . . . like a lion?"

"A what?"

13

Charlotte made a dismissive motion with her hands as she paced by the figure sitting in the blue and gold brocade chair in her cousin's sitting room.

"A lion, Caro, a lion. You know, one of those big gray beasts that lives in Africa. They have prodigious memories."

Lady Caroline Beverly looked confused. "Are you sure? The lion I saw at the menagerie was sort of a yellowish-brown color and no bigger than a very small pony."

Charlotte spun on her heel and paced a line back toward the fireplace. "Brown, gray, it doesn't matter. They come from Africa, and they have excellent memories. Just like Lady Jersey."

Caroline frowned. "I thought Lady Jersey's family came from Devonshire."

Charlotte stopped pacing, put her hands on her hips, and glared down at her friend. "What on earth does Lady Jersey's family have to do with anything?"

"You mentioned it! You said she came from Africa just like the lions."

"There are times," Charlotte said, breathing heavily through her nose, "when I find myself regretting that I returned to England. *Memory,* Caro, I likened Lady Jersey to the lion because of its exceptional *memory.* Just as she has."

"Oh. Does she? What about?"

Charlotte tossed up her hands and resumed pacing, reminding herself not to snap at the only person who had responded to her plea for help. "I can't afford to be discriminating," she muttered.

"No, you said you were quite pockets to let, but that doesn't explain why you're upset with Lady Jersey's memory."

Charlotte took a deep, deep breath, and sat on

the loveseat next to the brunette. "Caroline, listen to me very carefully. You remember four years ago when I left England to marry the Conte di Abalongia's eldest son?"

Caroline nodded her head. "Yes, of course I do. It caused ever such a scandal! Mama said it would all end in sorrow and that you'd come to a bad end, and for me not to even consider running off with Raoul the drawing master, which of course I wasn't considering because dearest Algernon was about to offer for me, and why would I want to be married to a drawing master when I could be a viscountess instead? Although Raoul did have the most attractive mustache—do you remember it? The ends came to two lovely points. And of course dearest Algernon tried to grow one just to please me when I admired Sir Ralph Henderson's mustache, but he did not seem to have much luck at it, although I rubbed pomade onto his lip faithfully every night."

A small headache pulsed to life at the front of Charlotte's head. She opened a window that looked out onto the tiny garden below and welcomed the sweet summer air, tainted though it was by the ever present hint of coal.

"I must admit I was glad when he gave it up. The pomade smelled of garlic, and you know, really, it's impossible to go to sleep when the person next to you has a garlic-perfumed lip."

The headache blossomed into something deeper. "Caroline, do you think we could get back to matters at hand—namely, that Lady Jersey has poisoned everyone's mind against me by recalling my romantic and dashing elopement all those many years ago?"

"Oh, but it isn't Lady Jersey," Caroline protested, smoothing the soft gray kid of her gloves. "At least,

15

that's what dearest Algernon said two nights past when we were at the opera and he was talking to Lord Collins. Have you seen your brother since you've come home again? He has the most divine mustache with just the shortest little beard, which I don't quite like, but I think you will find his mustache is all the rage. Many of the gentlemen are adopting them now. Except, of course, dearest Algernon. I told him I simply cannot endure more sleepless nights smelling the garlic on his lip."

Charlotte frowned in concentration as she picked through the other woman's mental meanderings. "What did my brother say to Lord Beverly?"

"About his mustache? Well, it seems he uses a special pomade that contains the glands of a—"

"No, what did Matthew say about me?"

Caroline pursed her lips as she searched the dark, dusty hallways of her memory. "Oh, yes, that. Evidently when dearest Algernon mentioned that I was calling on you today, Lord Collins told him not to allow it, that after The Event your father had made sure you weren't accepted in polite society, and he had taken it as a sacred duty to see his father's wishes carried out, and that he would be contacting Lady Jersey and other preeminent matrons to let them know of his feelings. So you see, it's not Lady Jersey's fault at all that you received so many cuts yesterday when you went out. I suspect it was all your brother's doing."

"That beast!" Charlotte stood, her hands balled into fists as she stomped over to the fireplace. The stomping didn't make her feel the least bit better, so she spun around and stomped to the other side of the room, anger seething from every pore. "I knew he wouldn't do anything to welcome me back into the family, but to deliberately sabotage my chances, why, that's . . . that's . . . that's a calligraphy!"

"A catastrophe." Caroline nodded. "Especially if you hope your plan to find a husband goes forward. What gentleman will offer for you if he knows your brother does not recognize you?"

Charlotte snarled silently and strode by, two fingers pressed to her forehead.

"Of course, you could always look outside of the *ton* for a husband," Caroline said tentatively.

Charlotte drew to a halt before her and gave a haughty glare down her nose. "Bite your tongue, Caro! I am an earl's daughter, the widow to the heir of a count, and I shall be a nobleman's wife, so help me! No, I shan't look outside of the *ton*, but I will defeat my brother nonetheless."

A look of interest sparked in Caroline's dark grey eyes. "How will you manage that?"

"It's evident that Matthew will not be quiet about my arrival in London. No doubt he's been carrying out his plans to keep me from my rightful place by spreading this foul slander at his clubs, filling the ears of all of the eligible gentlemen with warnings against me."

"I could ask dearest Algernon if he has heard anything," Caroline offered helpfully.

"Mmm." Charlotte twisted her borrowed handkerchief as she paced, her mind a whirl of thoughts. "There must be someone imperfidious to Matthew's evil plan. Who's in town, Caro? Unmarried and wealthy and titled gentlemen only, of course."

"Impervious."

"Who?"

"The word is *impervious*, not *imperfidious*."

Charlotte paused to glare. "Not you as well? What

17

happened while I was in Italy? Did some sort of language plague strike everyone?"

"But—"

"Did you or did you not agree to help me?"

"Yes, of course I did, but—"

"Even after my brother warned your husband about you being seen with me?"

"Yes, I told you that I reassured dearest Algernon that you were blameless—"

"Then would you kindly construe your mind to matters of importance, and not blether on about silly things such as mere words!" Charlotte shot her a penetrating glance before turning to the window to breathe in calming gulps of air.

"Constrain not construe," Caroline said softly.

Charlotte spun around. "What?"

Caroline blushed and lowered her eyes to the gloves twisted between her fingers. "Nothing. What did you want to know about the gentlemen?"

"Everything. Who is in town now, who has a fortune and title, and of course, whether they will look good against me."

"Whether they will look good against you?" Caroline blinked in surprise.

"Yes, yes, will they look good against me! That is to say, will our appearances compliment one another? Will we have handsome children? I must have a husband who will give me handsome children. Can you imagine having ugly children?" She shuddered. "It wouldn't be tolerable at all. Therefore, I must select a husband who not only has the fortune and position I require, but he must also have looks that will compliment my own."

Caroline gaped at her open-mouthed.

"Come along, Caro, I don't have all day, I have to make plans. Who of the gentlemen in town possesses suitable fortune, rank, and appearance to meet my needs?"

Caroline snapped her mouth shut. "I . . . you . . . well . . . there's Sir Everett Dillingham."

Charlotte seated herself on the loveseat and picked up an ebony-figured fan. "Everett? Is he still alive? Too old, Caro, much too old. He must be all of forty, if he's a day! Think of someone younger."

"Well," Caroline sucked on her lower lip in thought. "There's the Marquis of Chilton's son. He's cutting quite a swath in town."

"His eldest son? The Earl of Bramley? I thought he married Lucy Gordonstone?"

"Not his eldest son, his youngest. Lord Thomas."

Charlotte stared at her friend in horror. "Thomas? He's nineteen!"

"Well you said you wanted someone younger."

"Not infantile! I'm three and twenty, Caro. I would like a husband of an age with me, not one who still rides ponies!"

"I'm sorry, but I can't think of anyone else."

Charlotte snapped her fan closed. "Then think harder. I'm not an unreasonable woman, there must be someone with the title, fortune, and appearance to satisfy me."

"Well," Caroline drawled the word out as she eyed her friend carefully. "I did hear that there was a gentleman in town who might suit, but he doesn't attend many functions."

"All the better," Charlotte smiled, her dimples flashing. "He shan't object to my making a splash in society as is my due. What is his name?"

"I've heard it said that he has a terrible temper, and Mama once told me that he fought a duel over a lightskirt."

"That shows he has passion and an interest in

matters of the bedchamber. I swear, it will be a nice change from Antonio. Who is this gentleman?"

"Being an earl, most of the mamas have him in their sights," Caroline warned. "You will have heavy competition for his attention."

Charlotte's dimples deepened. "Let me worry about that. Who is this charming earl?"

Caroline hesitated, watching her friend warily. "It's someone with whom your name was linked five years ago."

"Really?" Charlotte drummed her fingers on the arm of the loveseat. "An earl? I don't remember attaching an earl to my court before I met Antonio. Which earl?"

"He wasn't in your court, as such," Caroline replied carefully. "The attraction was more one-sided . . ."

A face began to appear in the mists of Charlotte's memory. A long, lean, rugged face, perhaps not handsome by conventional standards, but a face that had great character, a face that had haunted her dreams for the last five years.

". . . although some said you would do the impossible and he would make you an offer . . ."

It was his eyes that she remembered the best. Deep, dark sapphire blue, almost indigo at times, with a distinctive black ring. Framed by two dark blond brows a few shades darker than her own hair, those eyes could pierce through even the most formidable appearances to see the soul.

". . . but then your cousin married and he returned to his estates in Scotland. I'm speaking, of course, of—"

"Alasdair McGregor, Lord Carlisle." Charlotte breathed the words as Caroline was about to pronounce them.

"Yes," Caroline agreed, still watching her friend closely. "The only man you were interested in that Season."

"Alasdair," Charlotte murmured, seeing again the face of the handsome Scot. "He was so very handsome, so dashing, so enigmatic. Everyone wanted to be seen on his arm, all the ladies fought to catch his eye."

"He seemed fond of you," Caroline said slowly.

Charlotte closed her eyes, swaying a little as she remembered the pleasure of dancing with him, of having him next to her as he drove her through the park. Once she thought he was going to kiss her, but they were interrupted before she knew what it was to feel his lips upon hers. "Alasdair McGregor. He was everything I wanted in a man."

She opened her eyes to find Caroline's knowing gaze on her. With a lift of her chin she rose and went to the window, staring blindly out at the garden as she played with the curtain tie. "And he still is."

Chapter Two

Alasdair McGregor was being hunted.

It had been a familiar sensation the last few days since he'd arrived in London. Mornings brought with them chits who mysteriously twisted their ankles on the steps leading to his front door (whereupon the chits immediately pointed out the necessity of a lengthy recuperative period inside his house). Afternoons occasioned women he was riding past suddenly falling into the miscellaneous bodies of water found in London parks, resulting in them screaming and thrashing about and calling upon him for assistance. And evenings drew to a close as warm, scented bodies of unentangled widows insinuated themselves into his bed without regard to minor points of etiquette such as invitation or inclination.

Dare had seen thirty-two summers in his lifetime,

was tall and broad enough in the shoulders as to cause the uninvited widows to lick their lips in anticipation of the pleasure to be found in his bed, and held the title of seventh earl of Carlisle, all of which made him fair game in the eyes of women of the *ton*, particularly those in the market for a husband.

"Batsfoam?"

"Yes, my lord?"

"I have a peculiar prickling sensation on the back of my neck."

"Again, my lord?"

"Yes, again. Any sign of her?"

The butler trailing behind his master paused long enough to briefly scan the street. He sighed as he turned a lugubrious face to Carlisle. "South-southwest, my lord. In a pink phaeton of such a virulent color that merely looking at it has given me a sharp pain on the left side of my head."

Dare muttered an expletive and lengthened his stride. "It must be Mrs. Benton. She's been trying to catch my eye for the last three days. How close is she? Do you think we can make Dunbridge and Storm before she catches up to us?"

Batsfoam, hired originally as a butler and now by a regrettable lack in the earl's fiduciary standing, secretary, valet, and draughtsman, squinted against the afternoon sun and gauged the distance to the solicitor's office. "Doubtful."

"Blast!"

The butler's shoulders drooped even more than was normal in his habitual slouch. Dark of eye and hair, with skin the shade and texture of a unripened lemon, Batsfoam moved through life at the center of a seemingly perpetual cloud of gloom. "We're doomed. It's no use, my lord, you must sacrifice me and leave me behind. My leg will only hold you up."

Dare immediately slowed down, turning to cast a questioning glance at his employee. A sergeant in his unit when they served in the 12th Light Dragoons, Batsfoam had done his part to keep England safe from Napoleon, but it had cost him his lower right leg. "Dammit man, why didn't you tell me your leg was aching? I would have hired a carriage."

Batsfoam shrugged a shrug that spoke of servitude, unworthiness, and emotions too depressing to be put into mere words. "I am but a lowly servant, my lord. I live to fulfill your slightest whim. Your commands are my commands. Should you require me to walk what remains of my leg to the thinnest slivers of skin and bone, why then, my every waking moment will be spent in accomplishing that task. My life is yours. I am humbled and grateful that you chose to place upon my frail shoulders the many tasks, chores, jobs, and responsibilities you have so graciously deemed fit for me. I prostrate myself with gratitude each morning that yet another day has dawned during which I will spend long, exacting hours working to make your life one of ease and comfort, and I go down on my one good leg, riddled as it is with rheumatism, each night to thank the Lord for sending me a master who does not condescend to coddle me because of the grievous and near fatal injuries inflicted upon me when fighting for my beloved country. It is with the profoundest pleasure, nay ecstasy, that I am able to martyr myself upon the altar of your happiness."

"In other words," Dare replied, his arms crossed over his chest, "you'd like me to hire a hack."

A momentary lifting of the ever present gloom indicated that Batsfoam would like just that, but just as quickly his usual dour, murky, abysmal expression returned. "I would not dream of imposing on your lordship in any such manner. Indeed, it would give my life the utmost meaning if you allowed me to throw myself before the razor sharp pounding hooves of Mrs. Benton's approaching team, sacrificing, as it were, my frail and feeble mortal frame so that you might escape without suffering such unpleasantness as might be experienced in having to tip your hat to her."

The earl rolled his eyes. Batsfoam had been with him for more than seven years, and despite the man's tendency to speak with significantly less than the respect due him, Dare wouldn't ruin the pleasure his servant found in being utterly and completely wretched. "It's good to see you in such a happy mood for a change, Batsfoam. Such a frolicsome, carefree attitude suits you. I must remember to dock your wages a few quid just to keep you from bursting into song on the stair in the morning as you go about your duties."

The corners of Batsfoam's lips twitched, but he had steely command over his expression and quickly pressed his mouth into its normal grim line. "As you desire, my lord. Alas that these frivolous few moments of jocularity are about to end with the imminent arrival of *a lady*. What is your will? Shall I cast myself to a certain bloody and unpleasant death under the horses' hooves, or will you suffer the cruel fate of gentlemen of your noble and honorable mien by greeting Mrs. Benton?"

Dare ignored the sarcasm that fairly dripped from Batsfoam's voice just as he always did, glancing down the street instead to where the lady in question was slowing her team in preparation to stopping before him. He squared his shoulders and resigned himself to the inevitable. "I shall reserve your sacrifice for another time, Batsfoam. As you say, I shall be forced to do the honorable thing and greet Mrs. Benton politely."

"Chivalrous to the tips of your noble toes, my lord," Batsfoam murmured, bowing obsequiously as he did so. "I shall just step back off the pavement into this pile of rancid, rat-infested refuse made up largely of offal and what appears to be droppings from a violently ill horse, so as not to sully the impression your lordship makes by tainting it with my unworthy presence."

Dare wondered briefly what he had done to deserve Batsfoam, but his attention was quickly wrenched from contemplations of his greater sins to the scene before him. Just as the pink carriage was slowing to a stop, a scarlet and black racing curricle swerved around the slower vehicle and came to an abrupt halt a mere foot from the tips of Dare's glossy Hessians, effectively cutting off the phaeton's approach, much to the dismay of its team and driver.

"Have you ever heard such language from a lady?" the driver of the curricle asked, a pair of cornflower blue eyes twinkling at him as her bonneted head tipped in inquiry. "You'd think she was from the stews the way she's carrying on! What exactly do you suppose she meant by saying I was no better than laced mutton?"

Dare's jaw dropped as he got a good look at the face under the wide brim of the blue bonnet. "You!" he sputtered. "You're in Italy! You ran off with some mealy mouthed son of a count, didn't you?"

"He's dead. I'm back." Charlotte dimpled at him before turning to face the phaeton behind her. "Mrs. Benton, I really must protest your shocking habit of driving up on people's heels. Not only is it rude in the extreme, but your horses are most ill mannered, and appear to be lunching on my cousin's butler's wig. Kindly remove them from our vicinity."

"Crotch!" Dare bellowed, catching sight of the figure clinging to the tiger's seat while beating off two horses clearly bent on eating his powered wig. The earl's eyes narrowed suspiciously as he glanced between Charlotte and the butler, wondering why a terrible sense of foreboding swept over him at the sight of the lovely blonde.

"Really, my lord, should you?" Charlotte murmured as she swept open her fan and adopted an expression of innocence that was not so far from the truth as she would like.

"Should I what?" he asked, stepping back as Mrs. Benton's horses, having consumed the wig, turned their powdery white noses to him.

"Speak about genitals."

He goggled at her, feeling as if he was a piece of driftwood caught helplessly in a whirlpool. With an effort, he swallowed and asked in a low, calm voice that was in direct contrast to his desire to shriek, "What the devil did you say?"

"Genitals. You brought the subject up, my lord, so you needn't give me that look of surprise. I am a lady. I would never approach a man and enter into a discussion of genitals. Well, that's not strictly the truth, perhaps I would under special circumstances, but not without him first introducing the subject, as you have just done."

"I have mentioned no such thing!" Dare snapped, outraged at such a patently false accusation. Him? Discuss genitalia? With a lady? He glanced over to see if Batsfoam had heard such an outrageous slan-

Katie MacAlister

der, but that worthy was engaged in discussing the finer points of field amputations with the behooked pirate Crotch whom Lord Wessex kept as a butler and general all-around thug.

"Yes, you did so," Charlotte said vehemently. She turned around on the seat. "Did he not bring up the subject first, Mrs. Benton? Genitalia?"

Dare ignored the unladylike comments spewing with increased venom from the pink phaeton in order to better extricate himself from what was turning out to be a horrible morning. "I did not introduce the subject of your genitals—"

"I should hope not," Charlotte replied with an outraged flare to her delicate nostrils. She smoothed her gown over her thigh. "My genitals are my own business sir, and they certainly have no relevance to you, no matter how hard you may try to introduce them into polite conversation. That is, they have no relevance to you at this moment, which, in fact, brings me to the very subject upon which I wished to speak with you."

Dare felt slightly dazed. He blinked several times, shook his head, and tried to focus on a sane subject of conversation. He failed. "What is Crotch—" he began, waving his hand toward the two servants.

"There, you see, you did it again!" Charlotte crowed, snapping her fan closed with a smug smile.

For a moment Dare considered the implications of throttling the woman before him, finally deciding she wasn't worth going to the gallows. "I meant Crotch. Crotch! Crotch the butler. You can't possibly mistake him, he's the one with the wicked-looking hook and a scar running from brow to chin. Wessex's butler. The thug Crotch!"

"I *know* who he is," Charlotte's smile went a little

28

terse around the edges. "But his name is Crouch, Alasdair, not Crotch."

Dare squinted suspiciously at her. "It is?"

"Yes."

"Are you sure?"

Charlotte thought for a moment. "Reasonably so. I might have misheard Gillian . . . no, I am certain it is Crouch. It wouldn't do at all having a servant named after one's personal regions."

"Ah. Well, then."

"Exactly. As that is straightened out, you may now beg my forgiveness for discussing my genitals in public. Lust after them as you might, I am not prepared to have talk of them on everyone's lips, not even you, although should you care to—well, we'll come to that in good time. You may now beg my pardon."

Dare stared at her for a long, disbelieving moment. "You, ma'am, are stark, raving mad."

Charlotte bristled, but Dare was not falling for such a display of righteous indignation. He shook a manly finger at her. "You always were slightly mad, and now I have proof. I have at no time, *NO TIME*, mentioned your genitals! You, on the other hand, burst into conversation with me about them at every possible moment! You're genital-mad! Not only did you bring the subject up in conversation—after narrowly avoiding an accident with Mrs. Benton's wig-eating horses—I do not recall ever stating that I lusted after your own particular . . . er . . . specimen. Indeed, Lady Charlotte." Dare took a deep breath, feeling a great deal more in control than he had since he first caught sight of Charlotte's lovely blue eyes. "Indeed, I hazard to say that you're obsessed with genitals! As such is the case, you will excuse me from further conversation and give me

29

leave to be on my way. I bid you a genital-free good morning."

With a sharp nod to Charlotte, and the merest tip of the hat to Mrs. Benton, who had given up trying to blister Charlotte's ears and was presently engaged in backing her phaeton with an eye to ramming her team into the black and scarlet racing curricle, he turned and started off for the solicitors' office at a brisk, no-nonsense pace.

"Wait, Lord Carlisle!" Charlotte called, flicking the reins across the well-groomed rumps of Noble's matched grays, sending the horses forward. Crouch and Batsfoam ceased discussing the relative merits of tourniquets versus cauterization as they leapt out of the way, Crouch swinging up behind the curricle as it passed him, Batsfoam ending up in the pile of offensive waste he had commented upon earlier. He stood and shook off clumps of sodden, odiferous matter, adding yet another nail in the cross he bore as his lordship's servant before lumbering after his master.

"Alasdair, wait! I have something to say to you!"

"I don't recall making you free with my name, Lady Charlotte," he said pleasantly, ignoring the sudden appearance of the curricle beside him. He continued to walk, aware that people were standing and gawking openly at the sight of Charlotte pursuing him. He'd be damned if he acknowledged her, though. He hadn't surrendered to any of the ankle-twisting, pond-diving, bed-warming schemers, and he certainly wasn't going to give a lesser hunter any sign she had him snared. "Now I know what a fox must suffer," he muttered to himself.

"Do you really? Being torn to shreds by a pack of slavering hounds and having your tail cut off, do you mean?" Charlotte asked as the curricle kept pace with him.

Dare fought the urge to smile. He had to admit that Lady Charlotte hadn't lost any of her delightfully unique sense of humor, the one attribute that had almost led him to offer for her five years before. She was so unlike the other young ladies out at the time, a fresh, lovely breeze of wit and charm in a room filled with unexceptional misses who were indistinguishable from one another. He had been captivated by the wicked glint of humor in her eyes, but events parted their paths before he could commit himself. Given the desperate state his life was in, that was all for the good, and all the more reason he should not now be recalling his fondness for her. He schooled his face into a scowl. "No. I was referring to the feeling of being hunted, chased, *pursued*." He added emphasis to the last word and chanced a quick glance at her to see if she caught his meaning, but her lovely brow was wrinkled in thought.

"Who is hunting you, Alasdair?"

He raised one dark blond eyebrow at her.

"Lord Carlisle," she quickly corrected.

"It seems at times, Lady Charlotte—er—what was your husband's name?"

"Di Abalongia, but you may call me Char. All of my intimates do."

"It seems, Mrs. di Ablagon . . . Alab . . . Alban . . . Lady Charlotte, that every marriageable woman within the bounds of the city of London has declared hunting season open, with me the game of the day."

"Oh, them," Charlotte scoffed, steering the horses around a stopped carriage blocking her path. "The marriage-minded mamas, you mean," she added when she had returned to Dare's side.

"And widows," he added with a particularly meaningful look that was unfortunately wasted upon his fair huntress.

"You are the subject of pursuit by women who wish to trap you into marriage?"

"Yes."

The office of his solicitor was a few steps away. He stopped and prepared to make yet another bow.

"And you don't wish to be pursued by them? Most gentleman are flattered when they are the object of a lady's attention."

Lord, she really was beautiful with the morning sun catching the curls nestled alongside her face, burnishing them into spun gold. His fingers itched to touch that warm golden hair, those smooth cheeks kissed by a hint of rose. He curled his traitorous fingers into fists. "I am not most gentleman. I don't have time for such foolishness. I am undertaking a project of the gravest import, and between my sister marrying in a week, and my work, I have little time for avoiding the matrimonial traps set for me."

"Hmm." She tapped one gloved finger upon lips that looked sweet as strawberries, her frown deepening. "You might almost say that your sad circumstance—being pursued by marriageable ladies—was interfering with your life?"

"That would be an accurate statement, yes. And now if you'll forgive me, I have an appointment with my solicitors. Batsfoam? Ah, there you are. Good lord, man, you're covered in dung! Did you roll in the stuff?"

Batsfoam glared briefly at Charlotte before casting a martyred glance at his master.

"No, no, it's of no matter." Dare forestalled what was sure to be forthcoming. "It's not sufficiently offensive for me to require you to throw yourself to certain death before the hooves of Wessex's grays. Do you still have the documents? Excellent. Shall we?"

"One moment, if you please, Lord Carlisle," Charlotte called as he turned toward the door to the office. "I believe I have a solution to your unpleasant situation."

It was Dare's turn to frown in puzzlement. "*You* have a solution?"

"Yes," Charlotte said with just the slightest air of preening herself. "I do. It's a very simple solution."

"Leaving town, I suppose. That I will do—"

"Not that," Charlotte interrupted him. "I know how much you would hate to leave London just as the Season is at its peak. No, my solution is much simpler, much more effective, and has many added benefits which I'm sure you'll appreciate once you put your mind to the matter."

Dare didn't bother to correct her misimpression of his desire to stay in town. He wanted to escape into the safe, dark, dusty warren that was his solicitors' offices, but try as he might to turn his feet and walk away, he found himself standing next to the curricle with one hand resting on the seat rail, unable to tear himself away from the dancing eyes of the woman next to him. "Very well, I will listen to your solution."

"It's quite simple," Charlotte repeated, her dimples flashing. "You are being pursued because you are unmarried. Therefore, you should marry me. All your problems will be solved."

Dare didn't know what he expected Charlotte to suggest, but proposing to him on the steps of

Messrs. Dunbridge and Storm was not it. The caught-in-a-whirlpool feeling returned. "Your offer is, of course, based on completely altruistic motives?"

Charlotte smiled a smile that would have brought a lesser man to his knees. "Yes, of course it is. I am ever altraphistic. All my friends say that about me. Why, only Monday last, my dear cousin Gillian—you remember her, she was the woman you helped kidnap—my dear cousin Gillian said to me, 'Char,' she said, 'you are the most completely almanistic woman I know,' and so I am."

Dare counted silently to ten. "You don't know what altruistic means, do you?"

"Of course I know!" Charlotte paused for a moment. "An exact definition has, at the moment, slipped my mind, but I am not so ignorant that I am unacquitted with everyday words."

"Unacquainted."

"On the contrary, we've known each other for five years."

Dare shook his head. Why he found Lady Charlotte's habit of mangling the English tongue amusing, he never understood, but he did and unless he took himself off and tended to business, he would no doubt find himself bemused into deep waters.

"Regarding your plan—"

"It's an excellent one, isn't it? And it has the happy coincidence of meeting my needs as well, for although I'm sure you'll be shocked to know that I find myself in immediate need of a husband, the truth is that you will suit me quite admirably." Charlotte batted long lashes over eyes so blue they would put a bluebell to shame, but Dare hadn't withstood three weeks of the most intense onslaught of marriage-minded women just to be caught in a snare made up of blue eyes, golden curls, and dimpled cheeks. With an effort he stepped back a few paces and made a courteous bow.

"As generous and selfless as it is, I must decline your offer of marriage. While I wish you the best of luck in finding another victim to your matrimonial plans, experience with the labyrinthine depths of your mind hastens me to state clearly and succinctly that my refusal is binding."

"But, my lord—"

"You need not continue to prod Cupid into aiming his nuptial arrows at me. I have no intention of marrying now, or anytime in the foreseeable future."

"If you will just consider the many and varied benefits of marriage to me—"

"I am flattered, but I must decline. Good day, Lady Charlotte." Dare turned his back and started up the steps to the solicitors' office, followed by a silent, but bright-eyed Batsfoam.

"Do you know, I think I liked you better when you were hatching nefarious plans against Gillian."

Dare froze for a second. That episode was a sore spot in his memory, certainly not one he wished to discuss with anyone, least of all Lady Charlotte. He continued up the stairs.

"Five years ago you weren't so stuffy and priggish! Five years ago you were interesting!"

He gritted his teeth against replying as he reached the top of the steps and opened the door. Two more steps and he would be inside, safe, away from the blend of temptation and aggravation that was personified by Lady Charlotte.

"Very interesting, in fact. I can honestly say that the day Gillian stumbled and tore off your kilt was one of the most *interesting* days I've ever spent. You're just not the same man you were then."

Five years ago he had just inherited his title, and had no idea of the extent of his predecessor's debts. Five years ago he wasn't facing bankruptcy and ruin. Five years ago he had a future. He turned to face the blonde watching him with clear eyes that were no doubt at that moment filled with scorn and condemnation for the man he had become. He allowed a grim, humorless smile to play about his lips.

"Truer words were never spoken, my lady."

Chapter Three

If a group of harlequins, accompanied by monkeys, dancing bears, and pantomime artists, had suddenly burst onto Green Crescent with every sinew of their bodies intent on entertaining and amusing the populace, they would have sobbed in despair at the notice given them by Lady Charlotte as she drove herself home. There were no harlequins, monkeys, bears, or pantomimists, however, leaving Charlotte's attention free to dwell on the events of the morning.

"Crotch?" she said after some thought.

"Er . . . Crouch, m'lady."

"Yes, of course. My apologies. Crouch, I'm going to want a footman to take a note to Lady Beverly."

"As ye wish, m'lady."

"It will be a very important note, Crouch. You must choose a reliable footman."

"All the footmen are reliable, m'lady."

"Yes, but this one must be especially reliable, for the note he will be entrusted with could mean my complete and unbound happiness. Lady Beverly is not yet aware of it, but she is going to assist restoring me to my rightful position."

"That bein'?"

Charlotte raised her chin as she turned the corner for Britton House, pulling up with a dashing flourish of her whip. A footman ran to hold the horses while Crouch handed her down.

"My rightful position is that of reigning Incomparable, of course. As Lady Carlisle, I shall once again be freely admitted into the arms of the *ton*. Once there, I will have no difficulty at all in obtaining everything I've lacked for the last four years—position, respect, admiration . . . Yes, this will be a very important note. Perhaps you should take it yourself. It must be delivered safely, for without Caro's help, I shan't be able to attend Lady Jersey's masquerade ball three days hence, and if I don't attend Lady Jersey's masquerade ball three days hence, I shan't be able to trap Lord Carlisle into a compromising position, and if I don't trap Lord Carlisle into a compromising position, he will never marry me, and if he never marries me—"

"Ye'll be hangin' about our necks in a bad skin, carpin' and bein' a right screw jaws until ye drive us daft," Crouch answered as he followed her up the front steps to the parquet-floored hall.

"Exactly," Charlotte replied with a polite smile as she handed her bonnet and gloves to a waiting footman. "Paper and ink to my sitting room, Crouch."

"Aye, m'lady. Will ye be needin' me to set Dickon at 'is lordship's 'eels again?"

Charlotte paused in the act of fluffing up golden

curls squashed by her bonnet. "I suppose it wouldn't hurt to know Lord Carlisle's movements. Forewarned is four-armed and all that business. Yes, please have Dickon continue to alert me to his lordship's appointments. It came in quite handy this morning to know that he was on foot and in what direction he was traveling."

"As ye will, m'lady."

Charlotte plumped up one last curl, eyed her hair critically in the small gilt-framed looking glass, then nodded decisively as she turned to the stairs. Her plan was good. It was logical and eminently practical, and she knew deep in her bones that it would be successful, assuming Caroline lent her a hand with one or two of the smaller points. "In addition, I'll need several sharpened quills, Crouch. I detest writing with a blunt quill. The noise of it makes my teeth itch."

"I'll 'ave Charles attend to that, m'lady. The quills, that is, not yer itchy teeth. Nothin' I can do about them."

She ignored Crouch's comedic venture and started up the oak staircase, pausing to add, "I feel quite in the need for a restorative cup of tea as well."

"Ye'll 'ave it."

"And perhaps some of those lemon cakes that Cook does so well."

"If ye like."

Charlotte stopped at the landing, glancing at the full-length looking glass reflecting her blue and cream gown with the scrumptious scalloped edging that had arrived from the skillful—and happily for her nearly empty purse, economical—dressmaker recommended by Caro. She tilted her head as she critically examined the lines of the gown, turning around to look over her shoulder. What she saw made her grimace. "I have changed my mind about the lemon cakes, Crouch. Just the tea will suffice."

Crouch squinted up the stairs at her. "Gettin' a bit wide in the saddle, are ye?"

"Certainly not!" Charlotte snapped, and gave him a good glare despite knowing it wouldn't do any good. Glaring never had any effect on Crouch.

The aforementioned just grinned, and ducked his head in an approximation of subservience that didn't for a moment impress Charlotte. With one last frown at the reflected image of her backside, she continued up the stairs to write her very important note.

Although the note had been dispatched and received safely, Charlotte kept the details of what she wanted from her friend until the two met in person the following day.

"This is a lovely room, Caro," Charlotte admired the champagne and rose satin Louis XIV suite. "How very clever of you to put these old things to use. Bruck, isn't it?"

Lady Beverly paused in the act of seating herself in an ornate low-backed chair. "I'm not . . . you . . . *what?*"

"Bruck. The furniture, it's Bruck. That's a style, you goose. French, I think. Good morning, Wellington." Charlotte swept aside a small pug from the settee and sat with a pleased smile, unaware of her hostess mouthing the word *baroque*. "How lucky you are in your situation, Caro. You have a husband who is not tight with the purse strings, a house on a fashionable square, lovely dark coloring that is always in fashion, and a neat figure that is shown to much advantage."

Caroline blushed by the unexpected compliments, unused to being referred to as lovely. She had always been aware of the shortcomings inherent in having an unexceptional face and rather awkward figure, especially when compared with Charlotte's perfection. "I . . . I hardly know what to say—"

"Then say nothing at all, sweet Caro," Charlotte counseled, drawing a small case from her reticule. "Silence, as we know, is molten. Yes, you are a lucky woman in that you have been graced in the physical and husband departments, but your greatest asset must be the happiness and satisfaction that comes from being a cherished member of the *ton*. You, dearest Caro, are indeed in the position to count your blessings."

"I . . . if you put it so, I suppose I am."

Charlotte nodded. "You can always trust me to speak the truth. And as I am doing such, I have no exhibition in stating that you are also a generous and kind woman, one who does not care to see those she's fond of hurt or left to feel less than wanted."

"*Inhibition,*" Caroline corrected softly, blinking in surprise at such effusive praise. "Why, Charlotte! That's very considerate of you to say so. To be honest, Mama said you were blind to the qualities of good in others, but I have always felt she maligned you."

"Alas, I fear you are correct, I have been sorely abused by many who misunderstand my true nature." Charlotte allowed an expression of profound martyrdom to settle on her face as she brushed a few stray dog hairs from her gown. "But say what your mother will, I have always seen your better side, Caro. Who else but someone as kindhearted

41

as you would allow an elderly dog with a propensity to dribble to lounge around on her best Bruck sofa?"

Caroline rustled in her embroidery basket for a handkerchief to dab back a tear brought on by such clear-sighted understanding of her inner self. "Thank you, Charlotte."

"Not at all. You deserve every ounce of happiness possible in your life. The question is, my dear friend, do you believe I deserve the same?"

"Of course you do!" Caroline sniffed militantly and looked ready to dispute anyone's attempt to say otherwise. "You're speaking of Lord Carlisle, aren't you? There's nothing that would please me more than to see you happily married."

"I'm glad you feel that way because I am about to make you very happy indeed!"

"Charlotte! Never say he's already offered for you!"

"No," Charlotte replied, a flicker of something very like obstinacy passing briefly over her smooth features. "Not as yet, but attainment of that very goal is how I will make us both happy."

Caroline leaned forward, her eyes puzzled. "I'm afraid I don't follow you. What can I do to help?"

An impish smile teased the corners of Charlotte's mouth. "It's very simple. The night of Lady Jersey's masquerade ball you're going to help me snare Lord Carlisle in a trap of such fiendish cunning, he won't escape it unbetrothed. To me, that is."

"Oh," Lady Beverly breathed, excitement lighting her eyes. She leaned her dark head closer to Charlotte's. "How will we do that?"

Charlotte gave free rein to her smile. Why shouldn't she? If anyone had a right to smile it was she, for she had thought up a plan of such outstanding cleverness, a plan so brilliant in its stark simplicity, it was truly wondrous to behold. Caroline, for one, was sure to be impressed. "It is quite easy, dear friend. During the ball, you and as many others as you can find will discover Lord Carlisle in a room alone with me."

"But," Caroline protested, "how do you know he'll be at the ball? He doesn't attend many events."

"Caro, do you honestly think I'd go to all the tiresome work, not to mention the risk of unsightly forehead wrinkles, involved in thinking up a plan if Alasdair was not going to be present? Lady Jersey's ball is the most important event of the Season, he's sure to be there with his sister, who is to be married a few days later."

"That may be so, but I've only seen Lord Carlisle and his sister once," Caroline said slowly. "I don't believe they attend very many balls and such."

"Then it will be up to you to ensure they attend this one."

She stared at Charlotte in confusion. "How am I to do that?"

Charlotte cast an impatient glance heavenwards. "Honestly, Caro, must I think of everything? Whatever happened to your initiative? I suppose you'll . . . you can . . . perhaps you could . . . oh, pheasant feathers, simply pay a call on Miss McGregor and tell her she must attend the ball or no one will come to her wedding."

Lady Beverly mused upon this advice for a few moments. "Will they?"

"Will who what?" Charlotte asked wearily.

"Will people not come to her wedding if she doesn't attend the ball? I'm not sure that one necessarily follows the other. Her wedding guests might not be at the ball, you know. The McGregors live a very quiet life, or so dearest Algernon says, and even if they didn't, I can't see people shunning Miss McGregor's wedding just because they did not attend Lady Jersey's—"

"Caroline Augusta Gwendlyspere Talbot," Charlotte interrupted, breathing heavily enough to drown out Wellington the pug. "Might we stick to the subject that concerns us, the subject of my happiness and your role therein? Your tasks are simple and few, and before you offer up one complaint, I'd like you to know that all of the work, the real work, will fall upon my shoulders. So cease this rabble about wedding guests, and focus your attention!"

"It's babble."

"I take extreme umbrage to such slander, Caro!" Charlotte exclaimed, stung by the unfair accusation.

"Well you shouldn't," Caroline replied somewhat crossly. For some reason she couldn't quite pinpoint, lengthy conversation with Charlotte always left her feeling thickheaded and dense. "I was merely correcting you. The word is babble, not rabble. I should cease *this babble* about wedding guests and focus."

"Well I'm glad you see that at last!" Charlotte cried, at the end of her patience. "Now, if you are finished baring your soul and admitting your sin of inattention, we can get back to the important issue of my future."

"I must admit that I don't quite see the fiendishly cunning element of your plan," Caroline interrupted. "You're a married woman—well, you were—and although I agree people would talk if they were to find you secreted away together, I cannot see how being seen alone in a room with Lord

Carlisle will result in his offering for you."

Charlotte's exasperated frown disappeared and her dimples dimpled. "Not even if I was found naked with him?"

Lady Caroline's jaw dropped, so complete was her surprise. Wordless with shock, she stared at her friend.

"I *told* you it was fiendishly cunning," Charlotte answered the silent look of horror. "I would never make such a claim lightly! Now, we have much to discuss, so close your mouth. I must have a suitable costume made up quickly—one that will not reveal who I am, since that fusty old Lady Jersey refuses to recognize me—and we must go over the plan of just how you will smuggle me into the ball, and then there's the crowd you must gather to witness Lord Carlisle's attempted debauchery of my naked person, and many other items. I have my memorandum paper here. I shall make a list for you so you won't forget your tasks."

"But . . . but . . . Charlotte! Such a daring, heedless, *bold* plan—is it prudent?"

"Prudent?" Charlotte scoffed at such a notion. "Caro, in all my three and twenty years, has *anyone* ever called me prudent?"

Caroline, her eyes still wide with disbelief, shook her head. "But—without any sort of clothing—"

"Don't worry about me," Charlotte said kindly, patting Caroline's cheek. "After all, they say that the faint heart never won bare lady, and Alasdair's heart is anything but faint, so how could the plan fail?"

Four nights later the moon was rising full, shedding its cold, mercurial light down upon the city of London, setting a ghostly glow upon the lamplighters who clambered up and down their short ladders as they lit the new gas lamps along the Pall Mall, casting the paving stones into variegated pools of black and silver through which carriages and horses plodded heedlessly as they went about their way, washing pale the portly figure of a man dressed in early Elizabethan garb as he climbed over the solid stone and wrought-iron fence surrounding the garden belonging to Lady Jersey. The moon, had she been able to express an opinion about what she saw from on high, would have no doubt commented that the portly man in costume was by his very actions suspicious. Rather than entering the garden through the gate as most people chose, the gentleman straddled the fence, vaulting down to the soft flowerbeds below with a distinctly heard, "Damnation! I'll get Caro for this!"

When, rather than strolling the graveled pathways as was the normal means of locomotion in a garden, the gentleman skulked about the shrubberies, racing from one clump to another, dodging behind topiaries shaped as fantastic beasts, finally emerging close to the stone steps leading up to the veranda at the rear of the house, surely any watcher would be well within his right to express surprise.

Truly, the gentleman was acting in a peculiar manner. From where he crouched next to the steps, he suddenly stood, fluffed up his ruff, tugged his doublet down over a pronounced belly, pulled a handkerchief out of his codpiece and brushed the dirt from his dainty white hands, and finally, after a quick look around to make sure no one was looking, hiked up his Persian silk stockings. What anyone would have been driven to say when this same portly man was arrested in midstep by the sight of a dark-haired young woman bursting from the

46

house and hurtling down the stairs is lost to us, but certainly the conversation that followed, hushed and whispered though it was, in all likelihood was not what would have been expected.

"Caro," the gentleman intoned urgently as the young woman dashed by him. Lady Caroline stiffened at the repeated hiss of her name, turning slowly to give the beruffed figure a cold and cutting glare.

"Sir, I do not have the honor of your acquaintance."

"You most certainly do. You piddled in my sand pit when you were only three. I remember quite distinctly how Matthew laughed when Nurse blamed me for the implement."

The silent, still figure of Lady Caroline, dressed charmingly in the wide panniers, rose silk, and silvered lace of her mother's era, came to life again under the influence of that familiar, if annoyed, voice. "*Incident.* Char? Is that you?"

The portly man moved from the shadow of the balustrade onto the middle of the steps. "Yes, it is me, just where the devil have you been? I waited at that gate for an eternity! You were supposed to unlock it at half of midnight, Caro! It's well after midnight now!"

"I'm terribly sorry, but dearest Algernon insisted on having a waltz with me. Charlotte," Caroline squinted to make out her friend's face in the shadow, "I thought your costume was to be of Good Queen Bess? You appear to be dressed as a man."

"Yes, yes, I changed my mind. I thought I would be less conspicuous if I were dressed as Henry VIII." She twanged the leather protrusion curving gracefully from her groin. "No one who knows me would ever expect to see me in a codpiece."

47

"No, indeed," agreed Caroline with alacrity. "Say what you will about your propensity for shocking the *ton*, codpieces are simply not part of your everyday apparel."

"And yet, in fairness," Charlotte admitted, "I must say it is very handy. Because I was so late waiting for Mme. Beauloir to deliver my costume, I did not have time to dine at home. Tremayne Three was kind enough to give me one of the horses' apples, which fit quite snugly in the codpiece. It is of no wonder to me that men wore them for so many years—they're much handier than a reticule!"

The two women considered that piece of male apparel in silence for a moment.

"Why do you suppose they call it a codpiece?" Caroline asked. "It doesn't look anything like a fish. Yours looks like . . . well, rather like an overly ambitious squash."

"It was the finest codpiece Mme. Beauloir had," Charlotte answered with dignity, stroking the smooth leather and brass object that, she had to admit, did somewhat resemble a squash. She was about to defend her codpiece's honor further, but the noise and light spilling out as a verandah door was opened returned their attention to the circumstance at hand.

"Take my arm," Charlotte demanded, "and pretend I'm a gentleman."

"You don't walk like a gentleman," Caroline objected.

Charlotte stopped at the top of the steps and pulled Caroline to the side where an urn erupted in a screen of greenery, providing a modicum of privacy. "What are you talking about?"

"No one will believe you're a man if you walk like a woman. Surely you must realize that. It's just common sense. Men don't sway their hips when they walk."

"Some do," pointed out Charlotte, squirming slightly as she adjusted her codpiece. "Drat the thing, it's tickling."

"True, but those aren't gentlemen we are supposed to know. What are you doing now? Char, you can't do that in public, someone will see you!" Scandalized, Caroline hurried to stand between her friend and the nearest group of people enjoying the cool night air.

"I can't help it," Charlotte muttered, her chin jammed against the starched linen of the ruff. "This codpiece is most uncomfortable. It's . . . moving."

"WHAT?"

"Shhh," Charlotte hissed, glancing around quickly before returning her attention to her nether regions. "It's as if there's something in there. Something other than my handkerchief, that is."

"Moving?" Caroline asked through her teeth, smiling a bit wildly at a couple dressed in red dominoes as they strolled past. "What do you mean moving? What could be in there that could move?"

"I don't know," Charlotte grunted, trying without success to unattach the buckles holding the polished leather piece onto her costume. "But I suspect something claimed occupancy while I was hiding in the bushes outside the gate waiting for you to let me in. Thus it is quite clearly all your fault that my codpiece is now rife with wildlife."

"Don't be ridiculous, what could climb into a codpiece? There's no room in there for anything but an apple!"

"Caroline," Charlotte snapped, turning abruptly so the codpiece whapped her friend smartly on the hip. "A family of dormice could have set up shop

49

in this dratted thing and I'd be none the wiser, so if you don't mind, I'd appreciate a little help evicting them from the premises so I can fulfill my destiny and become Lady Carlisle, something I simply cannot do if I have rodents inhabiting my groin!"

"Oh, good heavens," Caroline moaned softly. "We're doomed!"

"It's not that bad," Charlotte answered, placing both hands on the protuberance of the codpiece and tugging. "I just need help getting it off. The buckles seem to be frozen or caught on something."

Caroline, her back to Charlotte as she attempted to block the sight of her friend's codpiece-related actions, reached behind to tug at Charlotte's arm. "Char, stop," she whispered in an anguished, choked voice, trying as she did to summon up a smile. She raised her voice in a clear, "Good evening, Lord Carlisle."

Charlotte, for once alert to the nuances around her, froze and peered over Caroline's shoulder as she bobbed the earl a curtsey. "Damnation."

Dark, midnight blue eyes met hers.

"Quite," Dare replied.

"I . . . er . . . if you'll excuse . . . my husband is waiting for me," Caroline murmured apologetically, and with a worried glance at her friend, hurried off to rejoin the ball.

One of Dare's eyebrows rose as he studied Charlotte's costume. "Henry VIII?"

"Yes, how very clever of you." She turned as if to gaze in contemplation at the darkened garden, rubbing the codpiece on the railing in an attempt to force it loose. It didn't help. With a quick sidelong glance at the handsome man staring out into the garden next to her, she tugged at the obstinate bit of leather with what she hoped was unobtrusiveness.

Dare's second eyebrow rose as she realized she would need to practice her unobtrusive codpiece tugging skills in the future. Clearly this was one of those times when it was more prudent to admit her folly than to encourage the man whose children she would someday bear into thinking her the type of woman who would stand in darkness on a balcony and grope at her codpiece. "There's . . . I think there's something in there," she whispered, nodding toward the leather protrusion.

Dare pursed his lips.

"Something alive," she added, trying not to squirm under both his look of disbelief and the surety that it was hundreds of tiny little feet that were brushing against her sensitive flesh. Overwhelmed by the need to explain further, lest the earl think she was ten cards shy of a deck, she added, "I think something crawled in while I was hiding in the shrubs."

He blinked.

"Perhaps you would be kind enough to extract it for me? Lady Beverly assures me there is a private room at the end of the hall we could use briefly."

"Madam," Dare finally spoke, but in tones so frigid Charlotte expected ice to form upon his manly lips. "The contents of your codpiece do not interest me in the least."

"I understand," Charlotte answered somewhat ruefully. "I'm out of apples. I'm afraid I only had room for the one, you see. I didn't know you'd want one, too, and a two-apple codpiece just seemed a bit too extravagant."

She smiled, wondering briefly about the wild, dazed look about his eyes, finally putting it down to too much champagne. Gentlemen always had too much champagne at masquerade balls. In fact, she counted on that very fact to aid her in drawing him into her net. Her smile brightened as his look of confusion increased. He was no doubt so well oiled by now, she'd have no difficulty in proceeding as planned.

Dare paused in the doorway and scanned the ballroom for his sister, all the while he called himself every sort of fool. Try as he might to heed the warnings of the sane voice in his head, he was unable to resist the thought of spending a few moments in private with Charlotte. The predicament she was in was so ludicrous, so utterly Charlotte, that despite the harsh words he had spoken to her, it would take a group of strong men and quite probably several draft horses to keep him from the explanation of what she was doing dressed as Henry VIII with an animal stuffed down her codpiece. He couldn't begin to imagine what her explanation was, but he was certain it would be the most entertaining thing he had heard in a long time.

He spotted his sister standing on the fringes of a group of giggling girls. As he strode toward her, he justified his interest by pointing out to his doubting self that Charlotte was a widow, after all.

Rendezvous with men at balls were no doubt requisite in her set. A few moments spent alone with her would do her reputation no harm at all. There was, however, the matter of *his* reputation, and it was with an eye to that grisly relic he took the precaution of murmuring a few words into his sister's ear.

"Where's Mrs. Whitney?"

The small, dark-haired woman dressed as the infamous pirate Anne Bonney turned and smiled at her brother, her dark eyes sparkling with happiness. "She's dancing with David. Isn't this a lovely ball? I'm so pleased you agreed to let us attend, although it wouldn't have hurt you in the least to wear a costume. What are you looking so worried about? It's not me, is it? Dare, I'm perfectly capable of standing here by myself while David dances with his aunt. Unless, that is, you wished for me to join the set with you?"

Dare tweaked a dusky curl nestled next to Patricia's ear and ignored the teasing glint in her dark brown eyes. "Minx. I detest *ton* parties, as you well know. The only reason you're here is because I couldn't stand the incessant grizzling about not having anyone attend your wedding if you weren't present tonight, not that I see the connection between the two events. However, even if I wished to dance with you, I am not free. I have an appointment I must keep. I want your promise you'll stay here and await Mrs. Whitney's return."

"Oh?" With one eyebrow cocked in the manner of her brother at his most quizzical, she looked him up and down. He was an impressively austere man in his dress blacks, there was no disputing that, but he had about him an unexpected air of suppressed excitement that intrigued her. Dare was so seldom excited about anything other than his steam engine, surely if something—or *someone*—had caught his attention, it behooved her to learn more. "What, pray tell, do you have an appointment to do? You're not gaming, are you? No," she answered her question before he had a chance to protest her accusation. "No, you wouldn't do that, you're much too careful with your money to be throwing it away on nothing. Hmmm. Perhaps you are meeting with a gentleman who wishes to invest in your steam engine?"

Dare glanced nervously toward the door. He hated leaving his sister alone, especially since his entire future hung upon the goodwill of the woman acting as her chaperone, but he had promised Charlotte he would be with her momentarily. The thought of what might happen should she stroll into the crowded ballroom and announce that she was awaiting his help with her codpiece made his flesh crawl. "I must leave. Give me your word you'll stay here and wait for Mrs. Whitney until I return."

"Not a gentleman investor, I think." Patricia ignored his request, her eyes laughing as she tipped her head to better consider him. "For if you had an investor, it would not matter to you in the least whether or not Mrs. Whitney recommends you to her husband, and thus you wouldn't be so worried about placating her. Not to mention keeping your scandalous past from her ears." She tapped a finger to her lips, her eyes growing bright with interest. "If it's not gaming and it's not an investor, then it must be . . . good heavens, Dare, you're not intending to have an assignation with a woman, are you?"

"Well, I'm not likely to have one with a *man*," he snapped. "Now, will you—"

"It *is* a woman!" Patricia crowed.

Dare scowled as he abruptly shushed her. "If you can't behave any better than this in public, I'll think twice about giving my permission for you to attend any other such festivities."

"After next week, you won't have any say about where I go, but that's neither here nor there," she waved away her brother's objections. "Tell me about this woman you're meeting! Who is she? Do I know her? Are you courting her? Oh, Dare, I do so worry about who will take care of you after I'm married—please tell me you've fallen in love and are about to offer for a woman who will love you in return."

"Love." Dare snorted, momentarily distracted by that unwholesome thought. "That sort of foolishness is what comes from reading those novels you devour weekly."

Patricia watched her brother steadily for a moment, the light of laughter dying in her eyes. "No, I can see you're not in love with anyone, but I haven't given up hope that someday you will find the woman meant for you. I know you believe yourself too scarred by the events in the past to ever give your heart again, but truly, brother, not all women are like the one who hurt you. You must have hope. You must leave yourself open to loving again."

The blank, shuttered look that accompanied any reference made to the events of ten years past left Dare's face a cold, unyielding mask. "Yes or no, will you stay here and behave until Mrs. Whitney is free?"

There was no hope for it, he would not discuss the past. Patricia allowed herself an inner sigh of concern for him, but found a cheerful smile as she saluted smartly. "Aye, aye, *mon capitaine*. Hoist your mainsail and belay those worries, brother mine. I shall stay here becalmed until my own darling captain comes to hoist my anchor."

Dare paused as he turned to leave. "Patricia, just because you're marrying a sailor—"

"Captain, if you please, of the finest Whitney ship ever to sail the seas!"

"—captain, does not mean you must talk like Halibut Harry, the fishmonger's delight. And there had best be no anchor hoisting before the wedding," he warned, his eyes dark with meaning.

Patricia grinned and shooed her brother off. With a shake of his head at the folly awaiting him, he started for the small room off the darkened end of the hall that Charlotte had indicated. Surely it would be a simple matter to help her, one quickly attended to. He would assist evicting whatever it was that had taken up residence in her codpiece—women were so often squeamish about such things—then perhaps engage in a few moments of the particularly delightful form of word games that passed for conversation with Charlotte, after which, with a polite but firm excuse, he would take his leave. The nagging desire he felt to be near her would be assuaged, she would receive discreet assistance with regards to her codpiece problem, and none would be the wiser.

He was mentally forming the excuse he would use to make his escape when he entered the room. "My apologies for being delayed, Lady—mmrph!"

Dare didn't have time to do more than catch a glimpse of heated blue eyes before he was pulled into an intimate embrace.

With Henry VIII. A very well-padded, bearded, codpieced Henry VIII.

He unwound the arms clasped behind his neck in order to dis-attach his lips from the mouthful of scratchy red-orange wool that covered Charlotte's lower face. "I never thought the opportunity to voice this opinion would arise, but there is much to be said for women who shave."

Charlotte, dismay filling her eyes for a moment at his rejection of her advances, smiled instead. "I beg your pardon, I forgot about the beard. One moment, I'll remove it, then we may continue with the ravishing."

Dare shook his head in hopes of clearing away whatever it was that was keeping him from hearing her correctly. He knew Charlotte's verbal acrobatics were sometimes filled with leaps in logic that even a learned man would be hard put to follow, but the one she had just made was surely beyond even her fertile mind.

"About the problem with your costume—"

"That's been remedied," she replied, frowning as she tugged on the side of the wooly beard. " 'Twas just a leaf, not a family of dormice as I had suspected. Drat this thing. Crouch must have used extra glue on it. I can't seem to peel it off, and I ask you, how on earth am I ever going to attend to the ravishing in time if I'm wearing a beard!"

An ugly suspicion flared to life in Dare's mind. "Exactly whom do you expect will be ravishing you?" A morbid sense of curiosity forced him to ask.

Charlotte frowned as she muttered something about needing glue remover. "Pheasant feathers! You'll just have to keep your lips clear, is all. As for your question, no one will be ravishing *me*, Alasdair. I shall ravish *you*."

"*You what?*" Dare couldn't believe that even Charlotte, outspoken and uninhibited as she was, would suggest such a thing. A moment of honesty had him amending the thought to a disbelief that she would plan his ravishment in someone else's home, certainly not anywhere they could be easily . . . he sucked in his breath at the horrible realization that she had set a very clever snare for him, and he, a man who had prided himself daily on avoiding just such entrapment, had blindly walked right into her clutches.

"You needn't worry, I shall take care of everything. You won't have to lift a finger," Charlotte promised.

He stared at her, dumbfounded. Having removed the black and gold velvet doublet, she was spinning in a frustrated circle as she attempted to reach behind herself to untie the tapes holding a large pillow bound over a linen shirt. "Foo! I can't reach the dratted thing. If you could just unbind me, my lord, I will be happy to begin the proceedings. I don't imagine we have much time, and although my experience with ravishing gentlemen is limited, I assume it will take more than a minute or two."

Dare stared in continued disbelief, his emotions tangled and confused as anger and outrage battled with a very unwelcome desire to laugh. He should leave that exact moment. He should walk out of the room and leave Charlotte to whatever horribly convoluted plan she had hatched in that Gordian knot of a mind. He should turn his back on her and never see her again, never again feel the velvet brush of her voice, never experience the brilliant, brief surge of joy that swelled within him when he caught sight of her, and certainly he should never, ever hold her in his arms again.

It just was not sane.

"So be it. I'm mad," Dare growled to himself as he leaned against the door and crossed his arms over his chest, watching as Charlotte muttered and swore as she attempted to wriggle out of the pillow. He clamped down firmly on the wave of desire that swept through him at the sight of such unintentionally seductive movements, damning his eyes and his lust equally. No one would ever believe he could be aroused by a large, hairy, long-dead king, but with each wiggle of her rounded hips his desire, amongst other things, swelled. "This ravishment you're planning—do I assume it has something to do with your proposal of marriage a few days ago?"

Charlotte triumphantly kicked herself free of the pillow, turning upon him a look of innocence so profound it would make an angel feel impure. Dare wasn't fooled for a moment.

"Marriage? Proposal? Oh, that silliness! Good heavens, my lord, I'd forgotten all about *that*," she replied with what he knew were dimples beneath the beard. "No, this is totally unrelated."

"Ah. Would you mind, purely to satisfy my curiosity, informing me what exactly is the goal of your intended ravishment of my person?"

She paused for a moment in the act of unbuttoning her breeches. "You want to know why I wish to ravish you?"

Dare nodded. Yes, he did. He wanted her to admit that she was no better than the rest of the women in society. He wanted his disillusionment to be complete and inexorably final. He wanted to kill the hunger for her that grew stronger within him each time he saw her. By God, he needed to exorcise himself of her!

"Oh. Well. That. Er . . . it's quite simple, actually. You look exceptionally well against me."

A bubble of laughter threatened his iron control. "I do?"

"Yes," Charlotte gave him another beardy smile, and continued to work nimble fingers down the line of mother of pearl buttons on her purple and black breeches.

He resisted the almost overwhelming and completely irrational urge to take her in his arms and kiss away what infinitesimal bit of wits remained about her. "I see. I apologize for my incorrect deduction. I had imagined that your ravishment of me was part of a plan to trap me into marriage."

Charlotte paused. "Oh?"

"Yes. It had occurred to me—thankfully you have shown me the error in my thinking—that you might have arranged to be discovered with me here."

Her hand stilled upon the buttons. "Ah."

"In this room."

She blinked.

"In a state of extreme undress."

She licked her strawberry-sweet lips.

"That isn't the case?"

She raised an outraged chin and shot him a steely look. "I am sorely offended that you could think me capable of such heinous and unworthy acts, Lord Carlisle. You would think a gentleman would be pleased with an offer of ravishment, but no, you have to be obstinate and suspicious and ruin the whole experience! I'm of half a mind to not ravish you at all!"

One heavy gold eyebrow cocked in question.

"But I shall," she continued, nodding righteously as she resumed work on the buttons. "I shall overlook your petty thoughts this once, but don't expect me to be so generous next time."

"So your intention in removing all your clothing and making love to me is not to be discovered, compromised to the point that I will be forced by honor into wedding you?"

"I just said that!"

"Then you don't mind if I lock this door?" Dare turned the small brass key in the lock and pocketed it.

"Er . . ." Charlotte watched him warily.

"I thought you wouldn't. Where would you care for the lovemaking to take place?"

Her lovely blue eyes didn't even blink. "Er . . ."

"That couch looks comfortable. Or perhaps you would like to have your wicked way with me on the rug before the fire?"

She glanced at the fire. "Er . . ."

Dare gave her a scandalized wiggle of his brows as he strolled over to stand next to a large leather armchair. "Don't tell me you prefer more *inventive* positions? The armchair, perhaps?"

Charlotte looked with blossoming interest at the armchair. "How could that be possible?"

Dare couldn't help but laugh. She really was the most refreshing woman he'd ever met, uninhibited, direct, every word and deed unexpected, but he had had enough of playing her game. He had spent well over the few minutes he had allotted to attending her codpiece needs, and his future relied upon his keeping his sister's soon-to-be-aunt satisfied of his character and morality. "Lady Charlotte, I'm afraid I must turn down yet another of your charming but irregular offers. I have left my sister alone too long. If you will forgive me—"

Charlotte approached the leather chair, prodding gently at it as if she expected it to explode before her eyes. "How exactly does one conduct a ravishment in a chair?"

Both of Dare's eyebrows rose.

"Where, for instance, do the legs go?"

His eyebrows rose even higher.

"And what about the . . . instrument? How exactly is it wielded in such a situation?"

Dare mused upon his luck in having thick hair, for if he had not, his eyebrows would have found themselves at the back of his head. "Lady Charlotte—"

She stared at the chair with a puzzled frown, one hand holding her unbuttoned breeches together. "I simply cannot picture it. Not even in Vyvyan La Blue's famed *Guide to Connubial Calisthenics* is an armchair mentioned."

Dare opened his mouth to take his leave once and for all.

"I would have remembered such a thing if it were!"

He shook his head. He had to gather his wits, and do it now, else he'd be lost in the mad twirl of her thoughts.

"It wouldn't be an easy thing to overlook, and I paid diligent attention to the chapters on creative use of furnishings as Antonio was so very fond of brocade."

"Regardless—" *Brocade?* Surely he was not hearing her correctly.

"You wouldn't think a man would find brocade a thing of enjoyment, but Antonio loved to have me wrap him in long lengths of it, then use a carpet beater on him."

"I must be . . . did you say carpet beater?"

She nodded, tracing a finger down the curved back of the chair. "Yes, he said it made the brocade soft and pliable and soothing to the skin, although how he could appreciate that with all the twitching and spasming and moaning he did as a result of the application of the carpet beater is beyond my understanding."

He thought that was the least of what was beyond her understanding.

"Still, he looked forward to the brocade beating sessions, so I guess there must be some merit in what he said."

Dare took a good, firm grip on his wits, and made one last effort to save his sanity. "Lady Charlotte?"

Charlotte turned to him with a sweet, completely

misleading expression on her bearded face. "Yes, my lord?"

He looked deep into her lovely eyes, fathomless and clear, and he knew a yearning not felt since he was young and foolish and in love for the first time. But he was no longer young, and foolish though he might be, he had no place for love in his life. "Good evening."

"But, my lord . . ."

He walked to the door and unlocked it, glancing back over his shoulder to forever burn the image in his mind of the woman who had somehow, against his will, stayed in his heart after five lonely years. She was beautiful. Ethereal. A goddess, still as marble, clad in rumpled silk stockings, her ruff skewed slightly to one side with her exertions, the long lace fall of her linen shirt tangling with the hand that clutched her breeches together, the codpiece dangling in disarray. Her face was pale against the burning red of her beard, making her eyes glitter bright and clear as the bluest of summer skies.

He would leave town after Patricia's wedding. He would never see her again. "Goodbye, Charlotte."

The latched turned under his hand, forcing him to step back quickly lest he be struck by the opening door.

"Ah, Lord Carlisle, there you are. A little bird told me I could find you here."

Dare looked with growing horror at the smiling, suspicious face of his hostess.

"Lady Jersey. I . . . er . . ."

"Your sister was worried about you, weren't you, Miss McGregor?"

Dare took another step back as Patricia slipped in next to Lady Jersey. Both women looked beyond him to where Charlotte had scurried behind the chair. "I was. It's not like my brother to disappear when he promised me a waltz, although if you have some business with that gentleman, Dare, I am willing to forgive you the oversight."

Lady Jersey stepped farther into the room, inclining her head toward Charlotte as she held out her hand. "Sir, I do not believe I've had the pleasure?"

Charlotte, with a strangled sound and a quick indecipherable glance at Dare, reached out to take the proffered hand, but snatched it back quickly when her breeches started to slide down her hips.

"Good God in heaven!" Lady Jersey exclaimed, her sharp eyes missing nothing of Charlotte's rumpled appearance. "Lord Carlisle, I had no idea you are a . . . that you preferred . . ."

Thankfully the presence of Patricia put a halt to any further utterances. Dare opened his mouth to explain, but he couldn't. If he mentioned who Charlotte was, the parson's noose would be around his neck before he knew it. Yet if he didn't, Lady Jersey would be sure to spread word of his alleged sexual preference, which, given his luck of late, would find its way unerringly to the ears of the very straight-laced Mrs. Whitney, and that would spell a disaster from which he could not recover. He tried to rally his wits, but the full horror of the situation had struck him, leaving him with a sick, clammy feeling in the region of his stomach, hands that were suddenly damp, and the knowledge that if his goose was not yet actually plucked, it was next in line. Before he could do more than sputter an objection, however, the matter was taken from him.

"Lord Carlisle was merely helping me with my codpiece," Charlotte said in a deep, obviously false approximation of a male voice. Two more people crowded into the doorway as she cleared her throat and added, "That is, he was assisting in removing an object from it."

Dare's mind went numb around the edges. He hadn't thought matters could be made worse, but when Mrs. Whitney leaned toward him and in a scandalized whisper asked why a half-clad man was standing before Lady Jersey, he felt the leaden weight of despair clamp itself around his heart. Dare glanced at her, over to the sympathetic eyes of Patricia's betrothed standing beside his aunt, and felt the cold hands of the feather plucker approaching. He was caught. Ensnared. Trapped. It had come to this, to a choice. If he wanted any hope of selling his engine design to the Whitney shipyards, he would have to salvage the situation, and assuming his prayer for the earth to open up and swallow him whole was not going to be answered, salvage meant sacrifice. *His* sacrifice.

He took one last breath as a free man.

"When I say he was assisting me, I mean that he offered to look inside and determine what exactly was in—"

"What Lady Charlotte is trying to say is that she has done me the honor of bestowing upon me her hand."

Five pairs of eyes stared in surprise at his pronouncement. Dare looked calmly back at all of them, beyond feeling anything but stupefied.

"She? That person is a woman?" asked Mrs. Whitney.

"I knew it!" Patricia exclaimed, saluting her brother with her wooden saber before kissing him on his cheek. "I'm so pleased!"

"Best of luck to you, old man," said David the sea captain as he clapped Dare on the back.

"Lady Charlotte?" Lady Jersey growled as she turned to face the person in question. "Lady Charlotte Collins? The Lady Charlotte who ran off with an Italian nobody despite my warning her it would all end in despair? The Lady Charlotte whom I specifically forbade to attend my ball? The Lady Charlotte who, upon hearing my refusal, referred to me as 'that jealous old she-cat who wouldn't recognize quality if it bit her on the bottom'? *That* Lady Charlotte?"

Dare looked at Charlotte. She looked back at him, her eyes round with surprise. Then suddenly she whooped with delight and threw herself across the room and into his arms, murmuring into his ear, "I knew this would turn out well! I knew you wouldn't fail me! Now we will be wed and you won't be hunted any longer, and Lady Jersey will have to receive me, and I shall have gowns and go to balls and dance, and best of all, your instrument will be happy to apply itself while you delegate the armchair's usage to me."

"Demonstrate," Dare corrected softly, flinching slightly as the hunter's arrow pierced him with a mortal blow. The taste of entrapment was bitter on his tongue.

Chapter Four

"Truly, Alasdair . . ."

Charlotte stopped speaking under the look Dare bent upon her. She thinned her lips in annoyance. "We are betrothed. Must I continue to call you Lord Carlisle?"

Dare fought the familiar tightness across his chest and took an experimental deep breath. At least the shackles Charlotte had about him allowed him to breathe. "No, you do not need to call me Lord Carlisle, but if you must use my Christian name, please use the abbreviated version. No one but my mother calls me Alasdair."

She blinked. "What should I call you?"

"Dare."

"Dare? As in . . . *Dare?*"

"Dare." He signaled the horses to start and expertly guided them into the busy flow of traffic surrounding Covent Garden. "It's just four little letters. Even you should be able to remember it."

Charlotte tucked an errant curl back into her honeysuckle-crested bonnet, frowned for a moment, then turned to give Dare an outraged glare. "Did you just insult me?"

"Yes."

Her look of outrage grew. "Why?"

"Because I'm in a foul mood."

"Why?" she asked again.

Because he had been forced into offering for her. Because he had enough experience to know that what she wanted in life was not what he wanted. Because he knew that despite his acceptance of fate, their marriage would be a terrible mismatch, dooming them both to a life filled with misery, despair, and hopelessness. The Charlotte he remembered was silly and seldom looked beneath the surface, while he had been molded by bitter circumstances and had no patience with shallowness. Dare stared grimly ahead as he drove his team toward Green Park, where his sister had arranged to act in place of Charlotte's family to discuss wedding arrangements. He glanced at her out of the corner of his eye, expecting to see a righteously indignant Charlotte demanding he treat her as was her due, or a petulant Charlotte who wanted compliments to soothe his insult, or worst of all, a giggly Charlotte determined to jolly him into a better mood. Dare was a man who cherished his sulks, and he had no intention of being made happy when he wanted to brood.

What he saw in her eyes shook his faith in his right to make everyone around him miserable. She was nodding, understanding and compassion warming her blue eyes until they were so clear, he could see right through to her soul. He yanked his gaze away. He didn't want to see her soul. He wanted to be left alone to nurse the grievous injury she had done him, and he couldn't do that if he was forced to see beyond the shallow surface of her character.

She patted his arm nearest her. He stared down at the butter yellow glove resting on his sleeve as she said, "It will no doubt come as a great surprise to you, but I, too, have had occasion to give in to a pout. I've found them most refreshing, as long as they don't go on too long. Then they can cause wrinkles."

Dare straightened his shoulders and shot her a warning glance. "I do not pout, madam. I am, if anything, merely brooding over the many injustices done me of late. Brooding is not pouting. It's as far removed from pouting as is possible. Women pout, men do not."

"Pheasant feathers!" Charlotte scoffed. "It's a pout and nothing but a pout. And to what injustices are you referring? You don't mean our marriage, do you? Because if you do, I shall be forced to be offended and take action."

"What action?" Dare couldn't help but ask. He wrestled his bad mood back to its accustomed place. Just being in her presence gave him a sense of something so remarkably akin to happiness that it threatened to blow away the clouds of his foul mood. And he couldn't have that, because without his cloak of self-pity, he would have to admit to feeling things for Charlotte that were best left unrecognized.

"I should challenge you to a duel."

Dare jerked at the reins, narrowly avoiding driving over two unwary ladies' maids. He tossed an apology over the side of the phaeton before turning his attention back to his bride-to-be. "Obviously the stress of the last few weeks has taken its toll on me. My hearing has become quite unreliable. Would you repeat what you just said?"

"I said that if you meant our marriage and future together was an injustice, I should take action, and that action would translate itself as a duel. Pistols, I think. I never was any good with Matthew's sword, but I am reckoned quite a crank shot with a pistol."

"Crack," he corrected automatically, wondering if somewhere along the last day he had lost his mind. That or his life had turned into a French farce. Either explanation would make sense. "Ladies do not fight duels, Charlotte. Not with pistols, not with swords, not ever."

"I have never been one to follow the dictates of fashion, my lord."

Dare stared at her in disbelief. "Of course you are. You don't think about anything but what's fashionable and the latest shot with the *ton*."

Charlotte appeared to think about that for a moment. "When it suits me, yes, but often times what society says is reasonable and fashionable doesn't suit me."

He had to concede that point. Charlotte did exactly as she wanted, regardless of what anyone thought of her actions, whether it was wearing a beard and codpiece to a masquerade ball or running off with a penniless foreign nobleman. He sighed over his unconventional bride for a moment before admitting to himself that her originality was most decidedly an asset. Still, he wasn't about to start out his new life as a husband with his wife in the position of power. There was no better time to make it absolutely clear who would be in charge in their marriage.

"Ladies do not fight duels, Charlotte," Dare said in his best end-of-the-discussion voice. "Now, as I told you earlier, since you have no family present, my sister will be happy to help you plan your wedding."

"*Our* wedding."

"That goes without saying," he said with only a minor tightening around his chest. Maybe he would survive the experience after all. Maybe, after a few years, he would get use to his bondage and could look forward to, if not happiness, then a pleasant existence.

"And I notice you are the one who is taking great pains to avoid saying it," Charlotte pointed out. "I cannot help but feel, Alasdair, that you are not entirely happy about having offered for me, and yet I also cannot help but point out that it was, in fact, you who offered marriage, not I. Well, I did earlier, but you turned me down, so that doesn't count. Not really. Are you?"

"Am I what?" Dare asked, feeling only the tiniest bit bemused by Charlotte's amazing leaps of thought. He took pride in his ability to follow her, feeling certain few men could claim such an achievement.

"Are you happy that we are to be married?"

Dare flicked the reins and tried to think of how to answer her question. He wanted to tell her that he had only offered for her because she'd trapped him in front of the woman who could destroy his future, but he had enough honesty to admit that wasn't entirely the truth. Oh, she had trapped him, but he might have been able to bluff his way out of the situation, even with Mrs. Whitney viewing the proceedings with bright, inquisitive eyes. No, the truth was . . . What was the truth? He didn't want to wed her, did he?

He slid a glance at the figure beside him. He had wanted to make her his wife . . . once, five years ago. But that was before disaster struck, before he knew that he had little to offer a wife but an empty title and a mountain of debts. And he'd be damned if he went to a bride empty-handed, unable to take care of her.

"And yet that's just what I'm doing," he sighed, allowing a moment of self-pity.

"If you mean that what you're doing is avoiding answering my question, yes, you are quite correct. Really, Alasdair, I believe I'm about to be most offended. You can't even answer a simple question when I put it to you? Is there something about me that offends you? I know it can't be my appearance, because . . . well, modesty is a silly virtue I've always felt. Clearly my appearance is not at fault, and I know it can't be what I've said, because I haven't once mentioned any of the things that outraged you so during your discussion of my genitals, and I'm fairly certain it can't be this gown because it's my cousin's gown that I had altered, so really, if you're offended, it's Gillian's fault, not mine, and I don't think that's at all fair of you to be offended with her since she is on a ship somewhere and can't defend herself against your rude comments about her choice of gowns!"

It really was amazing, Dare thought to himself, that he was starting to understand how Charlotte thought. Oh, to be true, any lengthy conversation with her left his mind feeling a bit strained, but he really was getting the knack of the thing. He pulled the team to a halt before the small beige brick house he had rented for the time he was in London, and turned to tell her the truth. She tipped her head on the side, watching him with a gaze that seemed to see so much, and yet was the epitome of innocence. He thought of what his life would be like bound to a frivolous woman without a thought in her head for anything more serious than what gown to wear. He thought about sinking further into debt trying to support her. He thought about the dreams he had as a young man, now withered and crumbled to dust. He recognized the cold hand of despair touching his heart, and wanted to weep with the injustice of it all.

"Alasdair?"

He thought of all that until his gaze met hers, and then all he thought of was how indescribably lovely she was, how completely and utterly unique she was from every other woman of his acquaintance, and how he would rip to shreds any other man who thought to claim her.

"My lord?"

His jaw tightened as he acknowledged his unwanted feelings of possessiveness. So be it. He had made the decision, and now it was his duty to see it through. God alone knew how he was going to manage it. Marriage to any woman was not welcome, but to a woman so clearly bent on having her own way, regardless of his wishes . . . well, he would wed her and possess her, but in his own good time, in his own way. She'd just have to understand that he had no intentions of being trapped a second time.

"I am a simple man, Charlotte," he told her. "I would not offer you marriage if I thought either of us would live to regret it. If you are having second thoughts, please tell me now. Otherwise . . ." he leaped down from the phaeton and held out his hand to her. "... my sister awaits, and you have wedding plans to make."

"You are welcome to be married with David and me," Alasdair's sister offered, looking up with a smile from where she was embroidering her bridal stockings. "It won't be a big wedding, but you're welcome to share it. I think it would be very romantic for all of us to be married at the same time."

Charlotte thought it would be anything but romantic. Horrific, appalling, embarrassing, not-to-be-borne, a terrible waste of a day that was supposed to be the happiest in any woman's life, yes, yes, it was all that, but romantic? Faugh!

Patricia turned to her brother with a smile that sparkled in her eyes. "Dare, you wouldn't mind being married with David and me, would you? It would be such a lovely day. You could join us for breakfast at the hotel, and then we can all go down to the docks to see the ship. I'm sure Lady Charlotte would enjoy that."

On the contrary, Lady Charlotte was sure she would *not* enjoy that. Lady Charlotte was equally sure she would not enjoy any other events of that ilk. Lady Charlotte would go so far as to admit to an almost uncontrollable urge to wrap her borrowed lace handkerchief across Patricia's mouth lest other such suggestions burst forth.

"It might do," Alasdair said thoughtfully, one finger absently rubbing across his lower lip. Charlotte shifted to a slightly less uncomfortable spot on the worn settee, her gaze following his finger as it rubbed back and forth, her breath doing odd little palpitations in her chest as she noticed for the first time just how handsome his lips were. Lips, she had always felt, were lips. Functional, yes. Pleasing in an aesthetic manner, true. But she had never been a connoisseur of lips in the past, a fact she admitted with no little sense of regret upon viewing the fine specimens Alasdair bore. Clearly she had made a grievous mistake in overlooking lips as a source of enjoyment, his lips in particular, but that fault would be corrected immediately. Or as immediately as it took her to make him kiss her. "It would serve us both well. We could get both events over with in one fell swoop."

"I do not wish to be over in a fell swoop, whatever that is," Charlotte objected. Her musings upon the glory and greatness of his lips were abruptly brought to an end. She felt control slipping through her fingers, and it was not a pleasant sensation. She liked Alasdair's sister, she honestly did, but if that little mischief-maker thought she was going to do Charlotte out of the grand, glorious wedding due her, she could just think twice!

"We wouldn't dream of encroaching on your wedding," she told Patricia quickly. "That is your special day, the day everyone caters to your every whim, the day when you look your prettiest. You wouldn't want to share that day with another woman, would you?"

"I wouldn't mind," Patricia protested.

"Of course you would mind! You wouldn't want your husband-to-be comparing you to another woman, and seeing you in a lesser light, would you?"

"David would never—"

"That would be a terrible cavity!"

"Calamity," Dare offered.

Charlotte pointedly ignored him. "Your brother ought to be ashamed of himself for even suggesting

75

the idea to you. How dare he try to ruin your happy marriage?"

"No, Lady Charlotte, *I* suggested it to him—"

"How could you face the rest of your life with a man who thought you were second best?"

"But, but—"

"It simply is not tolerable! No woman should be asked to sacrifice herself thusly, not even for me. No, no, protest no more, dearest sister-to-be. It's quite clear to me that you must not have your day tainted by such unhappy opportunities as your husband seeing me looking particularly stunning in my wedding finery."

"Unhappy opportun . . . Lady Charlotte, I assure you that David—"

Charlotte turned on Dare, feeling confident that she had squashed the sweet, but sadly rather bossy, plan to cheat her of the momentous event she had envisioned ever since she put up her hair. She had been done out of a glorious wedding once, and she had no intentions of allowing that to happen again. "You really should apologize to your sister for trying to ruin her most important day, Alasdair."

The frown gracing Dare's manly brow deepened to something bearing an uncanny resemblance to a scowl. "I have nothing to apologize for, and stop calling me Alasdair. I've told you to use Dare, instead."

Charlotte brushed a miniscule bit of thread from her lemon-colored gown. "I'd prefer not to. It sounds silly."

"I'd prefer you would, and it does not sound silly." Dare rose from the chair next to his sister and went to stare moodily out the window.

"It does. You have a perfectly good name. There's no reason why you shouldn't use it."

He turned around to glare at Charlotte. "It's my name and I'll use it any way I want."

"You're acting childish!"

"And you're unreasonably obstinate!"

"Oh!" Charlotte matched his glare and raised it a notch. "I am not unreasonable or obstinate, you take that back! I'm simply pointing out how ridiculous you sound pattering on about a childhood nickname when you're an earl and an important person and about to become a married man!"

"It's *nattering*, and as the name in question is mine, I'll be called whatever I bloody well want!"

"You're shouting at me. I don't think that's called for in the least!" Charlotte marched over to the window until she was toe to toe with him. She poked him in the chest. "First you try to destroy your sister's sole chance at happiness, no matter how slight that might be when you consider that she's planning on tying herself to a man who is ready to spurn her at her own wedding for a lovelier woman, and then you're trying to make me cry by being beastly and cruel. Well, I won't do it!"

Dare grabbed her hand to keep her from poking at him again. She used her other hand. He grabbed that as well. Reading in his eyes no uncertain repercussion if she were to continue with the chest poking, she decided on a tactical retreat, withdrawing her hands from his and returning to the lumpy settee. "Really, my lord, you are the most argumentative person I've ever met!"

He ground his teeth and clutched with clearly visible white knuckles at the back of a nearby chair. Char watched warily as he struggled for control, relaxing when he regained it and finally unclenched his jaw long enough to say, "I don't know why our conversations always end up in arguments."

"Neither do I, Alasdair," she said after a moment's thought. "But I do have to point out that the fault truly is yours. If you wouldn't disagree with me, we wouldn't argue."

Charlotte's eyes widened as he stared at her with a wild look for a long moment. Then he turned on his heel and without another word left the small sitting room. "Well, really! How are we to discuss our wedding if he can't even remain in control of his emotions for a few seconds at a time?" she asked slowly, her ears still reverberating with the slamming of the door. "Has he always been so?"

Patricia seemed to have swallowed her tea wrong, for she was making odd little choking noises, and finally had to resort to a handkerchief to dab at the resulting tears. "No. He's not normally emotional, Lady Charlotte. He's usually quite the opposite. It seems that only when he's in your presence . . ." The words trailed off as Patricia choked again. Charlotte leaned sideways and thumped her back.

"You should be careful how you drink tea," she warned as she took up the paper and quill lying on the table before her. "There was a girl at Miss Bengyman's School who drank her tea wrong while the vicar was calling and it spewed out her nose and all over the vicar, his wife, two of their children, and a large gray Persian cat that happened to be passing. A most unfortunate circumstance for everyone involved. I believe the cat died. Now, let me see, you are being married on Sunday next, which means my wedding must be no later than Wednesday. Yes? What is it . . . Pigeonfroth, isn't it?"

"Batsfoam, my lady." The butler made an obsequious bow to the accompaniment of many cracking and popping noises that Charlotte felt were best ignored.

"Batsfoam, of course. How silly of me. That's nothing at all like Pigeonfroth, is it? Did you wish to speak to me?"

"Indeed, my lady. My lord, your soon-to-be husband and protector, instructed me to make myself of service to your august ladyship, and I, ever grateful for the trust he places in me, a mere servant, albeit one crippled in service to our good king, mad though he is, not that he can do anything about that, certainly no more than I can do about my own impairments, of which I have many and not limited to the tragic loss of my lower limb, am ever thrilled and delighted beyond human ken to fulfill his requests, no matter how my other duties may pile up. Thus it is that I abase myself before you, my lady, in offering my services, humble and no doubt unwelcome though they are." The man bowed again, this time so low his nose bumped into Charlotte's ankle. He apologized and straightened up with audible relief, pulling from an inner pocket a folded sheet of paper, which he presented to her with great flourish.

"Oh," Charlotte said, frowning at paper. "No, certainly your help is not unwelcome, although I am unsure of just what, exactly, his lordship expects you to do for me. What is this?"

"I believe, my lady, it is a list of dates and locations suitable to a person contemplating the act of marriage. His lordship had recently researched the very same for Miss McGregor's upcoming nuptials, and thought you would like to have the benefit of his labor."

"Excellent. Let me see . . . oh, no, no, Batsfoam, this will not do, not in the least. You see here that

Lord Carlisle has not listed any church of consequence. I couldn't possibly be wed in anything but a church of the utmost consequence, for if it is held elsewhere, no one in the *ton* will wish to attend. No, this list will have to be revised dramatically. I shall be pleased to do so now." She turned to Patricia. "How do you suppose you spell Westminster Abbey?"

"My lady, if I might humbly beg a fraction of your attention for a moment that I shall endeavor to make as brief as possible, there is more."

Charlotte looked up from where she was adding St. Paul's Cathedral to her list. "More churches?"

Batsfoam moved his features into one expressing regret. "Alas, my lady, no, not more churches. His lordship has asked me, in the guise of his man of affairs, a role I have the honor of bearing, in addition to that of butler, valet, draughtsman, knife-boy, and now, ladies' maid to your gracious ladyship, to ascertain the direction of your ladyship's most honored brother, Lord Collins, so that his lordship, a fine and honorable man, if one who tends to take such things a bit more for granted than I care to see, might ascertain the exact amount of your ladyship's dowry." He bowed and spoke the last word in such a reverent and hushed tone, Charlotte had difficulty hearing him.

"Alasdair wishes to ask Matthew about my what?"

"Dowry, my lady." He bowed again.

She blinked in surprise at him. "What dowry?"

He blinked back at her. "I am quite certain that ladies of your station and gentility often have bestowed upon them by some member of their family a sum of money or property that is customarily referred to as a bridal dowry."

"That may be so, but I don't have one."

"I do," Patricia piped up. "Dare sold out the last of some bonds or something to give it to me, although David didn't want to accept it at first, but Dare told him he had to take it, or he wouldn't agree to the marriage."

Both Batsfoam and Charlotte ignored the interruption.

"You don't have a dowry, my lady? Not even a small house tucked away in the country?"

"Nothing." Charlotte shook her golden head.

"Perhaps there are some government bonds you might have forgotten?"

"There is nothing, Batsfoam."

"Not even a groat or two invested in canals?"

"No groats, invested or otherwise."

"Your late husband . . . ?"

"Was kept on a very small allowance by the conte. It was just enough for a few sheep and the occasional purchases of brocade."

"No widow's stipend?"

"None. I had to sell the sheep to have the brocade cleaned so it could be made into a traveling cloak."

Batsfoam stared at the memorandum paper upon which he was prepared to write the earl's direction. A sweat broke out on his forehead. "A most calamitous event, my lady."

"Oh, not terribly so. The sheep smelled and the brocade was quite warm when I was at sea."

"I do not refer to the sheep, but to your lack of dowry."

"Oh, that. It's of no consequence." Charlotte waved away the servant's concern. "Alasdair might be upset because he can't add to his fortune, but I'm sure he is more than happy to take me as I am. While we are on that subject, please inform him

81

that although I know it's customary for the bride's family to pay for the wedding, I haven't any money, so he'll have to pay for that, as well as my new trousseau, which I will order just as soon as I am finished here."

Batsfoam's mouth worked silently a few times before he staggered over to a chair and collapsed into it. Charlotte gave him a brief frown to let him know what she thought of him sitting without being invited to do so, then returned to more important matters. "Now, looking back at his list, I must say that his dates are quite, quite unacceptable. Why, the earliest one is three months hence! No." Charlotte scratched out a list of five dates and made an addition with a bold hand. "Next Wednesday, I believe, will suit me admiralty."

"Admirably."

"Yes, it is. I'm glad you agree."

"But, Lady Charlotte," Patricia protested, "Wednesday is less than a week away!"

"Ample time for your brother to make the arrangements," Charlotte pointed out.

"But . . . but . . . such a hurried wedding . . ."

Charlotte looked up from creating a list of suitable wedding guests. "Only the really important people, I believe. I wonder what the Prince Regent is doing on Wednesday?"

Patricia blushed a delicate blush and shooed a still stunned, and noticeably reluctant to leave, Batsfoam from the room. She waited until he was gone to speak. "Lady Charlotte, you're not giving due thought to the date. A wedding in such a hurry . . . well, it can only cause talk! People will be speculating as to the necessity of such a thing!"

"Necessity?" Charlotte looked up from her list. "What do you mean, *necessity?*"

Patricia's blush deepened. "You are a widow, surely you must know."

Charlotte allowed her forehead to wrinkle briefly in thought. "I believe we must be speaking at cross purposes. What has my late husband to do with my marriage to your brother?"

Patricia wrung her hands, her face flaming with embarrassment. "Nothing, other than . . . well, if you insist that I speak frankly . . . intimate relations."

"What about them?" Charlotte eyed her soon to be sister with a small amount of concern. Patricia seemed to be upset about Charlotte's relatives, and although heaven knew Charlotte herself wasn't any too fond of her brother and her distant cousins, it seemed rather an odd thing to bring up objections to them now.

"People will think you had them. With Dare."

"That's ridiculous." Charlotte snorted, returning her attention to her list. "I am not even remotely related to you and Alasdair. Do you think the king would be offended if I were to not invite him?"

"No," Patricia said, pacing the floor before Charlotte. "You don't understand. If you and Dare marry so very quickly, people would be bound to talk about you."

"Well of course they'll talk about us," Charlotte reassured her in a soothing voice. "People always talk about me! Alasdair and I shall be the toast of the *ton*. How could we be anything else? A dashing, handsome earl and a lovely almost-contessa marrying in such a romantic manner is bound to cause envy in the hearts of everyone worth any consideration. I assure you I am quite used to being the darling of society. I shan't shame your brother, if that is your concern."

"Oh . . . I give up," Patricia said, gesturing defeat

with her hands. Charlotte raised an eyebrow for a moment, then decided not to point out that worrying just caused spots, and she returned to her list. For half an hour the only sound in the cozy sitting room was that of the quill on paper.

"Lady Charlotte?"

"Mmm?" Charlotte crossed Lady Jersey's name off her list. The rude comments she had delivered after she discovered Charlotte had attended her party in disguise were utterly and completely uncalled for. Charlotte relished the opportunity to give Lady Jersey a taste of crow.

"What . . . what is it like?"

Charlotte looked up. "Revenge? It's quite satisfying."

A startled expression flickered across Patricia's face before a dusky rose color swept up from her neck. "No, not revenge. Relations. *Marital* relations," she added for good measure.

"Marital relations? You mean your husband's relatives? I have no idea—"

"No, not that sort of relations, I mean . . . *relations.*"

Patricia's deep blush and her downcast eyes made a connection in Charlotte's mind. "Oh, you mean the joining between your womanly parts and his manly instrument? I'm sure I shouldn't tell you, but as my dearest cousin Gillian told me about it before I was wed, and as you are to be a bride next week, I shall just this once break the rule and tell you." She set down the quill and arranged her hands on her lap, then looked her sister-to-be in the eye.

Patricia leaned forward, her attention completely on Charlotte. "Yes?"

"It's messy." Charlotte nodded twice, then picked

up her quill and started double-checking the list.

"Messy? That's all? It's . . . messy?"

"Yes, that's all." Charlotte looked up for a moment, tapping the quill on her chin. "My cousin did have a good deal more to say about it, something about transporting her to heaven, but to be truthful, I thought it was just a messy business. Necessary, if one wishes to have children, and I wish to, but nonetheless, it's messy."

"Messy how?"

It was Charlotte's turn to affect a faint blush. She waved her hand dismissively. "There are bodily humors and such to be contended with. Not to mention certain . . . scents. My advice to you is to have a linen cloth handy. Two if your husband is particularly vigorous."

"A linen cloth?"

Charlotte nodded. "You will see. Messy."

"Ah."

Happily for all concerned, the subject was dropped in favor of a debate on the relative merits of Belgian versus Irish lace, a discussion that ended abruptly when Dare, shadowed by Batsfoam bearing Charlotte's revised list, came roaring into the room with a demand to know why Charlotte was attempting to drive him insane.

"I thought it only right since you earlier accused me of being mad, not to mention obstinate and unreasonable," she said placidly, considering and rejecting the fashion plates Patricia had presented her. As money was clearly no object with Dare, mundane fashions that any woman might have would not suit the future Countess of Carlisle.

When Dare sputtered indignantly at her answer, she glanced up at him to ask just what he was so upset about, but ended up staring in stunned amazement. He was coatless, cravat-less, his shirt-sleeves rolled up to expose muscled forearms that were as bare as the day he was born. His shirt gaped at his neck clear down to the top of his waistcoat, exposing a tanned column of throat that made Charlotte's mouth suddenly go dry. She looked between his neck and his arms, unable to decide at what she wanted to stare at more, the corded strength of his naked arms, all golden and warm in the afternoon sunlight, or the strong, tempting neck and glimpse of bare chest, with . . . good Lord, were those gilded curls nestled at the top of his waistcoat chest hair? She toyed briefly with the thought of swooning, but decided against it when she realized that if she swooned she wouldn't be able to stare, and at that moment, there was nothing more she wanted than to view his deliciously exposed flesh. Arms! Neck! Collar bone! Chest hair!

"Really, Dare, are you a savage that you must speak to your betrothed dressed in that obscene fashion?" his sister scolded him. "What Lady Charlotte must think of you, I shudder to think."

Charlotte knew exactly what she thought. She thought covering up all that glorious flesh was a crime against nature, an abomination, a travesty. She wanted to see more of it. Much more. All of it, in fact, every last inch of that golden, tanned, muscled flesh. Her tongue cleaved itself to the roof of her mouth just imagining it.

Dare's frown, directed temporarily at his sister when she demanded he rectify his appearance, returned to Charlotte, where it faltered in the face of her stunned expression. Charlotte dragged her eyes up from his neck to watch in fascination as his frown faded into a faintly puzzled look, flirted for a few seconds with smug male satisfaction, then deepened into an intense look that seemed to charge the air between them with almost tangible desire.

"My lord, if you would allow one so humble and unimportant, not to mention overworked and burdened, to explain . . ."

Charlotte and Dare both ignored the interruption. The tiny hairs on Charlotte's arms stood on end in response to his gaze; heat rose in her chest, then suddenly pooled low, down in her womanly parts. So surprised was she by the feeling, she almost looked down at them. That region seemed suddenly quite important, calling for attention in a manner she'd never encountered, certainly never in response to a man's look. One's genitalia wasn't supposed to do that, was it? Dare's gaze tightened on her and her womanly parts answered his silent call with a demand that she take them to him immediately.

"Lady Charlotte, are you ill? Dare, what's wrong with Lady Charlotte? Dare? *Dare?*"

Charlotte ignored her body's demand, unable to look away from Dare's unblinking gaze, shaken by the stark need written in his sapphire eyes, suddenly aware for the first time of the true power of her femininity. The emotions sparking between her and Dare were something infinitely more profound than the trivial, meaningless flirtations she had practiced in the past. This was . . . earthy. It was primal. It was shocking and exciting and utterly wanton. She wanted to touch him, to taste his skin, to feel his bare flesh against hers, and she ached, she positively throbbed for the application of his manly instrument. Her breasts suddenly, of their own accord and certainly without her permission, chafed in their stays, sensitized, heavy with the need to be stroked by his hands.

"My lord?"

Her breath caught in her throat, her nipples hardened and clamored for Dare's touch, joining a veritable cacophony of cries for attention from numerous other parts of her body. She wanted his hands on her flesh, touching her, warming her, easing the ache that he started so deep inside her. She wanted it all, and she wanted it right at that moment. She took a step toward him. His eyes glittered darkly as moved toward her, making a soft noise deep in his chest that answered the look in her eyes.

"Dare!"

"My lady!"

Two outraged voices cried out at the same time, breaking the spell. Dare frowned. Charlotte stepped back, her body crying out in silent frustration. She ordered her body to cease its lamentings and promised it that fulfillment would come next Wednesday night. "Perhaps sooner," she mused, her eyes once more on the banded muscles of Dare's arms. His fingers twitched in response.

"You see, Dare, Lady Charlotte is quite overcome by your uncouth appearance," Patricia said as she tugged Charlotte back toward the lumpy settee. "Come and sit next to me, Lady Charlotte, and we shall excuse my brother while he puts himself to rights."

Charlotte opened her mouth to say that wasn't in the least bit necessary or desired, but Dare had evidently remembered the reason for his returning.

"I have been working on my engine," he said to Charlotte by way of an explanation, "and I shall return to that just as soon as you explain this."

He held out her list of locations and guests.

"Your suggestions were unacceptable. You are an earl. I am the daughter of an earl, and the widow of the heir to a count. We cannot have our wedding in a small, poky church. Where would all the guests sit?"

"Which brings me to the subject of your guest list," Dare growled.

Charlotte gave him a triumphant smile. "The selection of wedding guests, Alasdair, is the bride's prohibitive."

"The word is *prerogative*, and that right is revoked when the groom is paying for the whole bloody thing, as Batsfoam informs me I am."

"Dare!" Patricia cried.

Charlotte jumped up from the settee and lifted her chin at him.

"Since you have no dowry, and no family to pay for the wedding, you will practice the utmost economy and organize it to my scriptures. *Strictures*," he corrected himself. "Good God, your tongue is contagious!"

"There's nothing wrong with my tongue," Charlotte snapped, at her limit for being insulted and yelled at. "Which you'd know if you took the time to kiss me. You didn't even do so when you offered for me, you beastly man, you!"

"You were wearing a beard," he snarled, stepping closer to her, the air around them both growing heated once again.

"Well, I'm not now," she answered, taking a step toward him.

"Fine!" he roared.

"Fine!" she agreed, her hands fisted, prepared to do more than poke him in the bare part of his chest if he didn't do the proper thing by her. She didn't have time to think of just what she'd do to his chest before his mouth took possession of hers.

"Dare! You can't!"

"My lord!"

"Lady Charlotte, you mustn't!"

"My lady!"

"Oh, Batsfoam, do something!"

"Short of warming up his lordship's bed, I am at a loss as to what you'd have me do, miss."

"Batsfoam!"

Charlotte ignored both of them, ignored the voice in her head telling her that virtuous women did not encourage men to kiss them, ignored reason and common sense and gave herself up to the pure, hot magic of Dare's mouth. Antonio had once or twice kissed her in the French manner, but the tentative prods and pokes with his tongue were nothing like Dare's kiss. He was everywhere, surrounding her, overwhelming her, one hand pulling her hips close to him, his thighs hard against her legs, her breasts aching and heavy again, pressed tightly against his chest. One hand tangled in her hair, pulling her head back until she was bent over his arm. But it was his mouth that captured and held her attention, his mouth that demanded and gave, coerced and teased until her eyes felt as if they would roll back in her head. He swept into her mouth, taking immediate possession, learning her taste, making her learn his. He was everywhere around her, inside her, the heat of him thrumming in her blood. She fought the sheer dominance of the embrace, tried desperately to pull air into her lungs, but her body would not answer to her any more. A whimper rose in the back of her throat even as she gave in, clinging to him, softening her lips against his as she matched his restless movements, wanting to twine herself around him just as her tongue twined around his. She wanted . . .

"ALASDAIR IAIN MCGREGOR!"

In a dimly lit, dusty corner of Charlotte's mind, she was grateful to Patricia for ending the kiss. The balance of her mind was furious and muttered things about people minding their own business, but hours later, as she sat in Gillian's best guest room, gingerly touching her lips, she recognized that Patricia was right to stop them. What she had demanded—a kiss sealing their agreement to wed—and what Dare had given her—a kiss that came close to scorching the blacking off her boots—were two different things.

"Still, it bodes well for the future." Charlotte smiled into the night. "It was a very effective kiss. I'll wager Alasdair won't need to look at Vyvyan La Blue's *Guide to Connubial Calisthenics* more than once or twice!"

Chapter Five

"This is the worst day of my life. Tell the carriage to leave, Caroline, it won't be needed, as I have no intention of going anywhere."

Silence met that pronouncement. Charlotte kicked at an innocent embroidered footstool and glared at the reflection of Caroline's maid, pressed into service to prepare her for what was supposed to be her day of days. Her day. Ha, she could just burst her stays laughing over *that* bit of comedy.

"You just have cold feet. Mama says all brides feel that way. Why, I myself was sick all over my dressing room on my wedding morn. Mama says there are only two times when it is allowable to be sick—your wedding day and when you're breeding." Caroline looked closely at her friend. "You're not breeding, are you, Charlotte?"

"Just a hearty dose of shame."

"I beg your pardon?"

Charlotte sighed and decided that while feeling sorry for herself might not be the solution to all her problems, it certainly couldn't make her feel any worse.

"How has this come to pass, Caro?" she asked, looking forlornly in the mirror at the lovely image facing her.

"Your marriage? Well, first you dressed up as Henry VIII—"

Charlotte glared her to a stop. "The question was oratorical, Caro, it wasn't meant to be answered. Truthfully, there's no answer to it, any more than there's an answer to the question of how all my plans could go so badly awry, how Alasdair could think to shame me in this manner, or how he could possibly expect me to take my rightful place in society if he carries through his nefarious plan to wed me in such an appalling manner."

Caroline studied her friend's midsection. "Are you sure you're not breeding? You sound just as dramatic as my dearest Algernon's sister Tess when she was carrying the twins, and that's saying quite a bit. Dearest Algernon said that Tess on a bad day could have out-emoted Mr. Kean."

Charlotte shook a rosebud at her friend. "I am having the worst day of my life and all you can do is go on about shooting the cat on your wedding day and staring at my middle parts as if I were going to burst suddenly into motherhood. Truly, Caroline, I think you could be a bit more sympathetic and aid my wallow in self-pity rather than trying to distract me with nonsense about actors and such! Today is promising to be a veritable blot of excuses on the humility of my soul, and it would only be kind of you to recognize that fact!"

"What?" Caroline tried to puzzle out the mangled last sentence of Charlotte's tirade. A blot of excrescence on the humanity of her soul? She shook her head and decided her time was better spent in calming the bride than trying to figure out what she was saying. Charlotte was clearly overwrought. She would focus her friend's attention on much happier thoughts. "Never mind. It matters not, Char. Those blossoms look lovely in your hair. The day is fine, you are the prettiest bride ever, and Lord Carlisle will soon be yours. You can't possibly be serious about not going anywhere—you're getting married today! Today is your most favored day, not one that will shame you. Everyone knows you can't make your wedding day the worst day of your life. It's a bad omen if you even think that."

Charlotte allowed her shoulders to slump just for a moment. As a solution to her troubles, self-pity clearly had failed; she hadn't even impressed Caroline with her woeful situation. This called for a new tactic. Where pity did not answer, perhaps a tantrum would. Charlotte straightened her posture and smiled at her reflection. Why hadn't she thought of this before? It was all Alasdair's fault. If he hadn't kissed the wits right out of her, she would have realized days ago that there was nothing like a good tantrum and show of temper to get results. Once everyone realized that she was serious about the appalling breach of manners Alasdair had planned on committing that very day, the situation would be righted to her satisfaction.

"I am not leaving this house. I refuse to go to the church, not because I have cold feet, not because I'm sick, and not because I'm breeding. Quite simply, my dear Caroline, I am not going to the church because I'm not getting married today," Charlotte said with a happy smile, dimples dimpling madly. She waved away the maid who was tucking rose blossoms into a mass of curls crowning her head. "You may cease that, Clothilde. I have no need for a headful of flowers, not until Alasdair rectifies his mistake."

"What do you mean you're not getting married?" Caroline clutched her hands together. "Of course you're getting married! You're in your wedding gown. Dearest Algernon is below with the carriage to take us to the church where Lord Carlisle is awaiting you. You have a wedding breakfast scheduled! You must get married!"

"Dearest Algernon can dismiss the carriage because I'm not leaving the house. In fact, I refuse to leave your bedchamber. I'm sure it will be no trouble if I stay here until Alasdair comes to his senses."

Caroline grabbed at the back of a rose damask chair and turned pale at the image of Charlotte in permanent residence. Dear heaven, she had to think, and think quickly! There must be some way to get Char out of the house and into the arms of her betrothed, where she belonged. Caroline's mind whirled madly as she tried to formulate persuasive arguments, calming platitudes, and soothing words. Unfortunately, her mind refused to cooperate. "Char, you're being too unfair! You simply must realize that it's unreasonable to cancel the wedding that you wanted, incidentally dragging me into your plans in order to achieve it, and making dearest Algernon agree to give you away, all because you are unhappy with the arrangements."

Charlotte's chin went up as she stood to face her friend. "The arrangements, as you well know, are not mine. They are *his*. *He* is the unreasonable one. *He* took them away from me when I insisted he could grind his economies into snuff and snort them." She paced for a few moments before plopping down on an overstuffed armchair. "Well he can just enjoy his arrangements by himself because I'm staying right here. Please ring for some tea. And perhaps some biscuits or tarts or a jam cake or two. And toasted bread, lots and lots of toasted bread. It doesn't matter what I eat now, I have no one to care if I get wide in the saddle."

Caroline's panic magnified tenfold at the obstinate look on her friend's face. "Char, you're making yourself upset needlessly. I'm sure Lord Carlisle cares about how wide in the saddle you are, not that I think that's important in a marriage, but still, I'm sure he cares about you and only wants you to be happy—"

Charlotte, remembering again the injustices he had perpetuated upon her in the name of saving a few coins, sprang out of the chair with an indignant flame in her china blue eyes, and began to pace before the window. "He doesn't care for anything but his precious purse. His slanderous comments about my extravagant plans for a memorable wedding were clearly the sign of a deranged mind, not to mention the lecture he read me about driving him into the poorhouse. As if that were possible! He is an earl, after all. Have you ever heard of a poor earl?"

"Well—"

"No, of course you haven't. Unreasonable, my garters! I'm not being in the least bit unreasonable! I am the most reasonable person I know, and I know a great many people!"

"But Char, I'm sure Lord Carlisle desires only your happiness—"

Charlotte gave an unladylike snort of disbelief

that felt so good, so right, she repeated it. "He made all the arrangements to be married at a tiny little parish church in Covent Garden with no one in attendance but you and that bossy Patricia, but that doesn't mean I have to be there! This is my wedding, too, and I'll be damned if I celebrate the most important moment of my life in an empty church!"

"Charlotte Honoria Eveline Benedict!" Caroline gasped. "Foul language on your wedding day is a bad omen!"

"God's teeth, Caro! My whole life is in ruins and all you can think about are bad omens? You have bad omens on the brain." Charlotte huffed as she stomped around the room.

Caroline, desperate now, faced as she was with the possibility of Charlotte making good her threat not to marry the earl, played her last card. "Have you thought of what everyone will say if you don't marry Lord Carlisle?"

Charlotte frowned at Caro as she paced by her. "There will be a delicious amount of speculation as to why I canceled the plans at the last minute."

Caroline shook her head, preparing to be merciless for the better good of her friend's happiness, not to mention her own marital bliss. "They will say Lord Carlisle jilted you. They will say he changed his mind about wedding you. They will say he found the very idea of marriage to you repugnant and unbearable."

Charlotte stopped dead and stared at her friend in horror. Her first instinct was to dispute such foul claims, but a moment of truth had her admitting that her star was not very high with the *ton* at that moment, and given the fickle nature of the members of society, it was entirely possible that reaction to her jilting Alasdair would turn out as Caroline predicted. She was a social pariah now; could she stand being pitied and laughed at as well? She shuddered at that unwholesome image and quickly rethought her strategy. Perhaps an outright refusal to marry Alasdair wasn't the solution. Perhaps there was a way to bring him to his senses and achieve her goal without having to run the risk of becoming an object of pity.

"Alasdair may think he can deny me my due, but I am a clever, intelligent woman who is not going to allow the minor tragedy of having accepted a pinchparing man so tight with his purse strings that he won't allow me to be fawned upon and idolized as is my right. I won't marry him until he begs my forgiveness and gives me a proper wedding, one with lots of people to admire me and congratulate him on his exceptionally good luck in gaining me as his bride!" Charlotte tossed the last few words over her shoulder as she marched out of the bedchamber.

"But, but . . . where are you going?"

"To the carriage. Really, Caro, are you so disorganized that you aren't ready to leave? We were supposed to be at the church ten minutes ago. Quickly, quickly! I haven't the time to waste if I wish to be wed today. Alasdair may look like an angel, but even he can't work miracles!"

Five minutes later saw the Beverlys' town chaise rolling down the street. Lord Beverly—after spending two minutes in Charlotte's company—opted to ride to the church. Inside the carriage, Charlotte spent most of the trip mustering the statements and demands she would present to her betrothed. He simply must see how important it was that they start off their married life correctly. She tried out a few of the choicer statements on Caroline.

"Honestly, Char, I don't think telling Lord Carlisle you'll see him hung by his toes if he doesn't give in to your demands for a proper wedding is quite the persuasive argument you mean it to be. Perhaps if you tried to reason with him—"

"He's a man, Caroline. Have you ever known one open to reason?"

"Well . . . dearest Algernon sometimes . . . he did stop trying to grow that mustache. . . . Regardless, I say if you just explained how unhappy you are with the arrangements, Lord Carlisle will be in a better mind to discuss the issue than if you threaten him with bodily harm."

Charlotte smiled a wicked little smile to herself. "I wouldn't harm his body, Caro, I like it. I like it quite a good deal."

"Charlotte!"

"Oh, you needn't look so outraged. If your Algernon were the magnificent personification of everything manly and virile as Alasdair is, you would be saying similar things."

"I would not! I would never speak of my husband in such a bold manner! It isn't seemly in the least!"

Charlotte dimpled at her friend and couldn't help but tease her a bit. "Really, Caro, you're the most circumcised person I know!"

"I am . . . circumcised? Did you say *circumcised?*"

"Yes, but only because you are. Very circumcised." Charlotte's smile faded at the sight of her friend's expression. "Caro, if your eyes grow any bigger, they might just pop right out of your head, and then where would you be?"

"Char—do you know what circumcised means?"

"Well, of course I do," Charlotte scoffed, then

thought for a moment. "I thought I did . . . yes, I know. It means to be overly cautious and hesitant. Doesn't it?"

Deep pink stained Caroline's cheeks as she looked anywhere but at Charlotte. "According to the passage in the Bible, to be circumcised means . . . well, it means . . . it's something they do to men. You know. It's when they snip off part of the man's . . . his . . ." Caroline gestured wildly with her hands.

Charlotte frowned in concentration. "His what?"

"You know, his winkle."

"His *what?*"

Caroline hushed her and looked nervously through the carriage windows before turning back to her friend. "His winkle. Dollymop. Dingle-dangle."

Charlotte sat back against the cushioned seat and rolled her eyes. "Honestly, Caro, you're a married woman. I can't believe you have to come up with so many juvenile euphemisms for a commonplace object you must see every day. We are, after all, adults. You can say it in front of me without blushing or going to such lengths as dreaming up words like *dingle-dangle!*"

"I know." Caroline looked abashed at her silliness. "I'm sorry. I won't do it again. You are absolutely correct. We are both married women; we can talk about such things openly."

Charlotte pulled out a tiny mirror and checked her reflection. "Exactly. As for the other, it's utterly ridiculous. You must have read the passage wrong. No man with any amount of common sense would allow someone to snip off his dinky."

Dare frowned at the pocket watch in his hand. His frown deepened as he glanced across the verger's small, musty room to where a carriage clock sat on a battered desk. Mindful that it was his wedding day, he kept the frown from moving into a scowl as he strolled with a nonchalance he was far from feeling to where Batsfoam stood behind Captain David Woodwell, Patricia's intended. He looked at the watch David was shaking next to his ear.

"Must get this fixed before Sunday," David grinned. "Wouldn't do to be late to my own . . . oh."

Dare closed his eyes briefly and rubbed his forehead. The watches all told him the same thing. They all foretold the depressing truth that today marked the beginning of a life spent wasting interminable long hours waiting on a woman.

He opened his eyes and heaved a martyred sigh of the doomed.

"Most fashionable ladies are late for events," David reassured him. "Patricia tells me it's just not done to arrive anywhere on time, and with brides . . . well, everyone knows how late brides are. They like to make a dramatic entrance."

Dare summoned a faint smile. He wished he had something pithy to say about the silliness of women and especially brides, but all he could think of was a strong recommendation to avoid the little darlings like they were plague-bearing lepers, and that was hardly the advice to be giving the man who was to marry his sister some five days hence.

"She'll be here," he predicted instead. "She worked too hard to snare me just to jilt me now. She's just punishing me for not spending every last shilling I had on a big wedding."

David smiled. "I know it must seem bad to you now, but Patricia is sure it'll work out. She thinks Lady Charlotte has a *tendresse* for you, and that's a good part of the battle, isn't it?"

101

Dare allowed his lips to twist into a wry approximation of a smile, and punched David lightly in the shoulder by way of thanking him for the consolation. He resumed pacing the length of the small room, stopping occasionally to pinch the bridge of his nose. He felt a headache starting to come on, a headache made worse by the noise from the yard outside the church. A circus was in town to perform for Tsar Alexander's visit, and it sounded like they'd decided to hold orchestra practice directly outside the church.

After Dare's tenth pass by the two men, Batsfoam spoke. "Would you care for me to ascertain the location of the lady you so honorably, if more than a little precipitously, offered to wed, not that I'm criticizing my lord's actions, not that that's possible since my brain could never even conceive of that notion, let alone retain it and expound upon it at great length, not when such a thing concerns one who is my better, as, indeed, my lord should know he is. In truth, I would rather cut off my other leg than make even the slightest criticism of the hasty manner in which you promised to wed a woman you barely know, let alone seem to feel any fondness for, not that fondness is required in a marriage, as I have experience to know, having been wed for seventeen extraordinarily long years to Mrs. Batsfoam before her untimely demise in a terrible accident caused by the Elephant Woman of Zanzibar on display at Mr. Trencherfoot's Gallery of the Unexplainable and Bizarre, who, as she seated herself on a bench, propelled the Tasmanian Bat Boy across the room directly into Mrs. Batsfoam's lap, whereupon she choked on her horehound sweet, thereby hastening her death three years later by palpitations to the spleen. Indeed, my leg would be a small sacrifice to put my lord's troubled mind at rest on the matter of his bride's willingness to wed him, and as my lord well knows, my very existence is inexorably fixed on making him happy. Shall I fetch a surgeon for the immediate removal of the one sound limb remaining me?"

Dare pursed his lips in apparent thought. "Whoever else is fickle in my life, Batsfoam, I can always count on you to be constant, ever a glad ray of happiness and cheer ready to light my solemn days and brighten every moment."

David made a sound suspiciously close to a snort. Outside the church, voices rose to a fevered pitch, cries of, " 'Ere, you, mind the bear, 'e bites" battling the sharp, tinny blare of several off-key trumpets attempting to play a triumphant march. Dare fought to keep in control the rising sense of absurdity at the situation. His lips quirked upward a moment later when Batsfoam, his head bent in humble approximation of subjugation, genuflected to indicate his leg and cocked an eyebrow. "The leg, my lord? It won't take but a moment to have it hacked off."

"Perhaps later, Batsfoam. After the wedding breakfast, hmm? Wouldn't do to put the ladies off their feed with a lot of blood and such."

"Dare!" Patricia burst into the small room, stopping just long enough to grab her brother by his arm and drag him toward the door. "Dare, you must come quickly. Lady Charlotte has arrived, but she refuses to leave the carriage until she speaks with you. Oh, and there's a monkey loose in the church, but the vicar thinks he has it cornered in the chandelier over the nave, so you're not to worry. Did you know there's a circus outside?"

Dare's shoulders twitched for a moment, but with

effort, he managed to square them and follow his sister out to the carriage with no more than a slightly bored look on his face.

"Ah, Carlisle, there you are. Spot of trouble with the ladies, don'tcha know," a slight, red-haired man standing next to the carriage said, looking distinctly relieved to see the groom. A shout of warning had the two men leaping out of the way when a camel trailing several silken scarves and a gilded rope galloped past them and up the steps leading into the church, pursued by three men who hurled a number of obscene threats and oaths at the animal's head.

"Beverly," Dare acknowledged with a nod as the two men resumed their place before the carriage. "I take it my bride has cold feet?"

Lord Beverly glanced worriedly at the church, then back to the carriage. The blinds were suddenly shoved aside, and Charlotte's face appeared in the glass. She beckoned to Dare.

"Er . . . something like that. I gather your lady has taken exception to something with the church. Wouldn't be surprised if it was the circus. Didn't know they held the things in a church. Doesn't seem entirely proper to me."

Dare made no reply, but opened the carriage door. "Good morning, Lady Beverly, Charlotte. Is there something I can do for you? Other than wed you, that is?"

"Yes," Charlotte said, grabbing his hand and tugging him into the carriage. Dare allowed himself to be pulled in. He settled on the seat across from her with a hard-won expression indicating only mild curiosity.

"I want to tell you that I'm not marrying you."

"Perhaps I'd best see if dearest Algernon needs

me. . . ." Caroline murmured as she tried to slide across Charlotte to the door.

"Stay where you are, Caro, I want a witness to this discussion."

"But, Char, this situation is between you and Lord Carlisle. I really think I should leave—"

Charlotte had the audacity to frown at him. Dare ignored Caroline and sat back, his arms crossed over his chest. "You're not marrying me?"

"No."

"You came all this way in your wedding gown to tell me we're not being wed today?"

Charlotte nodded. "That's right. I shan't wed you until you've come to your senses."

"I see." Dare nodded, even though he didn't see, not in the remotest sense of the word. Still, he was fairly certain that Charlotte would fill him in on all the minor points of her declaration, such as exactly why she had changed her mind after working so hard to trap him. He nodded again, then opened the carriage door and stepped out, narrowly missing being trampled by a small herd of harlequins. He took a deep, dung-scented breath, and waited for the inevitable.

"Alasdair!" Charlotte jumped out of the carriage after him, showing a healthy bit of leg in the process. She stormed over to him, favoring him with a glare that could strip the hair off a cat. He fought the urge to smile at the outraged look in her fathomless eyes, all the while acknowledging that her fury just made him want to kiss her.

"You can't just leave! You're supposed to beg me to marry you!" She looked so disgruntled, he had to fist his hands to keep from pulling her toward him and kissing the scowl right off her face. "You're not doing this correctly! You're supposed to plead

105

with me and sue for my favor, groveling and humbling yourself so I can tell you what you need to do to make me change my mind, and you haven't done any of that, and as I'm not getting any younger waiting for you, you'd best get to it!"

He did smile then. He couldn't help himself. It was one of the worst days of his life, the day he was to shackle himself to a woman he suspected he loved, but who would probably make every day of his life a living hell with her demands for attention and things he couldn't provide. Yet he couldn't keep from smiling at her. She was just so . . . damned . . . *Charlotte!*

Evidently she didn't quite see his smile as he intended. Her blue eyes flashed such heat at him as to ignite a lesser man, but Dare just gloried in her magnificence. Despite it all, all the sacrifices he was making, all the setbacks and heartbreak she was sure to bring him, she was his and his alone. No one else would be the recipient of the sparks flying from those beautiful eyes.

"Oooh! How dare you smirk at me!" She stomped her foot and poked him in the shoulder. "Aren't you even going to ask me why I won't marry you?"

He decided to humor her. After all, he had a lifetime to rile her up and enjoy the fireworks. It was better to calm her now so the wedding could proceed and he could return to work on his engine. He allowed his smile to fade, adopting a serious mien as befitted one who was about to grovel and sue for favor. He even added a courtly little bow for good effect. "I am all ears, Lady Charlotte."

The look in Charlotte's eyes metamorphosed from the white-hot heat of anger to the flushed glow of something much more intriguing as she ran her gaze over his shoulders and chest.

"Well, I wouldn't go that far," she murmured in a conciliatory tone.

He raised an eyebrow. "What are you talking about?"

A maidenly blush pinked her cheeks. Dare bit back the urge to throw back his head and laugh aloud with the joy of her. She never failed to surprise him—one moment she was saying the most outlandish things he'd ever heard, the next she was blushing like a virgin.

"You. You're more than just ears."

He fought long and hard, but at last he was able to speak without having to grab her and kiss her first. Now was not the time for kissing. Now was the time to get her into the church and wed her before she drove him daft with her innocent, highly seductive charm. Later, perhaps, he would allow himself to kiss her. Just one kiss, and a short one at that, given before he made it absolutely clear that despite the fact that she had trapped him into marriage, he had no intention of bedding her until he was good and ready. He put on his martyred face and bent his head to her. "Charlotte, I am distraught and filled with sorrow at this grievous news. What task might I undertake to encourage you to change your mind?"

She sighed with obvious relief, dimpling at him in a fashion that made his heart do odd little gymnastics in his chest. God's kidneys, but she made his vow not to give in to her wiles difficult! "I'm so glad you're being more reasonable, Alasdair. It's about this wedding you've planned."

"So I gather. I take it you have an objection to the church?"

"No. Yes. No, I don't mind it, although I do think it extremely unkind of you not to even investigate the possibility of Westminster Abbey being open to individuals who are not of royal blood. Truly, Alasdair, it's not the church I find fault with; it's the people."

Dare stared at her for the count of five. His amusement at her evaporated as the ache throbbing at the front of his head blossomed. Wearily he pinched the bridge of his nose again. "The people? *What* people?"

Charlotte nodded, clearly pleased with him. "Exactly! What people! There are none, no one except your sister and Caro. And Lord Beverly. And your sister's betrothed, and my cousin's servants. But other than those scant dozen, there is no one else. It is simply impossible for you to insist we marry with no one to watch us. Thus I have decided that I shan't wed you until the proper number of people are present to witness our most sacred oaths to each other."

"The proper number . . ." Dare shook his head, opened his mouth to say more, then thought better of it. Enough was enough. He had been as patient as a saint, but he had to take the upper hand with her, or he'd never again regain control of his life. The horrific vision of what life would be like with Charlotte in command fixed firmly in mind, he took his bride by her elbow and started toward the church, ducking under a rope dancer's rope set up between two pillars on the church portico. When Charlotte balked, he stopped and faced her. "Either you enter this church with me here and now and we wed, or you can leave and find yourself another fox."

"Fox?" A puzzled frown wrinkled her adorable brow.

He fought the need to smooth the puzzlement

away. If he wanted even a remote chance of happiness in the future with her, he had to stand firm now. Only by getting this marriage ceremony over with could he return to the important task of finishing his engine. Without the money that engine was sure to bring, their futures weren't just bleak, they were nonexistent. "Fox. Victim. Husband. Whatever you want to call it, but understand this, Charlotte, I will not pander to your whims and temper. Make up your mind."

"What?" Charlotte stared at him open-mouthed for a moment.

Dare leaned closer so only she could hear his words. "You wished to wed me. Now you will do so, or you will walk away from here a free woman. It's your decision."

"But, Alasdair—"

"My . . . name . . . is . . . Dare," he replied in the same low tone, his jaw set.

Her eyes clouded with tears as she obviously recognized the stalwartness behind his words. Despite his best intentions, he felt something melt in his chest at the sight of her lovely eyes filling, but a man couldn't give in to every pair of weepy eyes he saw, even if it felt like each tear was ripping open a gaping hole in his heart.

"Charlotte," he said, preparing to soften his words with a little judicious begging. It would be a blow to his pride, but that was already so tattered a little more damage wouldn't trouble him.

"Please, Alasdair," she whispered, her eyes shimmering with pain behind a shield of tears. "Please don't shame me in front of everyone. I couldn't bear it if you did. I just couldn't bear it."

"Shame you?" He put his hands on her arms and

tugged her closer, his frown deepening. "How is marrying me going to shame you?"

She waved one hand toward the church, two tears spilling over lashes suddenly made dark and spiky with sorrow. "There's no one there. No one! How can I tell anyone that we were wed in an empty church, that no one cared enough about us to see us wed but your sister and my friend?" She hiccupped. "How can I face anyone once they know the truth about our wedding, that you didn't care enough about it or me to have a proper wedding?"

He stared at her at a loss for words, unable to understand what she found wrong with the small, intimate wedding necessary due to economies and his own personal preference, but recognizing that whatever troubled her, it was of great importance. He had seen enough crocodile tears to recognize genuine distress when he saw it, and Charlotte's eyes were all but shrieking their pain to him. He took a deep breath, battling with the desire to maintain control of the situation, while unwilling to have her think he was a cold-hearted monster who cared little for her desires and wishes.

"Charlotte, even if I wanted to give you what you ask, it's impossible. We are to wed today, almost an hour ago to be precise." He ran a hand through his hair as he tried to think of how he could delay the wedding, deal with Patricia's upcoming nuptials, and still have time to finish the engine and test it before Whitney arrived. "To invite everyone you know would take days, weeks in the planning. I agreed to wed you now because it falls in well with my plans, but to delay—"

"It doesn't have to be people I know," she said quietly, one hand on his sleeve, a soft, hopeful look in her eyes that he had never seen. It called to him, drew him, made him want to promise her anything if only she would look at him again like that. "I don't want to delay the wedding any more than you do. I told you I had to be wed before your sister; it's only fitting."

He rubbed his forehead, willing the headache away as he tried to see a solution. "Then what do you want me to do, fill the church with strangers to witness our marriage?"

She was nodding even before he finished the sentence.

He closed his eyes for a moment against the trembling hope in hers, then opened them again. "This means that much to you?"

She nodded again, sniffling and dabbing at her nose with a delicate handkerchief.

"And if I do this for you, you won't pester me for gowns or more pin money, or the hundreds of other things that I won't be able to give you?"

Charlotte stared at him in surprise, the soft look replaced with a familiar glint that was pure deviltry. "Of course I'll pester you for those things, I'll be your wife. I realize you have not been married before, Alasdair, but truly, I see I must educate you in the duties of a husband. It will be my duty to ask you for things, and for you to refuse me, then to be swayed by my entreaties and encampments and so give me everything I want."

"Enticements," Dare corrected automatically, even as he struggled to keep his eyes from crossing at just what form those entreaties and enticements would consist. He pulled his mind from the vision of Charlotte lying in his bed, her creamy satin skin covered with nothing more than her hair, sated and pleasured until she purred. It took two tries, but at

last he could focus on the present, on the woman who didn't care who attended her wedding as long as there were people enough to fill the church. The thought of her plans sobered him immediately. "Charlotte, we are going to have to have a long talk this evening about your expectations. I have tried to explain to you that I'm not a rich man, and you will have to practice the most stringent of economies—"

"Oh, pooh," she waved away his warning and wiped her eyes, flashing a brief glimpse of dimple. "Papa used to say that to Mama all the time."

"Charlotte—"

"Will you do this for me, Alasdair?" she asked, her eyes soft and blue as a July sky. "Will you do this little thing I ask?"

Dare prayed for patience, then nodded.

"Oh, thank you, thank you," she squealed and threw herself in his arms just long enough to kiss him on the corner of his lips. He wanted to keep her there to improve her aim, but before his arms could tighten around her, she hurried back toward the carriage, avoiding as she did a row of tumblers and acrobats flipping themselves over scattered chairs and tables. "He's going to do it," she bellowed happily to Caroline just before shoving her friend back into the carriage.

"You'll be more comfortable waiting inside," Dare pointed out as he followed her, stepping over a collection of clubs and torches that would later be lit and juggled by the acrobats. He was a bit exasperated with himself for having given in to her unreasonable demand. If the ease with which she wrapped him around her slightest whim portended their future together . . . but no, he wouldn't think of that. Down that pathway lay madness. Instead he reassured himself that her request was a minor thing, a fairly simple request, one easily fulfilled in such a way as to keep her happy, and achieve his end as well. "It won't take me long to gather the . . . er . . . audience."

"I shall wait for you to complete your task," Charlotte said loftily, "and return when all is ready. Caro, instruct the coachman to drive us around the block until that time."

"I would prefer you wait inside," Dare said through softly grinding teeth. God's spleen, would she argue with him on every point?

"And have everyone see me waiting? Never!"

"You'll get tired of just riding around and around in a circle. Perhaps Lady Beverly would care to go inside where it is cool."

Inexplicably, Charlotte dimpled at him. "We're fine as we are. Caro and I were having the most interesting discussion of the Bible just before we arrived. I'm sure she has no objection to continuing it."

Lady Beverly giggled. Dare shot Charlotte a look that by rights ought to have sent her screaming from him in horror, but she just deepened the smile into a cheeky grin and added in a little eyelash-fluttering action.

"God save me from all women," he muttered as he turned back toward the church, reluctantly admitting to himself that her smile had kindled an unexpected warmth in his heart. Then he prepared to buy his bride an audience.

Charlotte stopped dead at the back of the church after taking one look at the audience her husband-to-be had purchased to witness her Most Important

Moment, intending on throwing the tantrum to end all tantrums.

"There is a monkey in the church," she ground out through her teeth, pointing to where a small monkey in a red hat and gold-fringed jacket was swinging from a sconce in the nave. "I might have been gone from England for five years, but I doubt if it has suddenly become the rage to have primates swinging from the walls at weddings."

"Er—" Lord Beverly said, gently tugging at her hand, clearly at a loss as to how to get the bride moving down the aisle toward her groom. "Well—"

"And that woman there, the one with the beard, she's positively wailing, and I don't even *know* her. This is supposed to be a joyous occasion."

"Eh—" Lord Beverly tugged again, shooting a helpless glance over to where Dare stood, his arms crossed over his chest, his eyes on the recalcitrant Charlotte. "I believe Lord Carlisle is waiting for you. . . ."

Charlotte refused to budge, turning her head to glare at the group of musicians in the far corner. "And the band! What on earth are they playing, live cats? Surely this is not suitable marrying music. Surely this is all wrong."

"Ah—" Lord Beverly took a deep breath, desperate now to fulfill his one (monumental, as it turned out) duty of getting the bride to the altar. "Look, there's the groom. Why don't you just stroll down there and take it up with him, hmm?"

"No," Charlotte said, flinching as the band hit a particularly sour note. "I won't do it. This just isn't at all what I had imagined. Dare will have to do better than this."

" 'ere, what's the 'oldup?" one of the rope dancers leaned back to ask. "We've got to do our show

114

for the Tsar this afternoon. Yer goin' to 'ave to 'itch yer carriage to a faster 'orse else we won't 'ave time to toast yeh with that fine ale 'is lordship there said we'd be gettin'."

Charlotte pounced on the one word that had any meaning for her. "The Tsar? You're performing for the Tsar? The one from Russia?"

"Isn't no other that I knows of," the rope dancer sniffed.

The light of victory dawned in Charlotte's eyes. She walked down the aisle quite happily after that, mentally forming exactly how she would tell Lady Jersey and other preeminent ladies of the *ton* how she had to hurry her wedding because the guests, her dear, close, personal friends, had an important audience with the Tsar himself.

She even forgave the monkey later for stealing her small bouquet of roses.

Chapter Six

Charlotte looked with a steely glint in her eye at her maid. Her maid looked back at her with a calm countenance. The new Lady Carlisle was not amused.

"You squeak," she accused. "I've never before had a maid who squeaked, and I don't intend to start now. I believe I shall find a new maid—one who doesn't squeak."

"I am devastated that I do not meet with your ladyship's most discriminating and no doubt exacting taste. My life, as I have told your husband— he who is my lord and master—upon many occasions, is devoted solely and completely, with humble thankfulness that he has seen fit to endure my attentions, to his happiness, a situation which I am thrilled to the very limits of my soul may now also be applied to your own gracious self. In short, my

116

lady, I live to serve you. If you are not happy with the unfortunate but alas, unstoppable noises associated with the new wooden leg I had made upon the occasion of my lord and lady's happy nuptial event, I will immediately dispense with it. I need it not to serve my lady in any capacity she desires of me, be it butler, valet to his lordship, boot boy, or in the most humble role of lady's maid to you. I am quite a prodigious hopper, as your ladyship will see—" Batsfoam hiked up his trouser leg in preparation to remove the offending wooden limb.

Charlotte stopped him the second she realized his intentions. She had no desire to see his leg, wooden or otherwise. "I'm sure you're quite a capable hopper, Batsfoam, but 'tis the truth that although I find the novelty of a squeaking maid difficult to bear, bear it I would if there were not a graver, more serious complaint to be laid at your door."

Batsfoam reluctantly lowered his trouser leg, his shoulders slumping into their habitual droop. He bowed his head in a close approximation of abject humility. "And that would be what, my lady?"

Charlotte wondered briefly if no one else thought it the least bit peculiar that her husband's butler should offer to serve as her maid. "Perhaps it is because Alasdair is Scottish," she mused aloud. "Perhaps it is commonplace in that heathen land to the north. You never know about a society that has men in short skirts. On the other hand," honesty compelled her to add, "I very much enjoyed the time I saw Alasdair in his kilt. And out of it, too, but I suppose that really goes without saying, don't you think?"

"My lady?"

"Hmmm." Charlotte shook off the image of Dare's

naked behind as seen the day Gillian ripped his kilt off, and considered Batsfoam for a moment. He didn't sound particularly Scottish, so perhaps the fault lay elsewhere. She worried about that for a moment, then decided it was more important she turn her mind to other things, such as having a maid, a proper maid, undress her so she could await her husband's connubial attentions. "Batsfoam, while it is true that I appreciate your willingness to help around the house as you can, I simply must draw the line at you serving as a lady's maid."

"If it is my noisome leg, my lady—"

"No," Charlotte reassured him as she opened the door to the hallway. Overall, she was pleased with the small room adjoining Dare's that had been assigned as her bedchamber, but she had strong feelings about the person who had shown her the room. "It is not just that. You force me to be blunt, Batsfoam, to wound you with words, something I had hoped to avoid with my new staff, at least for a day or so until we get to know one another better, but perhaps it's for the best that we clear the stair with this issue now and not later—"

"Clear the stairs? You wish me to dust the stairway?" Batsfoam looked surprised at the order. "Now, my lady? At this late hour? I believe his lordship will have need of my assistance with the rendering onto paper the design of a newly modified valve, but I will strive to meet your demands for stair care in between the many duties, tasks, and jobs his lordship is so gracious and kind as to heap upon my shoulders, riddled with rheumatism though they be. Nay, say not another word, my lady. You wish the stairs cleared, and so they shall be. Since I cannot serve you as your maid due to the uncouth and raucous noises issuing from my new leg, I shall endeavor to fulfill your every wish, desire, and whim, no matter how inexplicable and trying they might be. And now, my lady, I am off to clear the stairs, but before I do so, I will send up another staff member to take my unwanted place as your maid."

Charlotte, busy thinking about whether it was better to wait for Dare and his much anticipated manly instrument in her bed or his, missed most of Batsfoam's oratory, a fact which did not escape him. Should Charlotte have been looking at him at that exact moment, she would have seen something very akin to a light of challenge dawning in his eye. But she was lost in contemplation of the image of Dare's bronze skin, rippling with muscles and gilded with the finest of golden hairs, so she merely muttered, "Fine, fine."

It wasn't until later, when Batsfoam sent up Wills the scullery lad to act as lady's maid that she realized she would have to take charge of the household that very instant or suffer the most improper, and more importantly, *uncomfortable* life with Alasdair's heathenish staff. The good Lord above knew she, in an act fairly reeking of generosity and willingness to cooperate (not to mention desperation to get undressed and ready for the connubial action she anticipated with bated breath and wetted lip) had given Wills a chance, but he proved to be a sore trial to her patience when, asked to comb out her hair, he fainted dead away before even taking out one rosebud.

"He's gone too far this time," she warned the unconscious Wills a few scant seconds before she doused him with her wash water. He sputtered and came to life only to see his new mistress glowering over him, speaking in a voice that got progressively louder and higher with each word that slipped from

119

her cherry-kissed lips. "I have been patient with his eccentric ways, I have been understanding of his pinchparing habits, I have been everything a good wife could possibly be, but he goes too far in asking me to take on a twelve-year-old boy as my lady's maid!"

"M'lady?" Wills squeaked in concern, scooting backward across the damp rug, praying that Lady Carlisle wasn't about to bring the empty ewer down upon his head.

Char dropped the ewer, grabbed the boy by his wet ear, hauled him to his feet, and demanded to be taken to her husband.

"Oi don' know where 'e is," the lad cried, flinching as she steered him toward the stairs. " 'Onest, m'lady, oi don' know where 'is lordship is!"

Charlotte tightened her grip on the slippery ear. "If you want to see this ear again, you had better find out, hadn't you?"

The boy started to nod, decided that wasn't the wisest course of action when the future of his ear was at stake, and began to wail instead.

"Please, m'lady, Oi've told you Oi don' know where 'e is. You've got to believe me. Oi don' know and that's a fact. Please, m'lady, Oi want me ear, it's the only one Oi've got, don' take it away from me!"

Charlotte paused at the top of the stairs. The boy was openly sniffling now, wiping his nose on his sleeve. She released his ear and took hold of the back of his jacket, turning to march down the opposite end of the hallway, still retaining hold of the boy when she stopped before a door and knocked.

A tiny red-haired maid opened the door, gawked at Wills for a second before bobbing a respective curtsey to Charlotte. Behind the maid, Patricia rose from where she was seated at a low table, clearly in the process of being readied for bed.

"Charlotte? Is something wrong? Why is Wills crying?"

"He has something wrong with his ear," Charlotte said abruptly. "Where is your brother?"

Patricia stopped midway across the room, her hands fluttering in distress. "My brother? Dare? You want to know where Dare is? He's not with you?"

Charlotte raised her chin, narrowed her eyes, and pinned her new sister-in-law with a look that had Patricia taking a wary step backward. "He is not with me. Since I have only been in this house for an hour and have not yet been given a tour of the premises and since Wills seems to be obsessed with talk of his ear and wiping his nose on his garments in a manner that makes me want to do nothing so much as wash my hands, I must ask your advice. I am doing so now. Where might I find my husband, your brother, the earl?"

"He's . . . he's probably working on his engine. He does most evenings," Patricia offered, a questioning expression on her face. Charlotte was grateful it wasn't pity. She didn't think she could take pity at that moment.

"His engine? Oh, his little hobby. Where does he keep that?"

Patricia blinked a couple of times before shaking her head and stepping forward, smiling at Charlotte as she squeezed her free hand. "Dare works on his engine in what used to be the butler's pantry. It's below stairs, at the front of the house, where it catches the morning sun. Wills will show you the way."

Charlotte murmured a polite thanks and was turning away when she paused to frown at the boy in her grasp, setting him to trembling and sniffling again before she turned back to Patricia. "I cannot help but notice that your maid is a female."

Patricia looked between her maid and Charlotte. "Yeeeees," she drawled, confusion plainly writ on her face.

Charlotte's nostrils flared for a moment as a militant glint lit her eye. Then she nodded and headed off to the stairs, Wills in tow.

Five minutes later she was escorted by a remarkably cheerful Batsfoam into a small, dank room so far distant from the living areas of the house it seemed to be buried in the bowels of the earth. The room stank with the nose-wrinkling acid smell of burnt oil, mildew, dirt, and blacking, but what caught Charlotte's attention as she ducked to enter the low wooden door was not the smell, or the sight of a mammoth black machine that took up most of the available space, or the tables ringing the room, filled with strange tools, filthy rags, and pots of substances she couldn't begin to fathom. No, what caught and held her eye was the sight of her husband of five hours bent over a shaft sprouting out the side of the machine. He had stripped down to just his shirt and trousers, a fact Charlotte greatly appreciated as she stood blocking the doorway, her gaze happily feasting on the sight of material stretched tight across the long, muscled length of his leg. Not to mention the lovely contours of his behind. Charlotte took one look at that behind and instantly her womanly parts started clamoring for attention.

His attention.

"Oh," she said. "Oh."

Dare straightened up at the interruption and looked over his shoulder. His handsome face bore a familiar scowl, but Charlotte was too busy looking between his bare arms and neck and the large expanse of magnificent chest clearly visible through the shirt glued with sweat to every curve and contour to notice the scowl. A subdued cough at her back reminded her where she was, along with the latest round of grievous injuries done to her by the annoying, if mouth-watering, man in front of her. She tightened her hold on Wills and shoved him through the door ahead of her, looking around the small, dusty room as she did so.

"So that is an engine," she said, trying to sound interested in the horrible-looking conglomeration of mechanical bits that apparently held more allure than his bride.

"No, madam," Dare replied, reaching for a dirt-encrusted cloth to wipe the grease from his hands. Charlotte made a mental note to have his engine cloths replaced at the soonest possible moment. "This is an air pump, condenser, and boiler. It is part of my steam engine."

"That's what I said, it's an engine. It all looks so very—" Awful. Dirty. Boring. "—fascinating."

Dare stopped scowling and gave her a long, considering look. There was something in his eyes that suddenly had her anger melting, replaced with an odd, and hitherto inexperienced, desire to please him. She struggled for a moment with this strange new emotion.

"It is fascinating," Dare replied gruffly, giving her another long look before noticing the man standing behind her. "Ah, there you are, Batsfoam. You have yet to finish the drawing of the revised boiler. I'll need that before we run the first trial. Er . . . Charlotte?"

Charlotte, having just come to the decision that

her tender feelings for her new husband were due to novelty and nothing more, remembered just why she was standing in a smoky, ill-lit room, and so did not notice the note of hesitancy in her husband's voice as he spoke her name.

"Did you want me to show you what I'm working on?"

She opened her mouth to make a scathing comment, but the strange need to please him grew within her. Somewhat abruptly, she realized that Dare was no longer scowling, that his voice was warm and caressing, and his eyes were glittering with some glad emotion. She glanced at the machinery. She truly had no desire to hear about it, no desire in the least; she simply wanted to complain to her husband about his servants, get his approval to make the changes she deemed necessary, and have someone undress her so she could go to bed and enjoy the benefits of being married to a man who stole her breath every time she looked at him.

"I . . . I . . ." The last of her annoyance evaporated as his eyebrows rose in hopeful expectation. How could she refuse such an offer? She couldn't. Something inside her melted to a warm, satisfying emotion as she answered. "Why, yes, Alasdair, I would very much like for you to show me your project." Still maintaining a hold on Wills, she moved over to stand next to Dare and peered down at the open row of cylinders. "It looks very complicated."

"It is complicated. Marine engines are infinitely more difficult to design than traditional engines because of the problem of deterioration due to the constant exposure to salt water."

Charlotte eyed the engine with misgiving, tugging Wills over to examine the back side of the machine. "Is it dangerous?"

"There is always a danger when working with engines, Charlotte," Dare answered calmly. "However, I am confident I have located and fixed any flaws that might result in disaster."

"Naturally, I am concerned, but I must admit that it *looks* rather benign. Why is it you have chosen this project upon which to bestow your free time?"

Her emphasis on the last two words evidently did not register with Dare. He cocked an eyebrow at the grip she maintained on the back of Wills's jacket. "Is there something you want the lad to do, Charlotte?"

Her chin went up and her eyes narrowed. "On the contrary, my lord, there is something I want him *not* to do."

Dare rubbed his nose, leaving a slight smear of grease on his face. Charlotte stared at it, her fingers itching to wipe it off, to stroke the long planes of his face.

"What's that?"

"Hmmm? You have something just there . . . no, I'll get it." She brushed aside his hand and ran her finger down the long length of his nose. He stilled under her touch. Her breath quickened in response.

"Charlotte?" His eyes, she couldn't help noticing, had darkened to the color of the ocean on a summer's day. He took her hand in his, his thumb making gentle circles on her wrist. Her heart leaped at his touch.

"Yes, Alasdair?"

"Wills?"

She blinked, withdrawing from the fantasy of just what part of him she'd like to be stroking at that moment. "Wills?"

Dare nodded at the lad. "You said you wanted

him not to do something? What exactly would that be?"

"Oh. Wills. Yes, of course. Quite simply, my lord, I do not wish for him to be my maid."

Dare looked at her, disbelief rife in his mind-meltingly handsome eyes. "Your maid?"

Charlotte nodded. She'd decided to stand firm on this issue. If she started giving in to every one of Dare's eccentric habits, who knows where she would end up. "That's correct. I do not wish him to be my maid. He's too young, he knows nothing about dressing hair, and frankly, I doubt if he can care for my clothing in a manner suited to my position." Char leaned closer until her breath brushed his cheek. "The boy wipes his nose on his sleeve!"

"He does?" Dare asked, his breath mingling with hers as he turned his head to her.

"Yes," she said, immediately losing the train of the conversation. God's toenails, the man was so handsome it made her feel positively dowdy in comparison. Char took control of all her parts that were clamoring to be cast into Dare's arms and stepped back. She had to be firm, that was all, firm and resolute in the face of the most tempting man on the face of the earth.

Dare raised his eyebrows at her, and asked mildly, "Why would you even think of Wills as a maid . . . Batsfoam, come back here! You have drafting to do!"

"What do you mean, why would I think of Wills as my maid?" Charlotte was outraged by the implication behind his words. Clearly he didn't feel she needed a maid at all and was regretting the loss of Wills at his regular tasks. Well, if that were the case, he could think twice! "The boy was assigned to me, that's why. I'm sure you have other things for him to do. From what Batsfoam has told me, every member of your staff seems to be doing the jobs of three people, but nonetheless, I simply must have a maid. It is impossible to undo the tapes at the back of my gown without assistance."

"My most gracious and kind lord, I was just going to fulfill the other tasks that claim my time with the intention of returning to draft your new boiler design just as soon as I have seen to my lord and lady's comfort, health, and general well-being."

"Stay where you are, Batsfoam. Charlotte, I never said—"

"Not to mention my hair. And who will take care of my clothing? I am willing to cooperate to my fullest on many things, Alasdair, but on this I am adamant. I must have a maid!"

"I promised Cook I would assist him with the blacking of the stoves, my august and benevolent lord. And then I must check the coal, see that the beds are turned down and warmed, attend to the doors and windows, bank the fires, polish the silver, clean the knives, check the pantry—"

"If you take one step from this room, Batsfoam, you'll regret it, so help me God. Now, Charlotte, if you would just listen to me—"

"Your own sister has a maid," Charlotte said indignantly, poking him in the chest. "A female one, too. You cannot deny me one. Go ahead. Try to deny me a maid. I'll wager you won't find yourself with a leg to stand on if you dare try to deny me the simple necessities of life!"

"—and then there's the stables to be mucked out, the chimney pots to be checked, the privy door to be repaired—"

"CHARLOTTE!" Dare roared.

"WHAT?" she roared back, intent on giving as good as she got.

Dare breathed heavily for a few seconds, his hands fisted at his side, his jaw taut. "I have no intention of denying you a maid. I simply asked why you wanted Wills as your maid. Batsfoam—don't." Batsfoam, reading quite accurately the threat in his employer's eyes, stopped trying to escape and resigned himself to the inevitable.

"I don't want Wills as a maid!" Charlotte cried. Why had she never noticed that Alasdair was all beauty and no brain? "That's just the point. *I don't want* him as a maid, nor do I want Batsfoam. He is totally unsuitable, Alasdair, and even if you don't care if another man dresses and undresses me, I do! I won't have it!" She stamped her foot for good measure.

Dare slowly turned his head from his wife to the butler. "You offered yourself to my lady as her maid?"

A flicker of what might have been guilt was seen for a fleeting moment before Batsfoam's expression settled into its usual dour lines. "You instructed me to have the staff do as many jobs as possible in the name of economy, my lord. I felt the addition of a maid for the sole use of her ladyship would not be in best keeping with the sacrifices we are all making on your behalf."

"Her *maid*, Batsfoam?"

Batsfoam pursed his lips and tried to look contrite. He didn't succeed particularly well, Charlotte thought.

"Perhaps I did err in my reasoning, but I assure both my lord and my lady that I had only my kind and most generous lord's goodwill in mind."

Charlotte, all smiles once she realized that Dare

hadn't intended on foisting his butler on her as a maid, allowed her dimples free rein as Dare unburdened himself of a brief lecture to Batsfoam about what consisted of proper duties and what didn't, ending with the order to hire Charlotte a female lady's maid in the morning.

"I will draft a letter to the agency this very moment, my lord."

"If you do not return within ten minutes—" Dare growled.

Batsfoam assured him the note would take but the merest moment to complete.

"I'm sure Patricia's maid will help you tonight with . . . er . . ." Dare frowned at Batsfoam and Wills, waiting until they had left before gesturing toward Charlotte's midsection. ". . . with your gown and such."

She nodded and waited for him to make reference to his participation in the activities on the schedule for later. She waited in vain.

"Would you like me to show you what I'm working on now?" Dare offered. "It's just the air pump and a condenser, but you might find it interesting."

Charlotte thought that was hardly likely, but mindful of the newly born desire to make her husband happy, she bent forward to look at a collection of tubes, valves, and other assorted mechanical devices that Dare indicated.

"It's part of my double-acting engine. What you see here is just part of the engine; the whole thing is made up of a steam cylinder, a stern wheel, the boiler, and the air pump and condenser. Working together, they turn the connecting rod connected to a paddle wheel, and that propels the boat without it having to recourse to manual labor or wind."

Charlotte, first inclined to yawn at the sight of the

unintelligible mass of metal, couldn't help but notice the excitement in Dare's voice when he described—in terms she couldn't even begin to understand—the basic principles behind steam engine travel. She watched him closely as he talked and pointed out various bits and pieces to the condenser, explained how an air pump worked, and detailed the dangers involved in designing an engine meant to work with salt water. She listened and nodded, but all she really saw was how much regard he held for the project.

"This is important to you," she said in dawning awareness. "Very important, isn't it?"

He bent an admonishing eye upon her as he took another rag—clean, she noticed—and polished the glass face of a gauge. "It's important to both of us, Charlotte. The success of my engine means our success, no more, no less. Without it . . . well, without it our future is dark."

"Oh, you're over-exasperating," she smiled. "How can our future be dark? You are an earl, an important man, you have a lovely and charming wife who is sure to take the *ton* by storm, thereby doing great credit by you. I am sure to give you handsome children, assuming, that is, that your manly instrument is agreeable, and I see no reason why it should not be, not that I ever understood why Antonio's wouldn't even twitch for me, but truly, that is neither here nor there. We have a perfectly glorious future—what could possibly threaten it?"

Dare stopped polishing and shook his head for a moment, pinching the bridge of his nose as he said, "Let's take that slowly, shall we? In small chunks, so it's easier to understand. First of all, my title has nothing to do with our future happiness. All that I gained when the title came to me was a mountain of debts I couldn't possibly pay off in one lifetime, and three estates in such dire circumstances it would take a miracle to make them self-supporting."

Charlotte smiled sympathetically at her husband. Imagine believing an earldom had nothing to do with happiness. Still, he clearly had some strong feelings on the subject. An indefinable need to comfort him by some wifely means swept over her, generating a bright, shining idea in her mind. She *would* comfort him! He was upset, and she was his wife; therefore, it was her duty to comfort him. She wondered briefly how to go about doing that since she'd never actually comforted a man before, let alone a husband. Whenever Antonio was upset, he'd just go off to be with his sheep. Still, it couldn't be that difficult. People, she was sure, were comforted all the time. She was an intelligent woman. If she put her mind to it, she could deduce the proper steps needed to undertake a successful comforting

"Secondly, you won't be in town long enough to take the *ton* by storm."

Charlotte racked her brain for comforting gestures. From a distant corner of her mind the memory arose of when she was a little child, and of how her mother used to rub her back when she was ill. That was just what he needed! A tender smile graced her lips as she glided over to where Dare stood and placed her palm on his back, gazing up into his eyes with what he hoped looked like wifely concern. Inside, she was sure, it looked like desire, but hopefully he wouldn't notice it. She was almost certain that desire had no part in general comforting.

"Third, you seem not to be listening at all when

I tell you that I'm not a rich man, so I will tell you again: I am not exaggerating, Charlotte. I told you before we wed that you would have to manage with economizing most stringently. I don't have the money to buy you a new wardrobe, or take you on trips, or any of the myriad other things you will no doubt demand as your due. All the household are doing their part to help, and I expect no less from my wife."

Charlotte let her fingers wander over the muscled planes of his back, her entire being focused on the sensation of heat that flowed from his flesh through the soft linen of his shirt to her fingertips. She started rubbing small circles on his spine as her mother had done, but soon she was mapping out the terrain of his back with long, languid strokes that made every part of her aware that she was a woman, he was a man, and they were alone together. Legally wed. Able to procreate without censure or condemnation.

"Fourth," Dare stammered, his eyes a bit wild around the edges as she moved around behind him to use her other hand as well. She felt a bit flushed, but she was determined to see the comforting through to the end. It was her duty, and she was ever a dutiful wife. "About your expectations with regards to my manly . . . er . . ."

Charlotte was suddenly desperate to touch his flesh. She tugged at the shirt until it pulled free of his trousers, slipping her hands beneath to where his flesh beckoned and called to her.

"So hot," she breathed, running her fingers over every muscled bulge and valley, tracing the line of his ribs, overwhelmed with the sense and feel and scent of him until she had to lean forward and press her face against his shirt. "You make me feel so hot, husband. You make me feel as if I'm on fire."

Dare groaned and quickly ripped his shirt off even as he turned to gather her in his arms.

"Charlotte, it's very important that you listen to what I'm going to say," he told her, his breath hot on her lips, but she didn't have the time or energy to focus on his words. Words weren't important— the heat that was building inside of her was. Fire, she thought to herself as she molded her hands up his chest and over his shoulders. He was like fire in her blood, making her burn with desire and need and all sorts of sensual, shameful things that her womanly parts were demanding with each breath Dare drew. She threaded her fingers through his golden hair and tugged.

"It's your fault I'm on fire; do something about it," she demanded, tilting her head back, offering her mouth even as she wondered if she could stand the inferno his kiss was sure to cause.

"I'm sorry you're on fire," he said, his lips teasing hers with tiny little nips that made her squirm against him.

"Are you truly?" She rubbed herself against him, her body needing the hard touch of his.

"No," he said just before he claimed her mouth. Charlotte pressed herself even closer as his tongue swept inside her. She was eager to taste him, welcoming his outrageous demand that she submit to him. Charlotte had never submitted to any man in her life, but there was just something truly phenomenal about Dare—she thought it might be his tongue—that crumbled all her resistance until it was only the vaguest memory.

"Charlotte." Dare's breathing was hot and ragged as he tore his mouth from hers. She whimpered and tugged on his head to make him kiss her again.

"No, Charlotte, you have to listen to me." Dare seemed out of breath, angry even as he tightened his jaw. Charlotte leaned forward to kiss a trail along it. He moaned softly into her hair, his fingers flexing into her hips before he suddenly, inexplicably, *cruelly* pushed her away from the warm haven of his body. "Stop trying to drive me insane! A man can take only so much, woman! Stay there, right there, don't move an inch. Just stand right there and I'll stand here and then you won't drive me mad with your lips and . . . your . . ."

Charlotte, her restless body set aflame with the desire evident in his eyes, moved forward.

"STOP!" he yelled, and retreated behind the machine. "Stay there, and stop looking at my chest like that or I won't be able to control myself."

"But I don't want you to control yourself. I want you to be wild, just like your tongue when you kiss me. I've never thought a tongue could be so thrilling, but yours is. I like how it dances all over my mouth. I like how it strokes and teases and turns quite bossy with my tongue. And I can't stop looking at your chest, I like it. I want to touch your chest. I want to taste it, too. Don't you want me to taste it?"

Dare took a deep, shuddery breath as he ran an agitated hand through his hair. "God give me the strength to survive this night. Stop thinking of my tongue and my chest and the hot silkiness of your mouth and how your breasts fit perfectly into my hands and the alluring way your hips curve just right, and listen to me. What I have to say to you is important. It's vital that you understand me."

What with all the talk of hips and breasts and tongues, not to mention the wild, nearly uncontrolled look in her husband's eyes, Charlotte couldn't help but blink back disappointment that he wasn't attacking her and ravishing her on the spot, although she conceded that ravishment on a dirt floor was probably not the most comfortable of experiences.

"Very well," she said, clutching her hands to keep from reaching out to stroke all that lovely golden skin. "As you don't wish for me to taste you and touch you and perhaps stroke your manly instrument in the manner that Vyvyan La Blue says is most effective, then I shall stand here and listen to you."

Dare closed his eyes for a moment and swallowed hard. Twice. "Thank you."

"I will, however, continue to think about your tongue."

A tremor rippled through his powerful frame.

He gripped the machinery before him with both hands. He seemed to be having some sort of difficulty with his jaw, because his words came out tight and sharp. "I am a man of honor. When you trapped me into marriage with you, I was well within my rights to expose you and leave you to the condemnation of the *ton*. But I didn't do that. I didn't allow you to become an object of pity and scorn. I offered for you publicly, and I wed you publicly."

Charlotte nodded. She stepped to the side to better see his groin.

"You will admit that I could have left you with your breeches dangling around your knees, and walked away without further consequence to me."

Charlotte narrowed her eyes. She was familiar enough with male anatomy to know what she was looking at. She waited, watching for the sign.

"That I married you proves I have honor. That I

refuse to touch you until such time as I desire it, proves I am in control of my life regardless of your plans otherwise. I will not have a woman, any woman, dictating to me what I shall and shall not do. I realize you want children someday, that you ... er ... embrace the physical side of marriage, but you must understand that I will be the master in my own home." Dare paused for a moment, his breath hissing through clenched teeth. Charlotte leaned closer, her eyes on the tautly stretched fabric concealing his manly instrument. Her fingers itched to touch him.

"WHY THE HELL ARE YOU STARING AT MY CROTCH LIKE THAT?"

Charlotte jumped at the bellow, her gaze snapping up to meet infuriated blue eyes. "I was waiting to see if you twitched," she explained. The man certainly had a lot to learn about marriage if he didn't know all the specifics about bedding his wife. Everyone knew there had to be twitching before the bedding could begin.

Dare certainly looked a bit deranged as he ran a hand through his hair again, his eyes blazing, his broad, manly chest rising and falling with quick breaths. She wondered if she should comfort him again.

"Twitched? Did you say twitched? Do I understand you correctly? You are watching my crotch to see if my ... er ... *twitches?*"

Regretfully, Charlotte decided that now was not the time to comfort by physical touch. Instead, she would contrive to comfort him from where she stood. She smiled a calm, gentle smile that radiated soothing thoughts. "Yes. It's very simple, really. Would you like me to explain it to you?"

Disbelief, amusement, and resignation paraded

across his face. "Yes," he replied, crossing his arms over his chest and leaning one hip up against the machine. "Please. Enlighten me."

Charlotte had a hard time swallowing at the sight of all those muscles bunched, but she made an effort. She was, after all, supposed to be comforting him. The poor man was obviously clueless about how things worked in a marriage. As the wiser, more experienced partner, it was up to her to fill him in on the fine details.

"The harlot I consulted in Italy was most specific about what was necessary for a bedding," she began.

"Harlot?" Dare blinked a couple of times at her. "You consulted a harlot?"

"Yes, for Antonio. His manly instrument didn't work correctly, and so I went to a harlot to see what I could do to help it. Her advice was sound, I'm sure, so you needn't worry that just because it did not work on Antonio, it won't work on you—"

"One moment." Dare held up a hand to stop her. She clutched her hands tighter and made an effort to send calming rays of comfort toward him. "Are you telling me that your husband couldn't . . . er . . . couldn't maintain an erection?"

"Erection!" Charlotte beamed at him. "What a very good word that is. Apropos, too. Erection. I like that. Yes, the answer to your question is no, Antonio's manly instrument refused to erect for me."

Dare rubbed a hand over his face. His voice sounded as if it were stretched as thin as taffy. "You're a virgin?"

A faint blush made its way up her cheeks, but she ignored it. This was her husband she was speaking to. Such discussions as virginity and the erections of manly instruments were allowed with him. She shook her head.

"So he consummated your marriage?"

She nodded, happy that he understood. "Yes, the night we were wed."

"Just . . . er . . . just the once? He never gave you pleasure any other time?"

"No. As I said, his manly instrument didn't care for the erecting process. Which brings me back to the harlot—she said, and quite sensibly I think, that twitching indicates an interest on the owner's part. Your manly instrument seems to be capable of the erecting process. Thus I was watching for the twitching to tell me whether or not you find me toothsome."

Dare stared at her for a second before throwing his head back and laughing. Charlotte frowned. There seemed to be a pronounced note of hysteria in his laugh, and to be truthful, she didn't see what he found so funny. She was being as honest and instructive as she could be, helpful, too. How many wives, she wondered, would take the time to share their knowledge with their husbands?

"I was only mildly curious, you understand," she said with great dignity, ignoring her husband, who was still howling with laughter. Really, she was almost offended by his reaction to her offer of help. "Antonio's instrument didn't find me erect-worthy. I just thought I'd see how yours felt about the subject. And I must add, I think it's quite rude for you to carry on in this manner when all I was trying to do was give you the benefit of my experience as a wife of four years. Most men, I imagine, would be happy to have such knowledge imparted to them!"

Dare wiped his eyes and made an effort to stop laughing. "Charlotte, you might as well be a virgin for all the experience and knowledge of men you have."

Charlotte tightened her lips. He was laughing at her, *at her!* All because Antonio's instrument hadn't liked her. Tears pricked at the back of her eyes, but before she could do more than allow her lower lip to tremble, he was there before her, all golden skin and muscles and a wonderful scent that was pure Dare. He took her hands in his, kissing the back of each.

"I wasn't insulting you. I'm sorry if you think I was. I am humble and honest enough to admit that a part of me is pleased you are virtually all but untouched."

She allowed herself to be mollified and was about to bestow upon him her best dimpled smile when he went and ruined her good mood.

"But it changes nothing. I am in earnest, wife. I will not allow you to cozen me into your bed. I will bed you if, and when, I choose. No amount of kisses and seductive looks and teary entreaties will stir me. Do you understand?"

Charlotte stared at him in horror. He couldn't be serious. Could he? No. He was overwrought. He needed more comforting. He was worried about the something blocking something else in his engine that could explode. That was all. Still . . . "You're not serious?"

He nodded, releasing her hands as he turned back to his machine. He picked up his cloth and resumed polishing the gauge. "*You* wanted marriage, *you* trapped me into it, but *I* will be the master of my own fate. Now, it's late, I suggest you go to bed. Have Patricia's maid attend you. I will see you in the morning, when we will go over the household budget."

139

"But, but your manly instrument! It's erecting all over the place! Just look at it; it wants me!"

Dare refused her invitation to gaze upon his groin. Charlotte would have insisted, but she had to admit he looked as if he were at the end of his patience.

"That doesn't mean I'm going to bed you."

"That's . . . that's . . . surely that's not legal, is it? You can't *not* bed me!"

He didn't even bother to look at her as he spoke, the beast. "I can, and I will. Go to bed, Charlotte. I have work to do here, and you can't be of any help unless you know how to increase the efficiency of a marine condenser."

She gritted her teeth against the desire to tell him just what he could do with his inefficient condenser, but she told herself a good wife did not think such thoughts, no matter how much her pigheaded, obstinate, foolish husband might try to goad her into it.

Besides, a sudden vision had come to her, a vision of a book in blue leather with lovely gilt letters and marbled endpapers. Vyvyan La Blue, she was certain, would have a thing or two to say about husbands whose manly instruments erected at will and yet whose masters refused to put them through their paces. Vyvyan always had something to say, and the connubial calisthenics described had always looked so appealing.

"Very well," she said, her chin high as she skirted the machine. "I shall retire for the evening. Good night." She stretched up on tiptoe and placed a chaste kiss on his cheek.

He mumbled a good night that turned into a yelp as she boldly placed her hand on his crotch. His instrument twitched in response to her caress. She smiled a very, very smug smile as she turned and left the room without another word.

All would be well. He wanted her, his manly instrument was twitching as it should be, and as for all the rest of his outrageous statements . . . well, that would sort itself out in time.

Chapter Seven

Wearily, Dare climbed the three sets of stairs leading to his bedchamber, his mind filled not as it
should be—with a solution to the problem of the
obstruction of the free passage of heat from the
boiler to the water of the cold cistern—but with
thoughts of the warm, vital, utterly enthralling
woman who was now legally his. There wasn't a
person in the whole British Empire who would bat
an eyelash if he were to march straight into her
bedchamber and claim those marital rights due
him as her husband. Certainly Charlotte wouldn't
complain, he thought with a tired chuckle as he
turned down the hallway toward the bedchambers.
She all but stripped him in his workroom, and the
way her body melted against his indicated she
wasn't immune to his touch. If she only knew the
power she held over him ... he shook his head,

thankful she had no idea of the effect she had on his heart and soul. He glanced downward and ruefully added *body* to the list.

Of their own accord, his feet stopped before the door to her bedchamber. He found himself holding his breath, listening for sounds from the room. A powerful wave of desire washed over him as he stood gripped with indecision, wanting nothing so much as to fling open the door and spend the rest of the night making his wife happy. His lips twisted wryly as he eased the tight material of his breeches across the proof of his arousal. Just the thought of her so close, so tantalizingly near left his heart pounding with the effort to keep his needs under control, his whole body straining for release at the image of her awaiting him in bed, warm, welcoming, loving. . . .

He grimaced at the last word. That was the problem, she didn't love him. Hell, he doubted if she even *liked* him. She was physically attracted to him, but so were a good many other women, and while he had no complaints with a purely physical relationship based on mutual satisfaction, that was not what he wanted from a wife. A wife was different.

Not that he had *wanted* a wife, he pointed out to himself as he turned away from her door. But he had one now, and it was up to both of them to make the best of it. He wanted Charlotte to be a friend, a partner, someone who desired to share his life, not just his bed.

Dare hissed an oath as he strode down the hall to his small dressing room, cursing his foolish pride, cursing his need for something more than a lover. Why couldn't he be like other men and take what was offered without looking to engage her affections? He stripped off his breeches and boots, throwing them heedlessly in a corner before washing the dust and grime off his torso. Towel in hand, he glared down at himself. Despite the cold water he was still hot and hard and in desperate need of relief.

"Traitor," he growled to his arousal before stalking to the window, looking out at the empty moonlit streets, trying to ignore the demands of his body that swept all else from his mind. Certainly looking at a street would be safe. There was nothing out there to remind him of the warm, supple woman lying in the room next to his. No, there was just a street out there, a common, everyday sight. True, the crescent curve of the street reminded him of the sweet curve of her hips, but that was the merest of coincidences. And that the silvered light glinting off a puddle of water was just as bright as the sunlight striking her golden curls was of no account. Of course, there was the deep indigo of a shadowed doorway that mimicked her eyes as they darkened in passion when he took possession of her sweet, alluring mouth. . . .

"Dammit!" he snarled, dropping the drape and whirling away from the window. His arousal was throbbing now, actually *throbbing* with want and need and desire. He considered easing himself just so he could sleep, but grimly told himself he wasn't that desperate.

"Yet," he muttered with a curse as he blew out the candle and headed for his bedchamber. It was going to be a long night, this wedding night of his, but it would be better spent lying sleeplessly in his dark bed where everything he saw wouldn't remind him of his bride in the next room.

The bed loomed up, melting into the darkness of the room, the long bed curtains turning it into a yawning black embrace of heaven or hell, he wasn't sure which. He slid between the covers, ignoring the almost painful touch of cool linen across his heated parts, willing himself to concentrate on something not remotely related to the cries of need from his body. His engine, that's what he'd think about. Engines were masculine. Engines were hard, not soft and sweetly scented like a woman's welcoming body. Engines had long, steel shafts that fit tightly into waiting oiled bearings. Engines had pistons, lots of pistons, all of them pumping tirelessly, pumping and pumping, driving the shaft in a long, endless motion, building the pressure higher and higher until it was so great, the blow-cock triggered, releasing a great blast of steam. . . .

"Oh, Christ." Dare moaned into the arm flung over his face. He truly was going mad if even the thought of his steam engine did nothing but conjure images of Charlotte. God's carbuncles, his mind was so consumed with her, it even manufactured the sweet scent of her perfumed skin to taunt and torment him.

His entire body stiffened. Slowly he moved his hands, flexing his fingers, then turned his head toward the arm draped across his cheek and brow, the arm that most definitely did not belong to him.

"Charlotte?" he whispered.

"Mmm?" came a muffled, sleepy response from the shadowed side of the bed. The soft arm slid down his face to his chest. Dare cursed fluently in Gaelic as he leaped from the bed and grabbed for the flint.

"What the . . . Ow! Bloody chair . . . devil are you doing in my bed?" he roared at the disembodied arm lying in a pool of moonlight as he lit a candle.

"Hmm? Alasdair?" The soft glow of the candlelight revealed Charlotte sitting up, sleepy confusion on her face, her hair a mass of streaming gold that glinted as bright as a polished sovereign. "Oh, good, you've come to bed. I must have fallen asleep reading about the Beltane Fire."

Dare stared at his wife as she pushed the hair out of her eyes and stretched. Even covered with a virginal night rail, she was a goddess, a wanton temptress, Aphrodite and Venus rolled into one enticing package. He clutched the candle tighter and tried manfully to drag his hungering gaze from the soft swell of her breasts. "Beltane Fire?"

"Yes." She smiled and pushed back the bed linens, scooting over to the side of the bed he had just left. "It's one of the connubial calisthenics. I thought it looked particularly . . . dear God in heaven!"

Charlotte froze in mid-scoot, her eyes huge as she stared at Dare. All of him. Every last blessed inch of his hide. Especially the traitorous parts.

"I think the word 'erection' does not do your manly instrument justice, Alasdair," she breathed, her eyes luminous as they feasted on his arousal. "I'm thinking something more descriptive like monument or colossus or tarantula would be in order."

"*Gargantua* not tarantula," he snapped, dropping the candle as he scrambled to find his dressing gown. He could feel her eyes on him, touching his flesh, sending rivulets of molten desire through his veins until he thought he would go mad. Lord help him, he would never survive the night, let alone the few months he expected it would take before she had grown to care about him. He wrestled his dressing gown over a body that cried out for completion, and relit the extinguished candle.

He took hold of resolve that was slipping away with every rise and fall of her breasts, and set his jaw. He had to be strong. He had to be unflinching even in the face of the most tempting woman on the face of the earth. He had to stand firmly behind what he knew was right.

She leaned forward, the loose neckline of her night rail slipping down over one shoulder, exposing the creamy curve of her breast.

He had to be out of his mind.

"Oh. Why did you put that on? I liked you much better without it. You have nice flesh. It looks very touchable."

He swore that if he squinted he could see the rosy shadowed peek of her nipple through the thin lawn material . . . good God, what was he doing? He dragged his gaze up to her face.

The pink tip of her tongue ran lightly across her bottom lip. His eyes followed it. The world as Dare knew it darkened and spun for a moment. He wondered idly if he was about to swoon. He'd never heard of a man swooning outside of the battlefield, but then, no man he knew of was so close to going up in the flames of unrequited desire as he was.

"Alasdair?"

He opened his eyes. She was standing before him, a book clutched to her stomach, her breasts straining against the material pulled tight across them. He hadn't been imagining it earlier; he really could see the blushing crown of each glorious breast. His mouth watered at the thought of the taste of them, of the silky smoothness of her breasts, of the weight and feel of them in his hands, of the scented paradise her body offered.

"Is something the matter? Is it . . ." For the first time since he had met her five years before, she looked unsure of herself. She made a whispered choking sound. ". . . me? Is something wrong with *me?*"

She bit her lip and blinked rapidly, as if fighting tears. The resolve he held on to so firmly began to melt at the sight of his wife, his bright, effervescent, witty Charlotte standing before him believing herself to be inadequate. God's knuckles, what was he doing to her? She was all but an innocent, and his honor, his determination to be in control of his life was hurting her. How could he be so cruel to her?

"Dare? Don't you want to bed me?" The words, almost too soft to be heard, pierced his heart.

"I . . . I'm sorry, Charlotte." His voice was as rough as granite. "I tried to explain to you earlier. It doesn't have anything to do with my desire to bed you. I want something more than just your body."

She clutched the book tighter, tears trembling on her lashes. "I don't understand. What do you want if you don't want me? Is it someone else? Why did you offer for me if you want someone else?"

He shook his head, fisting his hands to keep them from pulling her to him. "I don't want anyone else. And it should be quite obvious, even to you, that I am not immune to your many charms. But you are my wife. I didn't want to take a wife because . . . well, for many reasons, not the least of which is I'm in no financial position to support a woman like you as she deserves, but most importantly because I didn't want to settle for a convenience, just a body to slake myself on. I expect more from my wife."

Dare willed her to understand. He couldn't say the words in his heart to her, not yet, but he hoped she would realize that what he wanted to grow between them was something more profound than just lust.

Her throat worked as if she were swallowing back tears. "You desire me?"

He nodded, unwilling to trust his voice.

"But you want something more from me than just . . ." She looked toward the bed.

His eyes glittered at her. "Yes. I want something more."

She bit her lip, an annoying habit in any other woman, but endearingly sweet and innocent in his wife. It melted his resolve even further. That his proud, confident Charlotte was standing before him unsure and insecure . . . his heart ached with the knowledge that it was his determination to have more, to have all of her that brought her to this, and yet he was unable to condemn them both to the misery that would follow if they settled for anything less.

"What do you want me to be?"

Companion, friend, wife, lover. "It's not so much what I want you to be, Charlotte. It's what we both should feel. I haven't seen you in five years, and we knew little enough about each other then. You put me in a position where I had to marry you, but that doesn't mean I'm willing to throw away our chance at happiness. I think we can have a happy life together, but only if we are first given the chance to learn about one another, to grow to . . . to have feelings for each other, something more than just the physical desire that we both feel."

Her eyes shimmered with tears. Then her gaze dropped to his feet as she made her soft admission. "I can't help the way you make me feel. My body burns for you. I want to touch you and taste you and have you touch me. My womanly parts tingle at the thought of you, Dare."

It was his name that did it; it was the soft exultation of his name off her sweet lips that pushed him over the edge. He told himself he was just going to show her pleasure, give her relief from desires that were, after all, entirely natural and wanted in a wife. He told himself he owed it to her to give her something since he couldn't give himself, but the truth was he just couldn't keep from touching her.

He scooped her up in his arms, reveling in the weight of her, his senses swimming with her scent and the texture of her silky hair, of the shy kisses she pressed to the column of his throat. Shy? His Charlotte? He would have laughed at the thought, but for her hands on his bare chest, stroking his skin with a touch that set fire to his blood. He moaned his surrender, dipping his head to plunder her sweet mouth.

His tongue moved boldly, teasing her, stroking her, sucking her lips into his mouth as he laid her on his bed, magically whisking away the suddenly unbearable material that separated her flesh from his.

"Magic." She sighed in happiness as the hot lure of his mouth returned. She tried to wrap her arms around him to pull his hard body against hers, but he resisted, murmuring instead a promise to please her. Please her? She wanted to tell him that he had far surpassed mere pleasure and was into uncharted realms of ecstasy, but she couldn't remember how to form words. Maybe later she would, when she wasn't being driven witless by the feeling of his mouth on hers.

Foolish woman, she thought a few minutes later when his lips had left hers. Foolish woman to think that it was just his tongue twining around hers that stole her wits. No, she knew better now. Her back arched of its own will as he licked and sucked a path down her neck to her collarbone, her legs tensing under his hand as it slid upward on her thigh. The skin on his hand was rough, but it felt wonderful on her sensitive flesh as she obeyed the silent command to part her legs. Her mind felt as if it were fracturing under the twin sensations of his mouth steaming a trail toward her aching breasts and the restless need building in the deepest center of her, directly in the path of his hand.

The cool softness of his hair brushed over her sensitive nipples as he traveled downward, his mouth hot on the underside of her breast, her mind fracturing even more when he took one breast in his hand while the other was laved in tightening circles of kisses, all while his fingers stroked a line up her thigh to the spot she ached for him to touch.

"Dare!" she groaned, her body moving of its own volition now. She felt as if she were floating in a sea of heat, flames licking at her, matched by the inferno he started so deep within her that her body wept tears of passion for him. "Please. Please."

Dare hovered over her, his head dipping in the valley between her breasts. She clutched his shoulders, wanting him, needing him, desperate to feel his hard body pressing into hers.

"Please what, love? Tell me what you want. Tell me what you like." His voice rasped along her heated flesh as his mouth closed over the hard, aching nipple at the same time his fingers found her sensitive folds. She heard his words, but they didn't make sense, nothing made sense, nothing but the feeling of his mouth and hands and the silky heat of his skin under her fingers. She arched beneath him, sobbing with desperation to feel him against her, but he slid down her body, pausing just long enough to suckle her other breast before kissing a hot, wet path down her belly.

"Dare! You can't stop! You can't leave me like this!"

His fingers stopped the delightful dance they were doing on her soft, sensitive parts, leaving her bereft, frustrated, wound so tight she was certain she would splinter into a thousand sharp pieces. "Dare!"

His hands were bold on her hips as he nipped her belly and looked up, grinning as he slid his hands down to part her legs wider. "Don't worry, love. I won't leave you. Not just yet."

"But . . . but . . ." Her eyes rolled back in her head as his head dipped down to her belly, suckling a trail of heat that lead straight to the focus of all her desire. "This has got to be sinful," she whispered, clutching handfuls of the bed linens as his breath scorched the outer edges of the needful center of her being. "I'm going to go to hell for this, I just know it. But oh, Lord, I don't care! Don't stop, please don't stop!"

His hair was the smoothest silk against her skin as his mouth possessed her in a way she had never dreamed possible. He was fire, he was lightning, he was quicksilver inside her, and she was dying, but oh, what a sweet death. She was no longer in any doubt that his tongue was the very best part of him as it worked magic on her sensitive, swollen flesh, touching her, teasing her, suckling her until she thought she would burn up in a bonfire of sensation. She had no idea she could burn hotter, but the minute his finger slid deep into her heat she blazed in a flame that was surely going to incinerate both of them. She heard a voice sobbing his name and knew it was her own, but could think of nothing but the bright, blinding moment of pure rapture as it exploded within her.

His name rang loud in his ears as she tightened around his fingers, her body shaking with the power of her orgasm. Dare pressed his face into her belly as she trembled, the need to plunge into her so strong he was nearly weeping. He hung on to his resolution by the merest thread, his body shuddering as it warred with his mind, his flesh crying out for the fulfillment it so desperately needed. He hadn't intended on going so far, of giving her so much of himself, but he could not stop, not when she tasted so sweet. He lay there for long minutes, his breath ragged as tears seeped from eyes closed tight, damply spreading on Charlotte's belly, his fingers holding firmly to her hips.

He left her were she lay, sleeping, warm and soft, her flesh beckoning and calling to him with a glow that crept into his heart and soul. He covered her, standing for a long time next to the bed, admiring the picture she made in the golden candlelight with her lips swollen from his kisses, and tears of joy still staining her cheeks. The tears were salty on his tongue; her skin was pure and sweet and tasted of something that was wholly Charlotte.

He left her, walking stiffly through the connecting door to her bedchamber, looking with abhorrence at the dark, cold bed. His body was tight and hard and hurting with a pain he didn't know was possible without a physical wound.

"Hell," he sighed, giving up the battle and climbing into the bed. He glared at his hand. It wasn't what his body clamored for and it wouldn't really satisfy him, but it might give him enough relief to allow him to sleep. He wrapped his long fingers around the aching length of his need, and prayed it wouldn't take Charlotte long to fall in love with him.

"I just hope I don't grow hair on my palms. I'd have a hell of a time explaining *that.*"

"Alasdair, you're being unreasonable."

"I'm not being unreasonable, I'm being practical, and my name is Dare. I know you can say it; you did last night."

Charlotte opened her eyes very wide and sent him a scathing look. "That was a special circumstance." The thought of just how special the circumstance was had her heart quickening and various parts of her body quivering in remembrance. She couldn't believe how the mere touch of his hands and mouth had transported her, but transport her they did, to some place she had never visited but was determined to visit again. Frequently. That very night. She eyed Dare speculatively. Afternoon was a good time, too.

"Be that as it may, I would like to point out that I've spoken to you several times now regarding the necessity of economizing, and regretfully, purchasing a new wardrobe does not fall under that heading."

"Dare, if you were to give Charlotte my dowry, she could buy—" Patricia started to say, but stopped when her brother glared across the sunny breakfast table at her. She busied herself with buttering a muffin.

Charlotte sent an appreciative smile to her sister-in-law, then turned the smile to a frown for her husband as she reached for the pot of chocolate. "Yes, you have mentioned that bit of ridiculousness frequently. You may rest assured you have made your point."

"Good," Dare said, turning his attention back to his plate of ham.

"Therefore, you may now give me what I want secure in the knowledge that you have done your part in protesting that you have no money with which to clothe my back, and authorize a visit to Mme. Terwilliger's. She is the latest crack in modistes," Charlotte told Patricia in a confidential tone.

Dare dropped his fork and stared openmouthed at his wife. "Charlotte, I am not playing a game with you."

"Well, no, of course you're not. It's not quite a game, it's more . . ." Charlotte waved a buttery knife. ". . . more a role. You protest you have no money, I pretend to believe you, then you give me what I want and everyone is happy."

Dare was shaking his head even before she finished her sentence. "Charlotte, I am not playing a role. I am not lying to you. I am not misrepresenting the truth. I am being honest, completely and utterly honest when I say that I do not have the money to pay for a new gown, let alone a whole wardrobe. I'm sorry to be blunt, but it's imperative you understand me once and for all. I . . . have . . . no . . . fortune."

Charlotte looked from her husband's tense jaw and glinting sapphire eyes to her sister-in-law. Patricia was nodding, her face twisted in sympathy. Charlotte felt a cold, clammy feeling in her midsection, as if someone had dropped a bowl of blancmange on her.

They couldn't be serious, could they? No money? Dare had no money? But that was ridiculous. He was an earl, and everyone knew earls inherited fortunes with their titles.

"No fortune?"

He shook his head.

"Nothing?"

He sighed and pinched the bridge of his nose. "Nothing."

She looked down at her plate of ham and potatoes, then back up to her husband, her mind too benumbed to take it all in. Nothing? "How can that be? How can you inherit a title but not a fortune? I don't understand! You're not just pinchparing?"

Sadness, regret, and guilt flickered across Dare's handsome face. Ire that had built up under his outrageous claims thinned when she saw the last. Perhaps he had been telling her the truth when he said he hadn't wanted to marry her because he couldn't support her. Perhaps he truly hadn't wanted to marry her. She quickly pushed away that horrible thought. Even if it was true, they were wed, and he would soon learn that she was an excellent wife, ideally suited to him, just as he was to her.

"I wish it were that simple, Charlotte. I inherited the title, true, but I also inherited my uncle's debts, a great many debts, which I am honor bound to cover. Our only hope of financial security lies in my success with the steam engine."

"That's where David comes in," Patricia added. "If Dare can sell his engine to David's uncle Edward, Dare will be able to pay off the debts."

Dare nodded. "With enough left over to begin recovering the estates. It will take time, but I'm confident that with hard work on all our parts, we'll see it through without too much damage."

"I don't wish to work hard and be damaged," Charlotte cried. "I wish to have a new gown for Patricia's wedding!"

Dare pushed his plate away and rubbed at his

forehead. "Can't you wear the gown you wore for our wedding?"

She stared at him in horror. "And have people see me in the same gown twice in one week? I think not!"

"It's a lovely gown, Charlotte," Patricia said quickly. "I'm sure no one would think any less of you for wearing it at my wedding as well. I think it's rather romantic, actually."

Charlotte glared at her, but transferred her glare to her husband when he added, "I doubt if anyone from our wedding will be in attendance at Patricia's, unless she's added Messrs. Rosencrantz and Windlestop's circus to the invitation list."

"No, indeed, I haven't. So you see, Charlotte, you will have nothing to worry about. You may wear your lovely gown and no one will know."

"I will know," Charlotte muttered to her breakfast. She looked up in time to see the pain in Dare's eyes before he threw down his cloth and pushed back from the table, making his excuses as he strode out of the room. Charlotte half rose in her chair, prepared to apologize for her comment, ashamed that he should see her acting like a petulant child, but he escaped before she could say anything. She sat back down, frowning. It wasn't fair. It just was not fair. How was she to know Dare hadn't any money? He looked just like every other rake in the *ton*, well-dressed but careless with his clothes, an air of noble negligence clinging to him just as it clung to every other family of blue blood. It was only the upstarts, the new money, the mushrooms who flaunted their wealth. How was she to know Dare really was on his uppers?

"If I'd have known that from the beginning . . ." she threatened, then stopped.

"If you'd have known what?" Patricia asked.

"Nothing." Charlotte sighed, unable to lie to herself. She had always wanted Dare, wanted him before she was married to Antonio, and wanted him a hundred times more after she returned to England. For a moment the visions of lavish balls and a dazzling wardrobe shown brightly in her mind. Then the warm, intimate memory of the evening past returned. Clothes and balls were, she thought with some surprise, only *things*. There was joy to be had in them, true, but the taste of bliss she had found with Dare filled her with a strange yearning for something more, something that went beyond the pleasure a pretty gown provided. Regretfully, she tucked away her dreams and braced herself to face reality. Lowering her expectations would not be easy, but she was never one to shy away from a challenge.

Righteousness and determination flared within her. "Your brother told me several years ago that I was nothing so much as a very pretty spoiled child. Well, he will not find me so now. If there is one thing I've learned over the past few years, it is that wanting something seldom makes it so. We will simply have to economize," she said firmly, tapping her knife on a peach. "I'm not quite sure how one goes about economizing a household, but I'm sure I can do it. It can't be that difficult. And besides, the servants are economizing already, so that will be of some help."

"Oh, yes, we've economized for the last three years," Patricia smiled. "We're all quite used to it, I can assure you."

"Excellent," Charlotte responded, her mind busy with ideas and newfound resolutions. In the midst of plans for cutting back on meals and canceling

158

her order for several new bonnets, a bright, shining image came to her mind. She studied it for a moment, pronounced it good, and smiled at her sister in law. "I shall start my economies by making a supreme sacrifice. I will inform Batsfoam he is to unhire the maid he hired for me."

Patricia blinked in surprise. "But you must have a maid! Who will help you dress? Who will do your hair? Who will mend your clothes and take care of them and see that they're washed and such?"

The image grew brighter in Charlotte's mind. "I shall take care of my own clothing. Don't look so shocked, Patricia, I am quite well known for my embroidery, how much different can mending a few tears be than embroidering? Besides, there can't be much to it. Francesca, my maid in Italy, was always finding time to go out and meet her lover. I imagine a few minutes each morning and night and I shall be perfectly suited."

"Perhaps so, but what about assistance dressing? You cannot do up all the tapes and buttons yourself."

Charlotte's smile deepened until her dimples danced. "My husband shall help me dress and undress. He, after all, is the one who insists on everyone economizing, it's only right he should do his part by attending to me himself. As for my hair, I shall adopt simpler styles as my cousin Gillian wears. Her husband always seems to approve of her hair despite its unfashionable color. Thus mine should be a great success. Now, tell me, when is Mrs. Whitney due to return from Bath?"

"Saturday, just before the wedding. She is taking the waters for her dyspepsia. She suffers terribly from upsets of an internal nature, and Lady Devonshire assured her that her upsets were quite cured

159

by taking the waters. I do hope they help. Aunt Whitney has been most uncomfortable after dinner."

"That's such a shame," Charlotte said cheerfully. "We shall sorely miss her presence here in these, your precious last few days as an unmarried woman. Indeed, I shall endeavor to fill your time so that you don't fret over her absence. Do you need help with the wedding?"

"No, Aunt Whitney took care of that before she left for Bath. I have a final fitting today for my wedding gown, and then there is nothing to do until Sunday."

Charlotte drummed her fingers on the table before rising. "I assume, then, you will not be transverse to helping me with a little project of my own?"

"I would not be *adverse* in the least to helping you, dear sister-in-law. How can I be of assistance?"

Charlotte took Patricia by the arm and headed toward the kitchen. "You know, of course, that the Duchess of Deal is giving an engagement ball for that pasty-faced daughter of hers whose name I never can remember."

"Lady Charlotte, yes."

Charlotte paused as she descended the stairs to the basement. "Charlotte? Her name is Charlotte? Well, the insipid little twit was misnamed, she's nothing like a Charlotte. Regardless of how poorly Their Graces chose to name her, her engagement ball is going to be the biggest event for the rest of the season, and I've already accepted—on all our behalf—the invitation she sent Dare. Now we must acquaint him of this fact, and then I shall take the servants in hand. They sorely need it, not that I am impruning your skills in the least."

Patricia giggled as the pair headed down the low-

160

ceilinged, dark hallway leading to Dare's work-room. "Thank you, Charlotte. I'm not feeing *impruned* at all, but I'm afraid Dare won't like your idea in the least. He hates the *ton*, he has ever since . . . well, since before he became an earl. I had a terrible time getting him to take me to Lady Jersey's masquerade. I had to threaten him with all sorts of things, finally resorting to crying before he agreed, and even then he swore it would be the only func-tion besides my wedding that he would attend for the rest of the year. I don't know how you plan to persuade him to go, but I can assure you that it will not be an easy task."

"I don't imagine it will be too difficult once I pre-sent my proposition," Charlotte said, halting before the door to Dare's workshop. "He'll have no way to refuse me once I offer to help him sell his engine to Mr. Whitney."

Patricia grabbed her arm as she was about to open the door. "Help him? How can you help him sell his engine to Uncle Whitney?"

Charlotte smiled a smile filled with her newly dis-covered awareness of feminine power. "My dear, I am a woman. No one can resist me when I put my mind to it. Even your brother could not withstand the onslaught of my full attention. Persuading your David's uncle to buy Alasdair's machine will be nothing compared to the coup I have just made."

Patricia mumbled a warning about the advisabil-ity of referring to Dare's marriage as a coup in his hearing, but she followed along docilely enough as her new sister bearded her brother in his den. Watching Charlotte handle Dare for the next few days was going to be an education, and she very much looked forward to seeing who would win their battle of wills.

Chapter Eight

"Truly, Charlotte, I don't know how you managed this miracle, but I'm so glad you did," Patricia whispered, squeezing Charlotte's hand as the pair slowly maneuvered their way through the crowd that littered the grand staircase at Henley House.

Charlotte thought briefly of the steadfast refusal Dare had first given, followed by gracious capitulation once Charlotte had sent Patricia from the workroom so she could ply him with kisses and pretty words. Truthfully, the words had little effect, but the kisses, oh, those kisses ... Charlotte glanced behind her at where her husband and David followed. The latter was smiling pleasantly, his eyes on his betrothed, while the former was scowling at her with an intensity that could blister steel. She paused for a moment to note just how very handsome he was in midnight blue, then blew him a kiss and turned back to the hall to remove her cloak and make her curtseys to those in the receiving line.

"Lord Carlisle, how pleased I am you could attend after all," the Duchess of Deal trumpeted down her long nose as soon as Charlotte and Patricia had left their cloaks. The duchess always reminded Charlotte of a long-faced pony she had as a child, and the similarity to those of the equine persuasion was even more pronounced with the passing years. "Miss McGregor, is it not? And you must be Captain Woodwell. You are most welcome, sir. My congratulations on your upcoming nuptials."

Charlotte waited politely to be acknowledged, relishing the moment of triumph. She had done what she had set out to do—she had married well and had regained her position, if not fortune. No one in the *ton* would slight her now, not without incurring Dare's wrath, and as he was in general a well-liked (if seldom seen) man, she knew his name would protect her. She flashed her dimples as the duchess condescended to notice her.

"Lady Carlisle." An infinitesimal tip of the head accompanied her dismissive glance.

"Your Grace." Charlotte smiled broadly, dipping into a deep court curtsey just to annoy the duchess. She rose and greeted the duke, gave her felicitations to the Marquis of Summerton, kissed the cheek of the unworthy bearer of her name, and proudly entered the crowded reception room on the arm of her husband. Candle flames flickered and swayed in the swirling air generated by so many moving bodies as they conducted that intricate dance of polite society meeting, greeting, and promenading. Delight shivered down Charlotte's back as she smiled at everyone. She had done it.

She had succeeded where everyone predicted she would fail. She had returned, on her own terms, and no one would ever again keep her from her rightful spot. Ah, but life was sweet.

"I'm back where I belong," she breathed, her eyes alight with joy as she savored her victory.

"I need a drink. I trust you will keep an eye on Patricia?" Dare asked as he disengaged his arm from Charlotte's clutch. "Good. Send someone for me when you are ready to return home."

Charlotte stared in horror as her husband of a day abandoned her at the moment of her greatest triumph.

"Oh, Charlotte, isn't it beautiful? Have you ever seen so many candles alight at once? I'm surprised no one has swooned in this heat. Why do you suppose the doors are shut? Wouldn't it be cooler if they allowed some air in? And the flowers? Who could have imagined so many white roses in all of London? Oh, Char, look, just look at that lady's gown. It's scandalous! You can see right through to her frillies! I must have one just like it after I am married. Where are Dare and David off to?" Patricia's face was aglow with excitement, in sharp contrast to the fallen expression of her sister-in-law.

Charlotte swallowed her disappointment, telling herself she didn't really need Dare present to enjoy herself, but even as the thought formed, she knew it was an untruth. Just being with him made everything seem brighter, more exciting, and when he left, it all turned dull and tarnished.

"Alasdair felt a bit parched in the heat and has gone for some refreshment. I believe David is keeping him company. The rooms are closed no doubt because the Prince Regent is expected, and I doubt seriously if your husband would appreciate you parading around in a gown like Mrs. Cutter's. She's a notorious widow, and is not in the least the sort of person you should emirate."

Patricia blinked for a moment, then grinned and took Charlotte by the arm as they wove their way through the crowd. "*Emulate*, Char. Come, you promised to introduce me to all the people Aunt Whitney would not allow me to meet. Let's start with Mrs. Cutter."

Charlotte spent the next hour in a unique position previously unknown to her—chaperone. While Patricia was not a flighty young thing to be watched every moment lest she bring herself to ruin, she was young, excited, and utterly thrilled with a world in which she'd had little contact. She also possessed a spirited sense of mischief that Charlotte realized, with some horror, bore an uncanny resemblance to her own. Never before had she been responsible for another, and she did not much care for the sensation.

"I have a new respect for what my poor mother must have endured," Charlotte grumbled to Caroline later as she intervened when Lord Briceland, a notorious rake responsible for many a young woman's downfall, would have swept Patricia off into a secluded corner of the ducal gardens. Caroline snickered.

"I am betrothed, Charlotte," Patricia protested as the two women dragged her along a cinder path edged with fantastic beasts rendered in topiary form toward the doors leading into the ballroom. "No harm can come to my reputation now. Lord Briceland has the dearest golden curls, don't you think, Lady Beverly?"

"Oh, yes, very much like that dashing Lord Byron's," Caroline agreed.

"Puts them up in papers each night like Byron, too, no doubt," Charlotte snapped, and came to a halt to face the giddy young girl facing her. She glanced around quickly, but there was little to be seen but a giant yew hedge marking the boundaries of a maze. "Good, there's no one around so I can speak freely. Patricia, I cannot have you dashing about making a cake of yourself in this manner. I really cannot. What would Alasdair say if I allow you to be seduced in the garden? What would David say? He's bound to object. Men do about that sort of thing!"

"They do, they truly do. Why, I remember the time shortly before I was wed when dearest Algernon caught me admiring Lord Selfridge's mustache—you remember him, Char, he had the most delicious blond mustache, almost silver it was—well, as it was, I was admiring Lord Selfridge's mustache and I felt I simply must touch it to see if it was as soft as it looked, and do you know, it was. It was very soft indeed, and I was much tempted to kiss him just to know whether the mustache tickled upon one's lip or not. But then dearest Algernon burst into the room ranting and carrying on in the most flattering way about me shaming him and giving away my innocence all for the sake of an attractive mustache—"

"Yes, thank you, Caro," Charlotte interrupted. "We take your point, assuming you have one. As for you, Patricia, I must insist that you remain at my side and take your cue from my conversations. Honestly, I would have never allowed you to read Vyvyan La Blue's book if I thought you were going to discuss the relative merits of the Minataur's Dance versus the Eight Heavenly Gates of Apollo with Lady Jersey! Ridiculously hidebound and old-fashioned though she might be, she *is* one of the leading ladies of the *ton*. One does not discuss connubial calisthenics with her!"

Patricia giggled. Charlotte glared at her and mused for a moment on the fact that she might be older by six years only, but she certainly *felt* decades wiser. "Do not giggle at me, miss! Giggling is for ninnies, and if you continue as you are, you'll end up like Caro here." She shook her finger with a stern countenance. God's elbows, wild as she was, she never was a ninny.

"Char!" Patricia objected, shooting a worried look at Lady Beverly.

Caroline drew herself up to her full height and looked down her nose at her friend. "I am not a ninny."

"Don't you 'Char' me in that outraged tone," Charlotte lectured her sister-in-law. "A ninny is as a ninny does, just you remember that! Besides, it is impolite to giggle in public."

"I have never *been* a ninny!"

"You said yourself we were alone here," Patricia said, trying to wipe the smile off her face. "No one can hear us, and I am sorry, but oh, Charlotte, you do make me laugh! Ever since you married Dare you've become positively priggish!"

"To be a prig is worse than to be a ninny," Caroline said darkly.

"Priggish!" Charlotte gasped, her eyes wide with outrage. "I am not in the least bit priggish! I am the most unpriggish woman in existence! Caro, tell her! Tell her that I am dashing and daring and do many things of a nature that is completely opposite that of priggish. Go ahead, Caro, tell her."

Caroline eyed her friend. "It is a well-known fact that ninnies keep company with prigs, therefore, since you claim I am a ninny, it follows that you are the living embodiment of priggishness."

"OH!"

"I think it must be the bedding that's made you this way," Patricia said thoughtfully. "Vyvyan La Blue says that lengthy and frequent bedding is recommended for shrews and women of a flighty nature since it balances their humors and eliminates their wild ways with the calming influence of motherhood. Although you certainly aren't a shrew or flighty, you must admit that since you wed Dare, you've become very circumspect."

"Hrmph," snorted Charlotte, bored to tears with the conversation. She leveled a stern gaze at her friend, who frowned back at her. Then she took her sister-in-law by the arm and headed off down the path past the torch-lit opening to the maze. "You shouldn't believe everything you read. In fact, I believe you should apologize to me here and now for saying I was priggish. Since your brother has not seen fit to do his manly duty by me, any circumspection I might have is due solely to the fact that your unthinking and careless actions are driving me to an early death."

"Charlotte!" Patricia gasped, stopping so abruptly that Caroline trod on her heel. "You can't mean that Dare didn't . . . didn't . . . that you and he didn't . . . but the way he looked at you! And the way you looked at him! I was sure he . . . I just cannot believe that he wouldn't bed you!"

"Shhh," Charlotte hissed, glancing around her. Although the three women were alone, standing between the foot of the stairs leading to the verandah and the opening to the dark and uninviting maze, one never knew who could be lurking around. "The fact that my husband refused to consummate our marriage is not a subject I wish made public. In fact, it's truly not any of your business what Dare and I do or do not do, so please forget I mentioned it at all."

"Char, you can't mean he didn't—" Caroline said at the same time Patricia said, "But, Charlotte—"

"Not another word! Look, there is David gesturing for you. It must be his dance. Go enjoy yourself. Caroline and I will be in momentarily. Do not, under any circumstances, repeat what I just said! I would die of shame if anyone found out that Dare refused . . . well, I would die if anyone found out."

Patricia assured her she wouldn't breathe a word to anyone, and hurried up the steps to fling herself into her betrothed's arms. Charlotte watched her for a minute, tempted to follow and make sure they spent the allotted time dancing and not sequestered in a dark corner, but quickly dismissed that idea when Caroline put her hand on her arm.

"Char, why?"

"Why what? Oh, why didn't Alasdair bed me?" Caroline nodded. Charlotte sighed and looked into the darkness while she tried to muster words to explain something she didn't quite understand herself. "He feels we need to know one another better. He wants me to be . . . oh, I don't know what he wants me to be. His friend, I think. He said he wants us to have tender feelings for one another before we engage in connubial calisthenics."

"That's rather sweet," Caroline said with a little smile. "I imagine most men wouldn't think of wanting to be their wife's friend before they did their duty by her. He must love you very much if he's willing to wait until you have similar feelings for him."

Charlotte rolled her eyes. "You *are* a ninny, Caro. He doesn't love me."

Caroline's hand tightened on her arm. "I swear to heaven, Charlotte, if you call me that again, I shan't be held responsible for my actions!"

"Call you what? A ninny?"

"Yes! I will not tolerate it again!"

"Really?" Charlotte asked with interest, tipping her head as she considered the angry countenance of her friend. "What will you do? Challenge me to a duel? Engage in fisticuffs with me? Tie me to a tree and shoot arrows at me? I've seen your archery skills, Caro. I wouldn't have much to be concerned about there."

"Don't be ridiculous. Of course I shan't do any of those things. No, I shall do something much, much worse."

"What?" Charlotte asked again, her curiosity getting the better of her. She knew Caroline well. A woman less able to say anything unkind or cruel did not exist. A flash of blue in the corner of her eye caught her attention as Caroline gestured wildly, her voice raising in distress.

"I don't know, something terrible, something cruel. No, I do too know what I will do."

Someone was coming from within the maze. Charlotte stepped aside, intending to pull Caroline after her so their conversation wouldn't be overheard.

"If you persist in calling me by that unkind and wholly inaccurate word," Caroline said in voice that pierced the night in righteous indignation, "I shall tell that awful Lady Brindley that your husband has refused to bed you because he is still infatuated with her."

Charlotte's mind skidded to an abrupt stop at the

sight over Caroline's shoulder. A woman emerged from the darkness of the maze into the golden pool of light cast by the torches. Dressed in midnight blue with a lighter blue overgown, Phylomena, Viscountess Brindley embodied the memory of every bad experience Charlotte had during her two Seasons.

"Did I hear my name taken in vain?" Lady Brindley's cool gray eyes examined Charlotte from crown to heels before she smiled.

Caroline gasped in horror, one hand covering her mouth as she stared with wide eyes at the woman Charlotte would gladly have seen struck down with a bolt of lightning.

"Oh, Char, I'm so sorry, I didn't know she was there—"

Lady Brindley smiled. Charlotte gritted her teeth and tightened her hands into fists.

"It can't be that bad, Dare," David said as he strolled into the card room from the dance floor. "I know you have no love for these things—God knows, I don't either—but we have to humor the ladies once in a while, and Patricia's in seventh heaven that Charlotte is going to introduce her to all the fashionable folk."

Dare tossed back a second whiskey and gestured to the footman for another with only a raised eyebrow and a grimace to indicate he heard his sister's betrothed.

"If you feel so strongly against attending balls and such," David said, "you shouldn't have allowed Charlotte to talk you into this one."

Dare took the proffered glass, saluting the younger man with it. "Talk? She didn't talk. Talk I could have resisted. Talk might have meant I had a chance to reason with her. Talk would have been manageable. What she did was much more insidious. She's a woman, and women don't think like we do. Always remember that, David. They take the shortest route to what they want, which, in most cases, means they use their perfumed selves to drive you to the brink of madness, forcing you— out of sheer self-preservation—to give them what they want."

David laughed again. "Do I take it, then, that your own good lady worked her wiles on you against your wishes?"

Dare allowed a smile to flirt on his lips before the memory of Charlotte at breakfast that morning returned. He was consumed with guilt when he considered the life he was forcing her to accept, overwhelmed with the worry that his steam engine wouldn't succeed. He took a gulp of the whiskey, closing his eyes against the burn as it worked its way into his stomach, wondering if he would ever be free of the yoke of debt that had settled on his shoulders when he inherited the title. Worse yet, he admitted to himself as he tossed off the last of the drink, he feared his future with Charlotte. Could he go through life in love with a woman who didn't love him in return?

"Dare?"

He pushed that thought aside and smiled a humorless smile at the concern in David's face. "I'm all right, just a bit tired. I've been putting in extra time trying to get the condenser running at optimum capacity before your uncle arrives."

David nodded. "You have another two months. His latest letter said he won't be here until September."

"Good," Dare replied, settling back to have a

comfortable talk about the world of marine engines. "I'll need every hour of that time to get it running its best. I've been thinking how best to demonstrate the engine, and I believe I have a solution—"

"Carlisle! Carlisle, where are you man? Has anyone seen—there you are. Come quickly."

Dare looked up in surprise at the flustered man who stood before him. "Beverly. Is something amiss?"

Lord Beverly's eyes bulged out in an alarming manner. "I'll say there is! You must come quickly. It's your wife."

Dare was on his feet and headed out of the gaming room before Beverly could blink. "Is she hurt?" he tossed over his shoulder.

"No, not at all." Beverly panted, trotting to keep up with Dare's long-legged stride. Dare stopped abruptly, grabbing the man to keep from running into him.

"If she isn't hurt, what is the hurry?"

Lord Beverly pulled out a silk handkerchief and mopped at his red face. "She's . . . she's . . . she's making a scene! You can't want that! She's your *wife!*"

Dare took a deep breath and turned back toward the comfortable leather chair he had been sitting in. "Is that all?"

"All?" Beverly asked in confusion. "All? *All?* Did you hear me? She's making a scene! In front of everyone!"

"Then I'm sure she's quite happy," Dare said with a grin to David. "There's nothing Charlotte likes more than an audience to one of her tempers."

"But . . . but . . . aren't you concerned? Don't you care?"

173

"Not really," Dare answered, resuming his seat. "To tell you the truth, I rather hate to spoil her fun. She's had so little the last few days. What is it this time? Is she telling Lady Jersey off again?"

Beverly stared at Dare as if he had a duck dancing on his head. "No, no, it's not Lady Jersey," he choked out. "It's Brindley's wife."

Dare's head snapped up at the name.

"Lady Carlisle seems to have taken exception to something Lady Brindley said, consequently dumping the punch bowl over her head."

Dare swore as he leapt to his feet a second time, dashing for the door with David and Beverly fast on his heels.

"The watch! Someone send for the watch!" Phylomena was screeching as he burst into the disordered scene in the ballroom. "She tried to drown me! You all saw her attack me! She's mad, quite, quite mad!"

"I am not mad. My hand slipped," Charlotte argued.

Dare pushed his way forward to where the most elite members of the *ton* stood in a loose circle around five people. The three clustered together—his wife, Patricia, and Lady Caroline—he ignored, focusing on the remaining two.

"Slipped? You held the punch bowl over my head and turned it upside down!"

"I was merely trying to assist you to a cup of punch. A full punch bowl is not an easy thing to handle, you know. I imagine anyone's hands would have slipped in a similar situation."

"I don't care what you say, you can't stop me from telling everyone that—Carlisle!" the bedraggled, punch-soaked figure in blue screeched, pushing away the man who had been attempting to comfort her. Three blue ostrich feathers hung down to her shoulders as hair formerly coiffed into sable ringlets dripped red punch down the front of her gown, her bosom bedecked with orange and lemon slices. If Phylomena hadn't one of the sharpest tongues and most vindictive natures he'd known, he would have been tempted to find the situation humorous. As it was . . . "Save me from that . . . that . . . madwoman, that hellion you wed!"

Dare put up a hand as she rushed toward him, his face tight. "I'll thank you to remember you are speaking of my wife and moderate your tone. We can discuss the situation after you have attended to yourself."

"Yes, truly, you are a mess." Charlotte nodded virtuously, showing her dimples for her husband. "Thank you for your support, Alasdair. You know how against my naturally shy and reserved nature it is to be any part of a scene. I am available for the next waltz if you wished to partner me, but do watch your step. Lady Brindley's unfortunate episode has made the floor quite slippery."

"Unfortunate?" Phylomena spat, glaring at Charlotte with a venom that was quick to fire Dare's anger. He stepped protectively in front of Charlotte, blocking her from his ex-lover's glare, his scowl fiercesome to behold. Lady Brindley, however, was not daunted. She took a step closer to him. "Unfortunate? The only thing *unfortunate* about the episode is that your husband didn't have the good sense to wed me when he could!"

"Or there is to be a country dance following, I believe. I should be happy to accompany you in that, if you prefer. I quite enjoy the lively nature of country dances." Charlotte tipped her head and gave him the full benefit of her blue-eyed attention.

Dare felt an absurd sense of admiration for a woman who thought nothing of pouring a bowl of punch over a rival. Still, a saner voice pointed out that it would probably be best to smooth over Phylomena's upset. He looked around for a familiar face. "Lady Beverly, if you would be so kind as to escort Lady Brindley to a room where she might receive attention . . ."

Caroline gave a little squeak of dismay, but obediently hurried forward and attempted to take Phylomena's arm. The latter snatched it back, snarling at the assembled crowd as a piece of garnish slid down the end of a soggy feather and fell with an audible wet plop on the floor before her. "I won't leave until she's taken by the watch! I will prefer charges against her! No one treats me in this manner, *NO ONE!*"

"I do hope the Prince Regent comes soon, so we might have the windows opened. I'm finding it a bit noisome in here," Charlotte said with a ladylike hint of boredom as she fanned herself. Only Dare saw the tense line of her mouth.

"NOISOME!" Phylomena shrieked.

Enough was enough. "Lady Brindley, you will retire now," Dare said firmly, his blue eyes steely in their resolve. He sent a silent message to Phylomena's escort, who nodded and took her arm. Caroline took her other arm. With only a moderate amount of cursing on Phylomena's part, they managed to steer her out of the crowded dinner room.

Almost.

"Do not think this is over," Phylomena dug in her heels long enough to warn over her shoulder as she was led out the door. "It is not! I shall make sure that everyone will know the truth! Everyone will know that you are bound to a deranged wife, a woman you find so repugnant you have yet to consummate your marriage. Everyone will know how you pine with love for me! Be assured I will have my vengeance!"

Dare heard the quick intake of breath behind him at Phylomena's words and wondered with a brief rush of irritability why Charlotte had mentioned something so private to the other woman. Surely she was aware of his past relationship with the twice-widowed Phylomena; he had been keeping her company when he met Charlotte, and he was under the impression that she would have rather died than condescend to even notice the older woman, let alone speak to her of something so intimate. But when, he wondered wearily as he rubbed the blossoming headache away, had his wife ever acted in a manner that made any sense?

An excited babble started up immediately. People moved away quickly, forming small groups to discuss this latest tidbit of thrilling gossip, tittering and casting periodic glances their way. No doubt it would be the topic of conversation for many months to come. Thank God they would have nothing to do with the *ton* after Patricia's wedding.

"I hope you're happy with the results of your actions," Dare growled to his wife. Her eyes were wide with surprise, but it was the flash of pain in them that stopped him from continuing. He couldn't chastise her, it would be senseless. She was simply being Charlotte. She could no more change than the sun could keep from rising each morning. The sooner he became resigned to her, the easier his life would be.

"I believe I would very much like to go home now," Charlotte said in an unusually subdued voice. Dare took a closer look at her. Her eyes weren't just wide, they glistened with tears, tears of mortification. He took her hand and pulled her after him toward the dance floor where couples were just taking their places for a waltz. As he swept her into his arms, he said, "Don't let them see you care, love. Smile at me as if none of them matter."

"But they do matter," she protested gently, her tears threatening to spill over. "They're the *ton*. They represent everything I have sought to return to. They represent success and achievement and every good thing. Even you must acknowledge that."

He couldn't help but laugh. "If you really cared for what any of them thought of you, my dear wife, you would not have *accidentally* lost control of a punch bowl while it was over Lady Brindley's head. The only achievement and success they represent has to do with the sheer luck of having been born into one of the noble class."

"But—"

He whirled her into silence for a moment. "Charlotte, they are only people, not gods. They have sins and failures and bad habits just as everyone else does."

She thought about that for a moment. "That may be, but they look perfectly elegant while they are sinning and failing and indulging in bad habits."

His gaze softened upon her lovely face as he noted the tears had disappeared unshed. "Appearance is not everything, my lady."

"Is it not?"

Her eyes were bright, brilliant as the summer sky, her lips parted slightly, beckoning him with a siren song to taste them just once, her curls tipped with molten gold by the candlelight, her skin not the pale, flawless alabaster so popular with ladies of the *ton,* but a darker hue, honey-warm and flushed with

178

life, as if she had spent time unprotected in the sun. "No," he said softly, almost without realizing he was speaking aloud. "I do not suppose you can understand what it is to look beneath an appearance when yours is so perfect."

She even blushed beautifully, her cheeks brushed with dusky rose. "I'm not perfect. My nose is exactly one quarter of an inch too long. My left eyebrow is unruly in the morning, and often requires a strict hand to conform it to the standards set by the right. One of my bosoms is larger than the other, too," she added with a morose sigh. "I was lopsided for an entire year when I was sixteen. I feared they would never match, and although they are more equitable, they are still not identical. I cannot begin to tell you what a trial it is to have unequal bosoms. It weighs upon my soul quite heavily."

Dare tried to hold onto a dignified mien, but it was a lost cause. He laughed again, shaking his head at his own folly, knowing that she did not see things as he did, that for her, appearance would be all. Inside him, deep inside where he kept his secret dreams, he mourned the dying hope that she would one day learn to value the things he did—honor, determination, strength in the face of adversity. He was honest enough to admit he didn't want to change her, just to help her to look beyond the obvious. Perhaps sometime in the future she might be able to see what he saw, but until then . . . "Charlotte, you are the only woman I know who has a soul made heavy by the state of her breasts." He leaned forward and whispered in her ear, "As an unbiased witness to them, I am happy to reassure you that any imperfections you might perceive are not visible to my eye. Or hands. Or . . . mouth."

She gasped, her eyes heated with passion before

she hid her gaze behind the down sweep of her lashes, her dimples flashing despite her attempt at modesty, her color still high. What a lovely contradiction she was—trying so hard to present an appearance of propriety, but her innate boldness and passion for life guaranteed she would never be like the other pattern-card women so cherished by society. He held her closer than he should, the scent of her stirring him, the memory of her soft, warm, inviting flesh calling to something deep inside him, forcing him to fight to keep from answering it. He had to give her time; he owed her that much. When she came to him, he wanted all of her, her heart and soul as well as that deliciously lush body.

He was contemplating just what he'd like to do to that very same body once she saw reason and fell in love with him when his thoughts—and their waltz—were interrupted.

"Matthew!" Charlotte gasped, the color fading from her face as she looked at the man who had tapped on Dare's shoulder.

A short, fleshy man with a washed-out version of Charlotte's glorious eyes bowed to him. "Carlisle, if you would allow me the pleasure of finishing this dance with my sister?"

Dare was surprised by the ferocity of his wife's grip on his arm, but he had no real grounds to refuse Lord Collins's request other than a general dislike of the man. Despite his lack of concern for what the members of the *ton* thought of him, it obviously mattered to Charlotte. It behooved him to bite back the refusal on the edge of his tongue and accede gracefully.

"Lord Collins," he acknowledged as he pried Charlotte's hand from his arm and presented it to her brother with a little bow. "I shall entrust my lady to your care for the rest of the dance."

His words were a warning, which Collins's narrowed eyes showed he understood. Dare smiled at the glare his wife was bestowing upon him and stepped out of the circle of dancers. Given the visions of mayhem that were all too evident in her eyes, he felt it best to make sure there were no more punch bowls at hand.

Chapter Nine

"I see you haven't wasted the four years of my absence," Charlotte said as her brother took her hand and, after counting under his breath, managed to move them into the waltz. "You look more than ever like Father."

She meant, of course, his portly figure, jowls, and huge muttonchop whiskers—a fashion she found ridiculous to the extreme—but Matthew, as usual, missed the finer nuances of conversation.

"No, certainly not. I never waste time, unlike some I could mention," the earl sneered, his eyes darting around at the other dancers.

Charlotte disliked dancing with her brother. He was neither light on his feet nor graceful (as Dare was), and he had no sense of rhythm, which meant they were often moving against the flow of music.

"How are Eleanor and the children?" she asked,

not in the least bit curious about her haughty sister-in-law and their three children, but driven out of politeness to ask.

"In the country, where they belong," he snapped, his pale blue eyes returning to her. "So you trapped Carlisle good and proper, eh? Silly bitch, you probably think you're clever, but you'll soon learn better."

"Ah, Matthew, you always have had such a grasp on the gentle art of social niceties, I'm glad to see that you haven't lost that talent while I've been away."

"Should have stayed in that damned country," he spat, muttering an apology when he collided with another couple. "Any other woman would have been too ashamed to show her face in society after she ran off with a foreigner, but not you. As proud as they come, and just as wild as ever, I'll wager. Father should have beaten some humility into you. Then perhaps you'd have the decency to stay away from where you're not wanted. But no, you must return and air the family's dirty linen in public. Well, you're getting your own now, ain't you? I understand your husband hasn't even bedded you. What a slap in the face that must be for you, eh? To know the man you trapped into marriage can't harden his rod for you?"

"Lower your voice, brother," Charlotte hissed through her teeth, forcing a smile to lips made stiff with anger. How dare he chastise her? How dare he judge her? What right did he have to say such odious things about Alasdair? "I will not debate this issue with you. I will not discuss my marriage or my husband with you."

A slow, evil smile stole over his face. "Oh, I think you will. When the time is right."

Charlotte shivered under the influence of his cold eyes on her, but smiled just because she knew it would irritate him. "What, exactly, do you mean by that melodramatic statement?"

His smile transmuted to a harsh bark of laughter that had many heads in the room turning to them. "You've made your bed, you stupid chit, now you'll have to lie on it. By yourself, since you married a man milliner, but lie on it you will. Carlisle impotent, who would have thought? Ah, well, hear me, sister—it'll do you no good to come to me for help when you discover the truth about the man you've married, no good a'tall."

She knew Matthew was a swaggering braggart, a cowardly bully who preyed on men weaker than he, but she also knew well he had a cruel streak that would not bode well for either her or Dare if he should take it into his head to do them some harm. Despite her inclination to answer insult with insult, it was best for Dare that she should swallow her brother's slurs and try to get to the bottom of his vague threats. Clearly the situation called for her to handle Matthew with the softest touch. She would be clever and very, very subtle. "Brother, you great boob, what are you blathering about? I know exactly the sort of man I married—one who is handsome and honorable and unlike you, can dance without stepping on his partner's toes—so unless you have something specific to tell me, please cease with these shadowy inamoratos."

Matthew rolled his eyes. "The word, you stupid slag, is *innuendoes.*"

"Since I suspect the word 'slag' is neither nice nor used in a loving, brotherly manner, I shall forego discussing your use of it and repeat my request—if you have something particular to say against my husband, please do so, but be aware that nothing short of Alasdair turning out to be the sort of man who eats small children for breakfast would induce me to turn to you for help or assistance. Even then, I would rather deal with a child-munching man than place myself in your power."

Matthew gave another cold bark of laughter, sending a little frisson of worry skittering across the somewhat sparsely furnished hallways of Charlotte's mind. "Oh, you'll find out in good time, my dear sister. And before too long, I'd wager."

What was he up to? she wondered as the dance came to an end. Rather than escort her back to where her husband waited, he simply dropped her hand and turned on his heel. It was a cut, and Charlotte knew it. Normally a cut from her brother would not have bothered her, especially not on *her* evening, the evening that should have been such a glorious triumph. But the cold shadow of worry about Matthew's words had joined with the shame of having her intimate marital details shouted to everyone. The evening was ruined.

She thought of bursting into tears right there, but Dare's softly whispered words echoed in her head. *Don't let them see you care.* Lifting her chin, she looked out at the figures around her, strolling, talking, laughing as if nothing life-shattering had happened.

But something life-shattering *had* happened—she had changed. She blinked for a moment, stunned by that unwary thought, then pushed it aside to examine it later. No doubt it was just a rogue thought, one of those pesky, troublesome thoughts that really had no place in her mind, but which were, to her dismay, appearing with a worrisome frequency.

It wasn't to be, however. The thought returned, and for the first time since she had come out, Charlotte felt herself distanced from the tightly woven threads of society. She stood outside it, able to see the strands of etiquette and manners that bound everyone together, blurring them until individuals could no longer be seen, and only the whole—a bright, glittering braid that made up the *haute ton*—was visible. She shook her head and tried to blink the fanciful thoughts away, but as her eyes roamed over the crowded room, she realized that her first thought was true: Time *had* changed her. She was no longer a part of Society. She was alone, an outcast, not part of the whole, but separate.

Her eyes filled with tears, blurring the image before her even more until all she saw was a swaying blur of color and lights, and for a moment she had an inkling of what Dare had said about looking beyond appearances. She truly was an outsider if she could see the flaws beneath the shining veneer of the *ton*. A sob of self-pity gathered in her throat, but stopped there as a tall blond man in black evening clothes emerged from the blur and strolled toward her.

Dare didn't blend into the *ton,* either. If she were an outsider, at least she was not alone.

Swallowing back the aching sob, she moved down the long ballroom until she reached her husband. Dare, stopped by an acquaintance, turned to her as she placed her hand on his arm.

"Enjoy your dance?"

"Not in the least," she said with a slight shudder. Swallowing her unhappiness, she dimpled prettily at the man Dare was speaking with, waiting patiently until he turned back to her, a question in his eyes.

"I wish to go home," she said simply.

He examined her face, concern darkening the deep blue of his eyes. "Because of Lady Brindley? I told you if you act as if nothing she said mattered, you'd give people less to talk about."

She rubbed her arms through the thin material of her overdress. "I don't think I can pretend not to mind much longer."

She lowered her eyes from his to look at the simple but elegant neck cloth that graced his neck. There was something compelling in his gaze, something almost magical in the way his eyes on hers made her want to confess every thought she had, every fear, and what was worse, every desire. She had a great number of desires where he was concerned, and she'd no doubt shock him with not only their sheer volume, but the quality of some of them. Vyvyan La Blue's Guide had been most thorough in examining the many connubial calisthenics possible, and although Charlotte had misgivings that some of the positions might not physically be possible without the aid of two or three strong footmen, not to mention a winch and tackle, still, they piqued her interest and she very much looked forward to discussing with Dare the relative merits of the Antics of a Burrowing Crane calisthenic versus the equally fascinating but more involved, Eruption of Magma From Vesuvius on a Late Summer's Eve.

"I will get Patricia," Dare said quietly. She could feel his eyes still studying her face.

"No, it would be cruel to make her leave so early." Charlotte twisted the wedding ring beneath her glove, reminding herself that she was responsible for her sister-in-law for the following few days. "There is no need to ruin her evening. We . . . we will stay."

"Are you sure?"

She glanced up at his eyes and raised her chin. "Yes, of course I am. Patricia is enjoying the evening."

"And you are not?" he asked, his fingers briefly caressing her chin.

"No. I was earlier, but now . . ." Her voice trailed off as his eyes burning into hers had its usual effect of wiping all thoughts from her mind.

"Now?" he prompted, his voice pitched low, intimate, wrapping around Charlotte with a soft blanket of warmth and comfort. The noise and music and chatter of the bodies around them faded as she gazed into her husband's eyes and saw only him.

"Now it does not seem to be as enjoyable as earlier," she admitted, rather against her will since she clung firmly to the notion that her triumphant return to society was everything. She felt frail, as if she had been ill for a long time, and only just now had the fever broken. Mayhap the fever analogy was more true than she knew—she must be feverish to be even thinking that she no longer fit into society.

Musn't she?

"Then we will leave," Dare said, his thumb brushing across her lower lip. She gave a little thrilled gasp, her lips parting, her attention torn between the anguish of her own thoughts, and the sudden flair of desire that left her wanting with every part of her body for Dare to kiss her. A sudden jostling of her arm reminded her where they were.

"I'll tell David to bring Patricia back later," Dare added, his eyes bright with desire. She thrilled knowing that he was as affected by their nearness as she was, and pushed away the worry over her mental state. She would deal with that later, once she had teased a few more kisses from her husband. "Perhaps Lady Beverly could watch over her?"

What a perfectly marvelous plan! Patricia could stay at the ball, and she could return home with her sultry-eyed husband and allow him to seduce her. Or perhaps, since he seduced her last night, it was her turn. She eyed him for a moment. What a very good thought that was. Likely a good seducing on her part was all he needed to clear out the cobwebs of his thinking regarding their nuptial activities.

"I shall ask Caro, but I'm confident she will have no objections to watching Patricia." She wouldn't if she knew what was good for her, Charlotte vowed as she hurried off to find her friend.

Charlotte thanked her lucky stars that Dare lived in an unfashionable area of town, one at a distance from Henley House. She waited until he rapped on the roof of the carriage before commencing her seduction.

"Charlotte," he had time to gasp just before she flung herself on him and captured any other words of surprise in her mouth. Since it was her turn to seduce, she didn't wait for him to take charge. She peeled off her gloves, spread her fingers through the silken strands of his hair, and grasping it firmly, pulled his head back just as he had done when he seduced her. His mouth was hot and alluring and she moaned her need into it as she twined her tongue around his, taking advantage of the element of surprise to taste him just as thoroughly as he tasted her. His fingers biting into her hips were the first sign that he had regained his wits; the fact that he flipped her aside, moving her under him until she lay half on, half off the carriage seat with him poised over her was another.

189

"I take it you are suddenly feeling better?" he growled, his breath hot on her lips. She kicked her legs up while pushing back against his chest until he toppled over onto the carriage floor. She followed him down, brazenly laying across him, her breasts heaving into his chest, pinning his hands to the floor next to his ears as she dipped her head lower.

"Much better," she said, nipping his lips as she demanded entrance.

He captured her legs between his, rolling her over until her back was pressed against the edge of the seat. She pushed him back, throwing herself over him and pinning him to the floor.

"Stay put, will you?" she frowned. Honestly, was any other husband in the world so hard to seduce? "It's my turn, you are obliged to do this my way."

She could just make out the look of confusion in his eyes through the dim light of the carriage lantern. "Charlotte, what are you talking about? I'm obliged to wrestle with you on the floor of my carriage? I don't remember that as part of our wedding vows. Or is this some new *ton*nish trend that you are determined to try? If so, I must object. This position is not only undignified, but it has the added detraction of causing a crick in my neck, not to mention the fact that I'm lying on a brick."

"Oh," she said, releasing her grip on his wrists to run her fingers into his hair. She sat up, straddling him. "I didn't know about the brick. Do you wish for me to get off you and postpone your seduction until a later time when there are no bricks and cricks to interfere with my plans?"

"That would be most magnanimous of you," he said, his hand running up her calf. Her breath caught in her throat at his touch. She placed a hand on his chest. Even through his shirt and waistcoat, she could feel his heart beating madly, almost as madly as hers was.

"Charlotte," he groaned, both hands on her legs now, above her stockings, his fingers teasing a trail up her thighs. "Oh, to hell with the brick."

One hand tangled in her hair as he pulled her down onto him, his mouth waiting for hers, asking, pleading, then demanding she give herself to him. Vaguely, in the back of her mind, she remembered that she had wanted to be the one in charge, that it was rightfully her turn to seduce him, but the hot magic of his mouth and the fires of desire his fingers were building as they stroked up her back and around to her breasts drove every other thought from her mind.

"God's breath, how I want you," he groaned into her ear as he kissed a lovely shivery spot on the side of her neck. "But we have to stop. Charlotte, you must stop. We can't do this here."

She sat up on him again, pulled away from kissing the area she'd exposed by tugging off his cravat. "Hmmm."

His chest heaved beneath her, his breath ragged and fast. That pleased her. "Hmmm what?"

"Hmmm, I agree that we can't do what I'd like to do here, but do you know, there was mention made in Vyvyan La Blue's *Guide to Connubial Calisthenics* of an act that is recommended for those who find themselves in a closed environment such as this carriage. Would you care for me to demonstrate?"

"Demonstrate what?" he asked, shifting slightly, reaching beneath himself until he extracted a brick from the small of his back. "Vyvyan La Who?"

She eyed him. He was so large, he didn't look

191

particularly comfortable crammed into the bottom of the carriage. "Blue. Sit up."

"What?"

"Sit up." She slid down his legs as he propped himself up, his back reclined against the wall of the carriage. She reached for the buttons on his trousers.

"Charlotte!"

"This is called The Alpine Shepherd Greeting The Dawn With A Song Upon His Lips. Vyvyan La Blue says if it is done correctly, you should emulate a Swiss youth calling down the mountain pastures to his sheep. Oh, my. I'd forgotten how very . . . *imposing* you are. But warm. Very, very warm. Now, let me see. If I recall the instructions correctly, I'm supposed to do this. I hope you don't mind. . . ."

His reply was muffled by the loud echo of the horses' hooves as they entered a tunnel created by a building that sat atop a stone bridge over the street. As they cleared the end of the tunnel, the coachman cast a curious glance at the groom who sat next to him.

"Did you hear that, Jem?"

" 'Ear what, then?" the groom answered.

The coachman peered around himself into the dark night. He shook his head and returned his attention to the horses. "Damned if it didn't sound like someone yodeling."

Charlotte sat in her husband's bed and steamed.

She was alone.

She was frustrated.

She was *furious.*

After she had gone to all the trouble of seducing her husband with mouth and hands, after she had brought him such pleasure as to call up half the sheep in the county, after all that, all he had done was carry her up to her bedroom, given her a chaste kiss upon her forehead, and left her there. He hadn't even stayed to help her out of her dress, and now here she sat, husbandless. He was probably down in the basement working on that horrid dirty machine of his. Well, she wasn't going to sit there and take such abuse! After she had suffered the trauma of having that old cat Lady Brindley tell everyone that her husband hadn't even bedded her, it was time she took matters into her own hands.

He was going to make love to her, and that was simply that.

She marched out of the bedroom in nothing more than her night rail, her feet bare. Down the stairs to the first floor she went, her head high, mouth set in a determined line. She continued down to the dark kitchen, empty of all but the cook's cat, then down further to the very lowest level of the house. She flung open the door to Dare's workroom and pointed dramatically at him, prepared to utter such scathing words as had never before left her lips.

The intended scathe turned to dust on her tongue as Dare, shirtless, a thick lock of blond hair falling over his manly brow, turned at the squeak of the door. Her finger, still pointing, wavered, as she drank in the sight of his bare chest, glistening with perspiration in the candlelight.

"Oh," she said breathily, unable to think of anything else but the desire to wrap herself around that chest.

Dare was not likewise struck dumb. "What the devil do you mean parading around in your night things, madam wife?"

193

"Chest," she murmured, her eyes huge.

"Have you no sense?" He set down a black, lump-ish thing—some part for the engine, the lucid part of her mind guessed—and glared at her.

"Bare chest."

He reached for a rag and wiped the oil and grime from his hands. Such an action caused his arms and shoulders and chest to move in a beautiful ballet of muscles and tendons. Charlotte grabbed wildly for the back of a wooden chair that stood nearby.

"Well? What have you to say to me?" Dare dropped the rag and started toward her. "God's teeth, woman, your feet are bare!"

"Not as bare as your chest," she gasped as he scooped her up in his arms. "Oh. You're so . . . hooo! Isn't it hot for May, though? Did I disturb you at your work, Alasdair?"

"Catch your death wandering around the house in the middle of the night in nothing but a scanty bit of lawn and bare feet," Dare grumbled as he started up the stairs. "Take that candle. Yes, of course I was working. What did you think I was doing?"

"But it's after two, and you really should be in bed. *With me.*" She added that last bit just in case he wasn't clear on the situation.

He stopped at the foot of the stairs leading to the second floor and looked down on her, his face shadowed. "Charlotte, we've been over this."

"Not to my satisfaction."

He sighed, then bent and told her to set the candle down. She placed it a few steps above them as he sat down in the small pool of light cast onto the carpeted stairs, holding her firmly against his chest, his hands warm through the thin material of her night rail. She snuggled into him, stroking the sweat-dampened hair on his chest. Truly, such an act would have repulsed her on any other man, but Dare even sweated in an attractive manner. Could any man be more perfect for her?

"Charlotte, I don't know what more I can say to make you understand how I feel. I want something more than just a physical relationship. I think you do as well. At least I hope you do, but until you know that for certain, until you know what you honestly want from this marriage, it wouldn't be fair to either of us to engage in those activities a husband and wife normally engage in."

"Arguing, you mean," Charlotte said softly, placing a gentle kiss on the curve of his ear.

He chuckled. "You know what I mean, wife."

Charlotte gave him a little smile. "You see, there is more to me than you had thought. I'm not just mind-meltingly beautiful. I can jest. I am interested in your machine, or I would be if you would explain it to me. I am economizing, and you'll notice that I have not once complained this evening about that sorry state of affairs. I am learned in the ways of connubial calisthenics. I have a good speaking voice, and a legible hand, and could be of great help to you in your business if you will just allow me. I am, in short, the perfect wife for you."

He leaned his forehead against hers and smiled into her eyes. "I have never doubted your qualifications, Charlotte."

"But you don't think I'm the perfect wife for you?"

His eyes were like blue fire burning on her tender flesh. "On the contrary, there is no other woman I would rather call wife than you."

Hope, dampened by his refusal to be seduced, flared to life again within her breast. "Then you want me?"

He pressed his lips to her palm, sending heat skittering down her arm. He shifted his legs, then placed her hand on his groin.

"Wanting you was never in question."

He was hard and long beneath her fingers, just as he had been in the carriage earlier. The heady knowledge that he truly did want her, that he reacted in this pleasing fashion to her made the hope within her burn brighter.

"I don't understand what more I can do," she whispered, searching his eyes for the answer. "I don't understand why it is you want me, and you know I want you, but you won't . . . won't . . . *do it*. I don't understand what's wrong with me."

He brushed his thumb across her lower lip. "Did you love your husband? Your first one, I mean."

She blinked at him. "Love Antonio? I . . . I . . . he was very handsome."

Dare said nothing, just watched her. She looked away for a moment, uncomfortable with what he might see in her eyes. "I liked him a great deal. To begin with. Once we arrived in his home, he . . . changed somehow. His mother was very domineering, you understand, and she wasn't pleased we had wed, and Antonio seemed far more interested in raising sheep than in me."

"Did you love him?"

"He was very handsome," she repeated. "He was tall like you, but much thinner, not nearly so broad, and he had very elegant hands and danced beautifully. I enjoyed it when he kissed me and had hoped that the other things would be as nice, but of course, we just had the once, and although it was nothing terrible, it certainly wasn't anything I would have written a sonnet about."

She could feel him smiling into her hair. "But did you love him?"

"No," she said miserably, her eyes on the fine gold hairs that lay on the top of his arms.

His lips caressed her temple. She sighed and leaned into him.

"I think you are confusing a desire for a physical relationship with deeper emotions."

"Shouldn't one desire one's husband?"

"Yes, you should." His hand slid up her arm. "But in our case, it's not enough. We've both had sexual relationships with partners we did not love—" He stopped her protest with a swift kiss. "Granted, in your case, it was a very brief relationship, but I'm hoping it was enough to make you understand that without something more meaningful, that without true affection, such a relationship can never be satisfying."

She looked up at him, suddenly realizing what it was he was saying. "You want me to say I love you."

He closed his eyes for a moment, his Adam's apple bobbing as he swallowed. "No. I want you to love me. There's a difference."

She curled her fingers into the hair on his chest. "What if I said I already did? Would you believe me?"

The blue fire glowed deeply in his eyes. She knew at that moment that he loved her, had loved her ever since they had first met, and that his love for her gave her an infinite power over him. "Yes. If you told me you loved me, I would believe you."

She could make him give her whatever she wanted. She could bring him to his knees. She could wring any confession out of him, demand any payment, and he would meet it, she could ask for any boon and be granted it. *He loved her.* If she lied to him, if she told him she loved him in return, he would bed her. He would believe that she loved him. Charlotte knew with a woman's knowledge of a man who had bared his soul before her that she could lift him up to heights of rapture he had never imagined or destroy him as easily as she could grind an ant under her heel.

Power flared brightly in her for a moment as he sat watching her, love filling his eyes, waiting to see if she would take the first step toward ecstasy or agony. She dropped her gaze and allowed the sensation of power to dissolve as she pressed a gentle kiss to the corner of his delicious mouth. "Good night."

She left him sitting on the steps as she headed for her own room, confused and annoyed by the myriad of emotions tangled up in a coil that resembled Dare's beautiful blue eyes. She wanted him more than anything she'd ever wanted, and yet his faith in her, his trust that she would cherish the gift of his love awoke strange new emotions within her. She could not return such a gift with deceit. He deserved more than that. He deserved her love in return, nothing less.

Charlotte snuggled into bed aware that for the first time in many years, she had put someone else's feelings above her own.

Oddly enough, it was not an unpleasant sensation.

Chapter Ten

"When did you first realize you were in love with Captain Woodwell?"

Patricia hid any surprise she felt at the question and instead flashed her sister-in-law a warm smile. She knew things were not as they should be between Dare and Charlotte, but she could see the love in her brother's eyes when he looked at his wife, and she had every confidence that Charlotte would learn to love him as well. "I believe I fell in love with David the minute I set eyes on him. He was so kind and funny, and when he spoke to me, he made me feel as if we were the only two people in the world."

"Kind . . . funny . . . only people in the world," Charlotte mumbled as she stood with her back to Patricia.

Curious, Patricia set the novel she was browsing

through back on the shelf and skirted her sister-in-law to peer over her shoulder. "What are you doing, taking notes?"

"Yes," Charlotte answered, closing a small leather-bound memorandum pad, tucking it and a gilded pencil away in her reticule. "I have decided to conduct an informal study on the matter of falling in love. I'm not quite sure how to go about it, and this seems the best way to understand the phenomenon. I am particularly interested in those signs that indicated to you that you were about to, or had already, fallen in love. Was it any one thing, or a sum of smaller indicators?"

Patricia swallowed back a burble of laughter. Charlotte looked so earnest, it would never do for her to feel as if she were the subject of amusement. "I believe it was a number of things: the way David made me feel, the fact that I wanted to share every event of my day with him, the sense that something was lacking when he was not near, the manner in which he filled my thoughts . . . it was all those things, and many others."

"Interesting," Charlotte said, a puzzled frown between her brows. She strolled down the aisle of Hookam's with her arm in Patricia's, nodding to the small groups of people collected around the more popular book offerings. Once she was assured she was out of hearing range, she dropped her arm and turned to face her sister-in-law. "Dare wishes me to be in love with him before he . . ." She waved an arm about in an inarticulate manner.

"Beds you," Patricia filled in.

Charlotte colored prettily. "Yes."

"Is that a problem? Do you not love him now? I thought you were very fond of him."

"I am. I am quite fond of him. I always have been.

He is so very handsome, and we look so well together, I know we shall have children who will be just as attractive as we are, but he will not give me those children if he does not believe I love him."

"Do you?"

Charlotte wrung her hands for a moment before she remembered she had on her last good pair of gloves, then sat down in a nearby chair with a *whoosh*. "I don't know. That is the problem! I desire him, in a connubial calisthenics sense, and I enjoy being with him, as you said you do Captain Woodwell, and I believe he is kind—although he might have told me he had run through his inheritance before we wed—and I know he can be funny, because he amused me very much five years ago, but as for the rest . . ."

Charlotte let her gaze wander down the long room. "I simply don't know. I do not feel as if I am in love, but I do want to be near Alasdair. I certainly want him to—" She looked up suddenly and remembered to whom she was speaking. "Oh, it is a tangle. If I am not in love with him, how am I to accomplish the feat?"

Patricia patted her shoulder. "I shouldn't fret over it, Char. I think if you're not in love with him now, you soon will be. Dare is very lovable."

"I hope so," Charlotte slumped in the chair as she sighed forlornly, then stiffened and rose to her feet. "Drat. There's that odious Mrs. Mead. She is Lady Bridgerton's sister and one of the biggest gossips in the *ton*. No doubt she is going to torment me with the happenings of last night. Smile, Patricia. As your brother says, it doesn't do to let them see you care."

Patricia nodded and curtsied politely when the lady in question sailed up to them, her maid and a down-trodden companion in tow. "Miss McGregor,

I am surprised to see you out only two days before your wedding. What can the earl be thinking?"

Charlotte knew to a very fine distinction the level of her abilities and charms. She was under no mistaken belief that she was the least bit bluestocking—she had never been a very deep thinker, unlike her cousin Gillian, and she had no intention of starting now. Being intelligent sounded exceedingly unpleasant. She knew that it pleased men to look upon her, and that many women were insanely jealous of her because of the circumstances of her breeding, birth, and appearance. Because of the last, she had often been the recipient of catty comments, snide asides, and slights that other less pretty women did not suffer.

She filed the cut she had just received from Neela Mead under the heading Jealous Acts and determined to ignore it just as she had ignored other such pettiness. With a lift of her chin that she knew would mark her as obstinate, she smiled. "My husband and I both feel there is nothing unseemly in the least in Patricia making an appearance in public with me. She is, after all, to be married, not bound for a harem where she will be secreted away from men's gazes."

The older woman gasped and turned eyes the color of boiled steel upon her. "You dare speak in public of that poor man you wed? For shame, Lady Charlotte. Your mother would die of mortification if she knew what a scandal you have brought upon your family name."

"I am now Lady Carlisle," Charlotte answered, gritting her teeth just the tiniest bit. "I don't see anything the least bit shameful in my marriage."

"A marriage in name only, or so I understand from Minerva Wentwater."

Charlotte was unable to keep from flinching at the name tossed at her. It was said that Minerva Wentwater was an even bigger gossip than Mrs. Mead, and Charlotte knew from sad experience with the sharp side of Miss Wentwater's tongue that such a thing was indeed the truth.

Mrs. Mead leaned forward as if to say something privately, but spoke in a trumpeting voice that was well pitched to carry down the length of the store. "Do you fear he will annul the marriage, dear Lady Charlotte? I confess that were I in your shoes, I would very much worry about finding myself once again unmarried. One cannot help but wonder if the tragic circumstance is due to a failing on Lord Carlisle's part, or—" She raked Charlotte from toes to crown. "—due to a distaste of engaging in intimate acts with you. Do you know that they are taking wagers on which it is at many of the gentlemen's clubs? I'm sure it will please you to be the object of speculation of so many gentlemen; you always did strike me as a little *desperate* in your attempts to attract their attention."

Patricia gasped at the insult. Charlotte ignored the gasp, laughing at the woman before her. True, her laughter lacked the quality of gaiety usually acquainted with such an act, but it was still laughter, and Charlotte was determined to work it for all it was worth. "Oh, my dear Mrs. Mead—if I were to procure a saucer of cream for you, would you pull in your claws and purr for us?"

"Well, really!" gasped Mrs. Mead, her eyes wide with shock.

Charlotte tipped her head to the side and tapped a finger to her lips. "Please do not discomfit yourself in such a manner, Mrs. Mead. If your eyes bulge any further, I am convinced they will pop right out of your head, and we should be obliged to tread carefully lest we squash them into pulpy little bits. Come, Patricia. I do not see any books here I want. I believe we will pick up your wedding gift to Captain Woodwell."

Charlotte marched off down the aisle leading a giggling Patricia, ignoring the stares and accompanying whispers of everyone as they turned to watch her. She knew she shouldn't have ripped into Mrs. Mead in that manner, knew that she would pay a dear price for it, but the spiteful comments and digs were just too much for her to bear. She made it into the carriage before she started shaking with the aftermath of her fury and humiliation.

"What an odious old woman!" she snarled unsure of whether she wanted to scream or cry. She decided on both. "How dare she say such cruel things about Alasdair!"

Patricia, climbing into the carriage behind her, looked surprised. "But, Char! She insulted you, not Dare!"

"Oh, pish," Charlotte said, fumbling in her reticule for the handkerchief that she had confiscated from Dare's bureau that morning. "As if anything she could say about me could hurt my feelings. She's just jealous of me, jealous and spiteful. That I pay no mind to, but when she says cruel things about Alasdair . . ." Fury like none she had ever felt boiled inside her. "Well, I shall not stand for it."

"What will you do?" asked Patricia, curious as to the fierce look on her sister-in-law's face.

"I shall simply redouble my efforts to fall in love with your brother. If I concentrate on the matter, I should achieve my goal by nightfall at the latest, don't you think? Then he will bed me and all the terrible, cruel things they are saying about Alasdair will be untrue."

Patricia's mouth moved as if she wished to say something, but no words came out.

"Yes." Charlotte nodded, just as if Patricia had agreed with her. "Nightfall by the latest. It simply is a matter of turning all my attention to the task."

Despite spending the remainder of the day attempting to fall in love with her husband, all Charlotte accomplished was an argument with him, the result of which was her banishment from his workroom.

"He said my mooning around him was distracting, Batsfoam. Have you ever heard anything so ridiculous? I never moon! I don't even know how to moon, and if I did, I'm sure I would do it in a pleasing and agreeable manner, not one that would annoy him." Charlotte climbed the narrow kitchen stairs up to the main floor of the house, Batsfoam thumping his way behind her. She paused on the ground floor and glared up the carpeted stairs for a moment before starting up them. "And that's another thing, why did he insist on you accompanying me to my sitting room? It almost seems as if he does not trust me to do as requested, and thus I must have a gaoler! Really, it is too much. Much too much!"

"Indeed, my lady, your lord, my good and kind master who saved me from the ignominy of unemployment by engaging me for not just one, but for so many jobs I have lost count, did seem to be a bit on the testy side this evening. Perhaps it is the weather. I myself feel the damp weather most strenuously in that portion of my limb which I left lying in a field in Poitiers, to the extent that it makes moving said limb difficult, if not impossible, as I attend the many daily requirements on my time, not the least of which is escorting your ladyship to her chamber as requested by my lord. Indeed, I am sure that climbing the stairs to escort you, a woman in the prime of her life and in what appears to be excellent health, or so it would appear to my eyes, old and weak as they are, will be beneficial and helpful to my unfortunate limb, as my master has only my happiness and well-being in mind as he asks me to carry out those tasks he personally selects for me. In God's truth, I would not be surprised if my limb should regenerate itself due to all the happiness and well-being I find from having the opportunity to escort your ladyship to her room, keeping from your person any and all dangers as you might expect to find as you move from the sub-basement to the first floor. I am almost certain I can feel my toes returning to life on that poor, misbegotten limb."

"Toes are vastly overrated. You are much better off without them," Charlotte said in a distracted voice, being busy with the regrouping of her thoughts and plans. She paused at the landing and turned to her companion. "Batsfoam, have you ever been in love?"

"Love?" He staggered back a few steps, apparently surprised at her question. "I, my lady? In love?"

Charlotte pursed her lips and continued up the stairs. "Yes, I wish to know. As you are Lord Carlisle's personal servant, I shall bare my soul to you."

The interested glint that always entered Batsfoam's eye around Charlotte glittered brightly in his normally melancholy eyes. "I am speechless with the honor you do me, madam. I am overcome. I am beside myself with joy. I am fair to bursting with pride at this most unexpected gift from your gracious self. I burn to know your thoughts, to share with you the unburdening of your soul, to support you in any and all endeavors to which you might put your estimable, and might I add, most unique, mind. I am, in short, your humble servant and await with bated breath and an eager ear to hear the missives of your soul. Pray, my good lady, tell me now before my heart should burst from the expectation and anticipation, leaving me a lifeless husk, a shell of my former self, dead here upon these very steps."

Charlotte stopped at the top of the stairs and raised an eyebrow at the servant following her. "Batsfoam?"

"Yes, my lady?" He bowed low as he clumped his way up the last of the steps.

"It is obvious to me that you read far too many flowery novels. They have warped your mind. It is most unbecoming to have a butler whose mind is warped. Therefore, I must insist that you limit yourself in the future to no more than one flowery novel per month."

His lips twitched as he bowed again, his head nearly touching his knees. "It shall be as you demand, madam. I shall struggle to fill the many long hours of free time I enjoy every day spent reading flowery novels in some other, more productive, employment. Perhaps I shall take up blacksmithing instead."

"An excellent suggestion." Charlotte nodded and allowed him to open the door to her sitting room. "Now, about my soul—as you are his lordship's body servant and thus in his confidence, I shall reveal to you that I have made it my goal to fall in love with him. I am endeavoring to do so now, but you were witness to that sad episode below."

Batsfoam's eyes opened wide with astonishment for a brief of moment, before he veiled them in his usual manner. "Indeed, madam?" he murmured.

Charlotte paced the length of the small cream and green room, her brow furrowed. "How he expects me to fall in love with him if he won't allow me to be of assistance to him in his work is beyond me, utterly beyond me. I cannot see what I did wrong."

"I believe, my lady, that Lord Carlisle found the fault not in your ladyship's intentions, but in the manner your assistance took."

Charlotte paced past him, still frowning. "He overreacted. His objections to my doing a spot of cleaning on that filthy engine were most ungentlemanly, and only because I am most determined in my attempt to love him was he saved from having his ears boxed."

Batsfoam bowed his head humbly, more so his mistress wouldn't see the unholy glee in his eyes rather than from any sense of subjugation. "I could be mistaken, but as I understand it, a certain amount of filth in the form of grease is needed to make the pistons move smoothly in their fittings. Without that substance present, the engine would not be able to work as it was intended."

Charlotte spun around. "Yes, but he said my interfering—ha! As if wiping off the dirt and grime found on the parts was interfering!—ruined the pistons. Still," her hands fluttered as if to push the thought away, "that's neither here nor there. The result of my well-meaning and tender concern is banishment. I must, therefore, find another way to fall in love with him. As you know him best, I was hoping perhaps you would have advice on the matter."

She looked at him hopefully. He looked back at her, more than a little nonplussed. "I . . . I . . ."

"Oh, come now, Batsfoam, you know Alasdair better than almost anyone. I cannot get anything out of Miss McGregor other than *when it happens, you will know it* and other such vagueness, but I expect better from you. You are privy to not only his intimate daily routine, but you act as his assistant with that engine. You must be able to tell me something that will aid my cause."

Batsfoam, for the first time since he had become Dare's servant, was speechless. Without thinking, he sat on one of the two matching green ladder-back chairs. "I . . . you . . ." He cleared his throat and suddenly realized he was sitting before his mistress. He stood and mumbled a brief apology. "I will think upon it, my lady."

"Good." Charlotte dismissed him with a nod and moved toward her writing desk. "But please hurry. There are only a few hours left until nightfall, and although surely I must almost be to that point, I don't want to risk the possibility that I might not be wholly in love with him before we retire for the night. It wouldn't be fair to Dare if I weren't."

"I will do my best, madam," Batsfoam intoned as he bowed himself out the door. He paused for a moment in the hall, whistling tunelessly to himself, then thumped his way toward the back stairs. He thought he might just be able to help his mistress's plans along.

Dare staggered up the stairs toward his bedchamber. He was exhausted and hungry, but had chosen to eat nothing more than a hunk of dried bread and a bit of stale cheese rather than sit across a table from his wife. He grimaced and rubbed the back of his neck as he dragged his weary legs up one step after another. His wife. Charlotte. The woman who was slowly but surely driving him mad. If it wasn't unbridled desire that was so unbearable he doubted his own control in her presence, it was the exasperation of her misguided attempts to help him with the engine.

Help. Ha! That was a novel word for her actions. No one but Charlotte would think to strip the lubricating oil from the pistons. Her bit of housekeeping had set him back at least two weeks, perhaps more while he cast new parts to replace the ones that had been destroyed.

His stomach growled hollowly as he trudged down the dark hall toward his dressing room, wearily aware that although he very much wanted to, he couldn't blame Charlotte for the damage. She had been trying to be of assistance, and despite the pain of seeing those pistons destroyed, his heart was warmed by her honest desire to help.

Perhaps there was hope for them after all.

Batsfoam was waiting for him, looking just as tired as he did.

"I thought I told you to go to bed two hours ago?"

"You did, my lord, but I would not be remiss in my duty to you, my most gracious and generous employer—"

Dare waved a weary hand and stopped the flow of what he knew would be a five-minute soliloquy. "Please, not tonight. Or rather, this morning. Just help me off with these boots and get yourself to bed."

Batsfoam did as requested and assisted his master into a faded, but still elegant, silk dressing gown before informing him that there was a problem with the bedding.

"What sort of a problem?" Dare asked, his hand

on the door, almost dropping where he stood he was so tired.

"There was a small fire, my lord. Nothing serious, and it was extinguished almost immediately, but not before the flames rendered the mattress unsuitable."

"A fire." Dare shook his head. He must be more tired than he imagined. "In my bed."

Batsfoam bowed his head in acknowledgment.

"There was a fire in my bed."

Batsfoam tidied up the basin and water pitcher.

"As in, flames? In my bed? An object situated well across the room from the fireplace?"

"It is most mysterious, my lord," Batsfoam agreed, setting Dare's boots aside to be shined later. "I cannot imagine how a fire came to start itself there, but the fact remains that your bed is unavailable for the evening. I thought perhaps you might desire sleeping on the chaise, and for that purpose arranged it in the appropriate bed linens."

"The chaise?" Dare asked dully, deciding he was simply too exhausted to pursue the subject of how a fire was started in his bed. "You want me to sleep on the chaise, the one that is at least a foot shorter than I am?"

"Alas, there are no other beds in the house. I would, of course, give up mine if your lordship were to insist—"

"No, no." Dare waved the offer away and taking a candle, staggered into his darkened bedchamber. The scent of burned linen was still heavy in the air despite the open window. He ignored the empty bed frame that sat hulking in the corner of the room and headed for the small red chaise now swathed in white linens.

"If I might suggest," Batsfoam said from the doorway to the dressing room, "my lady was saying only this morning how very soft and comfortable her bed was. I am sure she would be willing to share—"

"Thank you, Batsfoam, that won't be necessary. I'll be fine on the chaise. Good night."

"Good night, my lord. And might I wish you a pleasant and comfortable sleep?"

Dare mumbled something and collapsed onto the chaise, snuffing out the candle with an exhausted groan. The door clicked softly behind Batsfoam as Dare rolled onto his back, then onto his side, trying to find a comfortable position. He either had to lay with his legs crooked at an angle that he knew would become painful after a few minutes, or curl up with his knees bent, which would no doubt end up in leg cramps. He sighed and turned onto the other side, trying to prop the excess in his legs up on the chaise arm, but that just drove his side into the seat of the chaise.

"What is this thing stuffed with, gravel?" he grumbled as he switched ends in an attempt to find a spot that did not have sharp, pointy things digging into his flesh. Why on earth had he bought the blighted thing? Why had he never sat on it to ensure it wasn't lethal to human flesh? And who in their right mind would make such a devilish piece of furniture?

Visions of an inviting, comfortable, non-lumpy bed danced in his mind. Charlotte had such a bed. She wouldn't mind him using it, either. Truthfully, she'd probably be delighted, but it was the form her delight would take that had him turning again to find a comfortable spot. Better he should sleep all cramped and uncomfortable than to risk her seducing him again. After that episode in the carriage, and a day spent trying to not think about her, he knew he would not be able to resist the lure of her sweetly scented flesh.

A sharp stab to his kidney regions was the final straw.

"Damnation!" he snarled as he sat up, grabbing his dressing gown and shoving his arms into the sleeves as he stalked toward Charlotte's room. He had to get some sleep. He had to work twice as hard to make up for the lost time Charlotte's visit to the work room had cost him. If he was very quiet, and didn't disturb his wife, perhaps he could slip into her bed and get the few hours of sleep he needed. He didn't need much sleep, he thought groggily as he felt his way through the darkened room to the far side of the bed, just a little sleep, just enough so he could work without falling asleep.

Charlotte was a lump in the bed, but he stead-fastly turned his tired mind away from the alluring image of sinking into the soft linens warmed by her, and instead wrapped his dressing gown around himself and gently eased down on top of the bed covers. He was painfully aware of her body lying so close to his, not touching but close enough so he could breath in the scent of warm, sleepy woman. He prayed she wouldn't wake up, for he knew his wife—she took the straightest path between two points no matter what distractions lay along the way. If she should discover him in her bed, she would no doubt demand he do his marital duty by her, and he was conscious enough to recognize that the overwhelming attraction he felt for her, coupled with his traitorous body, would sound a death knell for his good intentions.

"Less temptation this way," he told himself, sti-fling the groan of pleasure as the soft mattress wel-comed his exhausted body. "I'll be gone in a couple of hours. She won't even know I'm . . ."

He drifted off before he could finish vocalizing the thought.

". . . here," Charlotte whispered softly from the other side of the bed. Moving carefully, she covered her husband with a light blanket, then curled up beside him, one hand protectively on his chest.

Chapter Eleven

Caroline watched her friend rip pages from her memorandum book and throw them to the small fire that had been lit in an attempt to throw off the gloom cast by the cold, damp June day so familiar to inhabitants of the south of England. "You look as if you hope to exorcise a demon by doing that," she commented mildly.

"The demon can exercise himself, I have much more important things to concern myself about. Caro, I am at my wit's end. I know that will come as a surprise to you—Lord knows I thought I'd never face the day when I couldn't think of some way around an obstacle—but this has me defeated, and I don't like the feeling one little bit."

Caroline made soft noises of encouragement.

Charlotte threw the last page into the fire and turned to stare out the window at the rivulets of rain

215

running down the glass. "I have never been defeated before. I have never once set myself to a goal and failed to achieve it. I have never, in all my years, been unable to have what I've desired. This situation is untenseable, and I simply shall not tolerate it any more!"

"What situation is untenable?" Caroline asked quietly, more than a little concerned by the look of confusion in her friend's eye. If there was one thing Caroline had always envied Charlotte, it was her sense of purpose, her knowledge of exactly what she wanted out of life and how she was to get it. The Charlotte before her plainly was not of that ilk; the Charlotte before her was made out of a common clay, the kind riddled with doubts and uncertainty and frustration just like any other mortal.

It warmed her heart like nothing else could.

"This falling in love business!" Charlotte wailed, throwing her hands up in a gesture of annoyance. "I cannot get a straight answer from anyone as to how to go about it, and obviously I'm not having any success by following my own inclinations. I have tried to fall in love with Alasdair, I truly have. I spent all yesterday at the task and was banned from my husband's presence as a reward for such diligence and hard work. Last night, when Alasdair finally came to bed—"

Caroline's eyebrows shot up.

"—he slept on top of the bed covers. *On top!* The only reason he was even in my bed was because Batsfoam had dismantled his under some pretext or another. I'm telling you, Caro, I am at the end. I cannot go on like this anymore. I can't think but for worrying about this problem. It's bound to give me wrinkles if it continues, and then where will I be? Unconsummated and wrinkled, *that's* where."

"Perhaps you are trying too hard," Caroline advised, watching as her friend started pacing the length of the room. Charlotte was forever pacing, Caroline noted to herself. It seemed to help her think. She wondered if she should try it herself at a later time. "Perhaps if you were to relax your attempts to fall in love with Lord Carlisle, you would have better success. Emotions are very difficult to force, Char. Sometimes you need to simply let them be."

Charlotte shot her a disgruntled look as she paced by. "Nonsense. My emotions will do as I tell them. No, my problem is much more serious— clearly, my mind is off. It is just not functioning as it should, and as I . . . are you all right? Did you swallow your tea wrong? Shall I strike you between your shoulders?"

Caroline waved away the offer and fumbled for her handkerchief, mopping up the aftereffects of hearing Charlotte insist her mind was off, just as if it was week old mutton. "I am fine. Pray continue."

"Well." Charlotte pursed her lips and tried to think how best to explain the unwelcome thoughts and emotions that chased around inside her. "I have in the past always known my mind. You will agree with that, won't you?"

"Oh, yes. Very much so."

"Yes, and knowing my mind, I've always been able to see logically what the steps were that must be taken to gaining that goal. That, also, you will agree with?"

"Well . . . I might take exception to the word 'logically,' but on the whole, yes, I believe you followed through as best you knew how."

"Exactly. Take recent events—I wanted to return

217

home to my rightful place in Society. I thought it out, realized I must marry again, and went about selecting a husband who could provide me with everything I wanted. I had a plan, Caro, a good plan, a plan that came to tuition, just as my other plans have—"

"Fruition."

"What?" Charlotte stopped pacing and cocked an eyebrow at her friend.

Caroline smiled into her teacup. "Nothing. Continue."

Charlotte shot her a dark look as she resumed her pacing. "As I was saying, my other plans succeeded just as well. So therefore, there must now be something wrong with my mind that I cannot succeed in a simple task like falling in love."

"I thought your plan was just to seduce Lord Carlisle?"

Charlotte paused before the fire, looking into the glowing coals. "It was, but that's changed. I . . . Alasdair . . . oh, it's too complicated to explain. You must trust me when I say it's imperative that I fall in love with him. The seducing will be no effort after that."

Caroline thought that Charlotte was well on her way to being in love with her husband, but wisely kept that information to herself. Charlotte, like the obstinate horse of fable, could be led to the water, but not made to drink unless she thought herself thirsty. "How can I help you, Char?"

"Well, if I knew that, I'd have a plan!" Charlotte replied grumpily, then spun around and slumped into a nearby chair. "Oh, forgive me, Caro. I don't mean to be snappish, it's just that everything seems to be going against me of late. I've never been so blighted in all my days."

"Blighted?" Caroline thought it time to administer a few truths to snap Charlotte out of what appeared to be a sickening wallow in self-pity. "You, blighted? I've never heard anything so ridiculous. You are the loveliest woman I've ever seen. Men have written poems to your beauty."

"And I have a husband who doesn't see any of it," Charlotte replied morosely, picking at the braid that ran the length of her gown. "He is forever nattering on about beauty not being important. He's just like Gillian in that respect—neither of them truly appreciates just how difficult it is to have a face that inspires lust in men."

Caroline thought it best not to pursue that avenue of thought. "And you have a husband, a handsome husband, the man *you* selected."

"Who won't bed me until I am in love with him."

"Bedding isn't everything, Char."

"Well, of course it isn't! I of all people am aware that a marriage can be conducted without any beddings. It's just that this time . . . I had hoped Alasdair . . . and he has all that lovely golden flesh . . . and my parts tingle, positively *tingle* when I think about him . . . oh, never mind."

"Mmm. Well, there's also the fact that you are a countess."

"A poor one. Alasdair's pockets are to let. I am *economizing!*" Charlotte pronounced the last word in a manner that combined shame and indignation most effectively.

"Still, you *are* a countess," Caroline pointed out.

"Yes, I am, and to be sure, it is my only comfort these days."

"You are . . ." Caroline cast her mind about for something else positive. "Oh! I know—you have been welcomed back into the arms of Society, and that was your main goal."

"I have been welcomed back. . . ." Charlotte restlessly rose from her chair and went to poke viciously at the fire. "Yes, I am allowed back into the hallowed ballrooms of the *ton,* but for what purpose? What good is it? I have been shamed before everyone, and Alasdair has had his manhood slandered. That horrible cat Lady Brindley made sure she spread the word to everyone." She stared into the fire, her cheeks warmed by an embarrassed blush rather than by the feeble flames. "If I had any doubts before that I no longer fit in the *ton,* I have none now. I am an outsider, a castaway, adrift in a sea of the unfashionable."

Caroline eyed her friend with renewed concern. "You don't believe you are a member of the *ton?*"

Charlotte felt tears pricking at her eyes for a moment. Then she straightened up, her jaw set. She would not let this best her. She had not survived four long years of living in the same villa as Antonio's mother just to crumple when her mind refused to cooperate. "I know I am not. Enough of this, Caroline, we are not getting anywhere. What I need now is a plan. Patricia will be married tomorrow. Alasdair informed me this morning that despite the fact that I have been shamed and made the object of fun by everyone who matters, he will not allow us to go to one of his estates where I might reign supreme over the locals. Instead we must stay in town as there has been some damage to the pistons and they must be recast or reformed or whatever it is that one does to pistons. Other than cleaning them, that is. Alasdair took great exception to my cleaning them. Thus, I am to be kept prisoner here in London, housebound, unable to go about in polite company until this latest scandal has died down."

"That doesn't sound so very terrible," Caroline replied. "It sounds rather romantic, actually, sort of a honeymoon where you and Lord Carlisle will be thrown into one another's company a good deal of the time."

"It would be ideal if my husband and I had a different relationship," Charlotte said as she picked up her memorandum book and flipped it open to a clean page. "But as I have a mind that has suddenly turned on me, a heart that is delinquent in falling in love, a body that wants to touch Alasdair in the most inappropriate—if very interesting— places, while my husband would rather work on his machine than dally with me, our time spent together is more a curse than a blessing. No, indeed, Caro, this shilly-shallying around is doing me no good. I must think up a plan, and you are going to help me do it."

Caroline watched Charlotte as she stared at the blank paper before her, a faint frown wrinkling her brow. "What I need is a perfectly brilliant plan, something unusual, something foolproof. Simply trying to fall in love didn't work, so logically, the next step must be to have assistance. But who offers assistance in falling in love?"

"Mama always told me who was acceptable to love and who wasn't. Perhaps she would advise you?"

Charlotte began to gnaw on the end of her pencil. "No, I know whom to love, I just need . . . oh, I don't know, something. A little push. A help, an aid of some sort. Something that will guarantee I fall in love with Alasdair."

"Something like a potion?" Caroline joked, her

mind on the copy of *Midsummer Night's Dream* she was reading to dearest Algernon.

Charlotte looked up, a beatific smile on her face. Her eyes lit up with that peculiar light that Caroline knew heralded another one of Charlotte's "brilliant" plans. She always worried when she saw that look.

"Perfect! What a stunningly, stunningly perfect idea, Caro! I shall forever be in your debt. Now, what do you think is more effective—a bewitching love spell or a love potion? Perhaps I should use both, just to be on the safe side? Yes, both is good. Now, where to find a witch . . ."

Caroline stared at Charlotte with a mouth that hung ever so slightly ajar. Never would she understand the paths Charlotte's mind took, not if she had a hundred years to do so.

"Charlotte?"

Dare leaned close to her, his breath ruffling her hair in a manner that made little shivers of delight go down her back. She kept her eyes on Patricia and David as they danced. "Yes, Alasdair?"

"Would you mind telling me what that is you're wearing around your neck?"

Charlotte looked down at the blue gown that matched her eyes, the gown she had worn for her wedding and had now donned for Patricia's nuptials. Barely visible above the bodice was a thin gold chain upon which hung the amulet the witch had given her.

"It is an amulet."

"Ah."

Patricia and David danced by in a swirl of adoring looks, rose lace, and forest green superfine. Charlotte almost envied Patricia her unblemished happiness, musing sourly to herself that her new sister-in-law hadn't had to survive the hell of the last few hours as she had. Long, painful hours during which she was both ignored and ridiculed by Patricia's guests, bound by etiquette and the desire not to ruin Patricia's wedding to keep her tongue behind her teeth no matter how strong the provocation was to do otherwise. And *that* was a sore trial, indeed.

"What sort of amulet?"

"It is the hind foot of a lovebird."

Still, she had survived all the catty remarks and cruel asides, whispered in tones meant for her ears. She noticed that both the remarks and asides ceased whenever Alasdair was around; no doubt he, as a man, was excluded from such unpleasantnesses.

Life was so unfair at times.

"You're wearing the foot of a dead bird around your neck?"

"The hind foot of a lovebird," she corrected him absently, glancing at the clock on a table set near the door. There was only one more hour to go; and then the wedding breakfast would be officially over with the departure of Patricia and David for his ship. One hour. One short hour, and then she and Alasdair would accompany the bridal pair to the docks, finally returning home where she would withdraw from Society until such time as it found some new bit of gossip to shred to pieces.

And, of course, there was still the little matter of falling in love with her husband.

"Birds only have two feet, Charlotte."

"Do they? How very fascinating."

"Two feet mean there are no front or hind feet."

"Perhaps lovebirds have four."

"No, they have two, just like every other bird."

"Perhaps this lovebird was of a rare, four-footed species little known to man, and thus, the hind leg of it would be considered lucky."

Dare gave her one of those looks that she had mentally termed his martyred look. She dismissed the leg question and fingered the thin chain around her neck, wondering if she shouldn't double the potions. Perhaps just taking it once a day was not effective enough. Sometimes she didn't see Alasdair for several hours after she'd drunk the rather pleasant-tasting brew. Mayhap it was wearing off before she saw him. She'd take an extra dose of it as soon as they returned home. It certainly couldn't hurt her; it was a love potion, after all. No harm could come of an abundance of love, surely!

"Charlotte."

She turned to look at her husband. He had one of his adorable eyebrows cocked. She was pleased to see that the tired lines around his eyes and mouth had diminished, no doubt because she had continued to pretend she was asleep when he crawled into her bed. He had looked so tired the last few nights, she could do nothing more than wait for him to fall into an exhausted sleep, then tuck him in and rest next to him, fighting the burn inside her that urged her to take advantage of his weakened state. "Yes?"

"Are you telling me that you have a dead bird's leg under your gown?"

She blinked at him. "I thought we had already established that."

He shook his head, running a hand through his hair in the manner she loved. She wanted to run her fingers through it, as well.

"I'm sorry, I thought I misheard you and felt it was better to correct the impression than to muddle

224

on thinking you had part of a dead animal stuffed down your bodice. I don't know why I'm surprised. I'm sure it is all the thing for fashionable ladies to be wearing legs of dead birds between their breasts, but on the off-hand chance it's not, perhaps you'd care to tell me why you are?"

"Oh." He wanted to know why? Drat. "It's . . . for luck."

His second eyebrow joined the first. "For luck?"

"Yes, it's for luck. For . . . er . . . you." She crossed her fingers behind her back. It wasn't really a lie, not a bald-faced one. If the amulet and the potions and the love spells worked and she fell in love with her husband, his luck would improve. It was bound to. How could it do otherwise with her at his side? "It's an amulet to . . . to promote the success of your engine." Again, another half-truth, not quite a lie.

He tugged on the chain until a small blue glass ampoule emerged from the depths of her bosom. He squinted at it. Barely visible through the dark glass was the dehydrated leg of a small bird.

"For luck," she said, meeting his blue-eyed gaze and suddenly feeling very warm despite the unseasonably chilly day. His eyes burned into hers, searing her, making her skin flush with the heat of his gaze.

"For . . . luck," he said softly, his fingers brushing the valley between her breasts as he tucked the amulet back into her dress. Her breath caught, then came fast, her breasts straining against her bodice as he slowly withdrew his fingers, trailing them against her soft flesh in a manner that made her legs go weak.

"Charlotte," he murmured, his eyes blazing as his mouth descended toward hers.

"Dare," she answered, tilting her head back, her lips parting to meet his.

"Come and join us," Patricia called as she and David waltzed by, abruptly reminding Charlotte that they were standing in full view of the entire wedding party. "You must have your wedding dance as well."

Charlotte looked away from her husband, embarrassed that she had so forgotten herself as to act the wanton in public, until the thought struck her in another manner. She had almost kissed Dare in public! Surely that was a sign the visit to the old woman who sold potions and amulets was not in vain. No doubt she was falling in love, for who else but someone in love would desire to kiss her husband in public?

"Shall we?" Alasdair held out his arm for her.

She glanced up at him from under her lashes, dimpling as she noticed the high color visible on his cheeks, placing her hand on his arm and allowing him to lead her out to the floor cleared for dancing. She swayed against Dare's hard body as he swung her into the dance, joy brimming inside her as she moved in time to the music, her heart beating wildly at being held in his arms. Forgotten was the mortification of the last few hours, forgotten was the nagging suspicion that she would never again truly be a member of the *ton*, forgotten was the worry over Alasdair achieving the success he so desperately sought.

It was all wiped clean from her mind as she fair hummed with happiness. She most definitely was falling in love with her husband, and given the notoriously fickle attention of the *ton*—new, more interesting gossip would no doubt soon engage their collective minds—things were most certainly looking up for her. She would soon be completely in love with Dare, she would welcome him to her bed for more than just sleeping, and after the rumors about her and Dare were no more, no doubt the foolish feelings of being an outsider staring in at Society would come to an unlamented end.

Life, she mused just before she gave herself up to the bliss of dancing with her husband, promised to be very pleasant, very pleasant indeed.

"The wedding went off very well," Mrs. Whitney said with quiet satisfaction. "It's a shame Nathaniel couldn't attend, but I'm sure he'll love Patricia almost as much as I do. She's the perfect wife for David. I wouldn't give him up to just anyone, you know, but they'll do very well together. I feel that in my bones, and my bones are never wrong."

Dare watched as his wife danced with his new brother-in-law, then turned to smile at the woman standing beside him. "They are very much in love. I'm sure they'll be happy together. David said Whitney was expected in August?"

"That is his plan."

"Ah." That gave him two months or a little more to fine tune the engine. If all went well, he might even be able to take some time off to devote to his wife. *Charlotte,* his mind whispered her name. His gaze wandered over to where she was smiling up at David. Perhaps if they had the time together, she would fall in love with him, and at last he could . . .

"McGregor! Been looking for you. Have someone you might be interested in seeing."

Dare turned at the sound of his name. Lord Collins stood in the doorway to the hotel room Dare had rented for his sister's wedding breakfast. Although he was aware Patricia had invited Charlotte's brother out of politeness, he hadn't expected to see Collins. He understood from less than oblique references made by others that Charlotte's brother had washed his hands of her when she eloped with her first husband.

"Collins," Dare said politely, giving the man the merest sketch of a bow. If the earl had any plans to upset Charlotte, he could just think again; she was having a hard enough time of it with the women making sly digs about Phylomena without having her brother add to her troubles. "I didn't expect to see you here. I hadn't thought weddings were to your taste."

The earl smiled a cold, ruthless smile and waved his pudgy hand toward a slender young man who looked vaguely familiar. "I am sure you weren't expecting to see us, but I thought as this was an event celebrating family ties, you would wish to have all your family gathered."

Dare looked at the young man, who arched a sardonic eyebrow and bowed with affected grace. He glanced back to the earl. "I'm afraid you have the advantage of me."

"That," replied Lord Collins with an oily smirk, "is exactly what I was telling young McGregor here."

"McGregor?" Dare narrowed his eyes at the arrogant young man in front of him.

"Geoffrey McGregor," the man acknowledged, a smile teasing his lips.

Dare went still at the name. "I had a cousin named Geoffrey," he said slowly, looking carefully at the man. He had the family's renowned blond looks, the same dark blue eyes, but where Dare's side of the family leaned toward tall and broad-chested, the man in front of him was slender and elegant. Still, there was no disputing that this man shared common blood. "My cousin died some five years ago, drowned when the ship he was taking to Holland went down in a storm."

"That is, I believe, the story that was told, but truth, don't you find, can be so much uglier?"

Dare's hands fisted at the undertone of insinuation in the younger man's voice. "Am I to understand that you claim to be Geoffrey Despenser McGregor, son of Robert McGregor of Perth?"

"I am he," the man said, his lips curling in a smug smile.

An unpleasant sensation in the pit of his stomach spread. Dare felt more than a little sick. "You did not drown while traveling to Holland five years ago?"

"Far from it. I was kidnapped and placed without my consent upon a merchant ship that was sailing for the Orient. The man who kidnapped me sold me into bondage until such time as I could work off his gaming debts to the captain. It took me five years to pay them and make my way back home, but as you can see, cousin, I have returned."

Oh, God, could life possibly get any worse?

"Matthew, what an unpleasant surprise to see you here."

Yes, yes it could get worse. Dare spent a moment madly wondering if he couldn't just scoop up his wife and dash away with her.

"Can I hope you mistook this for a gaming hell and will be leaving soon?" Charlotte tucked her hand into Dare's arm and glared at her brother. He closed his eyes for a moment, wishing she were anywhere else but standing next to him. If the young man before him was really who he said was . . . a groan slipped through his lips.

"There, you see, even Alasdair doesn't want you

here, and he's much more polite than I am."

"My dearest sister, I come to you with glad tidings." Collins's eyes were alight with vicious pleasure. Dare wrapped his arm around his wife and tried to steer her away from the news that he knew was going to devastate her.

"This is a celebration of my sister's wedding," he told the two men watching him avidly. "I would not have it marred by any of your *glad tidings*. If you would be so good as to call on me later this afternoon—"

"What are you up to, Matthew?" Charlotte resisted being herded away, looking between Dare's face and her brother's. "What devilment do you have planned now?"

"Devilment?" Collins spread his hands wide as if to show his innocence.

Panic welled up inside Dare. He didn't want Charlotte to hear the news now, not like this, not in front of everyone. "Wife, I insist that you go and mingle with your guests."

She wrinkled her nose at him in a manner that usually made him want to kiss her silly, but now just made him want to protect her from the hurt he knew was coming. "They are not my guests, they are Patricia's, and I have no wish to mingle. I want to know what nasty little surprise Matthew has planned."

"I am wounded that you would believe such a thing of me, sister, especially when I went to all the trouble of bringing with me one of your husband's cousins."

"Wife," Dare said in his haughtiest tone, the one he hoped Charlotte would recognize as not allowing debate, or at the very least, become offended by and leave him in a snit, "you have a smut on your nose. Go attend to it."

Charlotte rolled her eyes at him. "Don't be ridiculous, my nose would never tolerate a smut to land upon it. Alasdair's cousin, you say?"

Geoffrey McGregor, if it was he, took Charlotte's hand and bowed over it. Dare snatched it back before the other man could press his lips to her knuckles. He leveled his sternest look upon her. "Charlotte, I insist you leave us. Go talk to Mrs. Whitney. You were saying only yesterday you want to help me with the engine—go talk to her about what a far-seeing visionary I am."

She dimpled at him. "I'm much more far-sighted than you. Why I could read the sign for the blacksmith's shop we went to yesterday long before you."

Geoffrey converted a snicker into a cough. Dare eyed him coldly. "Nonetheless, madam, you will do as I ask."

"Why?" Charlotte asked, looking around him to study the young man. "Is there something about your cousin that would prohibit him from being introduced to me?"

"Ha!" laughed Collins.

Dare grabbed his wife and tried again to shove her in the other direction. She remained unshoveable. "Charlotte—"

"Is he not nice to know?"

"If you want to know the truth, sister dear—"

"—for once, would you please just do as I ask—"

"Is he riddled with vices or poor manners?"

"—the young man before you, your husband's cousin—"

"—without making a hissing about it?"

"Is he a ravisher of young maidens, a seducer of

231

innocents, a lascivious smutmonger tainted with all sorts of evil humors?"

"—his long-lost cousin, the cousin your husband clearly thought was dead, but he's not, and as that is so—"

Dare grabbed his wife and bodily forced her toward the group of people surrounding his sister. "Wife, I insist that you leave us now!"

"Is he a bad man?" she said, peering over her shoulder at her brother and Geoffrey.

Collins puffed his chest out and bellowed the last few words. "—*he* is rightfully the Earl of Carlisle, not your husband."

Dare's fists tightened to hard bands around his wife's arms. Damn Collins! Damn both of them! If the man was who he said he was—and Dare would be making sure the bounder had proof of his identity—then Collins was right. His cousin was the heir to the title and lands, not him. He didn't give a rat's arse about the title—it was an empty honor, saddled as it was with mountainous debts—but he knew that Charlotte set a great store by it.

"I wanted to tell you privately," he said quietly in her ear, his hand slipping up to caress the back of her neck. She had frozen at her brother's words, staring at the earl in wordless horror, the pronouncement echoing loudly through the room. A pregnant silence filled the air for a moment, then whispered exclamations swelled to a crescendo as the crème of Society turned to each other with glee to discuss the latest scandal, one that had unfolded so deliciously before them.

Life, Dare decided as his wife turned eyes wide with pain and disbelief upon him, could not get much worse if it tried.

Chapter Twelve

Charlotte sat huddled in her bedchamber, staring with unseeing eyes at the fire burning in the grate.

She wasn't a countess anymore.

The events of the day played through her head with the regularity of the clockwork bird she had been given for her seventh birthday. The beauty and joy of Patricia's wedding, the tedium and trial of the wedding breakfast, Matthew's arrival and subsequent pronouncement, the agonizing hour that followed, during which she had to stand before the knowing eyes of the *ton*, stripped of everything that mattered to her, the embarrassment and shame so great it was almost unbearable, and finally, the relief of seeing Patricia and her new husband off so she could return home and crumple up in despair.

She wasn't a countess anymore.

The fire cracked and popped just as it always did,

as if nothing significant had happened, and yet Charlotte felt as if the world had tipped upside down. It was as if life had suddenly become a series of disjointed events, related, but not connected with one another, familiar and yet strange. She was still Charlotte, but she was no longer who she thought she was. She was a wife, but in name only. She had been the daughter of an earl, the sister of an earl, the wife of an earl, but now her brother told her that she was simply Mrs. McGregor, an impoverished gentleman's spouse, and one she knew was not even particularly wanted or needed.

She wasn't a countess anymore.

What was Dare going to do? What was *she* going to do? How was she to settle into her life now that everything she had wanted and needed and planned for had been stripped from her? First the security of wealth, then her position in Society, and lastly the prestige of Dare's title . . . all she had left was Dare himself. And although she knew he loved her, it was a grudging love, a love he felt much against his will. He hadn't wanted to marry her at all.

Suddenly it was all too much for her. "How am I supposed to face this?" she sobbed.

"At my side," a warm voice answered her. Dare stood in the doorway to his room, his dressing gown tied loosely around his waist. "With that obstinate chin of yours held high and a smile on your luscious lips. Together we'll face the future, Charlotte. Together we can do anything."

She shook her head, defeat battling with the hope his words stirred within her. "You're not an earl anymore. I'm not a countess."

"No, but you're still my wife." He came into the room and knelt at her feet, bending his head over her hands to press kisses along the back of them. The brush of his hair against her skin started a familiar fire deep within her. His eyes when he looked up at her seemed to burn with the same fire. "You still have me. I am the same person I was. I flatter myself to think that it was me you wanted, not an empty title. Am I wrong?"

Charlotte looked deep into eyes darkened to indigo, and thought about what he asked, really thought about it. Had she married him just for the title? There were other titled men she knew she could have cozened into marrying her, but none so handsome as Dare . . . but no, that was appearance, and she knew now what he had meant about looking beyond the surface. The truth was that there were no other men who made her feel as Dare did, none who interested and challenged her, none whose touch left her breathless and excited and wanting more. She pulled one of her hands from his and placed her palm against his cheek. Tiny golden whiskers tickled her fingers as she drew them along the line of his jaw. "No, I didn't marry you for the title. I wanted you."

The muscles in his jaw flexed under her fingers as he turned his head slightly, just enough so her fingers grazed his lips. He opened his mouth slightly and swirled his tongue around the tip of the finger that sank inward. The touch of his mouth on her skin seemed to have the most amazing effect on her womanly parts—they suddenly clamored for attention as heat pooled low within her. She pulled her other hand free and slid her fingers through the silk of his hair, recognizing that something was building inside her, some awareness that was just out of sight, something momentous that began to blossom deep in her soul. She tipped her head down until her lips were almost touching his, until she could feel his breath upon her mouth. The pressure inside her built higher until, just as her lips brushed against his, the knowledge burst upon her like a glorious ray of sunlight in a black abyss.

She loved him. She loved him with all her heart and soul, with every ounce of her being, with every breath drawn into her body, she loved him! Tears spilled down her cheeks as she smiled against his lips, wanting to shout her love for him from the highest mountaintop.

"I'm so sorry, so very sorry about this, Charlotte," he said softly, brushing the tears from her face, pain flickering across his handsome face.

"I know you are," she whispered, sliding off the chair into his arms, her smile growing at the look of surprise in his eyes. "I love you, Dare. Isn't it amazing? I didn't think it would work so quickly, but it did, because I knew just a moment ago that I love you. I really love you. Don't you find it wondrous and astonishing that I feel this way? I do. I find it completely bemusing, but do you know, just now I realized that I loved you, even though that horrible man says you're not an earl anymore, not that I believe him—he's obviously a pretender to your title, a rogue and a scoundrel, because if anyone was meant to be an earl, you were—but still, that I could love you even *thinking* you might possibly not be an earl is so amazing, I am speechless, completely and utterly speechless."

Dare stared at her for a moment, then threw back his head and laughed, tipping over backwards until he was lying on his back before the fire, Charlotte draped over his chest, smiling down into his handsome face.

"You never fail me, wife. Just when I think at last

I know what to expect from you, you succeed in pulling the rug out from beneath me."

"Don't be silly," Charlotte smiled, kissing his chin, her heart joyous and happy at the sight of her husband laughing, warm with the knowledge that the love potion worked. She was in love! "I quite like this rug. I would never abuse it in such a fashion."

"Do you mean it?" Dare asked the moment his lips released hers.

"Yes," she breathed, her eyes lit with passion and love. She traced a finger down the opening of his dressing gown, exposing the length of his chest, reveling in the feeling of his warm flesh beneath her fingers, breathing deeply to fill her lungs with his wonderful scent. With an impatient noise, she pushed the dressing gown off his shoulders, then bent her head so she could press kisses along his collarbone. "Yes, I do mean it. It's my very favorite rug."

Dare chuckled as he pulled her close to his chest, then rolled over until she was pinned beneath him. "That's not what I meant, wife, and you know it."

She allowed her dimples to peek out at him. "Oh, you meant that other thing? The bit about my being in love with you? Yes, I meant that as well. Truly, it is a miracle, though."

His head dipped to taste that very sensitive spot behind her ear. Pleasure rippled throughout her at the touch of his lips.

"It is a miracle because I failed to give you what you wanted from me?"

"No." She tugged on his hair until he looked up. "You gave me what I wanted—a handsome husband, a return to the *ton*, consequence and position. It's not your fault that evil man devised a plan to try to take it all away from us. The miracle I refer to has to do with the fact that I was beginning to think my mind was slightly defective, and that I was unable to love, but I know now that such thoughts are sheer foolishness. My mind is just as strong now as it has ever been, which is a great relief to me, as I was unclear how I was to correct the defect and make it more to your liking."

Dare smiled down at her, one hand brushing a strand of hair back from her forehead. "Your mind is utterly unique, Charlotte, and I wouldn't want it to change one iota."

She stared up at him, silent, watching him as he watched her, extremely aware of the fact that his bare upper body was pressed against her upper body, his arms braced along either side of her head, his mouth, that wonderful mouth, only a few inches from hers. His head dropped slightly until his lips were brushing against hers.

"Wife, I think we would be more comfortable if we were to continue this in your bed."

"Oh?" Hope, desire, love, passion—the emotions surging to life in her were too numerous to be separated and named. "You are tired? You wish to sleep?"

His lips were sweet as honey upon hers. "No, I'm not tired, and I do not wish to sleep. I wish to make love to my wife."

Charlotte blew out a little breath of anticipation. "Are you sure? You were most adamant the other day—"

"I'm sure," he said, his voice husky with desire. "But what of you? Do you still want me? Can you want a husband who has failed so dismally to provide for you?"

"Yes," she said, unable to deny the need in his eyes, not that she had ever wanted to. "I have wanted you for the longest time, Dare. There are many connubial calisthenics that I would very much enjoy trying with you, especially the Montezuma's Pyramid, although I must say, the Hanging Gardens of Babylonia has much appeal to it, despite the fact that it looks quite involved what with the silken ropes and all, and I don't quite understand how the feathers come into play, nor the grapes for that matter, but I am convinced that we would find the exercise amusing—"

Dare laughed as he got to his feet, scooping her into his arms and carrying her to the bed. "I believe we'll leave Montezuma and Babylonia for another day. Right now I have in mind the desire to pay homage to my sweet wife in the best way I know how, without silken ropes or grapes or intricate positions."

"It Italy, it is said the most amazing things can be done with goat's cheese—"

The words stopped with a gasp as Dare ripped her night rail from her body. She stood beside the bed, naked, exposed, all her flesh there for him to see, gilded by the firelight . . . and suddenly, it didn't seem like such a shocking thing. She had never really thought much about her body: it was always there, it made her clothing hang well, and other than Crouch's slur against her backside getting broad, she had not paid it much attention. Now, however, her body seemed a wondrous thing, at least it was with her husband standing next to her, his eyes almost bulging out of his head as he looked at her. Her breasts were heavy and aching, her womanly parts were flushed, her skin, wherever Dare's gaze flitted, was sensitive and craved his touch. She leaned into him, almost purring as she rubbed her body against his, thrilled by the heat flaring in his eyes.

Suddenly, she wanted to see the rest of him, the parts that were covered by the lower half of his dressing gown. *The interesting parts.*

"I think the polite thing would be for you to return the favor," she suggested, her hands on the tie of his dressing gown.

"Gark," he said, his gaze still caressing her flesh. He looked rather stunned and made no move to remove his own clothes, so she pulled the tie free and with a rustle of silk against manly flesh, the garment fell to his feet.

"Oh, yes, *gark* indeed!" she breathed, suddenly understanding why her body had held him so mesmerized. He was so beautiful, the sight of his golden skin brought tears to her eyes. He was all hard lines, sculpted muscles, and great sweeps of taut flesh that called to her, begged her to touch him, pleaded with her to stroke her hands along every bulge and valley and long line of muscle. "You are so handsome, Dare, so very—oh, my, will you just look at that, surely it must be painful to be in that sort of a state—and then there's your chest! And your stomach! I have to say, husband, your stomach is a thing of beauty. You're just like one of those broken statues Lord Elgin brought from Greece, only you are much, much nicer to look at. Is your backside as nice as I remember—oh, it is! It's perfectly lovely, too! Might I touch it? Might I—hoo! How do you do that? What amazing muscle control you have. What do you think would happen were I to touch you right here—"

Charlotte, who had been happily frolicking in a land made up solely of a naked Dare, suddenly found herself on her back, sinking into the cool bed linens as her husband covered her front.

"Char," he growled, his mouth hovering over hers. She arched her back so that her nipples rubbed against the soft hair of his chest. "Are you planning on narrating the events of this entire evening?"

"Vyvyan La Blue says that communication during connubial calisthenics can enhance the experience for both husband and wife, and as I wish to please you in all ways, not just with my body, but with my mind, as well, because, you know, my cousin Gillian says her husband—Lord Wessex, you do remember him, you tried to kill him once or twice—Gillian says that Noble enjoys her mind almost as much as more earthly pleasures, although she didn't really specify just what earthly pleasures she meant, but I assume she meant those of a calisthenic nature, so yes, the answer to your question is that for your pleasure I am planning on narra— oh dear God in heaven!"

Dare effectively stopped his wife's babble with the simple act of taking her nipple in his mouth. She was silken fire, she was satin heat, she had the softest skin that burned like a fire in his blood. He was harder than he thought humanly possible. He wanted her so much he could almost cry with joy over knowing she was his, and she was here, and she loved him. His body shook with the need to bury himself deep into her heat, but he was a gentleman, and she was his wife, his beloved, the woman who would share his life. He owed it to her delicate sensibilities to gently prepare her for the intrusion of his body into hers; he must make sure she was well pleasured and physically aroused before she could receive him. He had to bring her gradually to the point of ecstasy so that she, too would experience the greatest act man and woman could perform together.

Her legs shifted beneath him. His head snapped back, all thoughts but one gone from his mind. "Now?"

Her eyes fluttered open briefly. "Dear Lord, if you have any mercy, now!"

He spread her legs, lifted her hips, and plunged into her all with one move. She shrieked and spasmed around him, hundreds of little muscles gripping him, squeezing him, caressing him in a manner he'd never experienced before, but which drove him to a frenzy. Sweat stung on his back as she raked her fingernails up his flesh, but all that did was make him more frantic, more wild with the joy of joining with her.

"Why didn't I marry you five years ago?" he wondered aloud, the words coming out remarkably like a groan.

"You were stupid," she gasped in reply, her fingers digging into the muscles of his buttocks, her hips thrusting up to meet his.

"I was," he agreed, his breath coming in gasps, too, pressure building inside him, a familiar pressure, but one so intensified, one so brilliant that it was almost as if his soul had been washed clean by her love. "Very stupid. Incredibly stupid. So stupid I can't even begin to—oh, Lord, woman, don't do that again or it'll all be over for me."

"Do what?" she panted, her teeth nipping the flesh on his shoulder. "This?"

Dare's eyes rolled back into his head, his body clenched tight as he thrust into her heat. "Not that."

She wrapped her legs around his waist, soft little sobs of pleasure escaping her lips as she pushed upwards, her hips against his, taking him in deeper than he thought possible. "Then perhaps . . . you meant . . . this?"

Her nails scored his back. A shiver of pure rapture shook him as he pulled her hips higher, piercing her very soul with his thrusts. "Not." He withdrew and surged forward again, earning a cry of pleasure from her as he did. "That."

Her head thrashed on the pillow as he shortened his strokes, intent on transporting her to heaven with him, desperate now as the pressure inside him threatened to burst.

"Dare!" she screamed, sobbing his name as her body spasmed around him, her legs locked tight around his hips, her eyes wild, her hands pulling him into her body until he thought they would never again be separate entities. Her exaltation triggered his, the orgasm bursting upon him in a starburst of euphoria that shook not just his body, but his soul as well. He heard his voice crying her name, felt her body tremble with her passion, and poured forth his life into her sweet keeping.

The wild rasp of her breathing mingling with the harshness of his was the only sound in the room. He lay upon his Charlotte, knowing he should move, knowing he was too heavy for her soft body, but loath to tear himself from her. Instead he rolled to the side, taking her with him. They spent long minutes locked together like that, hearts beating wildly as they struggled to regain their breath.

"*That,* my love, is what I meant," he managed to say, his heart finally slowing, his mind once again capable of thought.

"That? Oh, you mean this?" Her body rippled and tightened around him.

He squawked.

She smiled a smile filled with feminine knowl-

edge that would have worried Dare, but he was ex-
periencing too much pleasure to bother with an
insignificant thing like the fact that his wife could
wring him dry with just a flex of her muscles.

"Mmm. Very interesting. Before I investigate this
ability I have of making your eyes bulge, would you
answer a question for me?"

She pushed away from him as she spoke. He
wrapped one arm around her waist, and rolled onto
his back, pulling her on top of him as he did. Her
eyes opened wide as she sat up on him, looking
down to where they were still joined. "Your manly
instrument is still inside of me."

Pleasure rippled through him as she squirmed
slightly. "Yes," he said hoarsely, feeling himself
swell within her. "It is. I am. We are."

She frowned down at him. "I might not have a
great deal of experience doing this, Dare, but I do
know that men's erected bits become soft and
squidgy *after*. You, however, are not soft and
squidgy." She moved her hips in a little circle that
made Dare sure he had died and gone to heaven.
"You seem to be just as erected as ever. Have I done
something wrong?"

"Lord, no," he gasped, clamping both hands
down on her hips in an attempt to keep her from
continuing the innocently seductive moves that she
had no idea were driving him mad with desire.
"You're doing everything right. That's why I'm still
hard. Now sit still and don't move a muscle, especially—AAAAAGH! Especially *those* muscles!"

She grinned wickedly at him, then laid down on
his chest and propped her chin up on her hands.
"Is this better?"

He was still buried in her, the need to make love
to her again quickly rising within him. "Moderately

so. What was it you wanted to ask me?"

Her bright blue eyes considered him seriously for a moment. "Will you be honest with me?"

He rubbed his knuckles gently down the curve of her cheek. She turned her face into his hand and pressed her lips to his palm.

Lord, how he loved her.

"I will always be honest with you, Charlotte."

She took a deep breath. He tried to drag his attention from the blissful feeling of her body gripping him tightly, but it was difficult.

"I think something is wrong with me. Down there. In my womanly parts." Her gaze dropped to his neck. She couldn't look him in the eye when she made her shameful confession.

"Something is wrong with you? Wrong how? Are you in pain? Did I hurt you?"

She didn't want to tell him how defective she was, but he was her husband—in every way—and she was worried about her problem. She just hoped it could be corrected, and that he knew how to effect the cure. She didn't think she could possibly explain it to anyone else. "No, I'm not in pain . . . well . . . it's not pain exactly. . . ."

"Charlotte." Dare sat up suddenly, pulling her from him. She felt an immense sense of loss as he withdrew from her body, but what he did next was far worse.

He examined her!

"Please, Dare, I'm all right! At least . . . well, I'm not all right, but I'm sure it's nothing you can see, so would you please stop staring at me there? I assure you it's not that part of me that is the problem. Not entirely. Well, possibly it is the source of trouble, but I just don't know!"

She tugged on his head until he stopped prodding her private parts and looked up at her. "If I didn't hurt you, then what exactly is the problem?"

She looked at his chest. "I'm . . . defective."

"Defective?" He tried to raise her chin so she was looking in his eyes, but she kept her gaze clamped to his chest. "I don't understand. How is it you think you're defective?"

She took a deep breath. Sometimes it was best to get things over with quickly. "In Vyvyan La Blue's *Guide to Connubial Calisthenics* the culmination of the calisthenic is described as a moment whereby one is transported to elation upon a crimson tide of completion that rises higher and higher, foaming and bubbling around one until heaven itself opens up to pour down pearls of joy in benediction."

Dare's lips twitched and the muscles in his jaw tightened, but other than clearing his throat twice, all he said was, "And?"

She dropped her gaze back to his chest. "And . . . I didn't feel that."

He was silent for a moment, although there were odd rumbling noises from his chest as if he was struggling to hold some emotion within him. Disgust at her lack of fineness, no doubt.

She wanted to cry.

"Charlotte, I might not be the most experienced man in the world, but I know when a woman experiences an orgasm, and I can assure you that you did."

"Well, I don't know about this orgasm business, I haven't studied that, but I do know that although what I felt with you was wonderful, truly wonderful, indescribably so, it was *not* a crimson tide of completion that bubbled and foamed about me. What I felt was much more . . . common. It was . . . for lack of a better word, *earthy.* I know a lady should not feel such things, and I will try very hard to school my feelings toward those of the crimson tide of completion, but you must tell me how to go about it. Vyvyan," she said with a sudden frown at the bureau where the book rested, "is lamentably silent as to how one is to encourage all the foaming and bubbling and such, and eliminate the baser feelings."

Dare said nothing for a moment. Charlotte gathered her nerve and looked up at him, dreading to see the expected disgust in his eyes, but needing the comfort of his understanding. Hope rose again within her as she saw the laughter and love in his face as he stroked the line of her cheek, cupping her chin to kiss her very gently. Surely, she thought with a blissful sigh, he couldn't be disgusted when he was looking at her with such a tender expression?

"Charlotte, that moment—it's called an orgasm— *is* earthy. Lovemaking, real lovemaking, is not done with any elegance or refinement, or even sophistication. It's two people coming together in the most fundamental way, it's sweat and heat and uninhibited pleasure, and if you do it properly, when it's over you should need a bath."

Her eyes widened. "Not refined? Vyvyan La Blue makes no such note of this. A bath . . . yes, I suppose that what with all the moistness that ensues, that could be desired on the lady's part, but I had no idea it applied for gentleman as well."

He was grinning at her now, pulling her hand down the length of his chest to his groin. "How do I feel?"

She curled her fingers around the long length of him, suddenly feeling a bit shy. "Your chest is bedewed with perspiration."

247

"And?"

She remembered the feel of his back beneath her fingers. "So was your back."

"And?"

"And you're sticky. Here," she said, squeezing him slightly.

He traced a finger under her breast, then eased backward. "And how do you feel?"

She glanced down at the juncture of her thighs. "I suspect the same, although Mama always said ladies don't perspire, they glow."

Suddenly he was leaning over her, pushing her down into the soft blankets of the bed, his mouth close to her ear. She tipped her head to the side as he started nibbling on her neck.

"I gave you pleasure?"

"Yes," she whispered, her hands stroking his chest, finding the two little nipple nubs she had intended on examining earlier. "A great deal of pleasure."

"As you did me," he said softly, his breath on her lips now. She gazed into his dark blue eyes and allowed his words to eliminate her worry. "You're not defective, sweetheart, you're just full of passion." He kissed her deeply, pressing his body against hers, his tongue mating with hers just as intimately as his body had a short while before. "And I wouldn't want you to change one little bit."

Chapter Thirteen

"I think you're perfectly beastly, Alasdair."

"I am aware of your opinion, Charlotte."

"I cannot believe that you are the same man who introduced me to the pleasures of the organism last night. You are much changed by the light of day!"

"*Orgasm*, Charlotte. Are you planning on eating that last piece of bread?"

"You are breaking my heart."

"Regret it though I may, the sad state of your heart will not change my decision."

"But everyone is talking about us!" Charlotte passed a small silver rack containing toasted bread to her husband. How could the man eat when her life was falling to shreds around her? "Our names are on everyone's lips! I shall not be able to set foot outside this house without being shamed and humiliated! I cannot possibly survive in a society where I am the subject of ridicule and cruel speculations, and I think it's terribly insensitive for you to expect me to stay in town when you have three perfectly good properties we might retire to until this latest unpleasantness has been forgotten."

Dare calmly dabbed fruit preserves onto the cold piece of bread. "Shame and humiliation can only be felt when the someone's opinion matters to you, wife. You are the only one who can give people that power over you."

"But, Dare, why couldn't we go to one of your estates for a month or two?"

"Until I hear from my solicitors that my cousin is not the rightful heir of my uncle, ownership of the estates is in question. The only property I own outright is a small estate on a rocky little island off the coast of Scotland, and I don't think you would care for that overly much."

"Going to the country would make everything so much easier." Charlotte continued as if he hadn't spoken.

"Moving the engine to Scotland for a month, then bringing it back here for the industrial exhibition two months hence can hardly be said to make everything easier," he protested gently, helping himself to another serving of ham.

"You could work on your engine in peace in the country—"

"Something I can do right here."

"—and I can go about my duties as your wife—"

"Something *you* can do right here."

"—and we won't have to put up with sly innuendoes and nasty whispers from those we meet socially," Charlotte finished triumphantly.

"I have every faith that if you tried hard enough,

you could turn the other cheek to any whispers or innuendoes you might find distressing."

"Aaaaaagh!" Charlotte slammed her fork down onto the breakfast table and glared at her husband. "You are deliberately being obese just to annoy me!"

"Obese?" Dare looked at his plate, blinked twice, then smiled at his wife. "Obtuse, perhaps, but I hope not obese. Charlotte?"

Charlotte pouted at a quite atrocious painting of a man and his hunter that hung on the wall of the small dining room. "What?" she asked, snapping the word off with an edge sharp enough to slice bread.

"Have I told you this morning how beautiful you are?"

She allowed herself to be mollified just enough to glance at him with haughty disdain. "No, you haven't. I shall add that to your list of imperfections."

His smile deepened. "Have I told you how the sight of you lying next to me this morning gladdened my heart?"

The disdain melted in the warm glow of happiness resulting from his words. "No, you haven't. I consider that very churlish of you, too."

"Ah. Perhaps, then, I mentioned the extreme pleasure I found in undertaking the Egyptian Salutation to a Lady in the Full Glory of Morning with you last night?"

A small, very pleased smile curled Charlotte's lips as she remembered the joy of their first connubial calisthenic. It had been everything Vyvyan La Blue had promised and so much more. "I shall never again hear of Cleopatra's Needle without thinking of you," she murmured.

Dare had been quite correct, she mused as she

colored delicately and peeked at him through the screen of her lashes. If all went as it should, bathing was most definitely necessary afterward.

His eyes lit with a glint that was becoming familiar to Charlotte. She might have answered that look had not Batsfoam chosen that moment to bring in a fresh pot of tea.

"Will you be needing the carriage this morning, sir? I ask not for my own sake—I would gladly undertake the twenty-minute walk to the stables despite the fact that the lower part of my unfortunate limb appears to be resting on hot coals and several sharp pieces of glass, thus causing a sensation remarkably like agony to fill the limb itself, snake upward to my right hip, curl around that portion of the body commonly referred to as the trunk, venture across my spleen, throbbing deeply into my lungs, and finally culminating in a sharp pain behind my left eye—indeed, as I said, I would be happy to undertake the walk to the stables in addition to the many other tasks you have so graciously allowed me to fill my day with, but in truth I ask so as to ascertain whether the boy Wills will be needed to accompany the carriage. His livery suffered a most grievous accident when he fell into a coal scuttle. But should you, most beneficent sir, be requiring the use of the aforementioned carriage, I will add cleaning the lad to my extensive list of tasks to be accomplished today, tasks that you may be assured I will undertake to fulfill in such a manner as to leave you unaware of the mundane and tiresome day-to-day necessities I and others of your staff are happy to assume in order that your household runs with the clockwork precision you demand."

Dare pulled out his pocket watch and consulted

it. "Two minutes. I believe, Batsfoam, that is a record for you. Based on past performance, I wouldn't have thought you could work a mention of your spleen into a narrative that lasted anything less than six minutes. I commend you on your brevity."

Batsfoam bowed deeply to his employer. "I live, as you know, sir, for your pleasure."

"Then it should make you ecstatic to know that I will not need the carriage today. I will be spending the entire day working on the engine. I'm sadly behind schedule, owing to the mishap with the pistons, so I won't be going anywhere for a while. Charlotte? What are your plans for the day? I'm sure Batsfoam would be nigh on delirious with joy if you were to provide him with more of those tasks he is always nattering on about."

Charlotte looked up from where she was glaring at her innocent plate. "Surely you don't intend to spend the *entire* day working? I was hoping we might make one or two appearances in public together so as to stifle some of the rumors circulating about us. I thought perhaps a ride in the park—or a drive, if you can procure a suitably smart phaeton—followed by some shopping, and an appearance at the opera tonight would go far in proving to everyone that we are just as good as we were before that horrid man put forth his ridiculous claims."

Dare shook his head, the dark blue of his eyes brittle and hard. "I don't give a fig what the *ton* thinks of me, and I'll be damned if I feel it necessary to prove myself to them. I have to work on the engine, Charlotte. It is vital that I have at least a month to conduct trials with it before Whitney and the other Yankees come for the naval industrial exhibition, and in order to conduct those trials, I must first have the engine working. If I devote myself to it night and day for the next week, I will have it done in time."

"Perhaps you would like my assistance," Charlotte suggested hopefully. "I would be happy to cancel our plans for the day if you'd like me to help you with your machine. Nothing would please me more than to know I was of service to you."

Dare looked a bit panicked by her offer of assistance. "That is very thoughtful of you, but I will have Joseph to help me today and Batsfoam later to draw in the modifications I've made, so although I appreciate your desire to help me, it will not be needed."

He didn't need her. He hadn't wanted to marry her because he didn't need her. Charlotte swallowed that painful knowledge and merely nodded.

"There's no reason for you to change your plans," he added. "You can still take your ride and go shopping and go to the opera. You'll just have to do it without me."

"I don't *want* to do it without you." She frowned, heedless of the wrinkles that would no doubt result from such an extreme action. There were times when one just had to throw caution to the wind, and clearly this was such a time. "The point was for us to appear together, carefree and happy, not for me to appear without you by my side."

"I'm sorry, you will have to survive without my presence. Batsfoam is waiting, and as you heard him mention in excruciating detail, his abbreviated limb is giving him grief today—do you wish to use the carriage or not?"

She bit back her anger at his cavalier manner in dismissing the importance of the *ton*'s opinion. He was an earl, after all—no matter what that vile man claimed—and everyone knew earls were above such things as worry over what people thought of him. Still, she was his wife, and it was her job to see to it that his reputation, as well as hers, was of the highest quality. She would have to take on the task of ensuring it was not tarnished any more than it had been. "What about the Pretender?"

Dare set his cup down. "The what?"

"The Pretender." She waved her fork around in a vague manner. "That man who claims to be your cousin? What are you doing about him?"

"You were with me when I wrote to my solicitors. Until I hear from them that he is my uncle's son, I will do nothing."

"You can't leave something so important up to solicitors," she argued. "You have to *do* something!"

Dare dabbed at his lips with the linen and pushed his plate back, preparing to rise. "What exactly did you have in mind?"

"You must make him admit he's lying, of course! I would have thought that was evident even to a man who spends all his time in a dank basement with a smelly machine!"

Dare strolled the length of the table, then bent to press a kiss to her forehead. "The solicitors will investigate his claim, Charlotte. Until we know the truth, we will leave it in their capable hands."

"But—"

"We will leave it in their hands," he repeated, tipping her chin up and pinning her back with a look that did not invite debate.

"I will not stand by and allow that man to take away what's rightfully yours," she said, a mutinous warning evident in her eye. He could think again if he honestly believed he could glare her into subservience.

255

"The solicitors will see to it he doesn't," Dare said softly, then heedless of Batsfoam, brushed his lips against hers in a gentle kiss. "Stay out of trouble today. Batsfoam, I leave it to you to find out from my lady whether she wishes to use the carriage. I will be downstairs if I'm needed—which I trust I won't be."

"As you will, my lor . . . sir. I shall inform the staff of your intentions. They will be delighted to their very toenails, as I am, to hear we are to be graced with your constant, unceasing presence for the next week."

Dare gave Charlotte one last look that she met with flared nostrils and thinned lips. Then he took his leave and headed off to the bowels of the house.

"Has there ever been such an annoying, nettlesome, *aggregating* man?" Charlotte fumed, sitting back with an unladylike snort. Clearly Dare's insistence on refusing to deal with the situation left her with two choices—she could do nothing, tending Dare's house and waiting for his solicitors to prove the Pretender was just that, or she could take matters into her own very capable hands. Surely the removal of the Pretender should reinstate Dare and her back into the good graces of the *ton*. "And I have never been one to shirk my duty, Batsfoam."

"I do not doubt that for a moment, ma'am."

"I love my husband," she said, standing and fixing the butler with a militant glare.

His shoulders straightened under the influence of that glare. "As every good wife should, I'm sure."

"I will not allow anyone to abuse his good nature."

Batsfoam's head lifted in response to the equally militant tone in her voice.

"There are people out there who would think

nothing of doing so," he snapped out in his best sergeant's voice.

"Solicitors are well and fine in their place, but their place is not at Alasdair's side!"

"That is *your* place, not any other's," he agreed, giving Charlotte a brisk salute.

"Therefore, it falls to me to act on this matter."

"Yes, ma'am!" Batsfoam stood stiffly at attention, the creak from his wooden leg the only sound as Charlotte stared at the empty fireplace, a finger tapping on her chin. Finally, she nodded and turned toward the door.

"I will attend to this man who claims to be Alasdair's cousin myself. Once I do, Dare will see just how very useful and helpful I can be to him. Batsfoam?"

"I am here, ma'am, as I will ever be, no matter how much my unfortunate limb pains me, waiting to learn how I might best serve you and the master."

"I wish the carriage to be brought around at once. I have some calls to make!"

"I will be as quick as the wind the entire way to the stables, ma'am," Batsfoam said with another snappy salute, turning with a military fineness despite the ominous creak of his wooden leg. "I will be as the swiftest bird upon the wing. I will race as fast as a hare under the hounds. I will fly with the speed of a shooting star. My legs, the unfortunate one included, will be a veritable blur as I—"

Charlotte rolled her eyes heavenward, then interrupted before her ears were talked off. "Batsfoam?"

He tipped his head in obsequious inquiry.

"Leave now. I shall be ready for the carriage in one half hour."

He bowed until his nose touched his knee. Charlotte allowed herself a small grimace, one small enough to be effective without running the risk of wrinkles, and left the room mentally considering and casting aside any number of ideas regarding Geoffrey the Pretender. In cases such as these, Charlotte had always found that two heads were wiser than one.

"Caro will help me." She smiled to herself as she climbed the stairs to change her gown into something suitable for paying a call. "She's sure to. She has a great fondness for me, and can refuse me nothing. I can count on her to see me through this trying time."

"No."

"Caro—"

"NO!"

"But you haven't even heard—"

"And I don't have to! Charlotte, you have cozened me into one outrageous plan after another, but I must put my foot down now. I cannot help you."

"It is a matter of life and death."

"It is not, it's a matter of your pride. You said Lord . . . Mr. . . . . oh, what should I call your husband?"

"He is Lord Carlisle, but you may call him Alasdair if you desire."

Caroline looked appalled at the idea, so appalled she stopped where she was right in the middle of Hyde Park. Her maid and Charlotte's footman, both trailing at a discreet distance and chatting in a familiar manner that Caroline did not entirely approve of, sat down on a nearby bench. "I couldn't possibly!"

"Oh, pheasant feathers! You're making such a fuss over nothing! Very well, call him McGregor." Charlotte twirled her parasol in a determinedly unconcerned fashion and smiled at a pair of passing ladies. "Mrs. Hawkins is looking plump. Do you think she's increasing again?"

"I doubt it. Mr. Hawkins has been in Belgium this last year. As I was saying, if your husband has already contacted his solicitors about the matter, there is no need for you to go running off on another one of your hen-witted plans."

"There is every need, Caro," Charlotte said, refusing to rise to the hen-witted bait. She dimpled out of habit as a small clutch of dandies on horseback looked their way. The weather had turned sunny again, making it very pleasant to take a stroll through the park, especially since they were in clear view of Rotten Row so they could see and be seen. Still, she had a job to do. Duty must come before pleasure. Extracting a small memorandum book from her reticule, she slipped her arm through Caroline's and urged her in the direction she wished to go. "Solicitors are notoriously slow, and I haven't the time to wait on their pleasure. Besides, I'm not sure I can trust them to find in Alasdair's favor, as I will."

"But—"

"Only you can help me—you are a veritable mountainhead of gossip, Caro!"

"*Fountainhead.*"

"You must be aware of the very precarious position Alasdair and I are in at the moment. One more scandal and even I will not be able to salvage our standing with the *ton*. Thus I turn to you, my dearest and closest friend and confidant, for aid." Charlotte blinked quickly and dabbed her handkerchief at a nonexistent tear. "I have no one else I can turn to."

"I know full well you're not crying; you hate crying. Tears make your eyes turn red and swollen, and your nose becomes afflicted, and sometimes you get the hiccups as a result, so you're not fooling me into thinking that you'd weep now over something so trivial."

"Trivial!" Charlotte's glare was untainted by tears. "My life is not trivial!"

"Your life is not at stake here, only your pride—"

"My pride! Oh, I like that! How would you feel if your dearest Algernon suddenly found himself stripped of his title, disgraced and demeaned before everyone?"

"That wouldn't happen; dearest Algernon's father was viscount before him, and he has no brothers—"

Charlotte came to a halt, her fists clenched, her teeth gritted. She would not scream in public, no matter how strong the provocation. "My point, which you seemed to have missed entirely, is that this matter is one of extreme importance. You will at least grant me that."

"Yes," Caroline said with much dignity, pulling her gaze from a heavily mustachioed gentleman in order to give her friend her full attention. "I agree that it is important, but I do not think it is a matter of life or death, and because it is not, I am unable to help with whatever plan you have organized. Dearest Algernon was not at all pleased when he found out I assisted you at Lady Jersey's masquerade, and after the scene at the Duchess of Deal's ball . . . well, I'm sorry, but I must consider his position, as well as my own. I cannot help you."

Charlotte tugged Caroline's reticule from her wrist, pulling from it a small diamond-encrusted gentleman's watch that was a much cherished memento of Caroline's father, turning a small knob on the top of the watch face.

"What on earth are you doing?" Caroline asked, her bewilderment plain.

"I have set your papa's watch forward an hour. We will assume we have spent the past hour arguing over whether you will help me. It is now an hour later. You have been worn down by my brilliant arguments and charming wit and have agreed to help me."

Caroline blinked at her in surprise. "I haven't—"

"No, but you would if I continued. You know you would; you've never yet been able to withstand one of my pervasive arguments. So why don't we dispense with the need to waste an hour debating the point and move on to the part where you agree to help me with my plans."

Caroline looked as if she was going to argue the point. Then her shoulders slumped and she accepted the watch, tucking it away carefully in her bag before starting forward again. "The word is *persuasive,* and I'm not going to forget this, Charlotte, I'm truly not."

"If it churns your butter," Charlotte said with a bright smile. "I heard Gillian say that. Isn't it quaint? Now, as for my plans—"

"There's more than one?" Caroline asked in a voice faint with horror.

"Yes, I had a brilliant thought on the way over here, and I believe I have a solution to our problem with the *ton.* As you well know, they will continue to chew over this latest scandal—the one involving the Pretender—until something more meaty catches their attention. Therefore, I propose to present them with a morsel so tempting, all thought of Dare and the Pretender will be wiped from their collective minds."

261

"You've forgotten the original scandal, the one that came about when I inadvertently allowed Lady Brindley to know your husband hasn't consummated your marriage. And I should add that it is my own role in that sad business that is the only reason I will help you now. I owe you recompense for the damage I did you."

Charlotte let her dimples flash, a sweet blush of maidenly innocence that she always found particularly effective pinkening her cheeks as she spoke. "Sweet Caro, I knew you couldn't refuse me, although truly I do not blame you for that situation—Lady Brindley is just the sort of a woman who would stand about in a maze eavesdropping on people. Regardless, that bit of scandal is no more since Dare . . . well, you must take my word that it is no more."

Caroline's eyes brightened as she looked around them quickly to make sure they were not overheard. "Did he . . . ?"

Charlotte, with practiced ease, urged the blush to darken as she modestly cast her gaze down to her hands. She nodded. "He did."

"And was it . . . ?"

"Perfectly splendid, as I knew it would be."

Caroline breathed a happy sigh. "I'm so pleased for you, but must admit I'm a bit confused as well. Are you suggesting that you will create another scandal to draw attention away from the one regarding Mr. Geoffrey McGregor?"

"Exactly. You might not be the sharpest apple in the barrel, but you do have your wicks lit when it matters."

"I . . . sharpest?" Caroline shook her head. "Char, I don't understand why you would think creating

262

another scandal is the solution to your problem. People will still be talking about you—if not because of the Geoffrey McGregor situation, then because of whatever new scandal you cause."

"Don't be a goose, Caro, I'm not going to start a scandal about myself. It will concern someone else."

"Oh." Caroline continued to look confused. "How are you going to do that? I can't imagine anyone would care to have a scandal started about them. I know I should protest—dear Lord, you're not planning on using me?"

"Would I do that?" Charlotte asked, allowing herself a small moue expressive of wounded feelings.

"If you thought it would serve you, quite probably you would."

"Caroline Augusta Gwendlyspere! I would never deliberately engineer a scandal around you, and I am hurt and insulted that you would think otherwise."

"I seem to recall someone not a hundred miles from here who, when we were both at Miss Benjyman's School for Gentlewomen, used me as a scapegoat when she was caught climbing into the library window after midnight in the company of Ted the groom."

"Oh, pish, that was the merest coincidence."

"Coincidence? You told Miss Benjyman that I was spoony over Ted and that you were trying to stop me from eloping with him."

Charlotte frowned. "Caro, sweet Caro, might I remind you of the serious problem at hand? I cannot possibly be expected to remember every little event in my life, so if we might return our attention to the present—"

263

"I had to read sermons to old Mrs. Benjyman for an entire month, and you remember how horrible she was. She smelled of camphor and would insist on clacking those false teeth of hers when I least expected it. It was louder than a cannon shot."

"—I will be happy to tell you my plan."

"I was a nervous wreck after a few days. I ended up with a tic over my right eye for three months after that."

"Namely," Charlotte drew a deep breath and refused to argue with her sole remaining friend, "one concerning Lady Brindley."

That stopped Caroline in mid-squawk. "Lady Brindley? You plan on causing a scandal about Lady Brindley?"

"Shhh, do you want the whole of London to hear my plan? And who better to be the focus of a scandal? I couldn't very well go about involving someone innocent, not that the *ton* is overly ripe with innocents, but still, I would never deliberately hasten a scandal about someone who did not deserve it, and you must agree that if anyone deserves a little of the grief she's caused, it's Lady Brindley."

Caroline looked thoughtful for a moment. "I must admit I cannot fault your reasoning there. She certainly has gone out of her way to injure both you and Lord . . . Mr. McGregor. What exactly did you have in mind?"

"Well, do you remember telling me last week about the Marchioness of Welles's ball next week?"

A small frown of concentration wrinkled Caroline's forehead. "Yes, you said you detested Lady Welles, and you'd rather walk naked through Hyde Park than attend her ball."

"I've changed my mind. Prinny is supposed to be there, yes?"

"You mustn't call him that; it's disrespectful. The Prince Regent is Hypatia's godfather, and yes, he said he would attend her ball. Why?"

"The ball is sure to be a crush, for everyone who does not remember Hypatia as a spotty little girl inclined to tell tales will be there—in other words, it's the perfect setting for a scandal guaranteed to so shock and titillate Society. That foolish business with the Pretender will be forgotten in a trice."

"What scandal?" Caroline said with evident worry.

Charlotte smiled. Oh, it wasn't a particularly nice smile, she knew that, it wasn't the sort of a smile she would allow anyone but a dear, trusted friend to see, laden with smug satisfaction and just a hint of wickedness, but it was still a smile. She gave herself several points for the fact that faced as she was with the complete and utter destruction of her social life, she could still smile. "Lady Brindley is going to have an accident at the ball. Or rather, her gown is."

Caroline's eyes opened wide. "Her gown? You don't mean the one she was having fitted when I saw her at the modiste's?"

"Exactly that one. Or rather, a copy of it. That's where your help comes in."

"My help? My help with what?" Caroline's voice rose at least an octave in her distress. Charlotte explained her plan in such detail as to make Caroline's blood run cold.

When she was finished Caroline walked in stunned silence for a few minutes, blinking now and again at her friend. "You really have a very frightening mind. It worries me, Char, it really does. I cannot help but think of what havoc you could

265

wreak were your mind to one day snap. As for your plan . . ."

Charlotte strolled on with her arm through Caroline's, her mind at ease as the latter lectured her on the folly of her plan. With the matter of a distracting scandal taken care of, she could focus on the much more important matter of proving the Pretender's claim false. No doubt Crouch could help her there. Crouch was very useful when it came to things of that sort, things such as kidnapping and investigating people who made claims against earls, and the like.

"Alasdair won't like my consulting Crouch," she mused, incidentally interrupting Caroline's lecture, halting long enough to tear out the memorandum page of notes she'd written earlier for Caroline. "Certainly not after that silliness this morning when he tried to browbeat me—honestly, Caro, it was browbeating, pure and simple! There ought to be a law against husbands abusing their wives in such a manner—but then, as Mama was wont to say, what he does not know cannot hurt me."

"Er . . ."

Charlotte handed her friend the slip of paper, tucking the memorandum book away in her reticule before waving to woman near a large rhododendron. "There is Mrs. Whitney. She said she would be in the park today. For Alasdair's sake I must say hello, even if she is the most tiresome of women. It's been a lovely walk, Caro, and I take my leave of you secure in the knowledge that I have the dearest, sweetest friend in all England, a friend who I know will not let me down in my time of need. I shall spend a few minutes with Mrs. Whitney; then I must be on my way to set Crouch to investigating the Pretender. My best to your dear

Algernon. Jackson, come along and stop flirting with Clothilde, I have a great number of things to do today."

Caroline slumped onto a convenient bench as Charlotte waved cheerfully before hurrying toward a gray-haired older woman and her maid. There were times—such as when she went up against Char's indomitable will—that she felt as effective as a soap bubble against a herd of Charlotte's elephants . . . no matter what their color.

Chapter Fourteen

"You, sir, are a liar. You lied to your wife. You ought to be ashamed of yourself." Dare glared at the face before him, then threw his towel at the mirror and bent to splash water over his heated brow. Perhaps liar was too strong a word—he *was* behind schedule, and he *did* anticipate working around the clock on the engine so as to have it ready for trial by the week's end. Those hadn't been lies. Still, he could have easily carved a few hours out of his day to go riding with Charlotte in the park.

He glanced out the window. The sun was low in the sky, long shadows reaching across the street in an elongated parody of the house's shape. It wasn't too late; he could still take her to the opera. He had that box Patricia had pleaded with him to take for the season . . . it would take little time to send a footman to the theater. A slow smile curled his lips as he thought about spending the evening in the company of his wife. True, he'd rather spend that time in a less public place, one conducive to the activities that had, the evening before, left him wrung out like a well-used rag, but a visit to the opera would please Charlotte. Spending a few hours listening to a bunch of singers screeching in Italian was a small price to pay to give her pleasure.

He paused for a moment before the bureau drawer, a fresh neck cloth dangling from his fingers, his body quivering with the thought of giving his wife pleasure. Just imagining her response to him was enough to leave him hard and aching. With a leer that would have a harlot blushing, he quickly changed out of his oil-splattered work things and into garments more suited to a gentleman.

"Ah, Batsfoam," he said when that worthy wandered in a few minutes later. "I hadn't expected to see you above stairs so early."

Batsfoam retrieved Dare's recently discarded boots, now coated with coal dust, oil, and assorted grime, and inclined his head in acknowledgement. "Regardless of my other responsibilities—many and varied as they are—I am still your valet, and as such, it is my duty, nay extreme pleasure, to be on hand when you undertake that most onerous of tasks: clothing yourself. Thus you see me here, practically frothing at the mouth with excitement at the thought of making myself useful to you."

Dare smiled fondly at the man. Not even Batsfoam's usual dour countenance could ruin the happy anticipation that filled him when he thought of spending the evening with Charlotte . . . particularly the last part of the evening, the part when they would be alone, naked, his hands skimming all her lovely curves, making her eyes burn hot with that erotic mixture of love and passion that made him feel like a god among mere mortal men. This, he thought smugly to himself as he allowed Batsfoam to help him into a midnight blue coat that fitted him as closely as a sausage casing, was what he'd wanted from a wife all along—not just the sharp bite of lust, but the soul-deep satisfying warmth of a companion, a friend, someone he wanted to be with simply because he delighted in her company.

Someone who loved him.

"Do you know the whereabouts of my wife, Batsfoam?" He tweaked the neck cloth slightly until the simple arrangement met with his satisfaction.

"Lady Charlotte has been gracious enough to gift me with that information, sir."

Dare waited a moment, but when Batsfoam gathered up the boots and used linen in preparation to leaving the room, he cocked an inquiring brow. "Would you be so generous as to share that information with me, or is it some state secret that I'm not to be privy to?"

For the first time since Dare had met him, Batsfoam hesitated to speak. "Lady Charlotte is at Britton House, sir."

Britton House? Wessex's house? Although Dare no longer held Noble accountable for his mistress's death—indeed, his eyes had been sadly opened to the truth behind the late Lady Wessex and her cruelties, not the least of which was using him to cast blame onto Noble—he had as little to do with Wessex and his charming, if eccentric, wife as was possible. "Why is she at Wessexes' house? What did she tell you she was doing there?"

Batsfoam didn't flinch at the bellow, although he was willing to wager a sovereign that he'd be slightly deaf for a week because of it. "I was given to understand that Lady Charlotte sought recourse to the Earl of Wessex's staff for an unspecified undertaking, the staff here being, as the Lady Charlotte herself said, a bit over-burdened."

"Undertaking? What sort of an undertaking would she have for Wessex's servants?" Dare knew shouting at Batsfoam wasn't justified, but the thought of Charlotte running to Wessex—by means of his servants—when she wanted help made him see red. Dammit, *he* was her husband! If she wanted help, she could bloody well turn to him for it. Didn't she understand how the husband-wife relationship worked?

"As I do not have at hand a dictionary, I shall be forced to rely upon my own interpretation of the English language; in this case, the word *unspecified* is commonly given to mean . . ." The glare Dare turned on him caused the smart retort to wither on Batsfoam's lips. He cleared his throat and respectfully dropped his gaze to the boots in his hands. "She did not say."

Dare's nostrils flared for a moment as if he smelled something foul. Then he snatched up his hat and stormed out of the bedchamber. "I see I'm going to have to inform my wife of a few definitions of my own—*marriage, loyalty,* and *help* being three of them. Have Jupiter brought around immediately, Batsfoam. Send one of the footman for him, it will be faster."

Dare waited in the library, his riding crop beating out a tattoo on his leg as he tried to conceive of what would send Charlotte to Wessex's servants. Ultimately, the realization that no matter how long he was married to her, he'd never understand the way her mind worked calmed him enough that he didn't take out his temper on Batsfoam when he announced that the horse was waiting.

Wessex lived in a fashionable part of town, something Dare had never given a thought to until he rode the distance from his own modest leased abode in a rather overcrowded section of town to the wide streets and cream-marbled splendor of Britton House. He was suddenly uncomfortably aware of the differences between the circumstances of Charlotte's life before marrying him and the present. Regret flashed through him with the realization of how much she had given up, but it was easily pushed aside when he reminded himself that she loved him, not his title or money. That Charlotte had fallen in love with him despite living in a modest house with few servants and none of the trappings she was used to simply proved the depth of her feelings for him. He might not be able to worship her with riches, he thought grimly to himself, but he certainly could with his mind and body. Not to mention his help with whatever problems she found herself burdened with.

Such moody reflections ended in steely determination as he dismounted before the entrance to the large house. He tossed the reins to the footman who accompanied Charlotte's carriage in the role as coachman.

"Tie him to the back of the carriage."

"Sir?" Jackson's eyes opened wide as Dare started up the steps to the front door.

"I'll be back in a minute. With my wife. Stay here."

"Aye, sir."

"Lady Charlotte?" Dare asked grimly to the slight, golden-haired footman who opened the door.

The footman looked surprised. "No, I'm Charles. Lady Charlotte is a female."

Dare took a deep breath and unlocked his clenched fingers. "I'm looking for my wife, Lady Charlotte. Is she here?"

"Yes, sir." The footman blinked at him, a pleasant, but slightly vacuous, expression on his face.

Dare fought to keep from rolling his eyes. Or throttling the man. Either action had its attraction. "Might I see her? Today? *Now?*"

Enlightenment dawned. "Oh! You want to *see* her. If you will come this way . . ."

Dare strode past the man into the oak-paneled hallway and summarily ignored the footman when he held open a door to what was obviously a small sitting room used by guests awaiting attention by the family. He stopped at the foot of the stairs, put his hands on his hips, and threw back his head to bellow, "CHARLOTTE!"

The noise echoed most effectively around the long hall, up the stairs, and through the length of the second floor. The footman danced around him as his keen ears picked up the sound of a door on the floor above opening. He stomped up the stairs, ignoring Charles's suggestion that he wait in the sitting room. "Charlotte? I know you're here. You cannot hide from me!"

"Why would I wish to hide from you?" his wife asked as he reached the top of the stairs. "Alasdair, what are you doing he—oof!"

Dare knew his wife well enough to recognize the stubborn set of her chin. That chin decided him in an instant. He would forego explanations and get right to the point.

"I am collecting you," he said as he scooped her up and over his shoulder, turning carefully and starting back down the stairs to where his carriage waited. "There's no sense in arguing, woman, you are coming with me. Save your tears and tantrums, my mind is made up. You are coming with me."

"So I have gathered, Alasdair." Dare's mood lightened. She didn't sound upset or hysterical. Still, with Charlotte, you never knew. Better safe than sorry.

"Since I am forbidden tears and tantrums, would you tolerate a simple question?"

Dare stopped at the bottom of the stairs and allowed his wife to regain her feet, although he kept a firm hand on her arm lest she suddenly try to break away. "Perhaps, if it's pertinent to this situation."

"How very generous of you," she replied, but he had to admit she didn't look at all grateful. If the thinned line of her lips and the fire in her eye were anything to go by, he judged he was about to be on the receiving end of her temper. "Might I then inquire what the devil you think you're—oh, Crouch, there you are. Would you please fetch my reticule and memorandum book?—doing here, and why have you suddenly been taken with the desire to sling me about as if I were a sack of—" Charlotte waved her hands around to express her inability to finish the simile.

"Flour?" Dare asked at the same time that Charles the footman helpfully offered, "Bulldogs?"

Charlotte transferred her glare to the hapless man for a moment before returning it to Dare. He glared right back at her. "The question, madam, is what you are doing here?"

"I needed to speak with Crouch about something." Dare's lip curled in a snarl at her mention of the butler's name. She ignored his lip and continued. "Since you seem to have an abrasion to him, I thought it best to meet him here rather than at home."

"I have an *aversion* to him, wife—"

"Whatever you wish to call it," Charlotte interrupted, waving her hands again until Dare captured both of them in his. "It's a silly thing."

"It is not silly, the blasted thug kidnapped me."

"That was years ago!"

"He knocked me unconscious." Dare still had a scar on the back of his head where Crouch had used a lead pipe to immobilize him.

"Five years ago." Charlotte's hands twitched in his. He tightened his grasp on her fingers. "That's a very long time to be holding a grudge against Crouch."

"The coward had two men hold me down while he beat me on the head."

"Crouch is not a coward, Dare."

"Thank you, m'lady," a deep voice said behind him. Dare turned and narrowed his eyes at Wessex's brute of a butler as the man marched down the stairs, a dainty bead-encrusted reticule dangling from his hook. " 'As it 'appens, I needed the two other blokes to keep 'is nibs 'ere from killin' me. 'Eard enough about ye to know I'd be carryin' my 'ead 'ome in a basket if I'd tackled ye by my lonesome."

"I'm not quite certain—I never am with Crouch; the way he mangles the King's tongue is utterly atoastious—but I do believe he's praising you," Charlotte whispered in Dare's ear. He was distracted for a moment by the sweet sensation of her breath teasing his suddenly sensitive ear, but he quickly reminded himself he was outraged and angry, and outraged and angry husbands did not kiss

275

their wives silly in the presence of their rival's servants, especially ones who made it a practice to kidnap him.

"Regardless, I would remind you that I have good reason to demand you not continue your acquaintance with Crouch or any other of Wessex's servants. You have an entire house full of servants. If you need serving, ask them."

"We are economizing," Charlotte protested as Dare hustled her toward the door. She pulled one hand free long enough to snatch the reticule from Crouch's hook as they passed him. "I cannot ask our servants to take time from their employment to tend to my ... er ... little project."

Dare stopped and frowned down at her. He'd completely forgotten to ask her what was so important she had to seek the help of a roughneck like Crouch. Where had his wits gone? One glance into her lovely blue eyes was the answer—he was so besotted with her, he'd couldn't think logically when she was near him. "What exactly is the nature of your *little project?*"

"Oh." Charlotte considered him for a moment, then flashed her dimples at him. "I think it's best if you don't know. You're bound to not like it, and as I have engaged Crouch's help, I'm sure that I will have no further need for assistance, so truly, it is best if you were to simply forget about it."

He counted to ten, still felt like yelling, so repeated the process three more times before he managed to get out, "Statements like that are not the least bit likely to generate disinterest on my part. I insist you tell me what your project is and how Crouch is to help you."

Charlotte patted his arm and turned toward the door. "I'm trying to be a good wife to you—I'm only thinking of your happiness, Dare. The plan would upset you, so you must trust me that on this, ignorance is better. Thus, I shall keep you in ignorance, and all will be well."

"Wife—" he warned through gritted teeth, but it did no good. Nothing much did with Charlotte.

"My lips are silent on the subject, husband. You may take red-hot tongs to me, but I shan't divulge even the smallest morsel of information, and it's no good looking at Crouch in that manner, for his lips are just as silent as mine."

Dare handed his wife up into the carriage. He looked back at the pirate butler, who stood with his arms crossed over his chest, one hip leaning against the door frame. "Do I assume that my wife speaks correctly on your behalf?"

"Aye, sir. I've given 'er m'word."

"I see. In that case, just as soon as I have seen my lady home, I will return to . . . *discuss* . . . the matter with you in greater detail."

If Dare didn't know better, he'd swear a look of amusement flashed in the butler's eyes. "I 'ad a feelin' ye would be, sir. I'll 'ave the cook lay in a supply of ice."

Dare nodded and climbed into the coach after Charlotte. Life suddenly looked very good. He gave his wife a small smile, amused by the worried looks she was casting over at him as he cracked his knuckles and flexed his fingers. For once he was grateful for her stubborn streak; rather than forcing him to press her until she told him what she was up to, he would find out the same information from Crouch—with the added satisfaction of settling the score between them. His smile deepened into a grin as she started to wring her hands.

This revenge was going to be sweet, very sweet indeed.

"I appreciate the fact that you wish to attend the opera tonight, husband, but how are we to explain *that?*" Charlotte pointed, standing at what she considered a safe distance from where Dare lounged on the chaise in his bedchamber.

Her husband removed the thick piece of beefsteak from his face and flexed his jaw, grimacing in pain with the slight movement. "I don't see that we have to explain anything. It's no one's concern what I do with my face."

Men! As if no one would notice the swelling on his jaw. "People will want to know, nonetheless. I just hope Crouch is all right. I have need of him tomorrow—you did say you left him with nothing broken? Even so, I hope you didn't injure him so greatly that he is unable to attend to my project."

Dare had the audacity to look peeved. "You might at least pretend you are concerned about me. He did manage to get in one blow before I knocked him off his feet. And as for this mysterious project—"

"Nonsense," she said, bending over to examine his jaw. She gently felt around the swelling, then stood back to consider the overall effect. Perhaps if she were to put a little rice powder on the wound, its redness and accompanying swelling wouldn't be quite so noticeable. "I had no fear that you were in any danger with regards to Crouch. Not only are you an earl, but I have seen you unclothed. It's quite obvious it would take more than one man to render harm to you."

Dare looked pleased by her words, although heaven knew she hadn't meant them as a compliment. Would she ever understand how men's minds worked? She shook her head in silent answer to her own question. Men were far too illogical to even begin to reason with.

"Your project, Charlotte?"

She sighed. Illogical, and with minds that held tight to only one thought. "Are we back to that?"

"We are."

"Then we shan't make the opera because you will be too busy demanding that I tell you about my plan, and I shall be too busy detailing the many good reasons I have to not worry you. Shall I tell Batsfoam to have the carriage sent back?"

"No, you will tell me what it is you have planned. Then we will go to the opera."

Charlotte sighed again and sat next to him, discarding her gloves and fan. They would not be going to the opera. "Very well, we shall have it your way. We will stay here and argue the evening away when we might be having a perfectly lovely time at the opera. As for what you said, Dare, I would have thought that by now you had learned enough about me to know that when I intend to do my wifely duty and keep life's many little unpleasantnesses from you, nothing short of Judgment Day will keep me from the righteous and selfless path of marital devotion."

Dare rolled his eyes, discarding the beefsteak as he stood up and handed Charlotte back her gloves and fan. "Come along, selfless and devoted one. You can tell me what it is that you are planning on the way to the opera."

They argued all the way to the opera (or, as Charlotte noted to herself, he argued, and she merely remained steadfast in her determination to save him untold mental anguish), they argued on the steps of the opera, they argued their way into Dare's box, and they argued right through the first two acts of the opera itself, albeit in hushed tones so as not to disturb anyone else. Charlotte had to give her husband credit. He had tried every means possible to extract the information from her, everything from threats of dire, but unspecified, acts that Charlotte knew he couldn't possibly carry out against her, to pleas begging her to just set his mind at ease so he could concentrate on the pleasure to be found at the opera. Since only a week earlier Charlotte had heard him express in terms not for the faint-of-heart just what he thought of opera in general, she dismissed his pitiful plea as insincere, and warmed herself with the knowledge that she was doing the right thing by putting the need to keep his mental state calm and untroubled against her own desire for recognition of her unselfish acts.

Intermission arrived at last and with it came the end of Dare's patience. Charlotte was frankly surprised it had lasted as long as it had.

"Since you insist on refusing to answer a simple question when I ask it, I will assume you desire my absence. As I am behind in the adjustments to the steam valve on my engine, I will take this opportunity to satisfy your wish to be rid of me."

Indecision warred within her. If he left her by herself at the opera, not only would everyone see that they'd had an argument, but she would also be forced to face that which she'd been successfully keeping at bay all evening—the fact that no one, not one single person had called upon them in their box. They were being cut, and if Dare didn't care to recognize that fact, she would be forced by his absence to acknowledge it. Should she give in and tell him what he wanted to know, soothing his ruffled feathers and keeping him by her side so she could pretend they were on their honeymoon and did not wish to be disturbed by anyone, or should she selflessly put his well-being ahead of hers? She was tempted by the former since he did not seem to appreciate the sacrifices she was making on his behalf. It certainly was hard being noble when Dare didn't seem to realize he was being protected.

It was the last thought that decided her. He needed her, if for no other reason than to protect his reputation in Society. Since Fate had been so good as to give her what she'd wanted—to be vitally important to her husband—she would fulfill her destiny and serve him as best she could. On his behalf she'd tackle the *ton* head on and not concede failure until there was no breath left in her body.

She lifted her chin and met her husband's furious gaze with tranquility and serenity. "Very well. If you would prefer to work on your engine for the rest of the evening, then go home. Caro and Lord Beverly are here—I shall sit with them for the remainder of the opera."

Dare looked surprised for a moment that she had called his bluff, then bowed stiffly and held out his arm. He was very angry at her, that she knew, so she didn't try to jolly him out of it with dimples and sultry looks from under her lashes. Instead she allowed him to deliver her to Caro's box, giving the Beverlys only the briefest of pleasantries before curtly nodding to her and leaving. Dare might be angry now, she told herself as she settled herself in a gold and ebony chair next to Caro's, but she was confident that one day he would appreciate just how much she had sacrificed on his behalf.

"Lord Car . . . your husband seems very angry this

281

evening," Caro whispered over her fan as Algernon greeted a new arrival to their box. "Is it because you both are being cut?"

Charlotte shrugged and looked out over the edge of the box to the floor where the dandies and ladies of dubious reputation milled about. "To tell you the truth, I doubt if he's noticed it. No, that's not fair. Alasdair is a very astute man; I'm sure he noticed that no one had so much as bowed our way—he just doesn't care."

Caroline raised her eyebrows in scandalized semaphore. "He doesn't care? What people think of him? He doesn't *care?*"

" 'Tis most unnatural, I admit, but alas sweet Caro, that is my lot in life—wife to a man who is indifferent to people's opinions."

"But *you* care," Caroline protested.

"Of course I do . . . to some extent." Charlotte hurried on when Caroline's eyebrows, newly returned to their normal position, threatened to return to the top of her forehead. "That is, I care what people say—reputation is everything—but I shall never be a slave to etiquette as Society demands. I have ever gone my own way, and it's too late for me now to learn how to abide by rules. Besides, you know as well as I do that the *ton* loves an Original. They may fuss and gossip like cats about little scandals, such as my eloping with Antonio, but in the end, they love the very people they claim to censure."

Caroline didn't look convinced. "They don't seem to love you now, Charlotte." She shot a quick glance over her shoulder to be sure her husband wasn't within hearing. "In fact, dearest Algernon told me that the betting books are filled with wagers about you and Mr. McGregor."

"Oh, yes, I know all about that—that was Lady

Brindley's doing. They were taking wagers on when Alasdair would consummate our marriage. As you well know, the wager is now moot. Didn't your Algernon tell people that?"

Caroline's eyes grew wider. "Yes, he did . . . oh, Char, should he not have? I didn't tell him not to mention it, and you know what gossips men are."

"No, no, I was counting on you both to spread that particular tidbit, not, I hasten to point out, that it's anyone's business. Still, it was the only way to have those ridiculous wagers off the books."

"But, Char—" The words dribbled to a stop.

Charlotte transferred her attention to her friend. Caroline seemed to be at a loss for words, a condition unfamiliar to Charlotte. "Are you ill? Do you need my vinaigrette?"

"No, no, it's not that. . . . I . . . I . . ." Caroline's mouth bobbed open and shut like a fish pulled from the water.

"You what? Honestly, Caro, if you're going to sit and stare at me in that google-eyed way, the least you can do is close your mouth. Only ninnies sit at the opera with their mouths in flycatching position."

Caroline seemed to gather her wits. "The phrase is *goggle-eyed*, and don't start that ninny business again. I was simply trying to think how best to break the news to you."

"What news?" Caroline had all of her attention now. Lord Beverly leaned toward his wife and muttered something about calling on an acquaintance's box for a few minutes. Charlotte waited as patiently as she could for him to finish, then pounced on her friend as soon as the man had left. "Caro, so help me, if you're keeping something important from me, I shall tell everyone you stuff your zona with stockings—"

"Charlotte!"

Half of the house looked over as Caroline's outraged shriek pierced the din of conversation.

Charlotte snapped open her fan and proceeded to languidly stir the heated air before her. "You're just never happy unless you can cause a scene, are you?"

"I . . . you . . . Charlotte . . ." Caroline sputtered.

"Yes, now that you have the question of pronouns and proper nouns settled, perhaps you would care to tell me what news you have?"

Caroline glared at her with a regrettable mutinous look in her eye. Charlotte was just about to point out that ladies who wore mulish expressions ran the risk of their faces freezing in that manner, but was kept from that opinion by Caroline's furious whisper. "I shouldn't, I truly shouldn't tell you, you don't deserve to know at all after threatening me with such a blatant untruth—"

Charlotte leveled a critical glance on her friend's bosom. "You can't possibly expect me to believe that's all you."

"My bosom is neither here nor there," Caroline said with dignity as she opened her fan in a manner that hid the bodice of her dress.

"My point exactly—it's nonexistent."

"But I shall tell you," Caroline continued, albeit somewhat snappishly, "because your husband doesn't deserve to suffer. Dearest Algernon told me tonight that the wagers on the betting books are to do with Mr. McGregor, specifically, whether or not he is . . . he can . . . if he has the ability to . . ."

"What?"

"If he is impotent," Caroline whispered with a fiery blush.

"Impotent?" Charlotte asked, at a loss for what was making Caroline act in such a goose-ish manner. Perhaps she was carrying. Everyone knew women who were breeding were exceptionally goose-ish about things.

"Shhh!"

"Lord, Caro, Algernon must be quizzing you. Why on earth would anyone care if Alasdair was impotent with me? If you want to know the truth, I'm probably just as impotent as he is, more so in fact. Mama always did say I was shameless."

Caroline stared at her with googled eyes—or goggled, Charlotte couldn't remember which was the correct word—her mouth once again hanging slightly ajar. Suddenly Caro choked and fanned herself quickly, her gaze on the tips of her slippers as she leaned toward Char and hissed, "Impotent, not impudent. Impotent means physically unable to do your manly duty."

Charlotte felt her own jaw sag at the implication. She thought for a moment she might actually swoon as a result of the burst of fury that roared to life within her, and it was all she could do to moderate her voice so the word she spoke came out as a quiet demand, rather than a howl of wrath. "Who?"

"Dearest Algernon says it's no one person. The wagers are on all the books at all the gentlemen's clubs. . . . Charlotte, where are you going?"

She gathered her cloak from the chair behind hers, unable for a moment to speak. In a distant, isolated part of her mind she noted interestedly that her hands were shaking, although she was neither cold nor frightened. "Alasdair has taken our carriage; might I use yours?"

Caroline followed her friend to the hall behind their box. "Yes, of course you may. You don't look at all well; you really should go home and lie down."

"I will go home when I've seen to this latest outrage."

"See to it? You mean the wagers? How will you see to it?"

Charlotte pinned her summer cloak closed and collected her reticule and fan. A righteous anger filled her, giving strength to her purpose. She would not allow Dare to become the laughingstock of the *ton*. "I will see to it in the most expedient of manners—I shall go to the men's clubs and steal their betting books."

Caroline fainted dead away.

An hour later Charlotte stepped down from the borrowed carriage, waving toward its interior as Batsfoam prepared to close the carriage door. "There are a number of books on the seat. Please have them brought to the kitchen and burned."

"Books, madam?"

"Books, Batsfoam. Large ones, containing several pages, most of which are filled with foolish wagers made by even more foolish men who ought to know better.

Batsfoam glanced at the nearest book, which carried the name WHITE'S in a gilded, elegant script. There were at least seven more betting books he could see by the light of the carriage lantern. A rare smile touched the grim line of his lips as he gestured a footman to the task. "Eh . . . did no one see you while you were liberating the books?"

"They saw me, but I wore a domino, so no one knew it was me. Besides, the sort of men they employ at those clubs are not at all what I would call intimidating. Cowards, the lot of them. They positively whimpered when I brandished his lordship's dueling pistol. A baby could have stolen those books."

"Ah. That was very clever of you to wear the domino, if I might be allowed to offer my humble and unworthy opinion."

"Of course it was clever, you don't think I would do anything to make people talk, now do you? Is Lord Carlisle at work on his engine?" Charlotte asked as she unpinned her cloak and allowed Batsfoam to take it from her.

"He is."

"Very well." She paused for a moment as she stripped off her gloves, then shook her head at the pang of worry over her recent actions. "What's done is done."

"Ma'am?"

No, she was being silly to worry. No one had the slightest idea who had so boldly pushed past the porters of the clubs and dashed in to steal the books. Thank heavens Matthew had filled her ears while growing up with tales of the betting books. For once, she was grateful he was such a wastrel. "And even if someone was to recognize me, there's my little project; surely that will take care of any speculation that might be rice."

"Rice, ma'am?"

"Hmm?" She pulled her mind from worry about what would happen if word got out that she'd stolen the betting books and looked at Batsfoam before turning toward the stairs. "No, thank you. I'm

287

not hungry, although I would like a cup of tea sent to my bedchamber. And don't forget to attend those foul books. I won't have my husband's manly instrument impugned."

She paused when the butler appeared to have swallowed something wrong, advised him to have a drink of water, then made her way upstairs. With contortions that would do an acrobat proud, she managed to disrobe herself. Clad in Dare's cherry red silk dressing gown—she preferred it over the demure blue of her own—she curled up on his newly refurbished bed with Vyvyan La Blue's book and made notes about which connubial calisthenics were most suited to pacifying a husband who was in a sulk. She was mulling over the relative merits of Upturned Flowerpot Upon an Alabaster Pillar versus Cantonese Archery when a tremendous explosion rocked the house.

The floor beneath the bed shook as if the earth itself trembled, and in the throb of noise that followed, the sharp tinkle of glass hitting the paving stones outside could be heard. Charlotte sat for a moment, dumbfounded by the shock of the explosion. Then she was on her feet, racing barefoot down the stairs, calling her husband's name, ruthlessly pushing everyone in her path out of the way. The glass in the kitchen windows was missing, wood and plaster and pieces of twisted metal everywhere. The door to the stairs leading to the sub-basement hung drunkenly on one hinge, thrown backward toward the wall.

Someone called her name, but Charlotte ignored the warning, ignored the hands that reached to stop her. Heedless to the pain inflicted on her bare feet, she kicked debris off the stairs as she struggled to make her way downward, coughing and gasping in the thick cloud of coal and dirt and steam that filled the room. Her eyes streamed and burned as she searched desperately for Dare.

"Here!" a voice croaked from behind the remains of the heavy oak table Dare used as a worktable. "Joseph! Wills! Someone bring me a litter. And tell her ladyship—"

Charlotte was there in an instant, pushing Batsfoam out of her way so she could see her husband. He was covered in blood and black coal dust, dirt everywhere, shreds of wood and paper littering his body, small pieces of metal from the exploded engine piercing his skin.

Time seemed to stop and hold its breath as she knelt at his side, aware of the debris that pressed painfully into her knees, but uncaring in the face of the nightmare staring at her. Disbelief, fear, and anger all swirled around in her as Dare's blood seeped into a pool that soaked her legs. She gently touched the bloodied mess that was the right side of his face and shoulder, horror at the damage inflicted upon him mingling with joy that his chest rose and fell, indicating that he wasn't dead, he hadn't been taken from her . . . *yet*.

Dimly she was aware of Batsfoam shouting orders as he and the footmen dragged the larger pieces of twisted metal and wood from where they surrounded Dare. She shredded her night rail to bind the worst of his wounds, walking beside him, holding his hand tightly in hers as his unconscious form was carried upstairs. All the while her mind was spinning in a confusion of answerless questions. How could anyone survive such an explosion? How could his heart continue to beat after such a horrible event? How could he endure the loss of so much blood? A sob tore from her throat as she gazed at the broken body that was laid gently on his bed.

How could she live without him?

Chapter Fifteen

His wife was the devil incarnate.

"Good morning, husband! Isn't it a lovely day?"

True, she didn't have horns or cloven hooves or smell like brimstone, but Dare was convinced she was a handmaiden of Satan, if not the Dark Master himself.

"Of course, you wouldn't know it's a lovely day outside since you sit here in the dark. I'll just open these curtains and let the sunlight in."

Who else but the devil would derive such pleasure from his pain?

"You haven't eaten your breakfast. Dare, you must eat, you can't expect to regain your health if you don't eat."

She was smiling at him, dammit, her dimples blaring away as she tried to coax him into eating. She was always coaxing him to do something or other. He didn't want to be coaxed, he wanted to be left alone. In the dark. With no bright blue eyes to remind him just how much he'd lost.

He wanted to die.

"Dare? I've made something for you."

He closed his eyes . . . eye . . . and held his breath. If he pretended he was asleep, perhaps she'd leave him be. It had worked in a past. A couple of times. Not recently, though.

"Here it is! It's a new eye patch. Do you like it?"

Air moved in front of his face as if someone swung an object before him . . . an object approximately the size and shape of an eye patch.

An eye patch he needed to cover the gaping hole in his head where his right eye had once been.

"It wasn't easy embroidering your plaid colors, but I persevered, and I think the effect is really quite stunning."

There he sat—eyeless, scarred, his right arm limp, a complete wreck of a man. Useless, that's what he was. No, worse than useless—pitiful. He was a pitiful, useless, half-man, one who had failed his wife at every possible level of husbandness.

"The sporran, I believe, adds a particularly cunning touch."

Pitiful and pathetic, a shell, a former man, now good for nothing but sitting in the dark, taking up space, eating food that should go to better, more worthy, deserving men who hadn't ruined their lives and their wives' lives . . . *sporran?*

Dare opened his eye. "You put a sporran on an eye patch?"

Charlotte knelt at his feet, one hand resting on his knee. She held a red eye patch in one hand, decorated in such a manner that it looked like a miniscule kilt, complete with sporran. She must have worked for hours over it.

"Give it to someone else," he heard himself say gruffly. "I don't deserve it."

"Don't be ridiculous. I don't know any other McGregor who needs an eye patch." Charlotte flashed those damned happy dimples at him again. Her hand tightened on his knee, sending a sudden flash of warmth up his leg, straight to his groin.

That was another way he was bound to disappoint her. She wanted children. She had enjoyed their liaisons in bed. Now she was shackled to him for life, a pitiful specimen of mankind who would never be able to fulfill even her most basic desires.

If he had any honor, he'd take a pistol to his head and end both their torments.

"Leave me," he mumbled, leaning his head back against the chair and closing his eye.

"What did you say?"

"LEAVE ME," he said more forcefully, opening his eye just long enough to glare at her.

She studied him for a moment, then leaned forward between his legs until her breasts were pressed against his groin, her fingers trailing down the grapevine of scars that marked the side of his face. "Are you in pain?"

He was surprised to note he had an erection. He assumed he wasn't capable of one any longer, but the warmth of her soft breasts pressed against him, coupled with the faint lavender scent that teased his nose and the erotic glide of her fingers down his face stirred him as nothing had in the past month since the accident.

"No pain," he answered hoarsely, hope springing to life within him. If he could bed her, at least he would be of some use. He could give her pleasure, give her children, give her something to make up for the hell he had dragged her into.

She was no longer looking at his injuries, now she was looking at his mouth with an avidity that bespoke her own awareness of him. Heat blossomed within him as he leaned forward to capture her mouth, to taste her again, to sink into the warm haven her mouth offered. He slid one arm around her waist, pulling her tight against him, while the other hand ached to cup the back of her head, tipping it backwards, leaving her lips parted, waiting to be plundered. . . .

He stared with humiliation at his right arm. It hung limply at his side, refusing his order to tangle his fingers in Charlotte's golden curls. He couldn't even lift the leaden weight of it enough to put his arm around her.

"Dare?"

He let his left arm drop from her waist, slumping back into the chair, closing his eye against the disappointment—and worse, pity—he was sure to see in her eyes.

"Dare? Is something wrong?"

What a wretched end he had come to. Despair wailed within him as he realized that even if he had been able to will his injured arm into working properly, he couldn't pleasure his wife. No woman in her right mind would want such a pathetic mockery of a man to touch her.

"Husband, I realize you are frustrated because the strength hasn't returned to your arm, but Dr. Milton did say that he believed exercising it would help you regain the muscle you lost. Would you like to do a few of the exercises now? After you're done, I would be very happy to sit on your lap and kiss you."

He was only fooling himself to think it would be otherwise. "Leave me be, Charlotte."

"But, Dare—"

"Get out, woman! Why must you always be fluttering around me? Can't you see I don't want you?"

"But I want to help—"

"All I want from you is your absence!"

His words were hurtful, intended to cause pain, spoken with cruelty since he knew that was the only way he could drive her from his side. He fully expected her to snap back at him, to hurl harsh words at his scarred face, to run sobbing from the room. What he wasn't expecting was for her to press herself against him and kiss him gently on his lips.

"I love you, Dare. I always will."

He kept his eye closed tight against the tears that rose with her words and held his breath until he heard the door close behind her. With the soft click of the lock, he released his breath and stared dully at the rug beneath his feet.

The last thing he could bear was for her to see him cry.

"I am back, Batsfoam."

"So I can see, my lady. How was Mr. Crouch?"

Charlotte unburdened herself of her spencer. "Saddened that my plan for distracting society by means of the mortal embarrassment of Lady Brindley has been permanently delayed, but he agreed that I have more important things to tend to now than worrying about what people say. The visit to Dr. Milton was less pleasant. Has my husband eaten?"

"I regret that he has not, my lady."

Charlotte paused in the act of removing her gloves, and looked closely at the butler. His habit-

ual air of misery had been missing the last four
weeks, as if tending to his wounded master had
relieved him of his own self-absorption. Batsfoam
had worked just as hard as she had to keep Dare
alive those first few weeks, spelling each other so
one could rest while the other sat with Dare and
made sure the fever that set in didn't claim his life.
It had been a long, tortuous fight, but after two
weeks they silently celebrated their victory when
Dare's fever broke and he quickly began to regain
his strength.

Until the last week, when melancholy and de-
pression set in.

"Has he left his bedchamber?"

"He went to his study."

Batsfoam's eyes were dark with apprehension.
Charlotte frowned as she pulled off the second
glove. What was in Dare's study that had Batsfoam
so concerned? Dare hadn't left his bedchamber
since he was carried upstairs, more dead than alive.
Surely the fact that he left his room to go to the
study was a good sign.

She frowned over the memory of the morning as
she headed for the stairs. He had told her he didn't
need her. He'd rejected her attentions, couldn't
even bring himself to kiss her when she pressed
against him, but she had seen the self-loathing in
his eye and knew he was wallowing in an endless
well of self-pity. The physician had told her Dare
had healed physically, but his mind was now the
cause of worry. . . . "Damnation! His pistols!"

She leaped up the stairs, her heart pounding
madly. Why hadn't she had the sense to hide his
pistols? The answer echoed in her head as she
cleared the top step and turned to race down the
long hall.

She never thought he'd be despondent enough to contemplate taking his life.

"Lady Charlotte!"

She ignored Batsfoam's cry and flung herself into the small room at the back of the house that Dare used as his study.

He sat in the darkened room before the empty grate, a bottle of whisky at his side, one of his dueling pistols lying across his knee. With a slow, ominous movement, his head turned until he was looking at her. Her breath caught at the dulled look of hopelessness in his dark blue eye. He had given up. Dr. Milton had warned her that men either fought to live, or gave up and just wasted away. Despite all her care and love, Dare had chosen the latter path.

Well, he would have to think again! Charlotte stood before her husband, her hands fisted, anger like none she'd ever known filling her at the sight of the pistol on his lap. She loved him—he couldn't just give up like that! He loved her, too. Didn't that mean he would do anything for her?

"If you kill yourself, I will *never* forgive you," she yelled. "Never, do you understand? Never! I will make your life a living hell, or just you see if I don't!"

He blinked at her, then smiled a grim sort of smile that made her hand itch to slap it off his face. But she couldn't slap him—he'd been grievously injured. A good wife didn't slap her husband when he'd suffered a most traumatic event like surviving an explosion.

"If I am dead, you can hardly make my life a living hell."

The crack of her hand meeting his cheek shocked both of them. Batsfoam, standing in the doorway, gasped in surprise before suddenly grinning as he quietly backed out of the room and closed the door. Dare stared at her, disbelief written on his face. Slowly he set the pistol on the table at his elbow and one-handedly pushed himself out of the chair.

Charlotte refused to give ground to him. She stood where she was, pressed against him, her head tilted back to give him a glare to end all glares.

"You slapped me," Dare growled.

"Yes, I did. And I enjoyed it," she answered defiantly. It was true—she had enjoyed slapping him, a fact that should have shamed her, but the sad reality was that she was fed up with his self-pity. Dr. Milton had told her that very afternoon that unless Dare stopped pitying himself, he would likely not survive another month. Considering the pistol, she doubted if he would last even that long. "Indeed, I enjoyed it so much, I think I will do it again."

The second slap brought some color to Dare's face, but best of all, it also brought a murderous glint to his eye. Charlotte could have danced a jig at the sight of that emotion—until then, only apathy and despair had been present in his lovely eye.

"I have been wounded, madam. Do you take so much pleasure in my pain that you must add to it?" Dare asked between clenched teeth.

"Well, of course I do," she answered, raising her chin another notch, secretly smiling at the look of indignation plainly visible on his handsome face. "That's why I have not left your side these last four weeks. That's why I sat up all night, every night, for two weeks while you raged with fever. That's why I bathed you, changed your bandages, took care of your personal needs, fed you, wept over you, and pleaded with you to not give up, begging you to fight the fever until you returned to me. That is why, until today when I called on the physician you refused to see, I have not stepped foot out of this house since the accident. I did all that because I take *so very much* pleasure in your pain."

He had the grace to look ashamed, but it wasn't enough. The time had clearly come for him to make the decision, and by God, if he didn't make the right one, she'd make it for him.

"I will not go through the nightmare of having to pick out and train another husband," she told him, poking him in the chest as she did so.

"Train?" he snarled. "Do you liken me to an animal that must be trained to be made habitable?"

"I liken you to a man who is extremely pigheaded and obstinate, and hasn't a clue about what really matters in life. Until you realize just how blessed you are to have me as your wife—"

"I do realize how blessed I am . . . was," he shouted back at her, his face flushed with anger. "You are the loveliest, most amazing woman I know, dammit! I love you!"

"Then you had better start acting like it!" she said in a volume that a less-refined person might label as yelling.

"God damn you, woman, how can I? I'm crippled! Near blind! I'm worthless in every bloody respect! I have no money, no title, no social standing left to me, and now the last thing I had—a body worthy of worshipping you—has been destroyed. The only way I can show you I love you is to rid the earth of my pitiable presence and leave you free to marry a man who can give you what I can't."

She slapped him again, not very hard, but hard enough that he tensed his jaw, narrowed his eye, and grabbed at her wrist to keep her from repeating the action. She had to admit she greatly enjoyed shocking him out of his attack of self-pity. "How dare you! How dare you insinuate that the only reason I married you was for your money or title or social standing or your handsome face!"

He leaned forward until his hot breath fanned her face. "Can you honestly say you didn't marry me for those things?"

"No, of course I can't! What woman in my position wouldn't marry for money or title or handsome looks?"

A familiar look of resigned confusion came over his face as he released her wrist to rub his forehead. "You're saying you did marry me for the very same things I can no longer give you, and yet you're offended when I point that out?"

She peeled off his somber black eye patch and moved around behind him to tie on the new kilted one. "Red looks very good on you. I'm not offended that you know why I married you; I'm offended that you think those things still matter to me. Once I managed the feat of falling in love with you—no easy task, considering your temperament—everything changed. A woman in love doesn't care about money or looks."

She returned to his front, trailing her fingers down his lifeless arm until she caught his fingers in hers, bringing their joined hands to her mouth. She kissed each of his fingers.

"And does a woman in love not care about standing or titles?"

"Titles, no," she answered with dimples flying. "Standing . . . well, women in love reserve the right to retain their standing so as to better further their husband's successes. I really do think I've had as much of your self-pity as I can stand, Alasdair. Therefore, I will take Dr. Milton's advice and give you an intermatum: You will decide right here and now that you wish to continue living. You will realize that despite the loss of your eye and diminished strength of your arm, you are still a vital, important man. You will remember that you swore before God to cherish and honor me, and you can't possibly do that if you are dead or moping around in darkened rooms. I very much deserve to be cherished and honored. For that reason, you will kiss me and hug me and touch me in those womanly parts that tingle when you are near, and then you will bed me. Every night. Possibly two times a night once you regain your stamina. In short, husband mine, you will return to the Dare I knew and loved, and you will do so this very minute!"

Dare looked as if he wanted to smile, but was afraid to. Slowly the fire died out in his eye as he reached up to rub his thumb against her shoulder. "The word is *ultimatum*, not intermatum."

"I know," she said softly, allowing her eyes to fill with all the love she felt for him. "I just liked the sound of intermatum better. It's more forceful."

His lips twitched. "My beautiful wife. My beautiful Charlotte who deserves better."

"Yes, I do," she agreed, rubbing her cheek against the back of his hand. "I deserve a husband who is not a coward, a husband who doesn't know the meaning of surrender. I deserve a husband who loves me enough to fight for me."

"You deserve a husband who can give you want you want," Dare said softly, his shoulders slumping as his hand dropped from her shoulder. "What have I to offer you? I'm penniless, crippled and half blind. My title is in question, and our one means of salvation lies in a heap of twisted metal. You deserve far more than what I can offer you, Charlotte."

She refused to let him back away, wrapping both her arms around his waist, rubbing his nose with hers. "You told me once that appearance wasn't everything; I'm telling you the same now. Crippled and half blind you may be, but you're still *you,* and that's all that matters. And as for the other things . . . you'll have more money than I'll possibly be able to spend once you sell your engine. Your title might be lost—although Crouch is working diligently on the matter—but you still have standing in the *ton.* You might have lost one eye, but you have another, and Dr. Milton is convinced that you'll regain at least some use in your right arm if you set your mind to it. And as for your engine, I have every confidence that if you dedicate yourself to it, you could have it ready in time for the scientific exhibition."

He was shaking his head even before she stopped speaking. "There's only two weeks left. I couldn't rebuild the engine in that time."

She brushed her lips against his, smiling at the flicker of passion in his eye. "We'll all help. Batsfoam examined the engine and said he believed all that would need replacing was the boiler. You have a little more than two weeks—can you build a boiler in that time?"

Dare frowned, an act that made Charlotte want to cheer. He was thinking about it. She could see him working mental calculations regarding what would need to be done to have the engine ready.

"It would only take me a few days to rebuild the boiler, but that's not the problem. Obviously my design was flawed, or else it wouldn't have exploded under the pressure of a half-filled boiler."

"Then you will simply have to design a new one," she said helpfully, and kissed him again, this time her lips lingering on his mouth, her breath mingling with his.

"I can't—" he started to say, one arm snaking around her waist to pull her even closer. She rubbed against him, almost purring with the feeling of the hard, muscled planes of his chest and thighs.

"You can do anything you want," she answered, sucking his lower lip into her mouth. He groaned and pulled her tighter, grinding his hips against hers. "I believe in you, Dare. I believe you can succeed. I would never have married a man who couldn't keep me as I deserve to be kept."

"Little witch," he murmured against her lips. Her hands were busy until she had the buttons of his shirt free, sliding her fingers along the smooth, muscled planes of his back, along to the pleasing contours of his chest. Even after a month of illness and inactivity, his body was still hard with muscle and sinew. "If you think you can goad me into doing what you want—"

"Never," she breathed, nipping at his lips, wordlessly begging him to take charge. When he didn't, she murmured, "I do not goad. Seducing, however, is another matter. . . ."

Since he still wasn't kissing her the way she wanted to be kissed, she decided to take matters in her own hands—so to speak. She demanded entrance to the warm lure of his mouth, and when it was given, she ruthlessly invaded—tasting him, teasing him, stirring the embers of passion that burned between them.

With a groan, he succumbed to the fire, his mouth moving over hers with increased heat, his tongue doing all those amazing tongue things she previously believed she would never find the least bit interesting (but was happy to be proven wrong), his body pressed hard against hers, moving with a seductive slowness that threatened to drain all reason from her mind. His hand was everywhere, fingers one moment tugging her head back to angle her mouth for deeper penetration; the next they were skimming along the tapes at the back of her gown, tugging down the fine lawn until his fingers met her bared flesh. In the passion-fogged depths of her mind she remembered a scene from the past, and broke away long enough to push him backward, into the wine-colored armchair. She followed, pulling up her gown so she could kneel astride his thighs.

"Char, I can't—"

"Don't you remember?" she cooed, her hands working feverishly to free him from the confines of his shirt. "You promised to show me how to conduct a ravishment in a chair. I'm still curious as to the exact logistics of it all—assuming I'm correct in believing your erected instrument will function upside down, not that I've had any experience with upside-down instruments, you understand, but since your instrument appears to be straining your breech buttons, I gather you are pleased with the thought of being ravished in this chair. Therefore, I have faith that you'll make a most satisfying explanation of where the legs and such go."

Dare kissed the wits—those remaining—right out of her head before pulling his lips from hers and kissing a hot trail down her neck. "I can't do this, wife. I can't . . . I don't know that I can . . . you can't want . . ."

"Oh, but I do," she corrected, nipping his jaw as her fingers fumbled with the tightly strained cloth at his groin. "You cannot possibly imagine how much I want you, Dare."

"You deserve better than a half-man with a scarred face and a useless arm," he groaned into her bare shoulder as she released the last button on his breeches, pushing aside the material to take his hardness into her hands.

"I deserve you." She smiled, then gently removed his eye patch. He moved then, tried to stop her, his face twisted with anguish as the fingers of his good hand dug into her wrist. "Men! I'll never understand you. Such a fuss over a few scars."

His jaw tightened as she kissed the line of damaged skin that ran down the side of his face, moving upward until she reached his closed eyelid.

"No."

The word was spoken on a half-sob, only one word, but so filled with pain that it brought tears to her eyes. Tenderly she pressed a kiss to the slack eyelid. How could he imagine that something so inconsequential as the loss of an eye could diminish her love for him? "Yes. Until you realize that your injuries don't matter to me, yes." She kissed his eyelid again, and once again until he turned his head so he could look at her.

His eye was burning bright with the fever of desire, glittering with love and passion, but tinged with wariness, as if bracing himself for a blow. She smiled, and kissed the eyelid over his whole eye as well. *"From their eyelids as they glanced dripped love,"* she quoted.

Dare opened his eye, puzzled. She smiled. "That is from one of those musty Greek men Papa was forever fussing over. I don't remember which one . . . Iliad, I think his name was . . . but I do remember Papa reading him aloud to us. Mr. Iliad wasn't very interesting until he started talking about pouring sweet dew on tongues."

305

His lips curled ever so slightly. "I believe the gentleman in question was Hesiod, not Homer."

She leaned forward against him, pinning the rampant parts of him between them, cupping his face in her hands. "Does it really matter who said it?" she asked between little kisses to his cheeks and jaw. "Does anything matter but the fact that you're my husband, and I love you, and I want you to show me how the armchair ravishment you so temptingly teased me with a few months ago is managed?"

Dare fought within himself for a moment. The sober part of him, the part that knew he wasn't worthy of her, the part that counseled taking the coward's way out of his misery as the only possible way to free her, urged him to push her from his lap and retreat. Retreat to his bedchamber, to the darkness that hid his scars, even the ones that lay beneath his skin. But the warmth of his wife, the pressure of her against him, the love glowing from her clear blue eyes filled him with an emotion so strong it cut his despair to shreds. He knew he should force her away, but he was too weak to refuse the haven she offered.

She murmured his name as he fought with her gown until her breasts—those glorious breasts— were released, framed so charmingly in the green and cream of her gown and the lacy froth of her chemise. He cupped one breast in his hand, gently rubbing the pad of his thumb over her nipple until she groaned and arched her back. He swore silently as he gritted his teeth and tried to make his right arm respond to the need to touch her, startled when she took his limp hand and held it to her breast.

"Like the costliest silk," he murmured as he stroked her breasts, an amazing heat tingling its way down his fingers to burn strongly in his chest. His hand slipped out from under hers, but by locking every muscle he had, he managed to stop his arm as his palm rested against the swell of her hips, warm even through the fabric pooled around her.

"Do you know, I was going to say the very same thing about you," she answered, using both hands to caress the heated length of him. "Your manly instrument is so hard, and yet at the same time, your skin is so soft. It truly is an amazing instrument, isn't it? I mean, when it's quiescent, it's not much to look at. I would almost say it's comical when it just flops around and lies limply. But then when you make it like this, it's quite awe inspiring. How exactly do you do this, Dare? Did it take long to learn? Did you have to take lessons? I've seen animals, of course, but men are beyond the level of animals, so I cannot help but wonder how the erection business comes about."

Dare withstood her touch—which continued to explore his nether regions the whole while she was talking—as long as he could. He gritted his teeth. He tensed his jaw. He tightened his fingers into her gown. He thought briefly of anything that would take his mind off the fire she was building with every stroke of her fingers, but he knew he wouldn't last much longer if she continued to touch him.

"Charlotte," he said as sternly as a man who was on the verge of sexual ecstasy could, "if you don't mind, we will save the lecture on male physiology for another time."

She leaned forward until her soft breasts were pressed against his chest. "Do you promise?" she asked, nipping at his lips until he wrapped his hand in her hair and plundered her mouth. She was so good, he had to plunder her a second time, and only the fact that she was squirming restlessly against his hardness kept him from spending long hours paying homage to the wonders of her mouth.

"I always keep my promises," he murmured against her breast, just before his mouth closed over the delicate little morsel that beckoned him. He teased and nibbled the first nipple, her moans of pleasure filling his ears even as her fingers dug into the muscles of his shoulders. Then he turned his attention to the second breast, licking and suckling her until her breath was as wild as his. He untangled his fingers from her curls, enjoying her little shiver of delight as he stroked a path down her spine, sweeping his hand over her hip to tease the part of her he knew was aching for him.

"You'll have to excuse my personal parts," she gasped as he cupped her mound of Venus. "They're a bit moist. They seem to do that quite a bit around you. I was worried about it at first, but then I remembered how you touched me there on our wedding night, and you seemed to find the moistness a desired state, so I stopped worrying. Unless you don't like me being moist, and if you do, I'm afraid you're just going to have to—"

"You are babbling, wife," he said, groaning with delight as she sucked his tongue into her mouth. Flames of desire mingled with love, his need for her bound tightly to the joy that came with the knowledge that she was his, now, tonight, forever.

With one hand he lifted her as he slid forward into the chair, murmuring instructions in her ear as she reached between them to guide him into her silken depths, waves of pleasure rippling throughout his body as she sank slowly down upon him. A fierce sense of possession gripped him as he showed her how to move on him. She was his wife, his Charlotte, his brilliant, passionate goddess whose love healed him despite his desire to be left to die.

He had thought her the devil incarnate? Dare tore his lips from the soft curve of her throat and watched as she arched her back, her eyes wide with amazement as ecstasy claimed her, her song of rapture filling him, binding him to her until he couldn't tell where she ended and he began. Her love swept over him in a wave of heat so strong, it burned her name from his tongue as he gave way before it, pouring his life into her.

Soft, meaningless words were pressed into his flesh with gentle kisses and sweet breath. She wasn't a devil; she was an angel.

And he would never let her go.

Chapter Sixteen

Charlotte rested comfortably on her husband, her legs still locked around him, his breath slowing now, but still sounding a bit raspy in her ear. She shifted slightly, smiling into his neck at the feeling of his heart beating strongly against her. Who would have thought that such an intimate thing as his heartbeat in her womanly depths could bring such pleasure, such a sense of contentment that, she truthfully admitted, had less to do with the actual act than the fact that he shouted his love for her at his moment of climax.

She sighed, pleased that her seduction worked, happy to see something other than self-absorption filling his eye.

His arm tightened around her as she moved again. "I'd like to, love, but you're going to have to give me a little time. I'm not the man I used to be."

She giggled as she realized what he was talking about, then stopped, appalled that she had lost control of herself enough to be giggling. She never giggled; she made it a matter of pride that she was not a giggler. "Lord, I'm silly today," she mused, wiggling again on him. Deep within her, he twitched. She hummed with pleasure. He groaned as she circled her hips on him, another giggle building as the noise of their joining was clearly evident.

"I seem to be a bit more than moist now." She dimpled. Dare gave her a shocked look for a moment, then slowly, very slowly, his lips curved into a smile that deepened into a wicked grin.

"You, madam wife, are incorrigible."

"I know. But you love that about me," she answered with perfect composure, or as perfect a composure one could maintain while sitting impaled on one's husband's erected instrument. "Does this mean you've recovered? Are you going to stop moping around and get back to work on your engine?"

The dark glint of passion that had been building in his eye dimmed noticeably. With a bleak set to his lips, he gently pushed her off his instrument, helping her to her feet before setting himself to rights.

Charlotte took that as a sign that all was not yet well. She sighed as she tugged her gown back into place.

"Life, my sweet wife, is never as easy as it seems."

She frowned as he turned his back to her, staring out the window at the busy street beyond. "Is that a quotation, or are you simply making an observation?"

He shrugged, but did not answer.

Charlotte saw red for a moment. A long moment,

very long, long enough to relive the wonder of their joining, the fulfillment she found in his love, the joy that blossomed when she considered their future, but then the fury inside her turned to icy determination. "I have just spent the most marvelous half hour in your arms. We shared something rare and wonderful and important. I am willing to do whatever it takes to make you understand that my feelings for you have not changed since the accident, but now you are closing me out again so you can continue your destructive walk down the path of self-pity and misery." She picked up the pistol he had set on the small table. "So be it. If you're so desirous of obsidian, I'll give it to you."

Dare turned to find himself looking down the long barrel of his dueling pistol.

"I believe the word you are looking for is *oblivion*."

"I know what obsidian means," Charlotte snapped, using both hands to cock the hammer on the pistol. "And I assure you, if opaque, black nothingness is what you desire, you shall have it. Unless you agree, this minute, to stop pouting, I shall shoot you."

"I am not pouting. Dear God, woman, look at me, just look at me! I've lost my eye, the use of my arm, and my entire hope of saving us from the poorhouse. Is it pouting to grieve for the costly mistake I made? Is it pouting to know that I can never be what I was? Is it pouting to know that I've ruined not only my life, but yours as well? I'm not pouting, I'm mourning the loss of my manhood. How can I give you what you want, what you deserve, while I am in this pathetic state?"

"You can and you will, if you just stop pitying yourself and think about me for a change. Honestly,

Dare, any other husband in the world would be falling all over himself to please me, and yet you make love to me with such beauty one moment, then turn away from me the next as if I had an unsightly spot right in the middle of my forehead. I won't have it, do you understand? I simply won't have it. If you would rather die than live happily with me, so be it. I shall shoot you."

"You won't shoot me," he said with a martyred sigh, taking a step toward her. "You said yourself you love me. You can't shoot me if you love me."

"I shall. I'm quite serious in this, Dare. Look at my eyebrows. Do you see my frown? Frowning causes wrinkles; I don't undertake frowning lightly. That should be of some indication to you just how serious I am."

"You won't shoot me," he repeated, taking another step forward and holding out his hand for the pistol. "I'm not worth the trouble it would take to shoot me."

"Pheasant feathers!" Charlotte snapped in frustration, her fingers inadvertently tightening around the trigger. The pistol bucked painfully in her hands, the sound of the explosion reverberating around the room in a manner that left her ears ringing. She coughed the taste of powder out of her mouth and stared with horror at her husband.

"You *did* shoot me," he exclaimed, his voice full of amazement as he stared down at his leg. He touched his breeches, lifting his hand to show her the smear of red on his fingers. "By Christ, you shot me!"

"You wanted to be shot," Charlotte answered even as she dropped the pistol and threw herself at his feet.

"Not in the leg," Dare argued. "No one wants to

be shot in the leg, it's unmanly. A shot through the temple, now, that's suitable. But not in the leg, Charlotte, never in the leg. Ow! That hurts!"

"If you would stop squirming I could get a better look . . . oh, Batsfoam, there's been a little accident—"

"You shot me! Intentionally!"

"A little accident," Charlotte repeated with emphasis as she tore at the bloody hole in the outer side of Dare's breeches. There wasn't much blood, which, combined with the fact that Dare was still standing, gave her hope that she hadn't wounded him too grievously. "I didn't actually intend to fire the pistol."

"She told me she was going to shoot me," Dare said to Batsfoam. "She stood right there and warned me she was going to shoot me. Then she did. What sort of a wife shoots her crippled husband in cold blood?"

"One who is tired of his never-ending gloom and fitful depressions?" Batsfoam stared for a moment at Dare's kilted eye patch, then bent over to examine the exposed flesh.

"That's rich coming from you," Dare said testily. "Ow! Charlotte!"

"Rip that little bit of material away . . . there. It doesn't look too bad, does it, Batsfoam?"

Batsfoam pulled out a less than pristine handkerchief and dabbed at the blood welling from a small wound on the outer edge of Dare's thigh. "It does not, ma'am. I would say your shot went a bit wide. It looks as if the ball barely scratched the skin."

"She shot me!"

"Oh, stop being such a big baby."

"She shot me with my own pistol!"

314

"*Barely* shot you. I *barely* shot you with your own pistol. It is such a small wound, it's almost not there, isn't it, Batsfoam?"

"Indeed, ma'am, I would dare to say—"

"There, you see? Batsfoam agrees with me. It's almost an nonshot. Now, if you will sit down, I'll clean your almost nonwound and you can toddle off to your workroom and see what is what with your machine."

"Engine," Dare said in a decidedly surly tone as Batsfoam helped him to the chair. Charlotte relaxed. If he was making such a fuss over a little thing like being shot in the leg, he must be on the road to recovery. He hadn't so much as mumbled one word of complaint the entire time he was recovering from his other, much more grievous injuries.

"I shall want water and clean bandages and that tincture that worked so well on Alasdair's face." Charlotte considered her husband carefully. "And brandy, Batsfoam. He looks a bit shaken; I think his lordship would benefit from a stimulant."

By the time she had his leg cleaned, anointed, and bandaged and Batsfoam had assisted him into a fresh pair of breeches, Dare was arguing virulently with her. She delighted in every frown and glare, often rewarding his temper—sadly missing these last four weeks—with adoring gazes and light kisses, not to mention loving pinches on an area of his anatomy not visible when sitting.

"I won't forget this, wife, not for a very long time," he warned as he hobbled down the stairs toward the sub-regions of the house. "Possibly never."

"Good. Perhaps then you'll think twice about ever desiring to take your own life."

Dare glanced over at her, limping heavier than

was necessary. To tell the truth, he hardly felt the slight injury, but the shock that his wife, his Charlotte, had shot him—actually held his pistol on him and shot him!—put him in a petulant mood. She wasn't even looking the slightest bit sorry for her horrible deed. Oh no! She bestowed sweet smiles and sweeter kisses on him, caressing him and sending him little adoring messages with her lovely blue eyes until he wanted nothing so much as to pick her up and carry her off to his bedchamber where he could make long, slow love to her for the next few hours. Or days. Years had a nice ring to it, too.

"You know, that limp is really rather romantic," she whispered boldly in his ear as he held the door to the kitchen open for her. Her fingers trailed across the slack fingers of his bad arm as she entered the kitchen, an unmistakable look of passion in her eyes.

Dare sighed as he followed his wife down the last flight of stairs to the remains of his workroom. He wanted to wrap the chilly cloak of martyrdom around him again, blaming her lack of concern about wounding him, but he was a truthful man if nothing else, and so he admitted to himself that the fact that she had so brazenly shot him made him realize just how much she loved him.

And how much he stood to lose without her.

"Well? What do you think? Can you do it?" Charlotte stood aside and waved toward the remains of his engine.

Dare looked around the room, noting absently that someone had been in and cleaned up evidence of the explosion. The destroyed parts of the boiler were stacked tidily in one corner, the sturdy oak table that Charlotte had told him saved his life had been sanded and put back in its usual spot. He avoided looking at the engine itself, dreading the moment when he had to admit his dream was over, his hopes and plans for the future destroyed with one careless miscalculation. But eventually, there was nothing else to look at but Charlotte's hopeful face.

"Well?" she asked again.

He looked at the engine at last, slowly circling it, taking in the damage. There was surprisingly little to the body of the engine—his design had proven well in that respect, at least.

"Can you fix it? How long will it take? We'll all help, Batsfoam and all the staff and myself, so you needn't feel as if you are doing this by yourself. There's ten days before the scientific exhibition. With all our help, I'm quite confident you'll have the engine running spectacularly."

He caught the note of pride in her voice even as he leaned closer to examine a set of delicate valves. They moved a bit stiffly, but it was nothing that a good oiling wouldn't fix. He had a spare boiler— built while he was still making modifications to the design—so if just the boiler needed to be replaced, if nothing else was actually damaged, it might be feasible to get the engine back in working order before the exhibition. He did a few mental calculations, stepping back and absentmindedly removing his cufflink and rolling up the shirtsleeve on his bad arm, grimacing as Charlotte stepped forward to help him with the sleeve on his working arm.

"You're going to do it, aren't you?" she asked, her voice as soft as the caress she pressed to his cheek. He stopped eyeing the engine long enough to glance down at her. Her eyes were shining beacons of hope, pride, and love.

317

"I haven't a widgeon's chance in hell of getting it done on time," he warned her.

She dimpled at him. "You'll do it."

"It will take me time to work out what was the flaw with the boiler and design a new one, not to mention converting the spare to reflect those changes."

"A man of your intelligence? Pooh! I'll wager you already know what went wrong, and how to correct it."

His lips quirked at her words. She was right, and they both knew it.

"I'll have to work day and night on this. I won't have time to squire you around anywhere."

Charlotte's gaze dropped as she neatly undid the line of buttons on his waistcoat, helping him out of it so he was in his familiar work clothes of shirt and breeches. "That shan't be a problem, I assure you. In fact, I will give up all events so that I might stay home and be of assistance to you."

A refusal of her services was on his lips, but one look at her glowing eyes filled with happiness kept him from speaking. He had heard the note of pride in her voice when she informed him that she and the servants would all help him; he could no more dash that adoring look in her eyes than he could have shot himself.

That act he left to his wife.

"Your help will be appreciated," he said gravely, unable to keep from kissing the tip of her adorable nose before turning back to the engine. He'd just have to find her something harmless to do, something that would fulfill her need to help him and yet keep her from destroying anything—or worse, being destroyed herself should something again go drastically wrong.

"Nothing will go wrong this time," she said, apparently reading his mind. "Now that you know where the flaw in the design was, you can eliminate it."

"Mmm . . ." he agreed, reaching for a tool to tighten a bolt in the piston housing that had been loosened in the explosion. His mind was already filled with what needed to be done, and he was swiftly calculating how to correct for the overflow of water in the boiler when he heard the sounds of the door opening. He glanced up and smiled.

"Charlotte?"

She paused as she stepped through the doorway.

"Thank you."

Her head tipped to the side as she considered him. "For shooting you?"

He grinned. "For showing me just what I'd be missing if you weren't my wife."

"Oh, that," she said loftily, her chin raised as she sailed through the doorway. "I would have thought by now you'd realize you couldn't live without me!"

"What news do you have, Crouch?" Charlotte seated herself in Gillian's sitting room and looked expectantly at the butler standing before her. She waved him toward a blue and gold chair, which he took with obvious reluctance, easing his large frame into the small chair with an expression that showed he expected to crush the elegant piece of furniture into a pulp. Charlotte knew better. Her cousin, with an eye to the Black Earl's equally large size, had all the chairs in the house reinforced so that even those that looked delicate would hold an ox if they were so required.

Crouch rubbed the side of his nose with his hook. "It's not much news I 'ave to tell ye, m'lady. I sent the boys after the truth about Lord Carlisle—'im that's callin' 'imself Lord Carlisle—and so far they've only verified that 'e did come in on the *Mary Rose*, as 'e said."

Charlotte frowned. "That's all you've been able to find out in a month? That the Pretender was on a ship?"

"It's not easy trackin' down a crew that's been given a three-week leave, m'lady. I 'ad to send Thomas and Charles into the country to talk to the boatswain, and 'ire a couple of Runners to hunt down the other crew. I talked to the captain meself, but all 'e'd tell me was that McGregor joined 'is crew in Shanghai, tellin' some story about being kidnapped and left there, and that while 'e was obviously a gent, 'e knew 'is way around a ship all right and tight."

"That tells me nothing other than part of his fable—about having worked on merchant ships—is correct. It gives me no proof whatsoever as to his false claim against Alasdair's title. That is what I expect you to provide, Crouch!"

"I'm investigatin' the gent as best I can, Lady Charlotte. 'E's not been forthcomin' about showin' me proof of 'is ancestry—'e says 'e gave that to 'is solicitor and I 'ad no right askin' to see it."

"Ha! A convenient excuse, I call that." Charlotte tapped her fingers on the small table near her as she worried over what to do next. "I'm very disappointed in your investigation, Crouch, I don't mind telling you that. Very disappointed. I had counted on you to clear the matter up before his lordship regained his health, and now here it is four weeks later and what do I have to tell my husband but that his faux cousin apparently had served on a ship from England to China and back. I need not point out that many men have done such, and none of them are claiming to be Dare's missing cousin."

"No m'lady," Crouch said with humility that was only slightly ruined by the twitching of the scar that ran down one cheek to the edge of his mouth. " 'Is lordship's solicitor 'asn't any word?"

Her finger tapping began to take on a drumming quality. She frowned all sorts of wrinkle-inducing frowns whenever she thought of what Dare's less-than-useless legal representatives had said in their latest missive. "Nothing I wish to hear. He says the Pretender has proof of his claim, but he has yet to verify the details. Verify!" Charlotte snorted the last word as she snatched up one of Gillian's fans and fanned herself with vigor. "His solicitor isn't even trying to disprove the Pretender's claim; he's too busy trying to verify it. That's why I hired you, Crouch. To do what the solicitors wouldn't!"

"And I told ye I'd only take on the job if I was to find the truth, not fit the facts to suit ye."

"Oh, balderdash! I am quite confident that the truth and what I want to hear are the same thing. Only those fools Dunbridge and Storm don't have the wits to look beyond the obvious, and if there's anything my husband has taught me, Crouch, it's that beauty is on the thin sheep."

Crouch blinked at her as if she had suddenly sprouted wings and a halo. "M'lady?"

"Beauty is on the thin sheep. It means that you must dig deep to find anything but the superficial. It is a famous saying, from a famous poem, I believe. Papa read it to me once many years ago. I particularly remember him telling me it was a point I should remember, although I have never found thin sheep particularly attractive. I prefer the fat ones,

321

but I suppose 'beauty is on the fat sheep' doesn't quite have the same ring, does it?"

Crouch continued to blink at her for a moment. His scar twitched twice as he cleared his throat. "Erm . . . as to the other, m'lady, there is something . . ."

Charlotte stopped drumming her fingers, and with much gentility raised an inquiring eyebrow. "Something? Something that will prove the Pretender is a nefarious ne'er-do-well intent on lining his pockets with my Dare's inheritance, not to mention his title? Something to squelch his pretensions and evil plans once and all? Something I can present to those fools Dunbridge and Storm, and they can use to make him the laughingstock of the *ton*?"

"That's fer ye to decide. I've 'ad a man sniffin' around and 'e tells me that 'is lordship—'is pretend lordship, that is—is on 'is uppers."

"Uppers?"

Crouch nodded. "Word is that 'e's up to 'is blow-piece in vowels, all on expectation of receivin' 'is title and inheritance. 'Asn't a shillin' to bless 'imself, is what I 'ear."

"The bounder! No doubt once we prove he's nothing but a sham he'll try to foist his debts on us, saying it's all our fault things didn't work out for him. Men of his ilk have no shame."

"Seems to me a man that deep in debt would do anythin' for a few groats to rub together," Crouch said wisely.

Charlotte immediately took his meaning. "You mean it might be possible to bribe him into dropping his ridiculous claim?"

Crouch shrugged. "Might be worth the try."

"Hmmm. It is a good thought, but unfortunately, our present circumstances don't run to a blackmail fund, so we'll have to think of an alternative. In the meantime, I wanted to discuss a different matter with you—I take it Lord Wessex has you and the rest of the servants here on board wages?"

If Crouch looked surprised at the change in conversation, he didn't show it. "Aye, m'lady."

"Good, that means you're not doing anything important. I'd like you and every available servant to come to my house every morning. You may sleep here, of course, and I'm sure Lord Wessex wouldn't begrudge you the use of his carriage and horses while he's gone, especially since they would be used in my behalf. I shall expect you all promptly at sunup. Report to Batsfoam; he will tell you what duties everyone is to assume."

"Duties?"

"Duties. I've promised his lordship as much help as he needs with his engine, thus we must have more help to do the servants' work. You and the servants here can fill in as needed. The balance of your wages will be paid, of course. Gillian will no doubt wish to give me a wedding present—I shall simply inform her that your wages are to be that present."

"Yer all kindness," Crouch said with only minor scar twitching.

"Did you ever doubt it?" Charlotte ask as she drew on her gloves and prepared to depart.

"No, can't say as I 'ave. About the inquiry in Scotland—I take it ye'll be wantin' it to continue on, then?"

"Yes, definitely. I'm quite certain that investigation there will turn up the proof we need to show that the Pretender is not who he says he is. Tell your man there to continue until he has the proof I need."

"Aye. Is there anythin' else ye'll be wantin' me to do?"

Charlotte allowed Crouch to open the sitting room door for her. "No, I don't think so. Just be sure you and the men are at our house by sunup."

"Aye, m'lady."

She headed down the stairs, mentally drawing up a list of tasks to be accomplished before the day was finished: There was a very stern letter to be written to Dunbridge and Storm informing them that their services would no longer be required if they couldn't remember just who employed them, there was Caroline to visit and catch up with all the latest gossip, and most importantly, she needed to find time to sit down with some of Dare's books to study up on his engine.

"Oh," she said as she was about to mount the steps to the carriage. She turned back to Crouch, waiting politely on the pavement, his hook glinting wickedly in the sunlight. "There is one other thing—have you or any of the other servants any experience in marine engine design or construction?"

He seemed to choke on something—a molecule of air, no doubt, her cousin Gillian did that all the time—before he replied. "I'm sorry to be disappointin' ye, but none of the lads 'as that, m'lady."

"Pity," Charlotte said as she stepped into the carriage, and instructed the coachman to take her to Caro's house.

A tall, plump woman with graying hair stood presenting something green to Caroline. As Charlotte was announced, the woman whisked whatever it was into her skirts and made a hasty, red-faced exit.

"Has it come to this, Caro? Giggling in your sitting

room with Cook?" she asked as she nudged Wellington aside and claimed his seat.

"Oh, no! That is . . . it's just . . . there was . . . and it was . . . and she thought I'd want to see . . . oh, my!" Caroline dissolved into teary-eyed whoops of laughter as Charlotte adjusted her skirts. Wellington the pug wiggled happily at her, and after rubbing his squashed-in little face against her ankle, she relented and scratched him behind his stubby little ears until he collapsed with a sigh of pleasure, resting his chin on her foot as he drifted into a loud sleep.

"Are you going to tell me, or just sit there stuttering and turning fifteen shades of red?" Charlotte asked, eyeing her friend with lips pursed in the manner of an elderly spinster aunt whom she once shocked by asking whether it was true that babies came from a giant pumpkin patch.

"A dinky," Caroline gasped, mopping at her eyes with her lace-edged handkerchief. "Mrs. Robbins had a cucumber shaped just like a dinky. It really was most life . . . life . . . lifelike."

Charlotte watched as her friend dissolved into a paroxysm of laughter, well aware that there really was no one else she could call friend, and thus she had to wait out Caroline's cucumbral episode. She'd give Caro thirty seconds to snap out of it; then she'd take steps to sober her friend up. Water dashed in the face, she believed, had long been a solution to calming a hysterical woman.

Luckily for Caroline, such a drastic step was not needed. Under Charlotte's gimlet eye, she regained control over herself, with only occasional snickers and odd little snorts that required a quick dab of the handkerchief to the eye.

"At last! Honestly, Caro, I'd lecture you on the

ridiculousness of your action, but I suspect if I were to mention *cucumber* again, you'd be off in another bout of ninnified giggles."

The hated "ninny" word had the effect she anticipated it would. Caroline sat up straight in her chair and glared at her friend. "I am *not* a ninny!"

There were many ways Charlotte could answer such a statement; surprisingly enough, wisdom gained over the last few months guided her to taking the path that would cause the least offense. "No, you're not. You're a very dear girl who just has a silly side that in any other circumstances I'd appreciate more fully, not to mention be likely to join, but unfortunately, today I am not in a silly mood."

Caroline sobered immediately under both the unexpected kindness of Charlotte's statement, and the implication of her words. "What's wrong? Is Mr. McGregor worse?"

"Quite the opposite. When I left home, he was at work on his engine with Batsfoam, Wills, Cook, and the two footmen in attendance. He seems to have regained his will to live, for which I am profoundly thankful."

"Then why are you not in the mood to be silly? I've known you since we were little girls, Char, and you're always in a mood to be silly, whether you admit it or not. For you to be so serious indicates something most horrid is afoot, and yet you tell me your husband has regained his senses. . . . I'm confused!"

Charlotte gave in to the pout that had been hovering over her lips, dismissing the knowledge that pouting encouraged spots. If anyone deserved a good pout, it was her. "It's this tedious business with the Pretender. I had hoped it would all be cleared up by the time Dare was up and working again, but it hasn't. His solicitors are positively useless—I swear they're in the pay of the Pretender—and even Crouch has been unable to prove that the man is not who he claims he is. No one but I seems to realize just how important it is that the matter be cleared up. Without Dare's title, all his potential investors—his peers—will wish to have nothing to do with him. Mr. McGregor of Cairn Isle off the coast of Scotland may be a gentleman, but he does not carry the clout or importance that the Earl of Carlisle must surely command."

"Oh, pish," Caro said, her concerned frown easing. "Your husband will remain the same man whether or not he has a title."

"Well of course he will! That Dare will continue to be a most remarkable, exceptional man no matter what his station is not in question; the point is that Society is notoriously fickle, and you know well how easily they can shun someone on the slightest triviality. I am living proof of that."

"You eloped most scandalously, Char," Caroline gently reminded her.

Charlotte stood and worried the curtain cord as she gazed out the window at the busy street below. "But my husband will not elope most scandalously, nor will he have done anything to justify being made a mariah if the Pretender has his way."

"Pariah."

"That, too. You see my worry, Caro—I am helpless to do anything to help Dare with the one facet of life I have expertise in: Society." The glass felt cool against her brow, soothing somehow. Charlotte was suddenly overwhelmed with the urge to curl up into a little ball and let the world go on its way without her. She had never been one to back down from a challenge, but for the first time in her life she wondered if it was worthwhile to keep fighting.

"What does it bring you but more heartache?" she murmured.

"What brings heartache?"

"Life," Charlotte replied, closing her eyes and giving in to the pain that filled her. "It seems like all I've done lately is fight for what I want, but for what purpose? I fought to come back to England and ended up penniless and unwanted by my own family. I fought to marry Dare and ended up a burden around his neck, driving him deeper into despair with his worry about my life with him. I fought to show him that I would stand by him, that I love him no matter what happens, and yet everything positive in my life—Dare being the exception—everything I've fought for has been stripped from me."

"Char, I don't know what to say. If you need money—"

Charlotte smiled without the least sign of dimples. "That's kind of you, but it isn't necessary. Lack of money isn't the problem, not the true problem."

"Then what is?"

She sighed and sat down on the settee again, wondering how to express the feelings that had been growing steadily ever since she'd seen Dare. She knew full well that no lady ever thought the sorts of things she had been thinking, and she wasn't sure of Caroline's reception to her radical ideas. "The problem is that I'm not necessary. There is no rhyme or reason to me. I am needed by no one. Ladies of our class are useless, worse than useless, dependent on everyone for everything, from cooking their meals to dressing themselves. When's the last time you dressed yourself, Caro? Combed your own hair? You see? I'm no better than the rest of our class. All I've been raised to do is look pretty and entertain people and spend my husband's money. There's no future in any of that for me— Dare wouldn't notice if I suddenly sprouted an extra limb or two, there's no one left in the *ton* other than you who will acknowledge me, and I have to admit that a lifetime spent with the sole purpose of entertaining you is not what I'm looking for in a life goal, and as for spending money, there's nothing to be spent."

Caroline was staring at her with open-mouthed horror. "You can't mean that! You can't be serious when you say that we're not good for anything but looking pretty and entertaining people and spending money!"

"Tell me something else the ladies of the *ton* can do? Something worthwhile."

"Well. . . ." Caroline looked a bit flustered, biting her lip as she thought. "We can . . . we have . . . there's charity!"

"Spending our husband's money," Charlotte pointed out. "Can you think of nothing more?"

"Yes . . . no . . . oh, you're rushing me, I can't think when you rush me."

Charlotte sighed. "I fear there is nothing more. At least in my case there is nothing more. Dare is on the road to mental and emotional healing. I have no doubt that he could survive without me now. He has the servants to help him rebuild his engine, he has David's connection to assist him in selling the engine even if all his other investors lost interest, and most of all, he has the intelligence and charm and warmth to find himself another wife, one who will be just what he wants, not a wife who hoisted herself on him. *Foisted*," she corrected herself before Caroline could, blinking back tears that seemed to have been wept straight from her heart. "The truth is, I'm really not needed anymore now that Dare's well."

"He loves you," Caroline offered, dabbing at her own eyes with her handkerchief. "That is a sort of need, isn't it? And you love him."

"He loves me, but he doesn't have a driving reason to keep me in his life. 'Tis the truth that he'd be better off without me."

"You don't intend . . . you can't mean you'd . . ."

"No, of course not, don't be so megalomaniac. I simply mean that I believe the best thing—the best thing for Dare—will be to gain an annulment to the marriage, so he might live out his life in happiness. Even though my heart shall be destroyed by parting from him, I will have the satisfaction of knowing he will be happy."

"Oh, that's the most romantic thing I've ever heard," Caroline sniffled. "So brave of you! So self-sacrificing! You are the noblest woman I know, Char."

"I am, aren't I?" Charlotte agreed morosely, her lip quivering as the full extent of her sacrifice dawned upon her. "I cannot believe it has come to this, Caro, but I truly do want him to be happy, no matter how miserable his happiness makes me. It was fine when he needed me, but now . . ." She wiped at a tear that had crept down her cheek. "Well, there is no sense in crying, my path is clear. And now that we have that settled, I was hoping you'd have some tidbit of gossip about the Pretender that might direct me to other avenues of investigation, something I could use to sway public opinion against him. I shall make that my last act of kindness before giving Dare his freedom."

Caroline's naturally pale coloring paled even

more. She fretted a handkerchief as she watched Charlotte carefully. "Oh, dear."

"Oh, dear? What is it? What haven't you told me?"

"I hadn't wanted to tell you, but I suppose it is best if it comes from me, and Lord . . . Mr. McGregor doesn't hear of it elsewhere."

Charlotte brushed away the tears that had formed at the thought of her noble and selfless act. "Tell me."

Caroline fidgeted, something she rarely did, an action that instantly raised concern in Charlotte's mind.

"Well . . . oh, it's completely untrue, I want you to know that I realize that. Completely untrue! It seems that Lord Carlisle . . . that is, the man who claims to be Lord Carlisle, told Lord Keyes, who told Sir Albert Moray, who told dearest Algernon, that . . . that . . ."

"Oh, for heaven's sake, just spit it out, Caro!" Charlotte snapped, more concerned than ever.

"He said that your husband arranged for his kidnapping six years ago so he could take the title, and the estates because he was so poor and always coveted the title and Lord Carlisle has the proof of his misdeeds and he intends to bring Alasdair McGregor up on charges and have him hung for his crime and that the accident was just a convenient ploy to gain him sympathy and that he's not really injured, just too cowardly to face Lord Carlisle in public," Caroline said in a rush of words that stumbled over each other.

"He what?" Charlotte all but shrieked as she leaped up from the settee.

Caroline took a deep breath. "He said that your husband arranged for his kidnap—"

"No, no, you don't have to repeat those ghastly

lies. Dear Lord, he said all that? In public?"

Caroline nodded, her head swiveling as she watched Charlotte pace before her, eyeing the carpet critically to see if it would have to be replaced after Charlotte's latest round of ambulatory musing. Perhaps she should instruct Matthews to lay down a special matting in the pacing path whenever Charlotte visited. "In the clubs, yes. I imagine it's all over them by now. You know how Sir Albert gossips."

"I can't believe this, I just can't believe this. How can he say such a thing? That Dare would kidnap him? It's ridiculous, utterly ridiculous. No, it's not just ridiculous, it's . . . it's . . . it's asodyne!"

"Asodyne?"

"Yes, asodyne. That means it's completely absurd and unbelievable. Really, Caro, you should make an effort to study the English language. Your vocabulary is shockingly lacking."

"*Asinine.*"

"What?" Charlotte paused in the act of gathering up her things.

"The word is asinine, not asodyne."

She frowned. "Asinine? As in nine asses? Are you certain?"

Caroline nodded her head. "Quite."

"How very peculiar. Still, it matters not." Charlotte filed away that interesting fact and smiled, once more filled with a warm glow of happiness. "What does matter is that I have a purpose again. I can be useful. I need to go home, now, before Dare hears about this."

"How can you keep him from hearing about it?"

"I don't know, but I will have to, else he'll . . . he'll . . . oh, I don't know what he'll do, but I do know that it won't involve working on his engine, and that is what his focus should be right now. I suppose if

I ban any visitors to the house, and keep Dare at home, and screen his post, that should give me the time I need."

"To do what?"

"To take care of the Pretender once and for all, of course."

"But . . . you just said that you were helpless to do anything about him, that not even your expertise in Society could help Mr. McGregor—"

"Pheasant feathers! That was before I knew what foul lies that evil man has been spewing! Answer me this, Caro: Is there anyone in town more qualified than me to mount a counterattack?"

"A counterattack?" Caroline looked shocked. "You mean you will blacken his character?"

Charlotte snorted as she patted Wellington, standing to flash her friend a smile filled with portent. "As if that was possible. I shall simply ensure that everyone in the *ton* sees him as he truly is. That, my dear, shall be my new raisin debtor!"

"Raisin . . . you don't mean *raison d'être*—"

Charlotte sailed out the door, pausing long enough to kiss her friend on the cheek. "Thank you, sweet Caro. I don't know what I'd do without you."

With a flash of lace petticoat, Charlotte raced down the stairs and out to the carriage, her mind filled once again with plans for her husband. What a silly thing she was, thinking Dare didn't need her. Why, here was proof that she had a role to fulfill in life, a destiny that she intended to meet—Dare needed her keen eye and her sharp intellect and her ability to see things others missed to keep his life running smoothly and happily.

Charlotte settled back in the somewhat dingy seats of the rented carriage and allowed herself a small smile of satisfaction. The business with the

Pretender was bound to turn out as she hoped. How could life do anything but arrange itself to her pleasure now that she knew her husband needed her? All she had to do was keep Dare in the dark about the foul things the Pretender was saying, and all would be well. By the time the engine was ready and Dare was prepared to rejoin Society, she'd have taken care of his supposed cousin once and for all.

She smiled even as the poorly sprung carriage jounced and rattled over the road. Things were working out well after all.

Chapter Seventeen

"Batsfoam, fetch me when Johnson has the steam cylinder repaired."

"As you desire, sir. There are few things that will give me greater pleasure than to stand around the blacksmith's forge. You are kindness personified to offer me the opportunity to escape the sweltering heat of the day by allowing me to stand inside a small, confined shed containing the blacksmith's massive forge, not to mention the blacksmith's massive self, his massive assistant, and two massive sons, all four of whom will be manning the bellows in order to heat the forge to such a temperature as to work with the steel cylinder you wish repaired."

"Batsfoam—"

"I can imagine nothing I will like so much as to stand about on my unfortunate limb, perspiring freely, secure in the knowledge that I am doing my own insignificant part to ease your mind while you suffer through the trials and tribulations of lunching at your club, no doubt imbibing cooling beverages, dining on wholesome foodstuffs, forcing yourself to eat the fruit ice that I'm certain will be presented on this, surely the hottest day ever recorded in the history of Britannia."

"Batsfoam—"

"Even now I struggle to contain the joy that fills me at the thought of fulfilling your most gracious and thoughtful request. Indeed, were it not for the fact that I am even now wrung to the very limits of my poor, crippled body with the heat of the day, I should take the opportunity to turn a few hand-springs just to demonstrate my utter delight at the task you have set before me. Indeed, if you will just hold my hat for a moment, I will give the hand-spring a try, just so you may go off to your cool club with its cool, comfortable chairs and cool, mouth-wateringly tempting meals secure in the knowledge that you have made me, your most humble of all the servants, happy beyond human ken."

Dare knew how to play the game. Smiling was allowed if it was done properly, in a subdued manner, but laughing out loud would only wound Bats-foam's feelings, so he kept his chuckles locked deep inside and instead gave his servant a long-suffering smile. "I believe I'll survive the rigors of luncheon without forcing you into a show of acro-batics."

"Indeed, I would be most happy, sir—"

Dare held up his hand and took his stick from the carriage. "Just make sure Johnson does the job properly, and then fetch me when it's ready. And before you say it, no, you won't disturb me. I can't do anything until that cylinder is repaired, so I might as well wait at the club and catch up on what's been happening in the world while I've been recuperating."

Batsfoam made a half-hearted attempt to gain permission for the handsprings, but in the end he climbed back into the carriage and promised he'd keep a close eye on the blacksmith's repairs. Dare mounted the steps to his club feeling only the slightest pinch in his thigh where his wife had shot him.

He started laughing then, unable (or unwilling) to keep the laughter contained as he thought of his indignant Charlotte driven to shooting him in order to bring him back to his senses. How could he have even contemplated living without her? She was everything he wanted, everything he needed. Wife, lover, friend, nursemaid . . .

"Executioner." He chuckled to himself, shocking the doorman who took his hat and cane.

He spent a few minutes talking with an elderly member who remembered his father, then made his way toward the area containing deep leather armchairs situated so as to catch a breeze from the nearby opened window. There was mild amusement to be drawn from the fact that no one knew quite where to look at him—at his eye patch, the scars that trailed along the hairline on one side of his face, or his obviously limp arm—nor did anyone seem to know exactly how to address him, some calling him Carlisle as if to indicate their support, while others used his surname. It was the need to think about his cousin that was behind claiming the few hours it would take for the cylinder to be repaired. He had to think about what to do about Charlotte, and he couldn't do that with her very distracting presence at home.

Dare was no fool, he'd seen the writing on the wall before his accident; although he had no idea who had arranged for his cousin to be packed aboard a merchant ship bound for the Orient, he had no doubt at all that Geoffrey McGregor was exactly who he said he was, which meant the title and estates—such as they were—not to mention his late uncle's debts, all now rightfully belonged to his cousin. Truth to be told, he was better off without the title and estates—now all he had to do was take care of himself and Charlotte, and no longer would he need to throw money into the drain that were the estates. But Charlotte, his sweet, loving, eccentric Charlotte—she was determined to save the title.

"Hot out today."

Dare nodded to the elderly man sitting across from him as he took his seat in one of the leather armchairs, ordering a restorative beverage from the attendant lurking behind his elbow before turning his attention to the man who had spoken. "That it is."

"Ye're the Scot, ain't ye? The fellow everyone is talking about."

Dare allowed as to his ancestry and said nothing about his sudden fame. No doubt people were still discussing his terrible accident. It was impossible to ignore the subject since he was wearing an eye patch—an eye patch made by his loving wife's hands. This one was silver with blue piping, made to match his waistcoat of the same colors. She had presented it and several others to him earlier, pointing out with great solemnity that she had fashioned an eye patch to match all of his waistcoats.

Only Charlotte would think of color coordinating eye patches.

"Heard tell that other fellow, the other Scot, has called you out."

Dare's hand froze for a moment in midreach as he was about to take his glass off the tray the servant held. He took the drink and waved off the man before asking, "What did you say?"

The man opposite him was quite elderly, had to be near a hundred, with wild white hair, piercing blue eyes that looked remarkably lucid despite the age of their owner, and a strongly jutting nose that rose from the criss-crossed lines that mapped out the man's face. An ebony stick rested next to the man's leg, one gnarled hand trembling with gentle palsy next to the silver head of a lion that topped the stick.

"This other McGregor says ye were behind the kidnapping that sent him to China in order to take a title that rightfully would have been his. That true, boy?"

Dare ground his teeth. He had tolerated much in his life because it was fitting at the time, but never had he tolerated a slur to his honor or his name. "No, sir, it is most definitely not true. If my cousin has stated his intention to meet me on the field of honor over this, I will be happy to satisfy him. If he hasn't, then I will be even happier to demand his presence."

"Thought ye'd see it like that. Never were one to take a slight. Fought a few duels in yer day, haven't ye?"

"A few," Dare ground out, his eye scanning the common room of the club in hopes it would light upon the figure of his cousin.

"Don't think I'd be letting your lady wife know about it, though," the old man said thoughtfully, one twisted finger rubbing his chin. "Lady Charlotte's another chit with her own mind. Like as not she'd think of a way to put a halt to it. Best you keep your plans to yourself if you don't want to end up in Crouch's hands again."

Through an open doorway Dare saw a flash of scarlet that looked like it belonged to the elegant figure who had so publicly challenged him. He stood and bowed to the elderly man who was looking at him so curiously. He'd been saying something about Charlotte, but Dare hadn't time to listen to him now. He had a challenge to accept . . . or offer. "Thank you for your advice, sir—"

"Name's Palmerstone."

"It is much appreciated. If you will excuse me, I believe I see my cousin now."

A surprisingly strong gnarled hand on his wrist stopped him as he was leaving. Dare looked down at the old man, once again startled by the vivacity of his eyes.

"Don't forget what you've almost lost, boy. You'd be a fool to risk losing it again."

Dare fought the urge to frown, baffled by what the old man said until he dismissed his words as the meanderings of an elderly mind. He mumbled something placating, and strode off in pursuit of his cousin.

An hour later Batsfoam found his employer in the company of a short, red-faced young man who looked hot and nervous.

"There's nothing to it, man. Acting as a second is merely a formality."

"All the same, I'm sure my wife wouldn't like it. Still, a gentleman has his honor to think of."

"Exactly," Dare told Lord Beverly, and gave him an encouraging blow to the shoulder that almost dropped the younger man to his knees. "It's a simple matter of pistols at dawn. All you have to do is arrange the location and be sure a surgeon is summoned."

"In that case, I should be happy to act as your second."

Dare thanked him, then turned to his servant with a cheery, "Cylinder done, Batsfoam? Excellent. Let's be on our way, then."

As Dare strolled out of the black and white marble tile entrance hall, Batsfoam thumping a respectable distance after him, he was stopped at the door by a familiar (if unwelcome) person.

"Ah, McGregor. I'm surprised to see you up and about. From what my sister said, it sounded as if you were at death's door."

Dare bared his teeth in what he hoped was a polite smile at his brother-in-law. "It was due to Charlotte's most excellent skills that I stand before you today, Collins."

Lord Collins sourly looked Dare over, his narrow eye flickering from the eye patch, to the arm that hung limply at his side. A tiny smile that looked remarkably like satisfaction turned into a smirk. "We are all, of course, most grateful to hear the reports of your imminent demise are premature. Still, I'm surprised to see you here. I had heard that you had been issued a challenge and failed to respond. I wouldn't have thought that a man so cowardly would dare show his face in public."

The fingers of Dare's left hand clenched into a fist that ached to connect with Collins's pompous face. "You can't have it both ways, Collins. Either I was too ill to know there was a challenge, or I wasn't ill at all and too much the coward to be seen in public. As it happens, I was ill—would you like to see what remains of my eye?—and was unaware my cousin had called me out." He shook his head in mock sorrow. "This younger generation doesn't seem to understand the finer points of calling a man out, points such as challenging a man in person rather than announcing the slight to everyone but the party concerned. Still, Geoffrey's suffered some rather grievous circumstances in the past; I'm sure a little leniency is due him."

"Leniency?" Collins sneered. "Could that be the voice of guilt speaking?"

Dare took his hat and cane and with an effort, shoved neither article down his odious brother-in-law's throat. "I have no guilt whatsoever concerning my cousin, but you may rest easy that I don't take being called out lightly. I have men looking into the circumstances of Geoffrey's adventure six years ago and will soon discover just who is responsible. If there is nothing else, I will take my leave. I've lost quite a bit of time on my engine, and must return home to install a new steam cylinder. I shall give your regards to Charlotte."

Lord Collins looked as if he wanted to say something more, but Dare wasn't in the mood to be baited. He'd put up with enough of that from his cousin; he had no intention on debating the finer points on the doorstep of White's with his brother-in-law.

With a dashing left-handed twirl of his cane, he marched down the steps and into his waiting carriage, Batsfoam in tow.

"Home, John," he called to the coachman as he waved Batsfoam inside the carriage. "Sit down, man, I have a few things I want to say and I can't yell them out the window to you. First off, tell me what Johnson said about the cylinder."

Batsfoam duly reported the details of the blacksmith's examination of the damaged cylinder, and suggestions for strengthening it. Dare filed the information away for future use, then turned the conversation to the subject that was uppermost in his mind. "As you probably gathered, I have a dawn appointment tomorrow."

Batsfoam eyed Dare's wounded arm openly. "In that case, sir, I would say it's a very good thing you favor your left hand."

Dare was astonished. "That's all you're going to say? You're not going to give me a ten-minute lecture that alternately praises me to the sky while simultaneously pointing out that it would be the purest folly to honor a duel when I have only one working arm and eye? You're not going to go into a five-minute soliloquy on how difficult it will be for you and your wounded limb to find a new employer once I'm killed? You're not going to bring up all those many times when we were in the 12th Light when I told you not to take foolish chances and that it was absurd to be chasing death when he was only too willing to claim us? You're not going to say any of that, you're just going to tell me it's good I'm left-handed? Is that it, Batsfoam? That's all?"

Batsfoam smiled in a manner that on any other man Dare would have termed a grin. "I have no need to say all that, sir, you just did."

"I could still let you go, you know."

"But you won't," Batsfoam answered with a complacency that amused Dare. "You have need of me, at least until your engine is finished, for you yourself have said that no one else has quite the hand I do in drawing up the specifications."

Well, Batsfoam had him there. He leaned back against the soft cushions and with a concerted effort, managed to pull his bad arm up so his hand rested on his thigh. "We'll take your continued employment as a given. Now, as to this other affair, naturally it is to be kept from my wife."

"Naturally," Batsfoam agreed.

"And when she finds out about it, as she is sure to do since she is a woman and women always find out about a man's dawn appointments no matter how hard we try to keep it from them, you will do your utmost to convince her that the appointment is for the following day."

"I shall endeavor to put all my acting skills into a performance guaranteed to lead Lady Charlotte into believing that, sir."

"Excellent. Now, when we get home, I have several tasks for you on the engine. First, you'll need to test the condenser. . . ." Dare spent the next few minutes happily detailing what he wanted done that afternoon.

Batsfoam heard him out, then leveled a steady, dark-eyed gaze at him, speaking with the intimacy of one man who's seen another through a near-fatal situation. "I don't suppose there's any use in pointing out what will happen if the morning does not go as you expect?"

Dare's jaw tightened. He wasn't an unusually foolish man, he'd stared death in the face once or twice, and although he had recently sought the obsidian . . . oblivion—Lord, now he was thinking like Charlotte!—that death brought, he knew now that he would have never gone through with it. Just the thought of Charlotte filled him with a warmth and happiness he had only dreamt of. The vision of her lying in his bed, hair delightfully mussed, her eyes drowsy and sated, the gentle perfume of a well-loved woman teasing his nose came immediately to mind, making his fingers twitch with the desire to stroke her silky skin. She was his, every last square inch of her bound so tightly around his heart that he couldn't begin to separate her soul from his. No, death held no charms for him. He was too much in love with his wife, too fond of living to court death.

"Which doesn't explain why I'm so happy to meet my cousin over a pair of pistols, eh?" he asked aloud. Batsfoam was evidently thinking along the same lines, for he didn't look the least bit puzzled by the comment and just inclined his head in agreement.

"You seem to be singularly unconcerned about the event, which is not what I'd expect from a man with only one working eye as he faces a duel upon the morn."

Dare allowed himself a smile. "The truth is . . . well, as my wife would say, all that flitters is not gold."

Batsfoam raised his eyebrows. Dare's smile deepened into a cheeky grin.

Life really was looking remarkably good.

"I'm in hell, aren't I? I've died and gone to hell and no one bothered to inform me."

"Eh?"

"Nothing. How long ago did my husband leave, Crouch?"

" 'Twould be a just a few minutes ago, m'lady. Five minutes would be my best guess."

"Drat the man. How dare he slink off in darkness and leave me to be a widow all by myself? If I've told him once, I've told him twice, no one can kill him but me."

"That's a right interestin' attitude to 'ave, m'lady."

"It is the only attitude to have, Crouch, and you'd best be standing staring at the door and not looking around my bedchamber or trying to peep around the screen. I'm sure I'm breaking all sorts of employer-butler rules by having you in my chamber while I'm getting dressed, but as I have no maid, and as Batsfoam has gone off to see Dare killed, you'll simply have to be the one to do up the tapes in the back."

"Now, m'lady?"

"No, just a minute, let me get my boots on. Honestly, men! How could he go off to fight a duel and not tell me! He could have at least said *goodbye, nice to know you, I hope you have a good life without me.*"

"Mayhap 'e doesn't think 'e'll be corkin' off."

"Oh, I'm sure he doesn't; every man thinks he's invisible."

"Eh?"

"What?"

" 'E thinks 'e's invisible?"

"Yes, of course, what else would you say about a man who dashes off at all hours of the night to stand on a damp field and take turns shooting at another man, a man who has claimed everything you want and has spread the most malicious, foul rumors about you?"

"I might say as 'e thought 'e was invincible."

"Don't be ridiculous, Dare is quite easily seen. Now you may turn around and do up my back, and we'll be on our way. You did say you overheard that traitor Batsfoam state where the duel was to be held?"

"Aye, m'lady. The lads and me was just arrivin' as ye ordered, and there was old Batty and the McGregor gettin' into a hack, tellin' it to go to

346

Baker's Field. Then ye came barrellin' down the stairs yellin' and pitchin' a fit loud enough to be 'eard from 'ere to Banbury."

"Oh, do hurry. Dare already has a sizeable lead on us. At least you had the foresight to keep the carriage."

"It ain't easy doin' up all these fidgety bits with only one 'and, m'lady, but if ye'll just stand still . . . aye, there it is. Yer done, then."

Charlotte ignored her bonnet and shawl, grabbing her reticule and dashing out the door as she called over her shoulder, "Come along, don't dawdle, Crouch, I have a husband to save! *Again!*"

The ride to Baker's Field was not long, nor was it particularly arduous, but it seemed to Charlotte to last just shy of an eternity. What if she wasn't in time? What if that bastard killed Dare? What if her beloved husband was at this very moment lying on the damp grass, his life's blood draining away from him? What then?

"I'll kill him," she growled to herself as she clutched the seat in the carriage when it lurched drunkenly over ruts in the road. "If he's dead, I'll bring him back to life just so I can kill him for scaring me so! Oh, Dare! You stupid, foolish, idiotic . . . *wonderful* man! How can you do this to me? How can I mean so little to you that you'd go off without even saying goodbye, while you mean the world to me? How can you possibly want to die after spending such a miraculous night together?"

Charlotte sniffled into her handkerchief as she remembered the hours leading up to dawn. Dare had been a wild man, gentle yet demanding, forceful yet tender, bringing her again and again to the brink of paradise. "If you die, how will I ever again

347

know the joy of Churning Butter on a Fresh Spring Morn?"

Slowly a deep, dark rage overtook her grief and filled her with determination. If God were so gracious as to leave her Dare alive until she could save him, she would see to it that the beastly Pretender never bothered him again. She'd kill him herself if she had to, if that's what it took to keep Dare safe.

Such were Charlotte's musings as the carriage rolled on toward what she had began to think of as the murder ground. Before she had time to do more than mentally murder Geoffrey McGregor two or three times, the carriage had stopped, blocked by a newly arrived curricle. Charlotte peered out the window at the offending obstacle, then snarled an oath that she would never admit to knowing, and without waiting for Crouch to let down the stairs, leaped from the carriage and ran to the man climbing down from the other vehicle.

"Matthew! What are you doing here? Where's Dare? What have you done to my husband?"

"Charlotte! Dear God woman, what can you be thinking? You can't be here! Go home this instant."

Charlotte grabbed her brother by the neck cloth and shook him, not an easy task since he had several stone on her. "Where is my husband?"

Lord Collins's eye bulged slightly, reminding her of Caro's pug. "I haven't seen him," he choked out in between shakings. Charlotte loosened her grip. "I just got here myself. Now, release me. As long as you're here, there's something I wish to say to you."

She stepped away from her brother and looked around the field. A row of trees swaying vigorously in the morning breeze blocked her view, but she thought she saw two carriages through them. "Crouch?"

"Right behind ye, m'lady."

"Where is he?"

"Most likely beyond the trees."

She picked up her skirts and started off toward the carriages, ignoring her brother's demand that she wait and hear him out. "I have better things to do than listen to you tell me yet again that I've made my bed and now must lie in it." Better things like throttling her husband's murderer with her bare hands.

"That's just it, you foolish girl, I'm offering to forgive you and welcome you back to the bosom of the family!"

"All I care about is Dare and ending this stupid duel without him dying. Your bosom will have to wait until later."

"Dammit woman, it's you I'm thinking about! I can stop the duel!"

Charlotte stopped and turned to look at her brother. "You can what?" she asked baldly, waiting impatiently as he puffed his way up to her.

"I'll forgive you. You'll be reinstated to your rightful place in the eyes of the *ton.* You'll have everything you had before—position, a dowry, the force of our family name at your back—everything."

Charlotte glanced through the trees. She could see the figures of men speaking together next to the carriages. Her heart lightened considerably with the knowledge that the killing hadn't started yet. "You said you can stop the duel. Did you mean that?"

"I never say anything I don't mean, sister."

"Pheasant feathers, you do it all the time. What I want to know is whether you're telling the truth now. You can stop the duel? You can truly stop it?"

Lord Collins smiled in a way that made Charlotte's skin prickle. She'd never really liked her brother before. He was always a bit of a bully and a know-it-all, but for the first time she realized that she actively disliked him. He was an unconscionable beast of a man, and she suddenly had the desire to be away from him and his oily smile.

"I can stop the duel. All it will take is cooperation from you, my dear sister."

She glanced over at the trees again. The men were still talking. "Crouch, would you please go see if they are getting ready to start murdering each other?"

"Aye, m'lady."

Charlotte turned back to her brother. "What sort of cooperation?"

His oily smile widened. "Nothing very particular, certainly nothing you should balk at if you wish to regain your proper place in Society."

"And what would 'nothing very particular' consist of?"

"An annulment, of course, so that you might make a more advantageous marriage than to a penniless criminal. If you renounce McGregor for the liar and cheat he is, if you are willing to state that he's a dishonorable blackguard who tried to steal his cousin's title by having him kidnapped, and an impotent blackguard to boot, I will see to it that you have everything you've ever desired."

Charlotte stared at her brother, aware that her mouth was hanging open in surprise, but unable to do anything about such an unseemly expression, too astounded by his proposal to function properly for a moment.

"Impotent?" That wasn't what she was intending to say, but it was the first word that came to her tongue.

Collins nodded. His voice was smooth, persuasive as it coiled around her. "You can have it all, Charlotte: a new husband, one who can give you children, a title, money, position, power—it can all be yours. Just give me your word, and I'll go tell Carlisle that you've agreed to testify on his behalf against McGregor. You'll be a free woman again, but this time you'll have my blessing to smooth your path in Society. It can all be yours again, Charlotte, everything you've ever wanted."

Charlotte thought she saw the distant figures start to separate. She had to stop her foolish, honorable husband before he got himself killed; she had to take matters into her own hands.

"I see only one logical response to your plan," she told her brother as she peeled off her glove.

"I thought you might feel that way," he responded with a smug smile.

A fraction of a second later her fist struck his nose with every ounce of strength she possessed. She didn't wait to witness his reaction, but took off in the direction of the trees, following Crouch's path as he veered off toward the left. Judging from the cursing at her back, her brother was not far behind.

She burst through the trees just in time to see the Pretender aim his pistol at her husband. Then there was a familiar blast and a black puff of smoke belching from the pistol. Her heart stopped as her husband staggered, then clutched at his chest before dropping to the ground.

"Dare!" she screamed with enough volume to disturb a flock of birds roosting in a nearby tree. Another blast echoed as Batsfoam snatched up the second loaded pistol and fired at the Pretender, but Charlotte ignored Geoffrey as he fell screaming to the ground. Her eyes were focused on her husband's body. Somehow she made it across the field, flung herself onto Dare's chest, sobbing his name as her heart fractured into a million aching pieces. His coat had fallen aside to expose a huge red stain directly over his heart, but try as Charlotte did, she couldn't see through the tears enough to find his wound and stop it from bleeding.

"How could you do this to me?" she sobbed as she struggled with his neck cloth, her hot tears spilling down her cheeks to splash on her hands. "Do I matter so little? How could you be so careless with yourself? Oh, Dare, I love you so much, I can't go on without you, don't you know that you stupid, stupid man?"

"If you don't let go of my neck, you're going to strangle me, woman," came a whispered reply.

Charlotte stared down at her husband in shock, utter and complete shock. His good eye opened just enough for her to see a glint of blue.

"Dare?" she said hesitantly, her blood-stained fingers still buried in the folds of his neck cloth. "Dare?"

"Shhhh," he replied inexplicably, his eye closing again. "Act like I'm dead. Cry and wail a lot, you were doing a good job until you stopped."

His eye opened again, briefly, just long enough for him to say, "And I love you, too. I'll never leave you, Char. Never."

She stared at him, stared at his still figure beneath her fingers, aware dimly that others had come up next to her. He wanted her to act like he was dead? To cry and wail? He wanted her to *act* like he was dead? Act?

Slowly she pulled her fingers from his neck cloth and looked at them. They were stained red, true. But it was a curious red, a thin red, a red not at all like the blood she had stanched when he had been wounded in the explosion. This red was . . . well, it was false. And if the blood on his shirt was not real . . .

"Aaaaaaaaaaagh!" she shrieked as she threw herself over her husband's body, then shrieked again, louder, to cover up his grunt as she landed hard on his chest. She wailed, she ranted, she raised her fists to heaven and promised retribution on a God who would be so cruel as to take her husband, she did all but pour ashes on her hair and don sackcloth.

"Lady Charlotte, please, if you would just step back, I have seen many wounds. Perhaps I can help your husband."

Charlotte looked over her shoulder and glared at Lord Beverly for a moment before transferring her watery gaze to that of her brother. "He's gone, he's gone, that horrible man has murdered my beloved husband. Oh, woe is me!"

"Truly, my lady, I feel certain I can help him, if you will just move aside—"

"Go away," she hissed under her breath before loudly claiming she would die without her Alasdair.

"Here, you," Lord Beverly said. "Attend to your mistress. She is temporarily deranged and knows not what she says. If you will take Lady Charlotte to her carriage, I will see how badly you've wounded McGregor, although what the world is coming to when one's man shoots one's rival for one . . ."

"He's dead!" Batsfoam, to whom this last was addressed, shrieked as he knelt by Geoffrey's body. "I've killed Lord Carlisle! He's dead, dead, dead! Oh, that it would bring my beloved master back!"

"Dead? Both of them?" Lord Beverly wrung his hands.

Charlotte sighed. Clearly Lord Beverly wasn't privy to whatever plan Dare and, she suspected,

McGregor—no doubt his wound was of the same type as Dare's—had enacted. Thus, it was up to her to save the situation. With a heartbreaking sob, she threw herself upon Algernon, sobbing into his collar and clutching his shoulders in her attempt to keep him from examining Dare or Geoffrey.

"Listen carefully," she whispered in his ear while Crouch and Batsfoam quickly arranged a blanket over Dare's body, then did likewise for the other fallen man. "If you do not stop trying to see Dare's body, I will harm you in ways you cannot even begin to understand. Do I make myself clear?"

Lord Beverly stammered something as Charlotte peeled herself off him, turning to face her brother. She had no idea what Dare intended with his plan—she, after all, was only his wife, and thus not allowed the privilege of being made cognizant of his plans, a fact that she would punish him for later—but she knew enough to guess how to act.

"He's dead," she told the two men, her lower lip quivering of its own volition as she stood slowly. The words were so chilling, she had the strongest urge to peek under the blanket to make sure he was quite all right before continuing, but Charlotte was nothing if not determined. She fought that need down and trusted that Dare hadn't lied when he told her he wouldn't leave her. "They're both dead. You killed them. You killed my Dare."

"Killed them?" Lord Collins squeaked. "My dear, you are unhinged! I was standing with you when Carlisle shot McGregor, and your husband's gimp-legged man shot poor Carlisle."

"You might not have pulled the trigger, but you are responsible for Dare's death," Charlotte accused. "And for McGregor's, for that matter, for if he hadn't killed Dare, Batsfoam would have never retaliated. It's all your fault, Matthew, all of it!"

Of that, she honestly believed. Matthew was up to something. He looked far too pleased at the two men's deaths, and there was the curious matter of his attempt to bribe her into betraying Dare.

"You don't know what you're saying," Collins said dismissively, turning to Lord Beverly. "Best get hold of that fellow, Beverly. He'll hang for McGregor's death, of course, nothing for it. Tragedy that he killed an innocent man, but justice must be done."

"Justice? You speak of justice?" Charlotte interrupted. She had no idea of Geoffrey the Pretender's role in things, but she was becoming more and more suspicious of her brother. No matter where she turned in this mess, he seemed to pop up. Perhaps, just perhaps, his involvement went back further than she had thought. "I know exactly what I'm saying, brother. For instance, I know that you were the one to befriend Geoffrey McGregor when he returned to England."

That was safe enough, she'd had that bit of information from Crouch.

Her brother sputtered something about helping out a fellow peer.

"But you couldn't know he was the *real* Geoffrey McGregor," Charlotte said slowly, puzzle pieces suddenly falling into place as she spoke. "You couldn't know his claim was valid . . . unless you knew him before he was kidnapped?"

"Nonsense. Never met the man before."

A small glint of warning in her brother's eyes told her she'd guessed correctly. Charlotte ignored his protest. "How did you know each other?"

"None of your business. Beverly, I trust you'll stay

355

here with the bodies, and hold that man. I will fetch the magistrate—"

"Oh, but I think it is my business," Charlotte interrupted her brother again. The Pretender, now, she was fairly certain, was the true Earl of Carlisle. "It is, after all, because of *you* that my husband and another man have died. What was it, Matthew? Women? Gambling? Probably the latter. I seem to recall you begging Papa to help you out with a particularly steep debt about five years ago. Papa refused, saying it would teach you to gamble over your head if you had to sell off everything you owned to cover your gaming debts. I don't recall you selling anything, though. Just exactly how did you pay off the debts?"

"I . . . they . . . that's none of your business. You don't seem too terribly cut up over your husband's death now, do you, sister?" Collins sneered. "Mayhap you think my offer still stands, but it doesn't. You've made your bed, now you can—"

"Oh, for mercy's sake, get a new homily, will you? Crouch, when you were investigating Geoffrey McGregor, did you happen to run into a mention of my brother in connection with him?"

"Aye, that I did. Been meanin' to tell ye, but ye've been busy with yer 'usband. Both McGregor and Lord Collins went to the same gamin' 'ells. Lord Collins lost a goodly sum o' money to 'is lordship just afore 'e left for 'Olland. 'Ere, milord, ye'd best sit down, yer lookin' right green what with all the blood splashed around everywhere." Crouch grabbed Lord Beverly's arm, and helped him (despite the latter's protests) over to a distant rock.

Charlotte turned her attention back to her brother, her eyes narrowing as she studied him. She knew there must be a reason why both Batsfoam and Crouch were leaving her alone with her brother—clearly she was expected to worm an admission out of him. Thank heavens she had read so many gothic novels—she knew all about how one went about getting a villain to admit his guilt, and if there was anyone who fit the villainous character role, it was her brother. "Which brings up the question again, Matthew: How did you pay off your debt five years ago?"

"That, my dear, you will never know."

Charlotte cast a glance down at her husband's still form, then lifted her head to smile her most winsome smile. "Come, Matthew, we are alone here. Dare and McGregor cannot hear us, and I cannot testify against you. Satisfy my curiosity. Tell me how you settled that debt. Tell me what your role is with Geoffrey McGregor."

Lord Collins laughed and slid a sly glance over to where Batsfoam knelt some twenty paces away, ostensibly examining McGregor's body. Collins leaned toward his sister, his voice low and cold. "As you have asked so nicely, my dear, I will answer your question. There's nothing either of them can do to me now, and I certainly will stand in no jeopardy even should you tell the truth, for no one will believe the deranged ravings of my mentally distraught sister."

Charlotte tightened her lips, but held her tongue. Villains, she knew, simply could not resist gloating about their supposed cleverness. Thus far, Matthew was acting exactly as she expected.

"The debt you mention was owed to Geoffrey McGregor, who was, in fact, the real Lord Carlisle, but when Father refused to make good the debt, I did the only thing I could—I paid off a captain to make sure Carlisle wouldn't see England again, thus eliminating my unfortunate obligation to him. I hadn't expected the bastard to return."

"Why not?" she asked, wondering how she could be related to such a cold-hearted, monstrous man.

"Few men survive being pressed into the merchant ship Carlisle ended up on; the captain is known for his particularly harsh methods of instruction."

The words came from behind Charlotte. She smiled as her brother's eyes opened wide, his wet lips sputtering objections as Dare took his place at her side, sliding his arm around her waist in a gesture that was both affectionate and protective.

"That is an understatement if I ever heard one," Geoffrey McGregor, Lord Carlisle said with a wry twist to his lips, as he, too cast aside the blanket covering him and stood up.

Lord Collins stared in horror first at Geoffrey, then at Dare. "But . . . but . . . he shot you! I saw the blood!"

Dare looked down to his chest. "Oh that? Just a bladder of red ink. Geoffrey fired over my head. I expect if you look, you'll find the ball in the tree behind where I stood."

Collins looked from Geoffrey to Dare, his eyes wild. "I don't . . . I don't . . . how . . ."

"Oh, honestly Matthew, are you dense? It was a trap, set to catch you out. Even I could see that, once I realized Dare wasn't dead." She turned to him and gave him a good glare. "And don't think I won't have a few words to say to you about letting me believe you were going to your death without even saying goodbye to me."

He frowned his sternest frown at her. "Just as I will have a few things to say to you about following me to a morning appointment, madam."

Charlotte rewarded his frown with her dimples. "You can't intimidate me; you love me too much."

"I do, eh?"

"Good God, they're both alive!" Lord Beverly yelled, having just caught sight of the men. He raced over, Crouch at his heels. "I'm confused. You're not injured, either of you?"

"Yes, you do," Charlotte answered her husband. "Why else would you go to the extreme lengths of this polluted plan if it wasn't for me?"

"No, we're both fine. Neither of us is injured," Geoffrey told Lord Beverly.

Dare tugged Charlotte toward him until her breasts were pressed into his chest. "You're so clever, you tell me why I would dream up such a convoluted plan?"

"But why did you both pretend to be dead?" Lord Beverly asked in confusion.

"Really? *Convoluted?* That doesn't sound right." Charlotte's lips brushing Dare's as she spoke.

"It is, however, the correct word."

"No!" Lord Collins shrieked, and would have run had not Crouch suddenly appeared behind him, his hook glinting in the sun as it twisted in the cloth against Collins's neck.

"It was all part of our plan, Beverly," Geoffrey replied as he took a step closer to Matthew, ignoring the stream of snarled obscenities that came from the earl's mouth. "Dare and I talked it over yesterday. He pointed out how Collins here was manipulating me and suggested that the manipulation might go back further than either of us had realized. We agreed to trap him into admitting the truth by making him think we were both dead. Batsfoam was supposed to goad Collins into admitting that he was behind my abduction, since Collins was

359

sure to feel that as a murderer, Batsfoam could pose him no threat, but when Lady Charlotte came along—" Geoffrey shrugged. "She served the purpose far better."

"Very well, I'll believe you on the convoluted issue, but as for this other, you cannot make me believe you don't love me as much as you clearly do. No other man but one deeply in love would go to such lengths to protect his wife's reputation."

"You'd lost everything else," Dare murmured in between light little kisses. "I couldn't take away the last thing you had—the respect of Society. I know how much it means to you."

"The *ton* means nothing to me, husband." Charlotte looked up into her husband's eyes and smiled as she brushed a lock of his hair from his eye patch. He was wearing the one upon which she'd embroidered an open eye, the better, she had told him at the time she presented it to him, to intimidate those around him. "The only thing that matters is you. I would quite happily live at the very ends of the earth and never again step foot in a single ballroom or opera theatre as long as it meant I had your love."

"Oh. It was all a trick, then? The blood and the pistols and Lady Charlotte screaming like a banshee?" Lord Beverly asked.

"You can be assured you have that, Char," Dare said just before his lips claimed hers. She burned with his heat, and pressed herself closer to him, forgetting for the moment everything but the joy she felt when she merged herself with him. He tore his mouth from hers with a shaky laugh and held her at arm's length. "You make me forget myself, wife. McGregor—or I should say, Carlisle—I assume you can handle Collins without any further assistance?"

Geoffrey smiled at them both. Charlotte suddenly noticed a resemblance in his and Dare's smile, and decided to forgive Geoffrey for his unwitting role in Dare's loss.

"This won't affect your engine, will it?" she asked softly as she watched Geoffrey speak quietly to her brother.

"Losing the title? It won't make one peck of difference, love. I wasn't counting on the few men who were interested in investing in the engine. Only by selling it outright will we have enough to be able to return to Scotland and live our lives in peace." Dare suddenly looked worried. "You won't mind living in Scotland, will you, Char? It's not very stylish, and there's not a lot of Society—"

"Then I shall love it even more," she told him with a full-dimpled smile. "I think I've had enough of the *ton* for a while. I will be happy to simply be Mrs. McGregor. It will make a nice change, don't you think?"

"Yes," said Dare as he bent to taste her lips just once more. "I think it will make a very nice change."

Epilogue

Alasdair McGregor, former Earl of Carlisle, leaned against a stone pillar and watched his wife stroll toward him on the arm of his sister's uncle-by-marriage, accompanied by his brother-in-law.

"So, in the end everything turned out all right?"

Dare inclined his head in acknowledgment of the question.

"But what happened to Char's brother?" Patricia asked.

"He slipped away right after the duel and ran for the continent. Not even his wife knows where he went, but it's of little matter. His financial affairs are in ruin, and his reputation is in tatters now that the truth about his actions have been made public."

"And you and Char are the pets of Society?" Patricia teased. "How fitting that is!"

Dare shrugged, his eyes still on the graceful figure

of his wife as she meandered down the length of the building toward him. "I gather that is so, although Charlotte seems to care little enough about it." He shook his head briefly as he spoke the words. The truth was, he still couldn't believe that Charlotte would turn her back so wholly on everything that had been her dream for so long, and yet, that is just what she had done. She had gladly thrown herself into helping him work day and night to make sure the engine was ready in time for the exhibition. Even after it had been completed—three days ahead of schedule—she had not returned to her old routine of paying calls and attending social functions. Instead she spent the evenings at home with him. A smile flirted with the corners of his lips as he remembered just how many of Vyvyan La Blue's famed connubial calisthenics they had tried, the smile growing when he thought of how many remained as yet unexplored.

"You should have more faith in her," Patricia said, apparently reading her brother's mind. "Charlotte is madly in love with you, just as I hoped she would be. As long as she's with you, she's happy."

He looked away from Charlotte just long enough to smile down on his sister.

"I have every faith in my wife, little one. She once bragged that she would be of enormous assistance persuading your new uncle into buying my engine, and I'll be damned if she didn't do just that."

Patricia laughed and pinched his arm as his eyes lifted once more to watch his Charlotte. "Your engine sold itself, brother mine, although I will admit that both David and Uncle Whitney looked very full of themselves. No doubt Char is filling their heads with the worst sort of flattery. Even so, I will forgive her, for she has done the one thing I had never thought to see."

Dare cocked an eyebrow in question.

"She made you fall in love with her," Patricia said with another squeeze of his arm. "And now I can sail around the world with David and not worry about either of you."

Charlotte and Elias Whitney, owner of the famed Whitney Shipyards—and now proud owner of the McGregor Marine Engine—came to a halt in front of them, Charlotte transferring herself from Whitney's arm to Dare's with a flash of dimples at the former.

"We have seen everything there is to see," she told Dare with a familiar glint of pride in her lovely clear blue eyes, a pride that he knew was for himself. He didn't know what he had done to deserve her, but every morning he woke profoundly grateful that she was his. "And Mr. Whitney agrees with me that your engine is by far the most superior of any to be found. I think you should have asked much more for it, Dare."

"Charlotte," Dare scolded her. Whitney only laughed and shook his head at her.

"Don't 'Charlotte' me in that tone, husband. We're going to need every shilling we can get; after all, we will soon have extra mouths to feed."

Dare's mouth dropped open as he goggled at his wife. "Char—you don't mean—"

She smiled, her dimples in their full glory as she modestly dropped her gaze, the fan of her dark brown lashes resting gently on the faintly pink-tinged cream of her cheeks. "Yes, it's true." Her eyelashes swept up, exposing the merriment in her eyes. "I've invited Crouch and the rest of Gillian's servants to come up to Scotland with us to put that house of yours to rights. I hadn't wanted to tell you in so public a forum, but . . . well . . . the truth escaped me."

"Crouch! I won't have it!"

"From what Dare has told me of the house," she said to Patricia and David, "it's a veritable nare's messed."

"This time you've gone too far, wife. Shooting me was one thing, but this is too much!"

She ignored him, just as he knew she would. "I very much look forward to making it a home so we can settle down and get to work on Dare's next engine."

"You are not bringing that thug Crouch and his gang of miscreants to my home!"

"I'm my husband's assistant, you know. He couldn't do any of it without me. He tells me so every night."

"I forbid it, I absolutely forbid it!"

"We work very well together. We're thinking of modifying the marine engine for river use next. Don't you think that is an excellent project? It should make us quite a tidy sum, too."

"Charlotte—" Dare ground his teeth for a few moments at the thought of his mare's nest of a house put to rights with Wessex's servants, then gave in and wrapped his arm around his wife.

"Whatever would I do without you, woman?" he growled into her ear as the others quite accurately read the intention in his eye and politely moved off to examine a new type of propeller.

"You'd be a lonely, pathetic man whom no one talked to, and who ended up living alone without servants in a house with seventeen cats all of which were named William. When you died, the cats would eat you. Therefore, it is only fitting that you thank me now for marrying you and saving you from such a terrible fate, thus helping you to fulfill your destiny as England's premiere engine maker."

"Thank you, Mrs. McGregor, for saving me from being eaten by cats," he dutifully said, then pulled her behind the pillar to kiss her properly. "Now, about this hare-brained idea of yours to bring Crouch and all of the others with us to Scotland . . ."

Charlotte kissed the argument right off of his tongue.

GERRI RUSSELL

To Tempt a Knight

Brotherhood of the Scottish Templars

"Gerri Russell writes with a passionate intensity that will sweep readers straight into her richly imagined world."
—Jayne Ann Krentz

Sir William Keith owed allegiance to no one save the mysterious brotherhood of the Scottish Templars. But his task to protect the legendary Templar treasure brought him straight into the path of a bold lass who demanded he help find her kidnapped father, the treasure's previous guardian.

William dared not abandon Lady Siobhan Fraser to her enemies. She was his best hope for finding the holy artifacts—and a dire temptation to his vow of chastity. How long could he deny the ecstasy that awaited him in her arms? For he knew all too well it's the forbidden fruit that tastes the sweetest....

Coming this Fall!   ISBN 13: 978-0-8439-6259-8